Modern MAGiC

By P.L. Hight

For permission, contact **Belen Books, LLC**.

This is a work of fiction. Names, characters, businesses, places, events, locales, and incidents are either the products of the author's imagination or used in a fictitious manner. Any resemblance to actual persons, living or dead, wrongfully dispatched Persons of Magic, living gnomes, or actual events or places is purely coincidental.

ISBN: 978-1-959715-21-4

Library of Congress Control Number: **2023940878**
Published by **Belen Books, LLC**
St. Petersburg, FL | Winter Park, FL | Chicago, IL USA
Belenbookspublishing.com

Edited by Lisa Khelawan and Beverly R. Waalewyn
Cover by Belen Media Group

10 9 8 7 6 5 4 3 2 1

Printed in the United States of America

Dedicated to

Jessica, Jasamine, and My Menehune

This book began August 2009 and ended September 2009 over the course of fifty-two Magical days.

Enjoy!

"So, you think you know magic, then? Let me show you a thing or two about *Magic!*"

— Grant Chamberlin, 1672
Pax Consortia, Et al.

Modern MAGiC

CHAPTER ONE

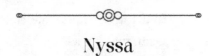

Nyssa

-1-

One day in July, something very peculiar happened that held no particular peculiarity more so than any other day or significant moment in time. The planets were not in some special alignment as they moved in their celestial paths, there were no two-headed calves born on *any* farm, *anywhere* in the world, and no one—not even the leprechauns—found a four-leaf clover that day. *That* day was just like any other blazing hot July day full of constant sun and muggy humidity when Magic exploded over the western suburbs of Chicago, and on that particular day, it just so happened to escape a sixteen-year-old girl named Nyssa.

When she woke that morning, nothing was out of the ordinary or different about that day than any other morning since summer vacation began. As usual, her eyes parted to the sun a whole ten minutes before her alarm began to wail.

She ate cold, bland cereal while listening to music quietly in her room, (once again, as usual), and then she showered, combed her hair, and brushed her teeth just like every morning to date. As she donned her work uniform in front of the tall mirror on her closet door, there wasn't even a whispering hint that the day was going to hold something grand. It was just another day of her growing up and proving her maturity (albeit her mind was not on such things now). Her muddled focus permanently resided within the sluggish pondering of whether taking on a summer job was truly worth it in the end.

With her head cocked to the side while sighing heavily, she convinced herself, once again, that it was.

It was her third trip to the parking lot when she paused at the lot's edge to regard the cloudless sky with disdain and then shot the sun the middle finger. Mid-July and less than a month into her summer job, and besides one afternoon when she covered for someone in receiving, her workdays comprised of hauling in row after row of carts. She was not the type to openly complain about the physical labor that her job entailed; that would be stooping down to the level of girls like Michelle Foster in Cosmetics, who would whine that her feet hurt from all the *hard work* that she did. Michelle would start complaining after the second hour, usually huffing about ankle pains—even though positions like hers came with stools to sit upon when customers were absent—and then spend the rest of her day sampling makeup.

No, Nyssa would never complain; she even took a more logical approach to her job as one filled with daily exercise instead of sitting around, but on days like that day—when her pores spouted more fluids than her body could take in or retain—thoughts of a cushy position inside was desired almost at a coveting level.

She sighed, dropping her poised center digit as she regarded the blazing sky once more, and then dug around in her apron to retrieve a piece of citrus chewing gum.

Throughout the day, she had seen many teens her own age out and about enjoying their summer break, seemingly without a care in the world. Based on the chipper moods, their mere presence at the Value Mart was one of choice and not one out of the laborious necessity to earn a paycheck as with her. At times she envied them with their day-to-day clothing ensembles and carefree hairstyles, all with destinations unknown, however free no matter what.

This was supposed to be her *Teen Summer*, a threshold point where she had crossed the divider line separating her from the early teen years and entered a time where her age gave her certain benefits for simply being older. Her first driver's license, event parties by the dozens, later nights followed by lazy mornings, and of course, the ability to start speaking her mind without the blow-off for just 'being a kid.' Not many of those things had happened yet, nor were there any events soon set on the horizon.

She had a learner's permit, but her mother had forbidden her the responsibility of an actual driver's license until she was seventeen. She had been to only two parties since the beginning of the summer (one of which was her younger cousin's so technically she axed that event from the list in her mind altogether). One benefit she did acquire was having full reign over deciding the hour she went to bed which she wielded mercilessly against the night owls: sometimes watching the sunrise before settling down. It was her choice, but she suffered the consequences the following mornings when her alarm would rip her from sleep even earlier than it had during the school year. And speaking her mind? Oh, she did that quite well, a champion at it to tell the truth, but she did so always through confrontation and at a considerable cost to her liberties.

"Oh, Nyssie?" the floor supervisor's voice crackled over the small radio clipped to her apron, tearing her from thoughts of her

3

summer thus far. His voice was shrill and nasal, sounding twice as nasally through the mechanical static of the set, making her shudder. "Are you there? Over."

Another sigh, eyes closing against the asphalt and field of cars before her, Nyssa unhooked the radio from her apron and depressed the key.

"Yes, Glenn, I am here," she replied, briefly curious to how her own voice sounded on the other end and then shrugged. "And it's *Nys*-sa, not Nyssie… Over."

"*Riighht,*" Glenn's sarcasm came back to her, and she could picture his round cheeks gleaming with a smile, while a hand sat tucked into his pocket just under his rounded, plump belly somewhere inside. The image made her cringe. "Any-who, as you know we are really busy today because of the sales, and we are running out of carts… again, over."

"I know, Glenn," her eyes rolling. "That's why I am out here in this furnace getting more of them."

"*Riighht,* well, can you pick up the pace a bit?" Glenn's sarcasm came stronger than ever, and Nyssa could almost feel the glow from his cheesy smile through the plastic radio set. "I have had three customers ask: '*Where are all the carts?*', and we do not want unhappy customers, do we?"

"Bite me!" she hissed without depressing the key and cursed twice under her breath. Calming, she produced a cheesy grin just in time for two would-be shoppers at Value-Mart to near before she delivered her proper retort.

"Of course, we don't want unhappy customers at Value-Mart, Glenn," her smile broadening like the *Cheshire Cat* while adding a little curtsy to the customers when they were right on top of her. "We wouldn't want that at all, or they might take their business elsewhere and find better bargains down the road at Walmart, *if* they had read the Sunday paper.

"Welcome to Value-Mart!" she finished towards the customers as they walked past her, slightly widening their berth. "Over!"

"What?" Glenn's voice raced back through the radio and Nyssa clicked it off.

With a deep growl rolling the back of her throat, Nyssa stormed into the sweltering parking lot, hands bunched in tight little fists and pumping hard as she stormed to the first cart corral, slamming one into the other to make a tight-fitting pack.

It was going to be a long, hot day.

-2-

By two o'clock, Nyssa had feverishly brought in line after line of carts as if she had been driving in herds of steel-meshed, wheel-mounted cattle with such celerity that the lot seemed barren of them. At one point, as her brow dripped heavy sweat like rainwater on glass, an elderly woman appeared to her side and insisted that she take better caution in the heat.

"You really should try to pace yourself, young miss," the woman said, brow bunched with genuine concern. Nyssa stood looking at the short woman for a moment and was amazed that at barely five-foot-one herself, the woman was shorter than her. "Young people can get heat stroke just like us old folks moving like that."

"I know," was Nyssa's simple answer.

Yes, it was hot, and yes, she was pushing herself well beyond a point anyone in current conditions should be, but it simply boiled down that at the time the heat wasn't on her mind, and now, after being reminded of it, it surely was going to be.

"Thank you for caring."

"You are welcome, dear," the woman nodded at her with a concerned once-over look, then produced a thin smile, regarding the blazing sky. "You would expect heat like this in the Southwest somewhere, wouldn't you? Well at least we can wish for rain, right?"

Off the woman went with her little legs moving steadily, and as the automatic sliding doors parted at the Value-Mart's entrance, her lightweight clothing blasted back as the rush of conditioned air greeted her. Nyssa watched her disappear amongst the rolling masses of shoppers inside and slowly regarded the sky, thinking: *At least I can wish for it.*

-3-

"Break time already?" A rough raspy voice sounded over Nyssa's shoulder as she sat on one of the benches just inside the store while holding a damp paper towel to her eye. She didn't need to turn to know that it was Roberta—the self-proclaimed staff monitor who ran the returns desk—standing behind her.

Ah, Roberta: there was a piece of this woman under every employee's skin, irritating the senses and causing discomfort like a jagged splinter. The only one who seemed to get along with her was Glenn because they both shared the same pastime of annoying other people, sometimes to a sadistic degree. Many disliked her because of her voice—heavy like sun-cracked leather from decades of chain smoking—while some due to her inquisitive purposefulness of minding other people's business. Despite the reasons, everyone under management had one agreeable dislike for her, and that was her loathsome trait of being a rat. If you did or said anything that may interest Glenn or the other supervising staff, you could be sure they would know about it, and Roberta did the informing.

"No, not yet," Nyssa mumbled back half turning, damping her eye with the paper towel.

"Oh, so then you are just relaxing then?" Roberta continued, studying her with an expression like a cat poised outside a mouse hole.

"I have to cool down," Nyssa snapped, her hand coming away from her face, exposing her sweaty brow. "You do know it's like an oven out there, right?"

"Oh, I am not saying anything!" Roberta protested, hands flinging up; her voice laced with denial and false pretenses and dared to produce a carefree laugh. "Oh my! Your skin is rather red and splotchy. I completely understand. I was just saying that you know how Glenn is about things."

"Yes, I know, Roberta," she ended the conversation as she turned away, the damp paper towel returning to her eye and her ears picking up the rapid clacking of Roberta's hard soled shoes on the tiles as she scurried away.

And I am quite certain he will hear about it in five minutes flat, she thought to herself gritting her teeth.

"Oh my God it feels so good in here!" a voice exclaimed somewhere behind her as the automated doors slid open, and two teenagers and their mother entered the store. *"Man, I could just stay in here all day!"*

So could I, Nyssa thought, her eyes picking up the shimmer of solar heat swirling in the air near ground level of the car park through the glass doors.

From the front pocket of her bright orange, semi-reflective smock—a horrible thing she had to wear in the parking lot so drivers could see her—she pulled a small white box that locked when you snapped it closed. She jiggled it back and forth, reassuring herself that she still had some pain pills. Her cramps had started that morning when she woke, low, distant, and persistent; the tell-tale sign for her that she was a day away at most from her period.

She hated the pre-symptoms more than the actual event because this not only meant the constant, ever-growing agony of bloating, but it also meant that she had two basic moods: complacency and rolling thunder (the latter was the dominant one, and no one wanted to be around her when that happened).

"Oh, Nyssie?" squawked Glenn's voice over the radio set, making her cringe.

"I know, Glenn!" she barked into it, her hand squeezing the set so tightly it seemed that she would crush it and then shut it off.

With a heavy irritated growl, Nyssa stood quickly; dropping the paper towel into the trash and then headed back into the inferno. As she passed the service counter towards the exit, she caught Roberta's gaze as the old bird half-assed arranged packs of chewing gum in a closed checkout isle, surprised not in the least to see the evil wench smiling.

Bitch just broke her tattletale record! Nyssa screamed inside her head and fought against herself from wishing horrible, wicked thoughts about the woman as a wall of heat slammed into her as she exited.

It's a good thing that she did not *wish* those things—especially for Roberta's sake—or this story would have taken on an incredible turn of events to say the very least.

-5-

After purchasing what may have been her fourth bottle of water from the vending machines, she decided to retrieve the straggler carts which dotted the lot's further edges.

At least concerning Nyssa, gathering the stragglers was her 'alone time'; a place where there were no customers, no co-workers, and most importantly, far out of the transmit/receive range of the cheap little radios. They had radios on the shelves, which boasted a five-mile range in any weather condition, but because they carried a hefty price tag, staff had to use the bargain-basement ones. For this reason, and only this reason, she was happy that management was a bunch of cheapskates.

Now she could pace herself and breathe, gathering up the *ones* and *twos* that sat off in the distance while reassuring herself of all the *Whys'* she took the job in the first place.

She loved music, which she had in abundance on her little *SanDisk* player but downloading songs costs money. There was also her clothing style, albeit not high fashion, but those too cost money. Nyssa also liked going out with the few close friends in her circle. That also came with a price tag, but most importantly, she was doing it to show her mother that she *was* responsible and *could* finish something she had started.

As she walked through the ocean of cars, seemingly lost in her own world while drowning in tepid water brought on by the humidity, Nyssa found herself wondering was all that worth it in the end.

Slowly she pushed four carts that she had gathered towards another one straddling the lot's curb at the furthest edge of the property, and mindlessly she regarded the small Bank of America branch building's illuminated clock in the adjoining lot. One moment it blinked at her 2:17; the next moment, it taunted her, displaying 102°F.

"This is *so* not right," she mumbled to herself, and pressed a palm deeply into her lower abdomen to quell her pulsating cramps. She exhaled seething air with a soft moan then glanced at the sky which held a solitary cotton ball-like cloud off in the distance. She prayed that it would move closer, perhaps blotting out the sun for even just a little while, but she knew it would more than likely burn off well before giving such an aid.

This was day eleven of the rolling heat wave, broiling Chicagoland mercilessly, leaving the night no comfort as the darkness held the day's temperature in a sultry soup of muggy humidity. Her mind flashed through her employee's handbook under 'Work Conditions,' and she could have sworn there was something in there about this crap, and if not, her mind spelled out the complaint that she would write to OSHA if she passed out under these conditions.

"This really sucks ass!" she growled, slamming the cart home into the awaiting collapsible rear of the four she had in line and then guzzled down the remaining water in her bottle. Grunting angrily, she tossed the bottle into a cart and delivered a swift kick to its rear and then shoved them into motion; snapping an acute glare at the sky and loudly spat out:

"I really wish it would rain!"

What Nyssa could only describe later as a jolt—very similar to striking one's funny bone smartly and directly—exploded and raced from her armpits, rounded the elbows, and blasted its way across her wrists and through the palms. There was a loud *Pop!* as it shot forth, forcing the carts to rear up like bucking horses, coming down hard on their wheels, toppling them over to their sides. She stood stark and shaken with her palms to her mouth as her eyes locked onto the rapidly spinning wheels, which hissed around their bearings; barely noticing the sharp startled squeal that had escaped her throat or the acrid odor of singed ozone floating about her like after a lightning strike.

Thunder, far away and distant, rumbled, coming to her in a low, heavy growl.

"What the—" she managed, stooping down next to the carts with her eyes transfixed on the spinning wheels which moved in a blur. She rested a palm on the mesh side of one of the carts for balance, pressing hard, and then suddenly snatched it back with a painful hiss as the heat there raced in, leaving hot red lines.

Thunder growled again, heavier, closer, calling out to her, drawing her attention as she slowly looked to the heavens. That once solitary white cloud, which seemed so insignificantly insignificant in a field of blue, no longer resembled a nice fluffy cotton ball. It now expanded and rolled like a thick wall of iron gray mud, erasing any hint of a pristine sky. Slowly she stood, her burnt palm resting in the other, her eyes wide and darting in an attempt to take in the expanding darkness as her mind filled with dread.

I really wish it would rain, echoed through her mind as she slowly backed away from the carts, and a sudden brilliant display of lightning and instantaneous thunder exploded overhead, giving her such a start that she squealed and pin-wheeled backward, almost falling.

"Holy crap!" she exclaimed, regaining a solid footing as her fingers gripped the sides of her hair, the burned palm quickly forgotten.

A wall of cold air blew across the parking lot, and she shivered involuntarily as the wave hit her. Refuse in the forms of discarded pop bottles, candy wrappers, Styrofoam coffee cups, shopping receipts, and spent cigarette butts that littered the lot began to shuffle and move as light breezes became gusting winds. The smell of rain began to weigh heavy in the air, and her eyes snapped back towards the bank in time to see the 2:21 hour blink away and the temperature displayed 79°F.

It's fallen more than twenty degrees! her mind screamed, attempting to find reason in this unnatural-natural insanity. Nyssa found the clouds again, marveling at how they rolled over each other while mixing and expanding, twisting, and dancing.

Briefly, she recognized one thing through all the chaos: it wasn't just rain she smelled on that particularly peculiar day, but saltwater rain, like during trips long ago when her family vacationed near the ocean.

Lightning flashed, and thunder exploded in a barbaric head-on collision of light and sound and then the rain came, torrentially heavy and instantly blinding.

Nyssa needed no more convincing than that.

She turned and bolted across the parking lot towards the Value-Mart, leaving the carts where they lay as her white and blue *Skechers* kicked up thick splashes of water behind her. By the time she had reached the inner lot closest to the store, her feet were blasting through an inch of water while twenty-five-mile-an-hour headwinds were hampering her retreat. Day had become night, unyielding heat had become a chilly waterpark playland, and under the bellowing thunder, Nyssa didn't realize that she was laughing and screaming the whole while.

As Nyssa appeared into view through the gray to the shoppers inside gawking out—her face stretched in a continual expression of childish glee—she side-skidded to a stop, snapped a glance back up towards the sky while cupping her hands to both sides of her mouth and screamed: *"Thank you!"*

Laughing, she skipped the remaining distance into the open doors.

CHAPTER TWO

Journey Through the Storm

-1-

A fluke storm, that's all it was, plain and simple. Something for the scholarly books as a blatant disregard towards the nature of scientific order which will keep meteorologists scratching their heads for years to come, and then some.

Things like that happen from time to time, much like having the sole winning lottery ticket with odds of multi-millions to one or tossing pocket change on a desk and for some reason based on the rules of *Chaos* and *Probability*, one of the coins lands on its edge and remains there.

Sure they do… they happen all the time… maybe at least once or twice a day…

Don't they?

Nyssa's mind played with these thoughts as she sat staring out the 331 Local Stop bus window, her eyes wide and gathering in all of the storm's possibilities while not seeing it either. Westland Mall shut down entirely, prematurely ending the business day for over a hundred plus stores, and for once, her bus packed to the seams. Luckily for her, the bus stop sitting one storefront down from her workplace was the end and the beginning of the route loop, so getting a seat was an easy blessing.

Her all-country *Schwinn* bicycle was fastened securely to the front of the bus in the courtesy carrier and getting a needed bath. Other than walking, it was her only mode of transportation save the off-schedule buses in her suburban town. She loved her bike—a silver and blue mountain-type model with twenty-six speeds that she had never had the chance to use entirely, which she lovingly named *Blue*—but on this day, as she rode the bus through the storm, the idea of reaching her stop and then pedaling a mile in this maelstrom was not a welcomed one.

The bus shuddered as gusts slammed against its broad flat side, drawing gasps amongst the forest of people sitting and standing. A man sitting next to her released a nervous, fear-laced chuckle and gave her arm a nudge.

"It sure beats the heat, though, doesn't it?"

Nyssa produced a thin smile to present a believable affinity of understanding, adding a nod for good measure. Her mind was too numb to bolster along the nervous double standard comparison the man had made, so she returned her attention out the window where a tangled mass of thick rain rivers crisscrossed the lightly tinted glass. Slowly, she rubbed her palms against her pants to soothe the tingling itch left over from the parking lot event.

Confused and shaken, Nyssa pressed her lips together tightly as her mind attempted to match the illogical pieces to the logical ones and still not finding a picture in the puzzle that the day had presented her with.

15

"Whoa! Another big one!" the man next to her exclaimed as the bus shuddered, nervously chuckling once again; his tone well past being anxious and teetering on the boundary of fear.

She wasn't afraid of the storm; she loved thunderstorms and often sat in her garage with the door open, watching them as they rolled through, but there was something not right about this particular one. It simply shouldn't be there—one-minute brilliant blue skies, the next a raging front—and the more she attempted to rationalize the impossible possibilities, the more it hurt her head.

None of it made sense.

Maybe a passing car clipped the carts which toppled them? She attempted, then shook her head.

No, the person would certainly have stopped, more than likely to chew her out for being careless and the driver would have demanded to see her boss.

Maybe you simply don't know your own strength? Her mind quickly added, disregarding the prior possibility and then shook her head once again.

She was strong for a girl, as so many people have told her, but she wasn't masculine by any standard. Although she played just about every sport both in and outside of school, she knew it was still highly improbable. The carts were simply too heavy, especially five of them interlocked.

Maybe— she closed her eyes to her own thoughts and listened to the storm blast away outside.

*

As the bus made its scheduled turn onto Ogden, a shockwave of gasps, '*Ooos*' and '*Ahhs,*' overcame the crowded space of the vehicle as the passenger's attention drew towards her side. The driver slowed and dipped towards the curb to avoid a large, downed oak resembling a massive piece of broccoli as it lay sprawled in the street.

Funny, they are as big below the ground as they are on top, her mind noted; her eyes taking in the massive tree which looked as if a giant had plucked the whole thing from the ground and dropped it there.

"Ladies and gentlemen!" The driver's voice came over the PA system nervously. "In the event that we encounter any downed wires, I am authorized to divert this bus to the next stop. If there are any downed lines near your stop, I cannot permit you to exit for your safety. Thank you."

Great! She sighed to herself, arms folding. *Be my luck that there will be lines down all over my stop!*

Eyes closing to the world, she breathed slowly, calming herself and damning her morning's haste by forgetting her music player at home. Focusing on her breathing, she slowly began to recognize the state in which all the riders were in, ranging from excited awe to absolute terror.

"I can't believe it!" One woman was whispering loudly to her bus mate from one of the sideways, aisle-facing seats. "Weatherman said it was going to be a burner for the next three to five days!"

Tick-tick-tick...

"Did you see how those clouds grew outward above the mall?" Softly but excitedly, a man not too far behind her spoke, his voice crackling over the consonants. "I have seen storms all over the world, from monsoons to hurricanes, and I ain't ever seen anything like that!

"*'There ain't no such thing as Global warming.'* Bah! My ass there is!"

Tick-tick-tick...

"This must be that *El Niño* or *El Niña* stuff, man," a young teenage skater-kid wearing all black and a T-shirt regarding something about having 'an effing great day' was telling his friend in the next row over and a few seats up. "I can't remember which one is which, but they both screw up the weather, man. I mean, whichever one does this stuff, ya know, man? Heard they once got hail the size of basketballs in California because of it, man. Fucking wicked stuff, man!"

Tick-tick-tick...

"My kids are home alone in all this," said an almost frantic woman loud enough that it seemed as if she was everywhere on the bus at once; her voice clearly straining near panic. "I mean, they are old enough to stay at home alone... fifteen, twelve and eleven, they are... but this storm... I mean it's so violent! And the power is probably out! It always goes out!

"Why isn't this driver moving any faster?"

Tick-tick-tick...

Nyssa sat and breathed deeply while listening but attempting to block it all out at the same time. She empathized with all of them, each having their own right to their fears and excitement, but for her, at that instant, it was nothing more than painful noise much akin to trying to cope with a migraine with a blender on. It was a dull pain that began to form in the middle of her forehead not too long before the storm came and a clear indication that she had been out in the sun way too long and was over-exerting herself. Now, it pulsated brightly at the back of her eyes like a distant flasher on a stranded automobile in the fog.

TICK! TICK! TICK!

"Is that your watch?" Nyssa snapped at the man next to her, her hazel eyes blazing into him. The man jumped as if she had slapped him and then he glanced at his wrist. There sat his imitation silver *Timex* with the second hand ticking away history.

"Yuh-yes, why?" he asked, shocked and puzzled.

"Nothing!" she growled, eyes shooting back through the window. "It's deafening… I can't hear myself think."

And that was that. No more nudges, no more nervous chuckles and clearly no more conversations between the two of them on their ride along bus route 331.

-2-

What is with you? she cursed herself, her stomach feeling bubbly and sour. She closed her eyes again, hoping to settle it, when she noticed the echo of her pulse in her ears. Nyssa had never experienced claustrophobia before that day—that eerie sensation that everything was closing in and trapping one within their skin—but at that moment, she knew all too well what those who suffered from it were talking about.

Exhaling heavily, she realized that she had been holding her breath for quite some time, and her head and chest burned with the hot, stale air.

With each thunderclap came another image in her mind: the carts, the sun, the heat, the parking lot, the old woman telling her to pace herself, the bank sign and that little ridiculous cloud sitting aloft in a field of blue. All of it completely irrelevant to this storm and yet all leading up to her simply saying—

"I wish it would rain," she whispered to no one, and her palms sparked.

Lightning exploded directly above the bus, accompanied by a loud and violent thunderous explosion that sounded like it had gone off inside the vehicle itself, shuddering it to its bolts. A loud culmination of gasps and shrieks raced through the tight spaces of the vehicle as the interior lights blinked on and off, and somewhere amongst them, two small children began to cry.

'I wish you would not do that again!' barked in between her ears, startling her.

"What did you say?" she said to no one in particular, attracting the eyes of the man next to her as well as several of the standing passengers as they held onto the above handrail. Her eyes darted amongst the cautious expressions which were attached to wry faces full of confusion.

'You heard me, girl!' came the voice again: feminine, commanding and stern.

Nyssa's eyes shot through a triangle-shaped space between two people and the back of the seat in front of her, meeting those of a woman with short black hair the color of a raven's back. She had the most brilliant green eyes Nyssa had ever seen, and they never blinked; the woman's focusing solely on her. For that moment, there was no sound or storm, and even the bus with all its passengers seemed to disappear. The woman was staring directly into her mind with the same blank expression her mother would give her if she were doing something inappropriate in public.

The woman's pupils narrowed, drilling into her mind.

'Once was enough, don't you think?'

Nyssa snatched her eyes from the angered gaze, finding her lap quite interesting now. At the same time, the all-too-familiar sickening feeling came over her as guilt-laced adrenalin pumped into her stomach. She fumbled with her fingers, one hand coming up and rolling through a damp curl in her hair, and then found her mouth as if trying to remove a hangnail. Cautiously, she chanced a glance back at the woman sitting sidesaddle on her seat facing away, reading a magazine.

Acid flared the back of her throat, bringing a wave of heat and sweat to her skin, for suddenly, Nyssa *really* needed to throw up.

Quickly, she snatched at the stop request pull cord and yanked on it several times, setting off an audible alert for the driver to halt at the next available stop.

She had to get off that bus!

Outside the winds continued to howl as the storm pounded and stomped its way across the area as the bus began to slow towards the curb, two whole stops away from her usual destination.

-3-

"Do you need a hand with your bike, miss?" the driver asked, mainly because he had to according to company policy and procedure, while secretly praying that the answer would be 'no.' He *had* to drive in the storm but didn't *want* to go out in it; the downed tree in the street a way back was a good enough reason for him.

Nyssa simply shook her head daring not to speak, fearing that if she opened her mouth to utter a single word, everyone on that bus would know *exactly* what she had had for lunch.

The pneumatic doors opened with a pressurized hiss, and Nyssa bounded off, her feet barely touching any of the steps, and into the heavy rain she went. Breathing heavily, she moved to the front and unhinged the locking mechanism securing *Blue*.

Heaving once, she freed it from the carrier and then swung the clasp back into place with a bang. Quickly, she moved from the path of the bus and stood on the sidewalk, panting as the engine revved up as started to roll. As the bus passed, she chanced a glance up towards the windows only to find the woman with jet-black hair and brilliant green eyes peering into her.

Thick sheets of rain came in the form of dark grays as her shoulders rose and fell rapidly, the nausea mounting, and although the riders of the 331 Local Stop bus were spared the inevitable, Nyssa threw up. Panting heavily while holding her midsection— strained tears commingling and combining with the falling rain—she cursed incoherently as she spat towards the off-red mass of cheesy baked ziti, garlic bread, cranberry juice, and two *Altoids*, which was quickly running off with the stormwater.

"Yummy," she managed past a shuddering cough, thanking herself for holding her breath while her stomach emptied itself so that none of it came out of her nose.

Straightening, she looked towards the direction she would have to travel in and sighed: there was a whole mile waiting for her in addition to the usual homebound distance. Slowly, she watched a sole car roll by at a snail's pace, its tires kicking up furrows of water that came up to its door panels as it crept by in the flooding street.

Soaking wet, Nyssa mounted her bike while a murmur of a thought, a wish perhaps herself, coursed her mind as she glanced at the raging sky above her. Stopping herself mid-thought, she thought better of it.

Slowly, she began to pedal through the deep water gathering along Ogden with her eyes focused on her front tire rolling.

-4-

When she reached the ordinarily busy intersection of Elm and Ogden—her would-be stop along the 331 route—she wasn't all too surprised to find the street barren. All of the traffic lights were dark, dead orbs sitting in their chassis, and just a little further down Ogden, where it declined towards a large *Walgreens* drugstore, she could see a lake of flood water which had pooled there, stranding several cars in more than three feet of water.

I guess the planners didn't think that one through, she thought distantly, remembering how during Hurricane Katrina, the floodwaters produced all the carnage they did because New Orleans was below sea level and then shivered at her thoughts in the rain.

There was no stranded bus waiting next to the street with its hazards on, as she had earlier assumed, halted in its advance due to downed power lines, just empty streets filled with the noise of the storm.

She made a slow right onto Elm, her eyes narrowing to thin slits as she headed directly into the eastward cold winds of the storm. Pedaling in this was no easy task, especially with the added resistance of her soaked work uniform, which clung to her like a heavily matted molding. Tan Dockers and white polo shirts made up a nice basic uniform which she didn't mind much; however, adding wet and cold to the mix? Well, let's say she was happy she had worn a bra that day.

-5-

Two blocks up she made a sharp right onto Persimmon Lane, a pretty tree-lined street which made an ideal course change towards home. Although it inclined, twisted, and curved a lot, which would make her trek home even longer, it was on higher ground and out of the direct force of the headwinds.

Nyssa had her future already planned out, which gave her the strength to push on. She would peel off the wet clothes, followed by a long, hot shower to melt away the cold. She would then dress in fresh, warm baggy clothes and get a tall glass of milk to ensure her stomach settled, and then music; lots of music.

The perfect end to a horrible day.

With eyes fixed on the prize and her front tire, she focused on her pedaling, rounding a downed branch on the walk, then suddenly let out a startled scream as dark masses entered the peripheral ahead of her. Grasping the brakes tightly and leaning inward, she side-skidded to a stop and came within inches of running into a couple walking a little dachshund whose curved, cord-like tail wagged rapidly back and forth.

"Sorry!" she blurted out, wiping water and hair from her face, her eyes happening upon theirs, which were wide-eyed and full of curiosity.

They were a youngish interracial couple not too unlike her mother and father: the woman of Caucasian decent, short, with a soft brunette tone and brown eyes; the man was a taller Hispanic, or perhaps even interracially mixed like her own dad, with a splatter of freckles on his cheeks. Wearing balanced summer earth tones comprised of shorts, tops, and comfortable warm-weather shoes, they were not dressed for the weather. The woman regarded her with a blank inquisitive look, while the man only produced a thin smile, broadening his trimmed reddish goatee.

"No worries," he said, smiling wider, pulling back lightly on the leash as the little dachshund attempted a closer inspection of one of her ankles. "No harm done. Having a nice ride?"

"*No!*" she spat out over the roar of the storm, and that's when it dawned on her, panging the inside of her mind and detonating a bomb of disquietude in her soul.

Slowly she looked them over, scanning them from head to toe to the little dachshund dog too, and then back up towards their eyes.

"You're dry!" she blurted out, rainwater spraying from her lips.

"And you're wet," the man replied not losing a beat, his smile broadening.

"*Noviciatus,*" the woman whispered as she leaned close to him, her eyes never leaving Nyssa's and the man simply nodded.

"*What?*" Nyssa begged, her eyes darting amongst these images of complete confusion.

"So why are you wet?" the man asked, dismissing the woman's comment.

"Be… because it's storming!" Nyssa was almost screaming it to compensate for the howling winds, her index finger pointing to the sky.

"She's not too bright, either," the woman added with a thin smile, finishing with a brief, exacting nod.

"Whu-what?" Nyssa stammered.

"See?" the woman confirmed, and the man gave her a slight nudge with his shoulder, and she silenced. His smile softened, eyes filling with warmth and then he took a deep breath.

"I know that it's storming, little one," he began, never needing to raise his tone, giving an eyebrow a quick scratch. "But *why* are *you* wet?"

Nyssa's mouth dropped as if on greased hinges, her mind narrowing to a filament of common sense. She had just a moment to look about herself to assure the mind that the weather was truly raging.

"What I am getting at," he corrected himself. "You *do* know that *you* don't have to be wet right now, don't you?"

For a moment, Nyssa thought that she was being put on, but then again, here they were, standing right before her: dry. Her mouth closed then opened repeatedly much like a fish expelled from its environment, then finalized all the actions by shaking her head.

"She doesn't understand what's going on," the woman spoke directly, and her expression softened as Nyssa's hand went to her stomach as her skin color changed. Quickly the woman thrust a hand into her pocket and produced a narrow cream and orange pack. "Gum?"

Nyssa shook her head.

"Trust me," the woman insisted. "It will help with that nauseous feeling creeping through your belly right now."

Reluctantly, Nyssa took a piece and removed the tan and gold wrapper, placed it in her mouth, and slowly began to chew. It had the flavor of butterscotch with lemon and a distant taste of warm buttermilk with a hint of raisins. It was an odd flavor indeed, one that she would typically recoil from, perhaps even spit out, but her stomach growled towards it hungrily, and she began to chew in rapid chomps.

"Careful," the man added with a smile. "You wouldn't want to bite the inside of your cheek now do you?"

A soft moan of relief escaped Nyssa's throat as she shook her head in reply. In moments her stomach completely unknotted and calmed, even the acrid taste of the earlier mishap had escaped her.

"Better?" he added, eyebrows up.

"Yes, thank you," she smiled, enjoying the refreshing wave of relief come over her.

"She has nice dimples," the woman added to the conversation and cracked a pleasant smile herself.

"She does indeed," the man concurred. "Well, shall we get on with our walk? Little Marley here has many a bush and tree to mark today."

Nodding, they rounded past her, with Marley immediately sniffing along a grouping of flowers near the edge of the walk, finding a scent he was looking for, and then popped up a hind leg and gave the blossoms a few rapid squirts. Nyssa stood over her bike, eyes wide with disbelief, watching the ground beneath them, which seemed to grow temporarily dry as the water parted and receded to the walk's edge, only to flow back into itself as their feet passed.

"What did you mean that I don't have to be wet right now?" she called after them, her voice attempting to best the noise of the storm.

The couple and the dog stopped, their eyes met, and then they slowly turned towards her.

"Simple:" the man replied. "Magic."

With that, they left her and continued their day; their hands finding one another like a definitive poster print of a loving couple while little Marley was busy sniffing out his next deposit point.

"Magic," she whispered to herself, her eyes trailing upwards towards the sky which played no part in the conversation nor cared regardless.

It was doing what was expected of it; it was raining.

CHAPTER THREE

Guilt Trip

-1-

Nyssa had walked her bike the remaining distance home; there had been no sense riding it any longer because all the sidewalks had become pools continuously bombarded by the sheeting rain, and the streets were rivers: fast and deep. Regarding being wet, she was soaked to the core long before getting on the bus in the first place, and another ten minutes in the storm wasn't going to matter much in the end. Yet, the real reason for walking the bike instead of riding it had nothing to do with the conditions; after the encounter with the couple and their dog, she didn't seem to have the mental strength to do anything else.

She entered her house by way of the attached garage, leaning *Blue* against some shelving sans the kickstand. She slowly moved through a small hallway separating the main house from the inner garage door, passing the washer and dryer and several neatly stacked boxes of *Wanted* but not *Needed* items that had been stacked there for six months since they moved in. Her stepfather will eventually get to move them the additional nine feet into the garage for storage… eventually.

The sound of the television met her first: loud and clear despite the noise of the storm.

"I just can't believe this, can you, babe?" The voice of her stepfather rose above the speakers, followed by some inaudible reply from her mother.

Nyssa stood in the small kitchen foyer, separating it from the dining and living room, dripping from every matted crease of her clothing, forming a decent-sized pool of water beneath her. Her mother saw her first as she shot a quick upwards glance from her magazine, then a second chance glance as her mind needed more information to process.

"Nyss?" her mother inquired, using the lazy pet name for her as she closed her copy of *Better Homes & Gardens*. Her stepfather glanced back over the sofa momentarily, gave her a double glance just as her mother had done, and then peered over his wire-framed glasses. The central air was still blowing despite the outdoor temperature dropping to a chilly 69°F, setting off uncontrolled shivers throughout her soaked body.

"Cuh-cuh-cold," Nyssa stammered and then set her house keys on the kitchen counter.

"I can see that," her mother stood and moved towards the kitchen with a rare expression of concern on her face. "You are soaked through!"

"Th-the st-storm," Nyssa shook with an arm rising and a finger slowly pointing towards the outside through the walls.

"Dear God, Nyssa! Why didn't you pick up the phone and call us?"

Bingo! the mother-tone Nyssa was expecting to hear.

"I duh-did!" Nyssa stuttered back, slowly shuffling her feet towards her room and trailing water behind her. "Phone wuh-wouldn't guh-go thr-through."

"No, no, no, no! Not on the carpet!" her mother demanded with a shaking head and moving fast; snatching open the hallway linen closet, pulling down a bath towel, and handing it to Nyssa. "You will get everything wet!"

Nyssa's eyes locked onto her mother's as the two of them reinitiated their ongoing battle of 'Alpha Female,' if their stares were truly sharp as knives, the house would have been a bloodbath. After a few moments, Nyssa simply added a 'thank you,' lined with razor blades dipped in arsenic, twice.

Her stepfather, Randy, approached with a wild spark illuminating his eyes as his mind pored over the events of the violent storm and the news broadcasts of it. Historically, since her mother and Randy met six years before, he had focused on being a kiss-ass to her mother, and his mood would emulate whatever her mother's was at the moment. If she was pissed, he was pissed; if she were happy, his spirit would follow suit, but not this time. Now the storm encompassed everything in his world, and as Nyssa looked at his wide, darting eyes, she could tell that this storm was scaring the crap out of him.

"I am sorry, Nyss," he spoke excitedly, and Nyssa bit down against saying anything about the nickname. "If I knew it was going to be this bad, I would have come and got you long before the streets flooded out."

Her real father hated the fact that anyone called her anything but her whole real name; a trait which she also carried after her dad once explained it to her as they sat having cereal one morning during a weekend visit.

"I named you Nyssa, not Nyssie, Nyss or anyway else you could bastardize your name," her father had said flatly. *"If I wanted you to be called Nyss, I would have named you that. Always be proud of your name, baby, it fits you well.*

Nyssa wanted to correct them both as she rubbed the towel through her matted hair, but she thought otherwise so not to reignite the battle which had been waging for years on the subject.

"Forget it," she said quietly, moving to the entrance mat for the garage and pried her drowned and bloated shoes and socks off.

"Why didn't you ask someone for a ride?" her mother asked, taking a seat at one of the counter stools, her face full of an expression of near disdain. Nyssa paused, her eyes relocking with her mother's and then shook her head. "Oh, that's right; you don't like any of the people you work with."

"That's not important," Randy said, waving a dismissive hand towards his wife, dividing their confrontation, and expressing a different approach than his usual siding with her mother. "I am just glad you made it home safely. This storm is bad... really, *really* bad."

Their mouths parted in disbelief as their eyes met one another as if assuring they were witnessing the same thing. For Nyssa, her surprise came because he was showing genuine concern for her wellbeing whilst her mother's gawk hung without commentary since he had just disregarded her passé daily bitching.

Wordlessly, he moved into the kitchen, retrieving a gallon of milk from the refrigerator, snatched a glass from the dish rack, and poured it nearly full. He quickly retrieved a small bottle of butterscotch flavored syrup from a tiny shelf of other syrups besides the coffee maker, plus a small flask of lemon extract from the spice rack. In a furor like a bartender preparing drinks in a busy tavern, he added a splash of syrup and a few drops of lemon extract into the milk, stirred it with a spoon which he tossed blindly into the sink, and then set the concoction on the counter before her.

Thirty seconds flat; worthy of an extra dollar tip if it had been a bar.

"This will settle your stomach, Nyssa," he said quickly, moving back towards the living room where the newscasters were droning on about the freakish storm, not looking back. "You should take a hot shower and get into some warm baggy clothes; that will stop the shakes."

The two of them watched him come and go, returning to the edge of the couch, leaning forward on his thighs, and intently holding on to every word coming from the set. Nyssa wasn't shivering any longer, her eyes slowly settling on the glass of milk waiting for her on the counter.

Milk, shower and warm baggy clothes, her mind whispered the words that Randy said, the same thoughts she had back on Persimmons Lane of what she needed to relax. All that was missing was the—

"Oh, your dad called while you were at work earlier," Randy called in from the living room, never turning from the television. "He said that he added money to your music account so you can download fifty bucks' worth of songs. He told me to tell you to enjoy and he will call you later."

What the—her mind began, and suddenly she felt nauseous again. Quickly she moved forward, grabbed the glass, and began sucking it down. Much akin to the gum from earlier, her nausea dissipated quickly into a fine mist of chilly, odd-tasting relief. Her mother—head cocked to the side like a curious puppy—noised a soft *'Huh'* and then slowly stood and entered the living room, sitting next to Randy while whispering something inaudible.

Nyssa was pulling the last drops into her mouth as she walked through the edge of the living room and down the hall to her bedroom, where she slowly began to pull off the soaked clothes as she headed into her adjoining bathroom.

As she held one hand in the running water while adjusting the knobs of hot and cold to get it just right, only two things kept looping through her mind: *'You know you don't have to be wet right now'* and her own inculpating, damning question of guilt, *'Are you doing all this?'*

With no answer to either quandary, she stepped into an entirely different type of shower than she had already experienced that day.

-2-

Randy was still sitting on the edge of the sofa with the remote control in his hand, bouncing between the *Weather Channel* and the *WGN Chicago* local news station when Nyssa quietly came into the living room.

"Where's my mom?" she asked, not really caring.

"Lying down…" he replied, pausing to take a swallow from his glass. "… her sinuses again… bad one."

She sat in the recliner, her extra baggy gray sweat shorts and shirt poofing up around her, creating an invisible cloud of fresh-scented dryer sheets and warm days. She had removed her contacts, replaced them with wire-rimmed glasses, and pulled her hair back into a long ponytail.

Nyssa usually didn't care for the news in any format, whether televised, broadcasted, or in print; it was always full of depressing local, national, and world events, and when anything positive happened, it always had the shortest runtime. Like her dad, she had been a fan of *National Geographic Magazine* for their amazing photography, but as she began to read the articles, even there, she could only find depression. From leopard seals in the Artic to wild dingoes in Australia, the history and nature of these beautiful creatures would fold out to her in picture and print, only to grow dark and sinister about how they are disappearing from the planet with the usual suspect: Mankind.

"Humanity loves misery, Nyssa," her father once told her when she had asked why people held on to news reports of war, murder, and mayhem as if it was their lifeline. *"It's sad and pathetic, I know, but people are always more concerned about a car accident on the side of the road than the scenery they pass along the drive."*

Randy's expression held the look of desperate obsession, occasionally licking his lips as he pressed the **RECALL** button on the remote, bouncing back between channels. She so badly wanted to call him out on his rapid channel switching—maybe even add a snooty two-cent comment in for good measure, especially since the scolding she receives for doing the same on lazy days. For now, she would bite her tongue this time; there was something so utterly odd about his nature today.

"This is just crazy, Nyss," he said and then shot her a quick, nervous glance. "I mean Nyssa… sorry."

Quickly, his eyes shot back to the television when the commercial ended.

"How bad is it?" she asked quietly.

"Really bad," he replied, and Nyssa sank back in her chair, swallowing hard. "There have been no reported deaths—quite a lot of injuries, though—but mainly the flooding and the winds. There are a lot of downed trees, and tons of people are out of power—somewhere close to a hundred and sixty thousand and climbing. I am just surprised that we still have power and phone. Speaking of which, your dad called while you were in the shower. He is concerned about the storm; you should try him back on his cell."

"Oh, thanks," she replied and took up the cordless phone which had been sitting on the coffee table and entered in her father's number without needing to look at the buttons. Listening, the call immediately went to a recording. "Hmm, it's going straight to voicemail."

"Oh, damn, sorry," Randy shot her several nervous glances. "He said he was about to get on a plane, but to leave him a message telling him you are okay. I told him you were, but you know; he wants to hear it from you."

Nyssa nodded and clicked the redial, listened through the brief message her father left for all callers and then she added her own message, happy and chipper as she normally did. She finished with an *'I love you'* and *'safe trip'* with the reminder for him to call her once he had landed, and then returned her eyes towards the set distantly.

"Oh, here we go!" Randy quickly readjusted his seating, leaning forward sharply and resembling a quarterback ready to receive the snap with only a few remaining seconds left in the game.

The words' **SPECIAL REPORT'** filled the screen, which immediately was replaced by an anchorwoman dressed in a gray business-like outfit, her eyes fixed directly on the camera and an open laptop on the tabletop in front of her. The upper left-hand corner of the screen showed the Chicagoland area broken down by county and region in a small rectangle window, and superimposed above that was the storm pattern in gradient colors with the word **DOPPLER** printed at its base in white lettering. Yellows towards the edges represent rainfall and light to moderate winds (the safe zones), and oranges and reds represent the storm's brunt. There were purples (lots of purples) near the core, but she did not inquire what those meant, fearing the answer. To add to Nyssa's already mounting dread, she acknowledged that the small rectangle picture was almost entirely red, orange and purple.

"If you are just now joining us," the woman began as Nyssa's eyes moved to the scrolling marquee at the bottom of the screen headed by a stationary bold posting: **SEVERE THUNDERSTORM**. Brief and to-the-point statements rolled by seemingly without end or repetition: *'AFFECTED COUNTIES: Kane, Du Page, McHenry, Cook...'* and so on. She had even seen Kankakee scroll by, which is sixty miles to the south. Other statements like *'Winds 30-50mph in most areas...'* and *'Gusts to 70mph...'* joined in, and *'Severe flooding'* brought goose bumps to her arms and legs. "You are likely aware of the massive storm front which has moved into the Chicagoland area."

"Shit," Randy whispered to no one in particular.

"Did, umm, like a storm front change direction or something?" she asked him hopefully as she rubbed her hands together.

"Nah, that's the weird part," he said, glancing at her; his face pale while holding the same nervous expression from before. "It just happened! I mean the weatherman was on earlier and he's completely baffled. One minute we were looking at another week of Arizona-like sun and then, *Blam!* Monsoon season in the upper Midwest! It's crazy!"

"Maybe it has to do with global warming?" she interjected, still hoping.

"I don't know, Nyssa," he slowly shook his head. "Global warming is one thing, and yeah, it has been making crazy weather, but this? This is Twilight Zone-type stuff here."

"…this storm would normally spell relief from the scorching heat wave that the upper Midwest has been enduring the last eleven days, but for many, this so-called relief is spelling disaster.

"We now go to weather-anchor Clive Carter who is coming to us live from Aurora; Clive?"

"This storm will surely go down in the annals of time as the storm of the millennium," the screen switched quickly to Clive Carter, a short black man dressed in a bright orange rain slicker which was being pressed against him by the wind and the rain; the little rectangle image of the storm's area was still in view seemingly there to taunt Nyssa's soul. A slight howl was coming across his microphone despite the wind guard covering the tip, which clearly expressed the wind conditions in his area, added by the sight of bending and twisting trees in the background. "I am standing here near the intersection of Main and Central, and as you can see in the background behind me, this storm is raging! It took our news van an extra hour to get here due to extensive flooding in the area."

"What are the conditions over in Aurora at this moment," the anchorwoman's voice came from off-camera to her.

Duh! Nyssa thought to herself, watching.

"Well, Anita," Clive continued, holding onto the hood to the slicker with one hand so to keep it in place. "As you can see, we are experiencing rather intense winds which are currently clocked at fifty-seven miles per hour.

"All of nearby Aurora is in complete blackout conditions, having lost power earlier when a Commonwealth Edison's power relay station in the area took heavy damage. This outage is affecting all surrounding areas including Downers Grove, Wheaton, Lisle, and many parts of Naperville as well.

"Take a look behind me," Clive continued, and the cameraman focused and zoomed past the newscaster to what resembled a river. "That's Central Avenue there and as you can see, it more resembles a raging river than a street at all.

"Local authorities have reported flooding upwards towards three feet in most areas and the water is still rising."

"Well, this isn't good at all, Clive," Anita, the anchorwoman, responded, the program snapping back to her with a small picture-in-picture square in the upper right of Clive, who looked as if at any moment would be whisked away to some far-off place like *Oz*. Nyssa's subconscious quickly followed her comment, producing her additional point of *'No shit.'* Luckily, her mouth didn't follow suit while Randy was sitting there. "I hope you can safely get out of the area."

"That's what we are hoping for too, Anita," Clive returned, holding fast to his composure. "We will see in—"

The image locked; completely pixilated in the corner.

"Clive?" the anchorwoman inquired, her hand moving to her earpiece hidden somewhere beneath her hair. *"Clive?"* No response. "Well ladies and gentlemen, we appear to have lost signal with Clive Carter and the news crew, but here is our own meteorologist, Alan Rickman. Alan?"

"Well ladies and gentlemen," Alan started while looking nervous and jittery. "Clive was certainly right about this storm, it is a doozie out there, no doubt about that. As we can see on the Doppler projection..."

The weather report carried on and Nyssa found herself looking at her hands which still showed red lines from earlier and mildly tingled. None of it made any sense and yet here it was. Her wish, her storm.

This is just nuts, she thought, her head shaking quickly in attempts to dismiss the thoughts. *I didn't make this happen... it just happened!*

I wish you would not do that again! Her mind recalled from earlier, draining her strength as she glanced back at the television, which showed montage shots of various degrees of area destruction with captions stating where the images came from. Aurora, Naperville, Downers Grove, Oak Lawn, Evergreen, Evanston, and all over Chicago itself; vivid, moving clips of downed trees, smashed cars under downed trees, battered homes under even more downed trees, shattered windows and flooding as if it were the end of days.

Nyssa's stomach crawled down to her shoes and hid there amongst the piggies.

"What we are experiencing, viewers, are the conditions that you would have had if you were in the area of the Atlantic where Tropical Storm Claudette had earlier gained enough strength to classify as a Category One hurricane." Alan continued, clicking his little handheld button, and the image zoomed out and away from the Chicagoland area, down and out towards the southeast and out into the Atlantic, filling the background space around him. "And what I mean by 'had' is, as we reported earlier, at around two o'clock, Claudette quickly lost momentum and was downgraded to a tropical depression like she was yesterday this time."

"Now, I know this seems a little far-fetched, Alan," Anita broke in, cameras switching rapidly between the two. "But is there any connection between the two?"

A blank pause.

"Well, Anita," Alan smiled towards the camera as it blinked back to him; a nervous smile on his lips, perhaps considering if his answer might prove to be a career limiting move. "That would be an odd connection indeed spanning several thousand miles, but right now the National Weather Service is looking into both of them."

The sounds of the news faded off and became senseless jargon as she sat staring at her palms. Randy had gotten up to retrieve another *Coke* from the refrigerator and returned, cracking it open without her even noticing that he had stirred. He was going on about how he was betting that many people were out there praying that their insurance premiums were up to date.

Nyssa swallowed hard as another pang of guilt slammed home and a sudden acid taste raced her throat again.

"I am going to go lay down," she said, rising quickly and moving towards her room. "I don't feel so good."

"Want me to mix you up another remedy?" he called after her.

"No," she said, pausing and turning back, her eyes squinting in curiosity. "By the way, where did you come up with that? You know, the drink?"

"Oh that," he replied, shrugging. "I-I don't know… it just suddenly came to me. Did it work?"

"Yeah, it worked" she said quietly and moved to her room, shutting the door behind her and crawled onto her bed.

Outside, the storm continued to howl, flash, and thunder; the rain hitting her bedroom window sounded like gravel poured on glass. Nyssa pulled the pillow over her head, held it close to her ears, muffled the storm noise as best she could, and began humming to herself. Quietly, uncontrolled nervous tears started to creep past her closed lids, and as she began to drift off, her mind could only question had she had anything to do with it all.

Stranger things have happened, Nyssa, her father's voice crept in as unconsciousness took over. *Stranger things have happened.*

CHAPTER FOUR

─○◎○─

Resolutions in the Moonlight

-1-

As Nyssa drifted to sleep in her bed, a tall woman stood by a large, opened window, looking at the moon. It was *her* moon, as she always regarded it, and it was waxing. The sight of it always brought the woman comfort much akin and not unlike a lost sea captain who sees the lighthouse's beacon through the heavy fog.

Safety, she thought to herself and then smiled brightly; silently mouthing '*Hello*' to it. The moon did not answer but she knew that it heard her words, and she dipped her head slightly with a respectful bow.

"Are you going to stop the storm, Lady Agatha?" A young woman's voice rose from behind her, stepping into the moon-glow. Agatha shrugged without turning; the long dark dress she wore followed the lines and curves of her body creating a perfect silhouette of her beautiful form in the moonlight.

"I don't know, Seema" she said, smiling at something between only her and the moon; gentle crow's feet showing at the edges of her eyes from years of smiling. "Marco tells me that this was the first peaceful day he and Amora have had in quite some time… even their little dog enjoyed it; yappy little thing that he is."

"Don't you think that it has gotten a bit out of control?" Seema stepped in closer, her mid-eastern olive skin gleaming brightly in the moon's reflection; her large, almond shaped eyes dancing in it. She had a small hair clip made of red flowers which was peppered with baby's breath in one hand which she was toying with as she spoke, then gently clipped it to the side of her short, jet-black hair.

"I don't know," the woman replied, looking at the young woman with a puzzled look crossing her face. Quietly Agatha unhooked the hair piece, adjusted it, and then clipped it back into place. "Chicago is such a dirty city... it could stand for a nice bath."

"But Lady Agatha," Seema continued, clear desperation filling her tone. "There's a *lot* of damage being done right now!"

"But they do have amazing gyros," Agatha said distantly, taking a seat at a large wooden desk while leaning back in the red leather chair; her stomach suddenly wanting the thin strips of goat meat, extra cucumber sauce, freshly cut onions on a warm pita bread (hold the tomatoes). "And their hotdogs are to die for... minus the ketchup, of course."

"People are getting hurt!" Seema was almost pleading now, moving to the front of the desk, her palms resting firmly on its mahogany surface.

"I know," the woman simply replied. "At least no one has died by what she has done. These are blessing we should count."

Seema paced the floor, her mind twisted and confused by the woman's calmness and passiveness. Does she not *see* what is happening, or does she not care? It was times like these that she dared to be brazen enough to shake the woman by the shoulders until she made sense.

"She can't control it!" Seema spat out rapidly. "She doesn't even know that she did it—"

"Oh, she knows," Agatha replied, her eyes trailing to the open windows and to her moon. "Or at least, she has a pretty good idea that it was her right now; poor child. One can always recognize their own Magic, even if they conjure it unconsciously."

"*Well?*" Seema stated, palms up at her sides, eyes wide and beaconing.

"Well, what?" Agatha blinked, honestly bewildered.

"Well, what are we or better yet, what are *you* going to do about it?"

Seema stood with an openly desperate expression which Agatha unpleasantly allowed her to stew in for a moment.

"Nothing," Agatha said simply.

"*Nothing?*" Seema blinked.

"Nothing," Agatha repeated, and Seema's eyes began to dart over her teacher's face so rapidly it was as if she was trying to count the woman's pores.

She expected some sort of offhanded answer from the woman, maybe something along the lines of *'We'll let it ride for a bit longer and see what happens'*, but *'Nothing?'* That came just as swiftly and unexpectedly as the storm over the upper Midwest had come.

"What do you expect me to do, Seema?" Agatha leaned forward in her chair and spoke softly. "Undo what another has done? You know that's completely against the rules, and you know what kind of consequences may come if I even try."

"But—" Seema tried.

"*And…* and this was *her* Magic, not mine, and although I have a pretty good idea, I cannot sense exactly where she brought it from."

"But—" Seema attempted once more but failed to get very far with it.

"Basically, every rule—especially the first rule—was broken this day." Agatha finished, crossing her arms. "She will have to send it back."

Seema was physically gawking at her, palms up and shifting, her mind dismal at the woman's retort. Perhaps it was *how* she addressed her concerns, so a better approach was in order.

"But she's a newbie," Seema calmed slightly, her tone dropping from desperation to a near controlled clarity. "She can *want* it away as much as she wants to, but that doesn't mean it's going to happen."

"*Newbie?*" Agatha smiled, showing teeth this time. "I didn't think people your age used words like that anymore."

Nope. Methodologies had nothing to do with the conversation at all.

"*Agatha, please?*" Seema's voice returned to pleading as she dropped all formalities and instigated another heavy sigh from the woman.

"Fine, fine, fine, Seema," she rose, hands rising in the air in irritation as she returned to the window. "I will send it back!"

"Thank you," Seema smiled, folding her arms; proud that after all these years she could still get her way through the tactics of whining it to death.

"But you hear me this, Seema!" Agatha spat out having been defeated by her own apprentice. "The girl will *not* learn anything by someone else fixing her problems, I will tell you that!"

"I am sure she will not, Lady Agatha," Seema said softly, satisfied and observed.

Agatha breathed in deeply as she closed her eyes; her left-hand extending outwards through the open windows and towards the direction of Chicago as her other hand slowly clasped the ivory brooch at her throat. Softly, yet inaudibly to Seema, Agatha's lips began to move.

"Lady Agatha?" Seema whispered with a pang of fear in her tone.

"Hmm?" Agatha paused, eyes pinched shut.

"Do you think the Anathema knows about her yet?"

Agatha sighed heavily, "You had better believe it."

In a blink her eyes and mouth shot cavernously wide as a golden showered shriek of a thousand eagles escaped her throat: sharp and piercing. Animals several miles away stirred in their nighttime activities; many a newborn woke to shrieking tears with images of a thousand pairs of flapping wings in their minds, and night watchmen were ripped from their snoozing, fearing that there might be an intruder to whatever they were guarding and decided to go look around.

After what seemed like an eternity, the shrieking stopped as Agatha's arms fell to her sides.

"It is done," she said softly, exhausted, the bright twinkle gone from her eyes. "I must go rest now."

Slowly Agatha crossed the room, heading for the door and paused.

"Seema?"

"Yes, Lady Agatha?" Seema asked softly.

"Contact them all," Agatha said and left the room.

"Absolutely, my lady," Seema whispered and watched her go.

CHAPTER FIVE

The Order of Anathema

-1-

Fingernails were rolling on a large oval table in an elongated conference room, clacking in a steady rhythmic pattern while the thumb stood idle against the swirled pattern of the brushed, stainless-steel top. It was an immense room, its walls lined with large, framed images of apparently great men and women throughout the ages, of which none were sitting there that day. No one was speaking, many dared not to breathe, but they all held the possessor of those tapping fingers as he sat at the far end of the table with his feet up on the curved edge, closest to the windows.

He was focused on nothing in particular.

Outside, the storm was passing quickly, leaving only rain-rivers running in tendrils on the glass.

"What a display of Magic," the man uttered, his rolling fingers continuing their beat. The other six people in the room suddenly found their eyes upon the tabletop before them or a pad of paper which they scribbled purposefully, yet illegibly.

"So," the man suddenly spoke, pulling down his feet and turning in his chair so that he was staring straight down the table length, his fingers crossing before him. "Does anyone have even the slightest inkling of how this happened, and why we didn't know of this child before tonight?"

Nothing.

"Hmm?" Seth questioned with an iniquitous smile, his face and eyes turning to the left and then to the right and only finding nervous glances in return. "Is 'no' the word for the day then? That's the consensus I take it?"

Once again: nothing.

"Well," he sighed, leaning back into the leather chair. "Then if no one knows, then I really don't know why I have gotten myself all excited then, for apparently it has been all for nothing." Leaning forward once again, he turned to the man to his right. "It is all for nothing, isn't it, Charles?"

Charles, a plumpish man in his forties who always wore bad tweed suits which enunciated his pale and red splotched skin, attempted to hold his gaze for as long as he could, then dropped his eyes back to the tabletop, licking his sweaty lips, "Seth I—"

"You what?" Seth screamed, a palm slamming into the surface top. "That's my name, now what? Whatever you are about to say had better be orgasmic or you'll know what it is like to live life after death!"

Charles' mouth snapped shut, his head shaking.

"No comment then, Charles," he said straightening then turned his attention to the young woman on his left. "And what of you, Mica; my fine picaroon of the World Wide Web? Nothing at all to be worried about, is there? No little chat rooms chatting away, or bloggers blogging about our little mishap and embarrassment today? *Hmm?"*

Mica, a teenage girl dressed quite Goth in nature whilst her counterparts—save Charles—wore one type of handmade designer suit or another, stared wide-eyed back into the gaze, her eyes rapidly shifting in their sockets. Her mouth parted, her tongue working out something in the small cavern, but nothing came from it. Her mind was scrambled with a million things to say, all of which made no sense for her to utter, yet he got his answer by the solitary tear that ran from the edge of an eye. She shifted nervously, pulled up a small, tattered gray teddy bear in her lap, and pressed it against her sternum.

"That, Mica, surprises even me," he breathed, reaching into his inside jacket pocket, and retrieved a highly decorative silver case.

Calmly, he opened it, drew out a cigarette set on the tabletop, and then closed it soundly, placing it neatly before him. Slowly, an index finger ran over the circular pattern press beveled from the inside; images of the four elements—Earth, Water, Wind, and Fire—arranged in a never-ending circle of eternity. The detail was impeccable, handmade almost two centuries before by a blind man who had an astonishing ability of seeing things despite the two caverns in his face where his eyes had once been.

"Aren't you supposed to be the elite of the elite?" he spoke passively to Mica as his eyes focused on the case, making her cringe. "You have at your disposal over twenty million dollars in computers, servers, routers and equipment of the like, plus enough bandwidth to host every computer on the planet, and you have nothing?"

Mica lowered her eyes to the tabletop before her, really wanting to cry.

Calmly, Seth retrieved the cigarette and leaned back in the leather chair, placing it between his lips and sparked his fingers, and in a dim flash, the tip became a glowing red coal. At that very moment, candles surrounding an effigy of Mother Theresa in a small church nestled in a quaint little area of Oaxaca, Mexico, suddenly blinked out without so much as a focused thought.

"You can let the tears flow, Mica," he said quietly, almost soothing, as he exhaled smoke. "You are not to blame here, little one. You are but a child yourself."

And with that she did, releasing the floodgates accompanied only by a single whimper. He leaned in with a gentle pat to her shoulder and then suddenly he bolted into a standing position, his eyes a blue fire.

"But not for all the rest of you!" he roared, setting off a wave of startled jumps along those sitting at the table. "Grown and trained: charmers, conjurers, enchanters, mages, seers, and warlocks! You... Not one of *you* have a single excuse!"

Seth stood, fists clenched on the table, his eyes blazing and a faint blue aura wafting off his clothing. A soft vibrating hum filled the air as the table tingled with his rage, causing any hands still on it to pull from the surface. Mouths hung, eyes gaped, and suddenly, all had to relieve themselves of internal waste in one fashion or another. Mica's quiet crying had become heavy sobbing behind her palms, drawing his attention.

"Look what you all have done," he said in a soothing voice and moved towards her. Gently he pulled her hands from her face which was wet and discolored from the thick eyeliner she wore. Gently he pulled Mica into a standing position, who at five foot one, came only up to his breastbone. "There, there, now, Mica, everything is alright. I am not cross with you."

"Yes, you are," she sobbed.

"No, I am not," he smiled soothingly.

"Yes, you are!" she cried it. "I can tell! You are *blue-ing!*"

"I am not towards you, I promise," he soothed, brushing the bangs from her eyes. "Listen to me Mica; you do not have to stay for the rest of this meeting, alright?"

"Uh-okay," she stuttered, nodding.

"Why don't you go wait in the car until this is finished," he produced a soft smile, using his thumbs to wipe away thick running lines of black eyeliner. "Aw, your makeup is running. Go now and fix it up. Have the driver retrieve my gift for you from the trunk. I think you will really like it."

"Yeah, okay," she sniffed and attempted a little smile back and began to move away to the double doors at the opposite side of the conference room. "Sorry."

Seth watched her go with her bear in her hand, her oversized combat-style boots making soft clunking sounds on the polished wood floor.

"Teens these days," he mused reflectively as she closed the door behind her. "I really need to teach that girl some fashion sense. Oh well..."

Seth trailed off into his thoughts, waving his hand towards a bank of flat panel screens cubing a wall. All of them came to life, each one showing the day's storm carnage from one different aspect and news station than the other. A soft, incomprehensible mishmash filled the room from twenty-five newscasters reporting the news: most in English, others in the languages of their home stations.

Slowly, he walked counterclockwise around the room, his body coming within inches of those who sat.

"Take a look, ladies and gentlemen," he spoke authoritatively, his fingers clasped together at sternum level, occasionally releasing one to motion towards the screens for effect. "This is what happens when an untrained conjurer does magic.

"Do you see the raw power of what this girl has unleashed?

"This is not the typical unconscious haphazard incident we have grown accustomed to where we see the bungling mishaps of some neophyte suddenly scoring a perfect hundred on a test or barely avoiding a tragic accident, no; here, ladies and gentlemen, is the demonstration of *real* power."

"The girl is strong, indeed," a voice spoke slowly and intentional, heavily German in accent and masculine. Seth turned slightly, enjoying his place in the conference, and smiled to the man in the silver-gray Armani suit.

"Not just strong, Karl," Seth added. "We are talking powerful. "Have you any idea how much mana it takes to channel a storm and then to *move* it?"

Sets of eyes held him, but no one dared to surmise or even speak. For one to ponder at a moment like this (and to be honest, those of Magic who ponder have been known to *Drift* and never return), could be dangerously close to making a lethal career path.

"To do what she has done," he continued, holding the room in subtle suspense. "Would take even the most gifted conjurer all their ability and prowess to even attempt it, let alone achieve. That's comparable to taking all the Magic present in this room combined and multiplying that by ten. Imagine all that power wrapped up in a Lilliputian-package no bigger and no older than Mica."

"That is quite the bold statement, Seth!" a woman hissed, leaning into view, and brightening. There was an unnatural shadowed hue to her features even in the brightest of light, and those who encountered her could never quite tell her age, or whether she was homely or attractive. She just was. Plain and simple. "A power like that would mean she is more powerful than the Order and decisively more powerful than you."

"That, Marana, is something I am proposing, yes," he replied, accompanied by a steady nod.

"*Rubbish!*" she leaned forward, her amber eyes glinting rage. "There is currently no one more powerful than the Order! I could crush this child with my pinky toe! You are referring to a child who is not due until the Next Coming and that event is many decades off."

"I am sorry, Marana," Seth turned to her with a peculiar look, almost inquisitive. "Did I bruise an ego here, hmm? Well, to you, I half-apologize, considering you are the one who sensed where all this came from. You did exceptionally well, despite the fact that a name, face, and location would be perfect knowledge to have right now. Other than that, if your feelings are hurt, I am glad because all your egos and vanities have brought us to this paradox we are in now!"

Marana recoiled, her features falling back into the natural shadows of her presence.

"And then what of it, Seth?" another one spoke; an older man with a well-manicured gray mustache which curled at the tips and large glasses added as he used a single digit to push them higher up on his nose. "Is that what she is? Is she the Next Coming, and if so, does this mean that the timeline is off?"

"Yes," Karl's heavy accent broke in. "Were the Seers of yore wrong?"

"Yes, is she?" came a flood of voices all at once. Seth scanned the room, and despite their ages and their abilities, he felt as if he was addressing a group of schoolchildren.

"Alright, everyone," he spoke softly, returning to his chair and taking his seat. "Before you all return to your sects panicked about the Next Coming and whether or not this teenage girl is just that, let me assuage any of your fears here and now. She is not, let me repeat: *Not* the Next Coming.

"This girl is a fluke… an accident… a bastardized child of Magic who simply has happened and now she is here. The *Who's* or the *Why's*, or even the *How's*, I do not know, nor do I really care, but the one thing I *do* care about is: '*A*', she is powerful beyond comprehension as you can clearly see. '*B*', she has had no training and probably doesn't even know what she has done, which I may add, makes her very dangerous to us and the Consortia and '*C*': she is *not* in our ranks.

"Out of the three, the one I am focusing on—which means that had better be the only thing all of you and your sects are focusing on—is '*C*'."

"But Seth," cried Marana. "All we know of this conjurer is that it's a teenage girl, she is untrained, and she is close, but other than that we do not know where to begin."

"I am not concerned about the limitations of your abilities!" he barked. "Hence why this meeting has been called because I need you and your people to focus on finding out who she is and where we can find her!"

"And what of *D*, dear Seth?" a voice from his right rose over the room, drawing everyone's attention.

Standing in the doorway of a side conference room stood a woman with short raven like hair and the most brilliant green eyes one could ever imagine. She was leaning against the door jamb, playing with a fingernail on one hand while holding a flip phone in the other.

"Pia!" Seth beamed, softening as he turned in his chair and leaned back, a leg pulling up and comfortably crossing the knee of the other. "It is so good that you could have made it despite the weather we are having.

"You know, you should upgrade your phone, my dear Pia. Join us in the modern age."

"It serves its purpose," she smiles as she long strode slowly from the doorway. "And the only root purpose of a phone is to make calls, albeit the occasional text or picture."

"Quite right," he smiled, admiring her casual forwardness without need of elaboration. "So… what is this *D'* you are referring to?"

"Oh, that's simple," she spoke nonchalantly, looking up towards a curled lock that hung over her brow, and she provided a quick puff of air from her lips to send it back into place. *"D'* is the fact that the girl doesn't have a clue what she has done. She suspects it, but that is all. *D'* also represents a concerning question: how did she send it back?

"Even more importantly, Lord Seth, *'D'* is pinnacled to understanding exactly *who*, if not her, *did* send it back?"

Seth sat slowly twisting the chair back and forth on its pivot, his fingers forming a steeple before his chin.

"I think *'D'* interests me quite a bit as well, Pia," he said distantly, his mind forming the shape of a woman who he has known for quite some time. She was not one of them, quite the antithesis actually; her Magic sat on the other side of the half-spin of life which constantly tries to bring order to disorder, only to come back around to Pia who would do with it as she wished. From what she introduced, Seth could picture what *'D'* was quite clearly, standing in the night's light and smiling at her moon while feeling quite proud of herself.

"Agatha," he sounded.

"Yes, Seth: Agatha," Pia replied, moving close to the table, opening her phone, and sliding it across to him. "And the path to *'C'* is that girl there in the picture... her name is Nyssa, by the way."

Seth's smile began to broaden as he stared at the image on the phone and soon, he began to laugh.

"Very well done, Pia!" he beamed as he stood while his eyes never left the still image of Nyssa. "Yes, very well done indeed!

"Ladies and gentlemen, this meeting of the Order of Anathema has concluded. You may all go back to your sects and covens and tell them that the great shift we have experienced will be rectified in our behalf shortly."

Slowly the members of the order rose, gathering their various belongings; each one carrying either a sense of elation, or spiteful irritation with them.

"Pia, Mica is waiting for me in the car," he said, smiling, handing her back the phone. "Please, join me tonight so that we may discuss many great things!"

"My pleasure," she smiled taking her phone.

"I will be down in just a few minutes," he said, glancing towards Charles, who was slowly placing papers inside a valise. Pia saw the blue glint race the surface of his eyes and followed his attention, finding Charles and returning to face Seth, who was smiling sinisterly. "I have a few things to take care of first."

"Hmm, have fun," she smiled back, reaching up and lightly stroking the side of his face. "I will see you in the car."

With that, Pia sauntered towards the door. As she passed Charles, she tapped him on his shoulder, mouthing 'Goodbye' and waved almost flirtatiously, allowing each digit to roll. Charles first looked perplexed and returned the smile with a little blushing nod.

"Until another time, Pia," he glowed, watching her go.

Charles gathered his remaining belongings and snapped the valise closed and then hurried towards the doors.

"Oh, Charles?" Seth called after him just as he was opening the conference room door. "May I have a word or two with you?"

He paused, his eyes finding his hand around the knob, the door partially open, and then shot a glance down the hallway where Pia was standing in the elevator as the doors slowly slid closed, smiling at him.

"Umm, yes, of course," he said shutting the door and as he made his way around it was in time to see the back of Seth disappear into the small side conference room which Pia appeared from.

"We will talk in here, Charles." Seth's voice came, muffled and distant.

"Oh, umm, fine, fine," Charles replied, feeling sweat creep to the surface of his brow and down the length of his back.

A royal reaming from the head of the Order was never pleasant to witness, and to be the receiver was even more brutal. This chat would be his sixth such lecture by Seth, and each time Charles prayed that it wouldn't be as bad as he thought. Slowly he began to move to the open door.

"I know you are quite angry, Seth," his words fumbled back and forth like so many keys in one's pocket. "And I-I, umm, can quite understand why."

There was only silence as a reply.

"I did my best to channel her once Marana sought her," he continued his explanation as he rounded the doorway and entered the smaller conference room, which was very dim; lit only by the lights of the city coming into it. "But the thing is, Jupiter is out of sync with Venus, and I am fresh out of eagle's talon and—"

Charles stopped four paces into the room before realizing it was empty, his heart dropping into his bowels. Across from the smaller conference room, which had only a round table large enough to seat six, a knee-level cabinet stretching the far wall, and a large plasma television mounted above it was a closed door containing a small washroom.

"Seth? *Seth?* Did you pop into the privy?"

No response came, not from the way of the washroom door or anywhere else. Charles stood alone in the small, darkened conference room, patting his damp forehead and upper lip with a checkered handkerchief. A small numeral-less table clock in the center of a cabinet ticking away all too audibly in the silence.

"As I was saying, Seth," he began. "I know I should have been on my game channeling the young girl, this Nyssa, but with the planets and me being under the weather again, I just couldn't seem to focus on—"

"Excuses!" growled Seth's voice from behind him, accompanied by the slamming of the conference door.

Charles spun so quickly he almost faltered, a brief shriek escaping his throat. There was no one there, only the closed door, and he slowly felt the nape of his neck growing warm. A growl, distant and throaty, began to rise behind him; his eyes growing wide and pulse-quickening to an accelerated heavy beat. Slowly, a shaking hand moved up his midsection, crawling along the buttons to his blazer, the fingers spreading to reach the amulet around his neck; his sole attempt was to alert his family that something dire was amiss. With the growl rising, the warmth on his neck growing to a sweltering humid air, his fingers finding the edge and then—

"Charles?" Seth's voice spoke softly and caringly.

"Yes?" Charles relaxed, turning, and before everything went red, all Charles could comprehend was teeth.

*

Pia stepped from the elevator onto the ground level of the building and was exiting the car when the scream reached her.

She paused, glancing back into the metal walled elevator car and then towards its ceiling where the shaft ran up the sixty floors, through a double set of steel doors, down the hallway, and through the oak doors to the conference room. Anyone else who might have been in the lobby that night would have heard nothing; the bare ears of your average person would not have picked up a thing, but to hers, she listened to each curdling crest and valley of the cry.

She blinked twice and smiled.

"Chomp-chomp, Charles," Pia giggled, and with a bounce in her step, she moved through the lobby to the waiting limo sitting out front.

-2-

Mica was a nonstop smiling chatter box since Seth entered the limo.

She had her gift on her lap as she sat next to Pia: a state-of-the-art laptop dubbed based on the raised plastic embossed words: *Vector Prime, produced* by one of the Order's many companies. By the look of the mess, there wasn't much patience opening the box; the floor was strewn with tattered wrapping paper, cardboard, and those annoying registration cards that no one ever filled out. Her mouth raced as she ran down the massive list of features that the thing came with, adding to the dialogue about what she could do with it.

"Two hundred and fifty-six gigs of RAM!" she beamed at Seth. "Oh… my… *Gawd!* No one out there has that much memory on a portable! Oh man, think about how much I can buffer in a massive brute-force attack!"

"It has built in L-T-E," he added monotonously, his eyes finding hers for a moment and then trailed off to the tinted windows to watch the streetlamps of Lake Shore Drive roll by. He was tired both mentally and physically and even his mana, his magical life-spirit, waned.

"I know!" Mica squeaked, producing a massive smile. "It picked up just about every WISP in the county! I even got two out of Madison, Wisconsin! Do you know how far that is away?"

Seth smiled thinly, happy to see that his gift was well accepted only to hear Pia whisper inquisitively what Mica had just said.

"Wireless Internet Service Provider," he addressed Pia quietly, whose mouth scrunched up in one corner of her mouth as she sounded out the acronym in her head.

"Ahh," she replied, satisfied that she could remain partially in the conversation. "Like, the internet, right?"

"Right," he nodded, his eyes trailing back to Mica who was months away from turning seventeen, he was watching a young toddler on Christmas morning indulging in gift heaven.

It humored him that in all ways Mica followed the Goth lifestyle—the music, the clothes, and the ever-present aura of darkness in delight—but the moment she saw anything geek, especially if it was a gift, her pure personality of that of a teenager needing to be loved, showed through. He watched as her slim fingers clicked away at the keys so rapidly that they seemed to blur.

Mica had been his apprentice since the tender age of two. Although the road usually is very long and hard between a student and the teacher of the Magic arts—even harder for those in the ranks of the Anathema, where wrongful Magic use is not the typical culprit in a pupil's death but that of a testy teacher who had finally lost their patience—Seth knew that he really did love her.

Since time immemorial, Seth had been well known amongst the Anathema for pointing out any behavior considered taboo by the Order, affection towards one apprentice being one of the top five on his list. Still, no one has ever dared to point out his double standard. When it came to Mica, if he showed her affection, no one dared to question or recite any of the rules... well, no one who is still in one piece amongst this planar existence any longer, that is.

"Do you realize I can hack anything, anywhere, and no one will be the wiser?" Mica addressed him, and despite the tears from earlier, the glint he always found in her was back. Her eyes narrowed, the edges of her mouth turned up in a wicked little grin, and softly Mica's eyes glowed violet, which meant her mind had already spelled out something catastrophic. "You had all my War Dialers and Snoop Progs loaded too!"

"And I am sure that you cannot wait to demonstrate that now can you, Mica?" Pia smiled at her, nudging her shoulder with her own only to receive one back. "What's a War Dialer anyway?"

Seth attempted a smile as Mica began to explain her hacker's rhetoric. Still, his mind was elsewhere, and his eyes happened upon the nappy little bear sitting securely bound by a lap belt in the seat between Mica and Pia. It was missing one of its little plastic eyes, which Mica had replaced with a three-hundred-dollar button she stole from a *Chanel* suit in a store he had taken her to many years before. He had vainly tried a few times to change her taste in clothing, but for everything he bought for her that was at the height of fashion, she took scissors to and made them whatever she wanted.

Money flushed down the toilet, he had scolded her on his last attempt with *Prada*, but her point was simple: if he wanted to spend ninety bucks on a T-shirt that she could get at *Marshall's*, he should have his head examined. He shrugged at the time and let her be, an odd confusion that a child in the presence of billions upon billions of dollars should be so frugal. Yes, she had made her point, and it did make sense in the long run, but like so many father figures, he had hoped that she would at least try.

"When are you going to wash that thing?" he inquired flatly and Mica paused, then followed his gaze to her little bear and then produced a perturbed expression of confusion.

"Wash Binky... my talisman?" she quipped, and Seth nodded. "Never, he's perfect the way he is."

A soft *humph*-ing sound escaped his throat as she returned her attention to the new laptop.

*

They rolled along silently to the sounds of the road and Mica's rapid clicking of the keys until she burst into a happy laughing fit.

"Oh, Teacher, thank you!" Mica exclaimed and moved across to give him a hug, but a small raise of a hand from Seth, as well as a gentle placement of Pia's hand on her knee, told her otherwise.

"Mind the bond, child," Pia said flatly, and Mica sat back in her seat, her eyes pained by the inability to express how she felt. As her eyes dropped quietly to the keypad, a brief silence fell over the car. "You never know who is seeking at the moment and who is watching."

"Iniqua nunquam regna perpetuo manent," words from memory rose in his mind as he held Mica with his eyes. It was the voice of his teacher from a time when his life was near its end after all the long years of the darkened Magic. The dying mage croaked as he lay on his deathbed, his body and mind torn and twisted by it leaving him

in a grotesque, bent form. Seth had been set in a chair near the old archmage's bed, watching life slip away, eager to claim the reins as master of the Anathema, a position which one was not grandfathered into but taken by brute, murderous force.

Seth's eyebrows rose inquisitively to the fading jibber-jabber of the old savant, and despite his desire to run the show, he respected the man; regarding him with a near fatherly air.

"It means: 'Stern masters do not reign long,' Seth… remember that when you have your own."

Seth did remember what his master had told him after all, and it only took the lives of his first four pupils to jog his memory of it well enough so the proper understanding of what was said flowed in. He had unyielding patience for Mica, for reasons he had never known, but it still boiled down to that in the heart of blackness, love could still flourish.

After a long silence, Mica looked up towards him, "Teacher?"

"Hmm?" he sounded.

"I am starving… can we order Thai when we get home?"

"I think that Master Seth has eaten already, didn't you Seth?" Pia produced a thin wicked smile of her own, her eyes locking onto his as he met her gaze. A quick shimmer of blue crossed the edges of his pupils then a thin smile cornered his mouth.

"Yes, Mica, I have already eaten," he replied openly.

"You did?" Mica said, puzzled, having been with him the entire day and never recalled him consuming anything other than three cigarettes, a handful of Altoids and loads of black coffee.

"Yes." He replied with a nod and a smile.

"Oh, and you missed a spot," Pia smiled, her index finger touching her own chin just below the corner of the lip in the place where Seth had a small red smear. "Right there."

"What did you have?" Mica continued.

"Swine," he responded, rubbing at his chin which got Pia smiling wider.

"And how was it?" Pia smiled brightly, biting over her lower lip to hold back her giggles.

"A little tough in places," he added. "And a bit fatty I may add."

That did it; Pia began to giggle despite herself and then turned her attention to the window where the giggles formed outright laughter. Seth simply returned his gaze to the passing lights and Mica shifted her eyes between the two attempting to figure out the joke. After a moment she shrugged it off, returning to the *Ins* and *Outs* of the new laptop.

"Well, I could just order for myself then, unless you are hungry too, Pia." She added never looking up. "Or better yet, I could convoke it *from* Thailand to us!"

"You can order via phone, Mica," Seth said blankly, his eyes and mind tired. "There has been enough Magic in the air tonight."

Mica's eyes grew wide based on two words he had said: **order** and **air**, and quickly pulled up a web browser which immediately blinked to a search engine where she typed in RESTAURANTS.

"Wow that was fast," she said to no one in particular regarding the speed of her wireless connection, and then immediately maneuvered the pointer using the touchpad to go to: CHICAGO… LOCAL… RESTAURANT… CUISINE… THAI and then double tapped the little pad to bring up the listings. Upon finding a place that delivered in their area, she pulled up their menu and salivated over their items.

'You know there is going to be hell and retribution to pay to the Merionethians, don't you?' Pia's mind reached out to his quietly as Mica carried on about what sounded so good and oh how she could eat two orders of this and that.

The Merionethians—so named for the former northwestern Wales capital region from which their sect originated—had long since tired of Charles' faults, flaws, and errors. Still, in the end, Charles was one of them, and based on the summary laws of the Order, only they could pass final judgment on him. In the long run, they would have more than likely banished him after another decade or two of his foul-ups, but this way—Seth's way—you could consider his banishment permanently *permanent*.

'It will be pittance,' he reached back to Pia's mind, lying.

Even in the chaotic world of the Anathema, there were rules. Above those rules, there were laws, and breaking those rules didn't always mean you were breaking any laws, but by breaking one meant that you were bending the other almost past its flexing point (and often, it took a lot of glue and twine to hold the pieces together). Seth was not above either; however, as the grand mage sitting as the Anathema's head, he had a lot more flex room to tempt the Fates.

'Well, business is business,' Pia added, shrugging, and if Mica had paid it much mind, it would have meant nothing other than her shrugging over things to herself. It was a two-way conversation, and she was not invited. *'The Merionethians will see that.'*

'That they will,' once again he lied, retrieving the cigarette case from his breast pocket and holding it between his hands for comfort.

It was a lie because of his motto that nothing is worth doing—business or otherwise—if there was no personal pleasure derived from doing it. He hated movies, especially the mob/gangster ones, where the line right before someone was blown away was: 'It's not personal, only business.'

Bullshit, he had once said, watching how in the movie, the person doing the killing always shot the victim in the head, a place where there was bound to be a mess. A messy kill was the sign of raw, innate passion, and passion derives from pleasure, and no one in this world could tell him that the killer in the story was not enjoying watching brains splatter from every fiber of his being.

Ultimately, Seth would express his decision based on that: business, and since they were all cutthroat businesspeople through and through, it would boil down to a simple logic: to expand business, sometimes it meant cutting loose dead weight. They would accept this ideology, yes, but with the added cost in retribution for the 'cutting loose' without permission in the form of either a million shares in one company or another, a span of untapped oil land, or the spurring of war in some far-off country.

Basically, something that results in renewing monetary value in return for life. They were all coveting bastards when it came down to brass tacks, and although none of them would outright admit it, it was because of this directive that the World of Magic was so screwed up in the first place.

"After three thousand years of Magic," the voice of his teacher came to him from his youth as a pupil after so many years of silence. *"No one has learned a damn thing, Seth, not even me and neither will you. It is our calling... it is our destiny... it is our addiction. We will build up all we can and ruin what is there for our own desires... let no one tell you otherwise."*

As they rolled on—Lake Shore Drive running out of lanes at its northernmost end, becoming Hollywood where one could continue straight west or make a right onto Sheridan towards Evanston just a few miles more to the north—Seth focused on his fingertip rolling over the symbols of everything that made up the Universe, or as the Anathema did everything in life: through carnage. They were simple symbols that can be further expressed by science or theology until one reaches the singularity of the atom or God himself, and neither would have it right because neither side of the fence ever listened to the other.

Seth sat quietly and glanced over his small party: Pia had closed her eyes but was not sleeping. Knowing her, she was seeking out continuous details about the girl as unobtrusively as possible not to attract Agatha's and her people's attention. Mica was finishing her food order, and Seth barely noticed that the girl was ordering at least two of everything off the menu. The laptop had an outstanding built-in microphone, and with the added *Zoom* communication software, she never had to lift a phone to place a call.

The limo slowed and paused at the intersection of Hollywood and Sheridan to allow a woman to cross, then turned onto Sheridan continuing north. Seth sounded a quiet *Hmm*, thinking about the Charles situation at hand, and then concluded that turning him into something like a mole-rat would have been the better solution.

-3-

Pia was sitting cross-legged on a padded footstool in front of the fireplace, her eyes wide as the crackling fire danced before her. Seth was not all too surprised to see her sitting on the stool instead of the plush leather chair that sat before it. Pia tended to lounge about or perch on items you would typically not expect one to find as a place of rest; desks, dressers, roofs of cars, and the occasional high tree branch if the air was just right. Usually, she would be curled up sleeping or tending to her fingernails which she considered her most highly prized feature, other times, it would be her short black feathered hair, but that would depend entirely on her *èlan vital*; the vital source and impulse of life which was filling her at the moment.

Mica was sitting at her student desk, which faced out towards the room, the wall behind it lined with books bound by old leather and fabrics. Many of the tomes came from animals that no longer walked the Earth or woven by cultures that had long since died or bred out through time. Most of her study came from them, a prime necessity for any student; however, she was reminded well by Seth that actual knowledge and skill are set by experience and not within the limited boundaries of covers.

To the right of this was a large framed black poster which had the typical anarchy symbol displayed in red in its center, and next to that was a poster for the music group *Rage Against the Machine,* a name which always puzzled him because He and They *were* the 'Machine.'

Mixed in with the older scholarly books of Magic wisdom was a hodgepodge of modern ones with titles containing words like *Unix, Novell, Microsoft, Linux,* Wi-Fi, *PERL,* HACKING, *DOS,* and DoS Attacks, plus many other words which Seth always referred to as 'geek-script.' To the side of the desk sat a mini-rack that held several thin blue-green *Cisco* devices which blinked and pulsed green and amber lights, which Mica had explained were routers, switches, load balancers, and firewalls, which Seth barely understood.

Her new laptop was sitting before with an external keyboard, mouse, and three large widescreen flat panel monitors; save these few items. Every available space was covered with cartons, trays, and take-out boxes from some local Thai restaurant. With one hand, she busied herself with the mouse—moving, pointing, and clicking away—while the other held the chopsticks, plastered in various sauces.

Seth paused momentarily as he entered the room to regard the little eating machine at the desk while it multitasked and wondered how the child's mind sometimes worked. She wasn't quite eating as it were; more like devouring whatever came within chomping distance of her mouth, and he was not surprised to hear the occasional, *Mm-hmm* noise gurgling in her throat as her head nodded to something that her brain found interesting on the screens.

Shrugging, he moved across the polished wood floor and onto the large ornate runner sitting in its center.

"I take it you had enough money then, Mica?" he asked absently over his shoulder. Mica paused in mid chomp of a large mass of sagging cellophane noodles which was dripping a thick brown sauce and raised a finger which moved with her nodding head, swallowed, and then gasped for air.

"No, I just *nudged* him a little and gave him a piece of paper," she said, that wicked little grin reappearing.

"Mica," he said irritated, his head shaking as he approached Pia from behind, his hands moving in the air. "I had expressed that there was to be no more this evening."

"But you were showering and changing," she replied innocently. "It was only a little nudge, Teacher, almost an afterthought."

Seth didn't reply; he simply didn't have the strength to make a real issue out of it, and in the end he really did not care. She was quite talented in many areas of Magic, more so than he was at her age, and when it came to her power of suggestion, he had never known her equal.

Early on with Mica, Seth had to focus hard against her powers of suggestion because it came so pure and naturally that its potency delivered a blow so severe that it could cause brain damage. A child has very few needs at two years of age, but when they need them, it is always '*Right now.*' He would catch himself doing and giving her things that he normally wouldn't have dreamed of—treats, toys, knives, the neighbor's new puppy, and the pony at the zoo (which crapped in the foyer and chewed on his favorite rug)—and when he *would* realize that it was her *nudging* him along, he was always met by that thin, wicked little smile of hers.

He would anger quickly, filled with thoughts of casting the child in the middle of the *Yondsphere*, but in the end, he was simply looking into the face of a younger, feminine version of himself, and his heart would always warm.

In the servitude of Student to Teacher, pupils rarely ever left the close side of the instructor, especially once they had begun to learn anything of any importance (and with the Anathema, anything dangerous), but for Mica, that clause was heightened swiftly at a very young age.

When she was three years old, Seth had taken her to a carnival out of necessity, not so much as for her to enjoy. He had important business there to conduct, but he wouldn't have dared to leave her in the care of another out of fear of what she might do to them. Her company was pure proxy while he met with two Elders of the Anathema, and during the meeting, Mica slipped away. When Seth had finally found her, she was sitting on a patch of grass with a tray of cotton candy set out before her, eating the spun sugar as if she hadn't a care in the world, and he knew she had none.

The vendor to whom it belonged, however, was forever changed that day. The man had told her she didn't have any money so she couldn't have one; mistake number one. He then told her she should not be walking about without her parents—mistake number two—and upon his third mistake he explained that she was a spoilt little brat and to push off.

When Seth found the man huddled and shaking between two carnival rides—mumbling something incoherently about donkeys with blood dripping from his nostrils—it was evident that she pushed him so hard that it had scrambled his brains.

She had wanted one, plain and simple, and she had wanted it 'Now!'

Seth stopped on the edge of the rug next to Pia, his hands sliding into his pockets. He said nothing at first as his eyes accompanied Pia's on the crackling flames which were slowly dying away.

He was exhausted.

For the last several weeks, the Anathema had been busy culminating the final touches to another great retooling of the world's mechanical gearing. The Big Three American automakers had been steering too far away from their agreed-upon direction of using the Order's large deposits of oil. All of them were hell-bent on introducing new fuel-efficient hybrids, which stood to have an impact on the auto market by monumental proportions, mainly to counter the release of so many Japanese cars which boasted the same efficiency.

This could not be allowed.

This new directive and their reneging on an agreement echoed almost blatant disobedience; the mere thought of how it was going to affect the bottom line was deplorable. All of them needed to be taught a lesson in the form of a really good financial spanking. The first order of business was to remove them from the Top Selling lists, and the next was Federal Bankruptcy.

This is how the Anathema operated since the sixteenth century when the Order first formed and how people like Seth had for thousands of years before then when their way of Magic had so many other names. He thought of this as the flames danced before him, his mind trying to picture Victus Anathema as he burned at the stake in 1535, just a few years after the Church with their ecclesiastical authority—as well as the spoken language itself—had adopted his surname as a vile word equating to *bête noire*: abomination... condemnation... vigorous denunciation... Cursed.

"Are you seeking her again, dear Pia?" he asked quietly, his eyes moving with the flames never blinking.

Slowly, Pia's head cocked to one side, her neck twisting upwards and towards him at an almost inhumanly possible angle. Her pupils were as wide as black pearls, the edges filling the iris almost completely with a thin rim of green.

She blinked at him twice and then returned her gaze to the flames.

"A lot of people are seeking her this night, but they cannot find her," she purred as she rested her hands on her knees and narrowly curved the arc in her back, stretching. "But for now, I see her, and she sleeps."

"Others like who?" Seth asked quietly, his tone not alarmed in the bit.

"Many others including our own," she purred back. "That is all that I can see, but she is not sleeping well."

"Oh?" Seth sounded looking at her.

"No… she has a good heart, and her dreams are restless with guilt."

"The storm?" he continued, eyes returning to the flames which were threatening to go out.

"She sees all that has happened as all-too coincidental," Pia answered, her head cocking to the right, eyes narrowing. There was a dull pain deep inside her mind as she sought, finding barriers there in the distance… strength. "Marco and Amora didn't help the situation any."

"Then they know of her as well," Seth surmised in almost a whisper and cursed to himself. He had been hoping that Agatha and her coterie had simply diminished the storm out of their persistent and irritating interference, which they had been so accomplished in doing so over the years. A mere 'good-doer' deed and nothing more, but hearing those names meant everything he feared: *They* knew about her too.

"They've known of her for quite some time, well before she was born." Pia whispered back. "But they have only watched her from a distance; wanting and waiting for her to age beyond the ability to instruct."

"That doesn't make any sense, Pia," he spoke, turning towards her and kneeling, attempting to capture her eyes with his own. Something was not right in this and well out of balance beyond the all-present lopsided World of Magic, and what Pia was telling him sounded absolutely preposterous. "Why would the Consortia ignore such things? She is so powerful!"

"Precisely, Seth," she smiled, her head slowly and seemingly mechanically turning towards his, the pupils seeming catlike, the green of the irises beaming. "She is so very powerful, and they still remained distant until now."

"Why?" he asked full of confusion.

Pia's smile broadened to almost insane limits.

"Because they fear her as well."

-4-

Seth sat quietly alone before the fireplace, his heels resting on the stool in which Pia had made her perch, watching the flames slowly diminish. He was alone now with his thoughts as he sat in the large parlor room, the cigarette case resting on one thigh with his hand safely resting on top of it.

Pia had provided him with every detail of the day which led up to her finding Nyssa *'Purely accidentally and incidentally, of course'* as she had expressed modestly, shying away from his direct stare with a thin smile on her face. There was nothing that Pia did 'accidentally' or 'incidentally,' and Seth was not buying it despite her innocent look. All too often in the past, Pia would produce items people didn't know they were looking for in the first place simply by *'sniffing the air'* as she put it. She was a *Myriad-Haruspex*, a multi-seer that did not require inspecting a sacrificed animal's entrails to do what she did. On top of that, she was a magical mongrel because of her shape-shifting ability.

Simply put, Pia was a rare breed amongst the sects, yet not belonging to any of them directly. However, her presence was welcomed—usually under somewhat suspicious eyes as the greeter often wondered if she had direct business with them or as a rogue agent for someone like Seth—at any of their tables. Many felt weary towards her because she was the last of her kind, knowing that someone truly unique has much to lose and will do anything to keep what they have. Mainly, if you care to get right down to the truth behind the mistrust, they were troubled because she *was* the last of her kind, especially since she was the one who made sure she *was* the very last.

They would all open their doors and welcome her regardless of the hour because when a *Myriad-Haruspex* made a house call, that individual had seen something that may just concern you in the end.

For now, Pia spent most of her time in the presence of Seth and the Anathema, partially out of faith in his ideology of the Order but mainly because she had fallen in love with him so many years before. She had never told him directly, but he knew it; there had been times when he needed to *see* what she saw so Pia would open her sight to him, which meant allowing him inside. Once their minds were one, every sensation of togetherness glowed, and on occasion, despite the difficulties to prevent it, she would show him pieces of her affection. She would never side or turn against him even if the threat of pain and death loomed over her, and he knew this well, and so did all the other sects, which added to their distrust towards her.

"*Flagrare*," he whispered and the flames in the hearth swelled and climbed with a soft *whoosh*-ing sound. Somewhere in the world at that moment, something that needed those flames suddenly no longer had them, and if it was a 'have-fire-or-die' situation, well, Seth didn't really care.

Seth had contemplated leaving both Pia and Mica where they had fallen asleep—Pia from pure exhaustion from her seeing endeavors and Mica from a cross between over-gorging and soy sauce overload—simply for their physical company but then thought better of it. Instead, he roused them both and sent them to their rooms, for he needed quiet time to think. The 'now' only consisted of his thoughts on what to do about Nyssa and, inevitably, about the Consortia, who had the better hand in the game. If Pia had been right and the Consortia truly *did* fear the girl, then Seth had no choice but to be weary.

'*I could just kill her,*' he had spoken to Pia's mind earlier as his options came sparsely. '*That will assure the playing field remains unlevel in our favor.*'

'*You could,*' she had echoed back through his mind. '*But by doing so you are proffering that we have already lost our chance to have her.*'

'*And taking any risk to have her is wise?*' he had asked back, his mind looming in turmoil.

'*It might prove safer than trying to kill her, my Seth,*' she simply replied, and the conversation had ended.

As the night waned towards morning—his body succumbing to the day's fatigue—those last words continued to roll through his mind like bowling balls in an antique shop, smashing and crushing age-old ideals he had held to fast over the years.

CHAPTER SIX

A Call from an Old, Old Friend

-1-

Nyssa's eyes parted slowly to the sounds of chainsaws.

From her bedroom window, she would typically look directly out onto busy Oakdale Avenue, which bustled with cars and bicycles alike, wondering where they were heading, but not that morning. That day the street was lined with Streets and Sanitation vehicles sitting in several inches of water, one of which trailed a woodchipper. It looked as if all hell had broken loose out there, and from what she could make out from a distance, at least six trees were down.

Poor trees, the conservationist part of her mind acknowledged, and slowly she crawled from her bed, glancing at the clock, which steadily read 10:22 am.

Oddly enough, they had not lost power during the storm.

*

The smell of cooked bacon met her as she walked into the living room stretching, the aroma setting off her saliva glands and producing a growl in her stomach.

She had slept well and long through the night, but it had come so swiftly and heavily that it had plummeted her into such a deep sleep that she still felt tired. She stopped briefly in the living room where the television was droning on about the 'freakish storm of the millennia.' Although the undeserved feeling of guilt had left her through slumber, the images on the screen at least produced a sensation of coincidental uneasiness in her.

She moved on, led by her nose and the sensation of smoked flavor in the air and towards the kitchen.

On the counter was a bowl with an upturned saucer on top of it, doubling as a cover. Stuck to the bottom of the saucer was a blue *Post-it* with her name on it, written by Randy's hand.

"I know it's been way to long!" Her mother's voice surprised her as it came through the kitchen windows from outside. *"We haven't seen you in so long; you have to come for dinner."*

"Why is she home today?" Nyssa said absently to herself as she removed the saucer to find a nice size pile of hard-fried bacon sitting on oily paper towels. Smiling, she grabbed up two pieces which disappeared quickly into her mouth. The first bite sent the sweet-salty taste of it racing through her, and the next chomp took the whole piece in, followed by the next.

Pausing, she returned to the bowl and took three more and then moved to the kitchen door to the backyard.

-2-

The garden was not so much a yard as a patch of wide grass and a wooden deck that dominated the space. It was nowhere near the size of her grandparents, whose house sat on a two and half-sized lot in the city, with a backyard big enough that she used to run herself sweaty in. She slid the door closed behind her, latched it—a requisite laid down by her mother to prevent the nasty bugs from entering—and moved towards the deck railing to see what was happening.

There was a decent-sized pile of broken branches and twigs which Randy had collected and neatly grouped near the garbage cans next to the garage. He was busy scooping out water from her mother's rose bed with a plastic drinking cup, and although it was at ground level, the wood sidings which corralled the roses from the rest of the yard allowed the rainwater to collect and pool there. Her mother was standing off the side with a pair of work gloves tucked under one arm, which she had no intention of using since Randy was there, and the cordless house phone pressed to her ear. She was wearing a bright smile which Nyssa rarely saw, and somehow this made Nyssa feel uneasy. Her mother talked and moved with such lazy grace while having the conversation, so she knew that her mother was enjoying the conversation, another rarity.

"And how is Seema doing?" her mother inquired, tapping Randy's shoulder, and then motioning towards a spot in the garden in which Randy simply nodded without looking at her.

Seema? she thought, her mind trailing back to when she would have been in the fifth or sixth grade when she last summered with her mom's college friend, Agatha, and her adopted daughter, Seema. *Wow, that's a name I haven't heard in a long time.*

"Hey Nyss… I mean Nyssa," Randy acknowledged her as she approached, a piece of bacon snapping in two between her teeth. "I see you found the bacon I made earlier… good."

"Yes, thank you," she replied, swallowing, feeling a bit odd considering since she was thirteen, her mother and Randy always told her to make it herself if she wanted it. "Wasn't expecting it."

"Oh," he said, smiling as he looked up at her. "Let's call it a little bit of making up from your harrowing day yesterday. Sorry again for not coming to pick you up."

"No worries," she shrugged and then squatted near the edge of the bed. There had to have been close to four inches of water pooled inside of it, with leaves and twigs bobbing along the surface like little imaginary boats. "Are Mom's roses going to be okay?"

Randy licked his lips, his eyes reviewing her mother briefly and then whispered towards her, "To be honest, I think they've drowned."

"Pity," she added flatly and then shrugged again.

This was her mother's prize garden which had produced blue ribbon roses at various contests her mother would submit them. The blooms were beautiful and spectacular, but they were also the very plants that formed another wedge between them. It was Nyssa's and Randy's job to weed it, to water it, and to chase the occasional squirrel from its edges, and every time one bloomed with the slightest deformity, the fault somehow rested with them. In many ways, the garden represented her mother's unyielding attempts to fit in as the proper suburban wife and mother. To Nyssa, it meant yet another teen-angst for her to someday grow out of, seek therapy, or one day write a book about.

In short, Nyssa despised it.

"Don't let your mother hear you say things like that," he said, head down while his hand followed a rhythmic motion of scooping, then pouring. "I happened to say in passing this morning that she should have taken my advice of letting me put in a small, above-ground green house, and she almost ripped me a new one."

Pity, she thought to herself, wanting to rip him a new one on many occasions in the past, but chose to say nothing.

"So why are you and Mom home today?" she continued.

"Well, I called off because your mother got called off," Randy sat back on his haunches, wiping his brow. "Her job called and told her not to come in because of the road conditions and the flooding. The moment she saw her garden well, you know, then I called off work. I don't feel guilty; the office is basically closed today because of the storm and by look of the streets, I don't think I would have gotten very far to begin with."

"Oh," she responded absently, her head slightly cocked to one side as she concentrated on what her mother was saying into the phone.

"Of course, she remembers Seema!" her mother beamed, turning towards the two of them near the garden. "You remember Seema, don't you Nyss?"

Nyssa nodded and attempted a smile as her mother turned back to her conversation.

"Is Mom talking to Auntie Agatha?" Nyssa inquired.

Auntie Agatha—so assumedly named for her mother's college friend, Agatha Turrell—was a pleasant woman who was exceptionally educated, world-traveled, and for most of Nyssa's young life, the epitome of a woman which Nyssa wanted to emulate. Nothing was accidental about the woman; every motion and step was full of natural grace and calculation, every word enunciated with clarity, but never afraid of using a contraction, and a smile that could soothe any pain. Agatha was everything Nyssa had associated with stories of the etiquette of headmistresses. She also held a beauty Nyssa knew would only become more pronounced and graceful with time.

"Yeah, for nearly an hour now," Randy nodded, setting the scooping cup down for a moment and lifting a mug of cold coffee that had been sitting off to the side. "She must have heard about that crazy storm and got worried."

"It's been a long time since I saw them," she spoke to no one in particular. "It's odd that she would call now over a storm. I mean, I got her card when I graduated from grade school, but I mean, we have had bad storms before."

"I don't know," Randy shrugged, setting down the mug and returning to his mundane task of scooping water. "I have a buddy who's kind of the same way. Won't hear from him for years and then suddenly something would happen in Chicago, and he'd give me a call just to see if everything was okay."

"So, they're going to visit?" she asked, shrugging as her mind returned to the current phone call.

"Sounds like it," he replied. "Which means we will be busy until then making the house spic and span for them."

"Hmm, how did she know our number?" she mused, her attention towards her mother.

"What?" Randy inquired, distracted.

"I mean, we got a new home number when we moved here," Nyssa continued, the *Nancy Drew* sleuth inside her chiseling away at the facts. Although cell phones were the modern norm, a home phone was an unspoken requisite by the standards of her mother's upbringing. "And we have always been unlisted."

A shrug came from Randy; his future of cleaning, fixing, reorganizing and furniture moving filling his mind.

"And I mean, this is the workweek," Nyssa continued. "How did she know that Mom would even be home to take the call?"

"I don't know, Nyssa," Randy shrugged again, scooping water. "Maybe your mom wrote her and told her of the new number, and for being home, well, maybe she just had a hunch, ya know?"

A hunch, Nyssa's mind played over the word as Randy scooped the water and her mother beamed into the phone. Her mother was smiling so wide that Nyssa wondered if the expression would freeze like that permanently.

On the other side of the house, the sudden high-pitched buzz of the woodchipper came to life as it mercilessly ate the large branches as they were fed into it.

-3-

Twenty minutes later, her mother exited the rear of the house and stood on the deck with her hands on her hips triumphantly. On her face was the same oversized smile she had from earlier.

"Now *that* was a breath of fresh air!" she beamed, her eyes dancing between the two of them.

"Oh?" Randy inquired his eyes on her. "Did you have a good conversation?"

"Did I?" her mother laughed, stepping from the deck and stopping directly over them as Randy set down the scoop and Nyssa plopped another handful of debris into the pile she was forming. "Of course I did! It is so good to hear from an old friend!" "So, are they coming to visit?" Nyssa asked, wiping her hands.

"Yes!" her mother glowed. "Her and Seema."

"When and for how long?" Randy asked, attempting to sound excited while his mind began preparing a quick list of chores that he would surely be made to do.

"Day after tomorrow," her mother laughed, shaking her head while Randy's mind pushed the chore-throttle ahead a little in his mind. "They are staying only for the weekend. She said on the next full moon, can you believe that? Agatha is such a nut!"

"So, I take it they are staying here, then?" He added, knowing the answer to that already.

"Of course!" her mother announced, giving him a perturbed look. "Where else would they stay? Do you think that I will have them stay at a hotel when they are like family?"

"No, I suppose you would not," he finished, hope diminished while clearing the mental slate free of all other duties beyond getting the place ready for guests.

"Of course, I would not," she concurred firmly. "Alright then. Nyss? I need you to finish up out here while Randy and I go inside and prepare of list of things we are going to need."

"Figures," Nyssa sounded, not trying to be heard but not trying to hide her disdain all the same.

"Nyssa!" her mother snapped angrily; a time when only her mother ever called her by her full birth-name. "We all need to pull together and pitch in to make this work!"

"Okay, sorry," Nyssa muffled without sincerity.

"Good, now, Randy, give Nyss that scooper and come with me," she said as she turned towards the house moving quickly and Randy slowly stood and handed over the cup. "Now, there are a lot of things to be gotten and… Nyss, do they still have that sale of sheets and towels at your work?"

"I guess so, why?" Nyssa shrugged.

"Good," her mother nodded, sliding the patio doors open. "Later we will go and pick some out, and get a new bath set to go with them. How much is your employee discount again?"

"Twenty percent," she added with a soft gulping sound.

"Great, that will help a lot!" she continued as she disappeared into the house. "And you thought your job was worthless."

Nyssa knelt and watched as they disappeared into the house with the screen door sliding close behind them, and she wondered to herself if it was now a good time (or not) to tell her mother that she had quit her job as the cart jockey the day before.

Shaking her head as her attention focused on the pool of water in the garden, she decided that that would be a *No*.

-4-

Nyssa rode her bike to *Walgreens* three blocks away from her home to get the odds and ends her mother needed, turning down the possibility of a ride there from Randy, which produced a disappointed look on his face. The rejection didn't hurt him, but he was disquieted that his one way out of his wife's designations of mounting chores had been shot. For Nyssa, even though she never put off a ride if she could get one, especially in the summer months with all the heat, she had been more interested in seeing the carnage left after the storm.

Street crews were out everywhere, removing downed trees and branches from the roadways, and just a block from her house, all traffic had been diverted by red and yellow-painted sawhorses due to downed power lines. They wore bright reflective waders as they tromped through twelve-inch flood waters. Luckily for her, the sidewalk was on much higher ground and was only wet despite a few puddles.

She stopped briefly to peer down the block to where the electric company's trucks were sitting and uttered a mild expletive in disbelief towards that general direction. Almost every single house had some display of the storm's fury, whether by the lawns littered with tree limbs or blown-in picture windows. She swallowed hard against the swelling guilt rising in her chest and turned away from the sights, and as she headed towards Ogden, a group of people had gathered in one yard, talking.

"I don't know," a man in his early forties with wide-rimmed glasses was speaking as he stood closest to the sidewalk, one arm crossing his chest, the hand planted safely in the armpit, while in the other he held a mug of coffee. "Look at the last twenty to twenty-five years with all the pollution, over-cropping, wasteful use of fossil fuels and then look at the weather we have been having. No one can tell me one doesn't have something to do with the other."

"I agree," a frail form of a younger woman, much too frail for her apparent age of late twenties was nodding; occasionally waving her hand towards her knees where no-see-ums were agitating her. "Big Oil has a large part in it… they are running most of it."

"And the strip mining; I hope this new President can do something about all that…" the voices trailed off as she passed them slowly, rolling her eyes.

She didn't know any of them but saw them in the neighborhood often as they drove their large SUVs to run errands, and all of them had immaculate lawns that never knew the quench of thirst. These were the exact sort of people Nyssa despised the most: the hypocritical ones who took part in all the things they complained about, only to sleep soundly at night with a sense of innocence because they donated to the carbon tax.

As she coasted along, only producing pedal pumps necessary enough to prevent herself from toppling over, her mind continued to roll over the previous day's events. In contrast, various levels of emotions rolled with it. She knew she had nothing to do with it, and coincidences were a part of everyday life. However, she could not help but feel that she has been immortalized in some surrealistic blame.

It was just a freakish storm! *She commanded her thoughts and reflected upon when Katrina slammed into the Gulf years before causing widespread death and mayhem. Even then, no one expected the storm to do what it did, but look at what happened. Coincidence: that freakish occurrence of events that occur at the same time by accident but seem to have some connection truly is a daily event, and regardless that someone could do the math and put the odds at billions to one, the fact remained that they did_happen, nonetheless.*

Shrugging as she rode, she would leave it where it lay (or at least attempt to anyway).

-5-

Nyssa was returning from the store just as slowly as she went, for all of Ogden Avenue was suffering from lack of power, and the store windows stated such by their signs. It didn't matter to her because, unlike Randy, who was trapped in the house with her mother, she had managed to escape the housework even for a little bit.

As she turned off from Ogden, she slowed to see a black cat sitting in the middle of the sidewalk, blankly watching her. It wore a collar that seemed too elaborate for it being an outdoor pet, but the creature's brilliant green eyes caught her attention. The feline straightened its back just as Nyssa rolled to a stop a few feet from it, and the two of their eyes met, the cat blinking from time to time.

"You know you could get squished out here," Nyssa scolded. The animal simply responded with a lazy blink.

Shrugging, Nyssa half walked/rode to one side of the walk to round the blinking black obstacle, but as she drew close, the cat stood, walked two steps into her path, and then sat down again.

"Do you *want* to get hit? *Shoo!*"

The cat did nothing but blink at her once more.

"Dumb cat," she whispered and heaved at the handlebars so to pass on the other side, only to have the cat match her direction by moving in her path again.

Yes, it wants to get squished, she thought, knowing very well that she wouldn't dream about running it over, and glanced at the flooded street.

"*Move!*"

"She just wants your attention," a gentle voice from over her shoulder spoke, and Nyssa turned to find the face of a teenage girl not much older than she was.

She was dressed in dark colors, which Nyssa compared to the Emo-kids at her school who listened to nothing but dark music, lived in their depressing worlds, and cut themselves just to be alive (or at least dressed the part in a poser mentality just to fit in the clique since the idea of bleeding oneself also involved pain). She had a pleasant voice, and her smile gave Nyssa at least comfort that the girl wasn't confrontational.

"She gets like that from time to time."

"Oh," Nyssa sounded, watching the girl approach.

The young woman squatted down, lifting the creature from the walk. On the girl's hip, where a thick black leather belt was looped through the eyes of a dark-colored skirt, hung a nappy little gray bear with mismatched eyes which drew smiles from Nyssa at the originality of her fashion.

"Is she your cat?"

"Well, if you know cats," the girl smiled. "You would know that they are the ones who own us and not the other way around."

"Yeah, I do," Nyssa returned the smile and extended an open hand. "I'm Nyssa. I have never seen you around before, are you new to the area?"

"Nice to meet you, Nyssa," she smiled back, adjusting the cat's weight on her arm and shaking Nyssa's hand. "I'm Mica, and no, I am just visiting my aunt; she lives in this building."

"Oh, well nice to meet you," Nyssa nodded, her eyes scanning the three flat apartment building and then found the eyes of the cat peering into her. "Were you here yesterday during the storm?"

"No, I came in this morning with my mom," Mica replied, stroking the cat's head. "We got a little worried after watching the news. I live in the city."

"Me too!" Nyssa beamed, knowing if anyone in the burbs said *The City* they meant they were from Chicago. "I was a Southsider, what part are you from?"

"North side," Mica smiled. "Go Cubs."

"Go Sox," Nyssa shot right back and the two of them laughed. For those who do not know Chicago, that is how the city is majorly split.

If you met a Sox fan, you pretty much could assume they were from the Southside of the city, and with the Cubs, you had the opposite, leaving the East and Westside an almost even toss-up where their loyalties lay. For those Cubs fans on the far Southside, well, there are oddballs everywhere (silly mortals), but you could live on Mars and love the Sox.

"Well, I grew up there; been out here for a little while," Nyssa continued. "I miss it all the time."

"Yeah, there's a lot to do there," Mica nodded, setting the cat down on the walk.

The cat licked its paw for a moment then circled her, rubbing her tail along the girl's calf.

"Couldn't imagine being a creature of the city living out here… must get pretty damn boring."

"Tell me about it," Nyssa sighed but smiled.

Nyssa was not a spitting sailor when it came to profanity, but whenever she met someone her age that not only cursed from time to time but actually *knew* how to curse, it always brought a certain relief to the conversations.

"It took me a while before I could fall asleep at night… too damned quiet out here, especially at night."

"I could imagine," Mica smiled, eyes focusing on a spot right between Nyssa's eyes as she swallowed, concentrating: *'Makes me feel like I am in a cage.'*

"Makes me feel like I am in a cage," Nyssa absently spoke and then continued on her rant about the burbs.

'And there's nothing to do but hang out at the mall,' Mica's mind said.

"And there's nothing to do but hang out at the mall," Nyssa added to her rant.

'And I want to eat sushi while standing on my head while a penguin slaps me on the nose,' Mica smiled.

"And I want to eat sushi while standing on my head while a penguin slaps me on the nose!" Nyssa exclaimed.

"What?" Mica smiled, almost losing her composure, and laughing outright.

"What *what?*" Nyssa asked, eyebrows rising.

"Chicken butt," Mica followed quickly, choking back her laughter. "You said something about a penguin."

"I did?" Nyssa asked followed by Mica sounding a lazy *Mm-hmm.*

She stood blankly, eyes shifting in her sockets, her mind flashing between the conversations about City life and the sudden want for sushi. An odd feeling ebbed over her, one of being lifted effortlessly from the ground, while a dull ache began to form in the center of her brain. She slowly shook her head to aid the sensation's passing and then regarded Mica again.

"Huh… that was odd… never mind… mind got away from me a bit. I guess I didn't get that much sleep after all."

"Storm kept you awake?" the girl asked as one eyebrow rose, her eyes locking now on Nyssa's; pushing: *'Feeling guilty are you, Nyssa?'*

"Yeah," Nyssa's eyes dropped, her stomach turning into a knot, her presence quickly becoming crestfallen and somber. "Didn't mean it."

"Didn't mean what?" Mica asked, relaxing.

"Huh?" Nyssa blinked.

"Never mind," Mica smiled, satisfied. Seth had promoted so much apprehension about this girl that even Mica had worried that her gifts would have no effect, but it was obvious that they did.

'Stop toying with her!' a voice boomed in Mica's mind, startling her. *'Plant the seed!'*

"Fine," she spoke to her feet where the cat was staring right up at her.

"What?" Nyssa inquired.

"Oh nothing," Mica said quickly, nudging the cat with her boot. "Pushy, smelly little animals… attention getters each and every one of them… keeps nudging me. I guess she wants to go inside so she can eat old bologna then lick her butt."

Slow and long the cat growled at the girl with focused eyes.

"Oh, yeah, my dad had cats," Nyssa reminisced. "They were the same way. Well, it was nice to meet you, Mica; gotta get going to help my mom out with some chores."

'Now!' The voice screamed, and Mica jumped, her hand shooting out and taking Nyssa firmly by the wrist.

There was a brief expression of surprise and defense in Nyssa's eyes until they met Mica's, which had gone pitch, the centers flowing with little violet embers.

"I want you to listen to me, Nyssa," Mica spoke deeply, her voice seemingly very far away and echoing. "I want you to listen to everything I have to say and then do all that I say..."

As the one-way conversation went on, the cat raised its leg above its head and started to clean itself. Nyssa traveled up and up, her mind seemingly leaving her body as a cold sensation filtered through her, tingling.

No, I don't want to go with them, her mind sounded robotically. *I want to stay with Mom and—*

She was falling back down swiftly, the coolness being replaced by warmth, faster and faster her mind fell, gathering in nothing but seeing everything.

Someone around her screamed *Ouch!* A cat hissed and screeched. The metallic clangs of a bicycle hitting concrete sounded, and as her mind dimmed, her ears echoed with the sounds of a little dog yapping away.

-6-

Nyssa rode her bike home quietly and without incident, barely noticing a street crew hauling up a downed streetlamp from the floodwaters. She went inside, placed her mother's money on the table unspent, looked over a note stating that her mother and Randy would be out for a while, and then went and sat on the couch, eyes looking blankly ahead of her.

*

That night, Nyssa simply didn't sleep, she was comatose.

CHAPTER SEVEN

Old Friends

-1-

By the day after tomorrow, everything in the house had either been cleaned and sterilized or replaced entirely. In many ways, Nyssa was perfectly happy with this.

Every little decor her mother had picked up from various garage sales or liquidation specials, which Nyssa felt to have been tacky, suddenly seemed so to her mother as well. Nyssa reluctantly bit back her comments of *I told you so's* and simply went through the motions. On the other hand, Randy was looking forward to the whole thing being over with, considering his role had been primarily the muscle and the gopher. At that moment, he was hauling out boxes filled with smaller broken-down boxes from their purchases to store in the garage while she and her mother sat on the sofa, taking a break.

"Now you do remember this, don't you?" her mother positioned the photo album closer to Nyssa to get a better look. In the picture was a smaller, brighter-faced capture of her swinging on a swing; her face full of glee as her long hair flowed behind her.

Nyssa blinked, her eyes finding her youthful ones in the image, frozen in a time when days were much happier for her.

"Actually, a little," Nyssa produced a smile and gently nudged her mom's knee with her own without realizing she was going to. Her mother jerked slightly, surprised herself by the instant and minute show of physical affection, returning a smile as well.

"Ah, here are the ones I wanted to show you since you don't seem to remember your Auntie Agatha that much." Her mother continued after a moment of silence as she flipped to a central cover in her scrap album.

She had at one time been exceptionally gifted, making scrapbooks and photo albums that friends and family had quite coveted. Whenever the holidays neared, many wished secretly in hopes of receiving one. This had been when her mother felt young, the world could still be her possession, and personal hobbies were allowed considering they did not distract her from the prize.

Since the divorce, she has never made another one.

"*Escape to Agatha's*" her mother read aloud the cover and smiled brightly in the glow of her best work. Nyssa found herself smiling as well as her eyes darted over the complex detail of the work.

The craftsmanship was exquisite, its facing page consuming the entire vision of the eye yet still having more to show. The page was heavy with glues layers of multi-colored cut pieces of paper and cloth, sanded smoothly on the sides to form a pleasant bevel. There was a large tree in the center, which her mother had used actual thin pieces of bark to make up the trunk and main branches, and at the end of each was a circle, oval, or square in which the cover backing had been cut out to show faces from the page beneath. From left to right was a younger image of her mom, then her, a picture of Agatha looking at the camera with a thin Mona Lisa smile, and the last sat a small girl with large almond-shaped eyes, and short jet-black hair, a large smile void of the front teeth.

Nyssa leaned in slightly and then smiled to herself.

"Seema!" Nyssa chirped as the memories began to bloom.

Her mother had gone distant, looking at the cover and her eyes looking at no one particular piece or another. Her fingers rolled over bits of string, an acorn shell, and dried colored leaves which had been permanently locked in place with glue and a heavy lacquer varnish.

"Yes, that's Seema," her mother sighed, attempting to flip the page.

"What used to be there?" Nyssa asked stopping the page turn, her finger going towards the center of the tree towards the top of the trunk where a blank oval sat. Her mother glanced slowly to only meet her eyes.

"Just an old picture," her mother said quietly and turned the cover to another crafty designed page in which her mother had gone to great detail to make personalized borders.

Nyssa kept quiet as her mother's silence fell over the moment. She knew exactly what was there; there had been a picture of the three of them there once: herself, her mom, and her real dad.

Suddenly a high-pitched giggle rose from her mother, nearly startling her.

"Look at you! Aw, you were no taller than this!" Her mother's arm extended in front of her, the palm lying flat and slightly angled up to exaggerate the height.

In the picture, she stood near a very ornate and colorful garden, poised with a butterfly resting on her open palm. She was wearing a broad smile and brilliant eyes of purity as she awed at the colorful insect which had entrusted her as its roost. Crowning her head was a ring of small clover flowers, which she later remembered was a thing she enjoyed making for herself. She had been standing on the garden's edge, and in the background behind her sat a blurred out-of-focus shape of a white stone bench, and to the side of it was a blurry garden gnome.

"I was cute," she sounded quietly with a smile.

"Yes, you sure were," her mother added, turning the page and for a moment Nyssa wondered should she be insulted at the 'were' and then shrugged it off.

The next page had many pictures, large and small, matching its facing page in order—many images contained mostly shots of either Nyssa alone or with Seema, hugging or huddled together. One particular picture showed her and Seema squatted down and intently looking at something on the ground, their eyes full of curious wonder and innocence.

"What are we looking at?" Nyssa asked, leaning forward to see if she could make it out.

"Oh, you girls had corralled a Japanese beetle with leaves and sticks," her mother spoke softly, her tone laced with gentle, reminiscing thoughts. "You two were set on interrogating the poor thing."

"Huh?" Nyssa sounded looking up. "What do you mean?"

"Oh, if I remember exactly, you two were convinced that the beetle was a scout for some wicked kingdom. It was attempting to spy on the garden and you two were going to make it talk."

"What did we do with the beetle?" she swallowed.

"You guys let it go… eventually," her mother chuckled in the memory. "Only after you both were convinced that it meant no harm to the fairies."

"Fairies?" Nyssa's face twisted in a look of pure confusion.

"These," her mother said, pointing to the other page where her mother tapped the glossy surface of another picture. There was a picture of Nyssa and Seema sitting cross-legged near a reflection pond, and dancing around them were ornate garden fairy figurines suspended in place by long, thin glass tubes.

"Oh," Nyssa sounded not recalling them.

"You used to go on about the magic in the garden," her mother recollected. "And about how you and Seema were their protectors, along with this fellow."

Nyssa followed the tapping finger to the edge of the picture to see the shady form of a little garden gnome. She blinked, looking back at the previous photo to see the out-of-focused capture of the same little gnome. Curiously, she glanced over all the pictures, and in one place or another, there the little guy stood.

"Did I used to carry the gnome around with me or something?" she asked.

"What do you mean?"

"Well, look," Nyssa pointed out from one picture to the next. "He's like in every picture like some sort of *Where's Waldo*'-gnome book."

Slowly her mother followed Nyssa's finger and sounded a curious *'huh.'*

"I don't know... maybe there were a lot of garden gnomes. Curious though, it looks like the same one in every picture. Funny."

Crash! Heavy sounds of metal and breaking glass startled the two on the sofa which drew their wide eyes towards the back of the house, and then quickly followed by, *"Oh shit!"*

"Clumsy as an ox," her mother whispered, shaking her head. "You okay, dear?"

"Yes, I'm fine!" barked Randy from the garage.

"Nyss, will you go see if your father needs any help?"

"Stepfather," Nyssa said flatly, standing; the short-lived mother-daughter bonding ended. "And it's Nyssa."

Slowly she moved through the house towards the garage, knowing that her mother's eyes were burning daggers through her back the whole while. The flares of sudden irritations and bursts of rage towards her mother and Randy have been increasingly frequent lately, especially in her attempts to conform to ideals only her mother and Randy followed.

She hated herself for her thoughts, especially when they would turn to ill conceptions. Still, luckily for everyone, she had never wished her mother to drop dead (however, under heavy duress in the past, she had wished her mother to go screw herself, and well... how about if we leave that at that).

-2-

It was 4:00 pm exactly when the doorbell rang, and her mother jumped up so quickly that Nyssa swore that her mother suddenly had to pee. When the door opened, all Nyssa could see from the foyer perspective was blurred arms delivering hugs, shoulder grips and more hugs.

"Agatha!" Her mother was screaming, her entire face stretched into the form of a gaping smile. "You look so good!"

"Christine!" Agatha replied, delivering another hug.

Nyssa was standing close but not too close, for those fast-moving elbows could potentially knock her flat. Just behind and to Agatha's left stood Seema, her eyes bright and a perfect smile on her face wearing a simple blouse of neutral tan with a slight shimmer to the material. She wore a pretty hairpiece made up of tiny red flowers; the edges were peppered sporadically with baby's breath_accents. She looked primarily at Nyssa, and her eyes sparkled with fond recognition.

"*Nyssa!*" Seema's smile broadened and she dipped in between the chortling women, arms extended before her.

Nyssa met her grasp, absorbing the loving hug, and there was genuine tender warmth behind it, that of sisterhood. She could do nothing but glow in the moment as a soft tear formed in the corners of her eyes.

"Oh wow, Nyssa! It is so good to see you!"

"You too," Nyssa returned softly, almost whispering as they parted, their height almost identical, their eyes locking onto one another's.

"And you got your nose pierced!" Seema glowed, her eyes dancing over the face of her once departed sister.

"Yes!" Nyssa giggled; her fingertips gently touched the small gold ring through her left nostril. "My mom and I did ours together and—"

"You are crying child," Agatha's voice said softly, and Nyssa dapped at her eye.

"I am?" she asked, taking a step back and then looked at her fingertips came away damp. "I guess I am."

"Well, come give me some of that tenderness too," Agatha said, arms rising.

"Auntie Agatha," Nyssa beamed and moved into her arms.

They held each other firmly as a soft hum filled the air, which tickled the hairs on all present. Perhaps it was just the tenderness of the moment that tugged at the heartstrings of the group or leftover static in the air from the now-passed storm, who knows. They all smiled at the sight as a gentle breeze flowed inwards through the doorway and delicately ruffled the loose edges of clothing and hair.

For the briefest moments, however, ever so peculiar, a soft golden aura flicked and shimmered between the two.

Seema cleared her throat drawing a thin peek from Agatha's closed eye.

"Oh come, come, come," Agatha hurried dismissively in case anyone noticed. "Why don't we step inside out of the breeze?"

They moved from the entranceway into the foyer, shutting the door behind them. Across the street from Nyssa's house, a black cat sat in between two bushes, watching.

As the door closed, the cat stretched forth its hind leg and began to nurse a small bite wound just above its paw.

-3-

When her mother really put an effort into it, she could cook quite well.

They had sat down to dinner at 5:30 to an assortment of meats, starches, and veggies; the main course was roasted duck with orange-curry glazed asparagus steamed with fresh lemon and ground pepper. Nyssa could not recall eating a meal at home this good since before when her parents were together, and even then, one thing or another had been either under or overcooked to some degree. The entire spread was magnificent and had been laid out like some yuletide family event, and the first fifteen minutes were filled with verbal exchanges of someone asking someone else to pass something along. Seema seemed to enjoy it most of all, devouring all that was passed and then some.

"You have quite the appetite, Seema," Randy introduced his observation with a smile. Seema looked up shyly and then glanced at Agatha who gave her a little wink and a smile.

"Everything is really good," she blushed as she tucked a morsel to the side of her mouth.

"Oh, don't blame her, Randy," Agatha smiled, taking a sip of iced tea with lemon. "Seema hates everything prepared in our house."

"No, I don't," Seema protested guiltily, retrieving her glass of iced tea and swallowing her mouth clean. "I like the muffins."

"Ha!" Agatha laughed, leaning back. "And that's all she eats, but before I got good at conjuring up a good batch, she said she was going to use them as skipping stones on the pond."

A round of laughter rose, producing a blush and a shrug from Seema who finished it up by snagging two black olives from the condiment tray: popping them into her mouth.

"Well, I take it as a compliment, Seema," Nyssa's mother smiled, leaning over and softly gripping Seema's shoulder warmly. "Now if I can get that one to eat what I make, well, that would be a blessing."

"But you hardly cook anymore," Nyssa retorted, feeling a flare rise up in her chest.

"Well, this is true," her mother conceded without a fight, but the glare that shown in her eyes told Nyssa all that was needed to be said and that was to behave. "I have been quite busy lately with the shows."

"And how is that going, dear?" Agatha inquired shifting towards her slightly in her chair and the two of their conversation carried off on their own.

Randy had heard the tone in Nyssa and saw the eye daggers fly back and forth across the table between the two. He cleared his throat as he excused himself, gathered up some dishes, and disappeared into the safety of the kitchen.

Nyssa found herself sitting quietly in her chair in a pronounced slouch, alone with her thoughts and not wanting to be there anymore. A mixture of guilt and anger rolled around each other like light and dark clothing in a dryer. She knew that this was neither the time nor the place for the bitch in her to show its ugly face, but another side of her simply wanted to dump another cup of lighter fluid on the already crackling flames.

With a fork, she began rolling a pea around a clear spot on her plate.

"Hey, Nyssa," Seema whispered to her with a smile. "Wanna see a magic trick?"

"Uh, sure," Nyssa produced a smile and straightened in her chair.

"Okay, cool," Seema smiled, quietly turning in her chair so to better face Nyssa. "Great, now here's what you do…"

Seema licked her lips and moved in closer to Nyssa speaking softly. She spoke clearly and directly to her, her animated eyes moving and shifting, occasionally chancing a peek at Agatha who seemed none the wiser. Nyssa followed the instructions to the letter.

"Take a black olive with your right hand and hold it in your palm… yeah, just like that. Now close your hand into a ball, but don't squish it, okay? Good. Now, hold it there. I am going to pick up a green Spanish olive and hold it in my right hand, see?

"Okay, what I want you to do is close your eyes… good.

"Now, you must picture the green one in my hand, not the black one in yours; actually, don't even think for a moment that you are holding anything at all. Now, I want you to picture that you are holding the *green* one, got it?"

Nyssa nodded and a thin smile spread over her lips.

"Good," Seema said quietly, but excitedly.

"What now?" Nyssa almost giggled, eyes closed.

"Take hold of my left hand with your left hand," Seema instructed, and blindly Nyssa felt for Seema's palm and found it. "Good, now open your eyes."

"Okay," Nyssa followed as instructed and opened her eyes to find Seema's looking right back at her."

"Ready?" Seema said excitedly.

"What now: abracadabra?" Nyssa giggled.

"Not quite, but you'll see," Seema spoke near bursting with excitement. "Here we go... *Gumpen.*"

A pulse—much like an uncontrolled twitch—raced from Nyssa's right hand, up the arm, and across her body as their hands sparked, forcing her to jerk suddenly while producing a startled cry. The table jostled akin to someone kicking one of the legs, shaking the glasses, and disturbing the dinnerware. Nyssa's mother uttered a small, surprised cry, tearing the two women from their conversation.

"Nyssa!" her mother hissed alone.

"Seema!" Agatha made the lecture tone a duet.

The two girls sat looking at their elders and their eyes dropped, and they turned and faced the table.

"You scared the life out of me!" her mother finished.

"You know the rules about Magic tricks at the table!" Agatha scolded right along with her.

The girls whispered a sullen apology, then the two women went back to their conversation accompanied by the occasional sideways glance.

After a moment of silence between the two, Seema glanced to her side and spoke-whispered out the side of her mouth, *"Look in your hand."*

"What?" Nyssa whispered back.

"Look inside your hand," Seema finished and retrieved her glass of tea. Slowly Nyssa brought her arm up and placed the back of her fist on her thigh and then slowly spread her fingers. Once she was convinced no one was fixated on her, she dared to look down, and sitting there in the middle of her palm was a green Spanish olive with the pimento glowing red at her.

"How in the—" Nyssa started, eyes wide with disbelief, shaking her head. She looked up, hoping to find a reason only to find her Auntie Agatha smiling at her as her mother droned on about roses and their upkeep.

Agatha gave her a little nod and a wink.

-4-

Nyssa had quickly excused her and Seema from the table, where her mother simply waved them off with a smile as the two women played catch up. As they hurried out of the dining room, Agatha quickly called after Seema, uttering only three words, "No more Magic."

Nyssa rushed Seema into her bedroom and shut the door behind them.

"How did you *do* that?" Nyssa begged quickly, flipping on her MP3 stereo, which acted as a chassis for her player. Immediately *Wallflowers* by One Headlight began to play as Nyssa pressed the little '+' button several times to increase the volume. Regardless of the music's volume, she spoke in a whisper. "That was amazing!"

"Umm, it was just a trick I picked up," Seema shrugged, eyes shifting over items in Nyssa's room to divert their attention to.

The room was laid out in a hodgepodge décor of an older teen to that of a small child, the occasional stuffed animal and little kid's trinket or bobble resting amongst physics books and lava lamps. It was small compared to her room back at Agatha's estate, but for a medium suburban home, it was pleasant, and oddly enough, decorated with the same age-defining items.

"That was no trick," Nyssa was shaking her head and pulled Seema down with her so to sit on the edge of her bed. "And what did you say, *Glumpen*, or *Gumpen?*"

"*Shh!*" Seema sounded, her hands coming up to Nyssa's mouth, startling her, and Seema's eyes shot towards the door, waiting. After a moment Seema relaxed and leaned back on her palms, stretching out her back. "This is a really nice room."

"Thank you," Nyssa said quickly and then returned to her questions. "So, what did that word mean?"

"It's Low German," Seema said quietly, sitting upright, her eyes wide and dancing towards Nyssa, a thin smile on her lips. "It means *'jump'*."

"Jump?" Nyssa blinked and looked at her palm. "That was real? It *did* jump?"

Seema held Nyssa's eyes briefly and then shrugged passively, unsure of the correct answer. She stood and walked about the bedroom, her fingers touching item after item, occasionally pausing long enough to lift one for a closer examination and then moving on to the next.

"I suppose that depends on what you consider *'real'*." Seema said quietly, looking.

"Can you do any more tricks?" Nyssa's eyes begged.

"Just some things," Seema shrugged, her tone full of modesty. "I really do like your nose ring."

"Thank you, but you're changing subjects," Nyssa added with a very anxious tone. "Like what kinds of *things*?"

"You heard Lady Agatha, Nyssa," Seema whispered sharply over the music. "She doesn't want me to do any more tricks!"

"So, then it was just a trick, right?" Nyssa's chest fell, her eyes going to her palm.

"Let's just say for now—here—it was just a trick," Seema said with a smile and moved along the shelves of odds and ends that made up Nyssa's personalized décor.

Nyssa was studying her palm, her eyes focusing on the spot where the olive had sat just where her lifeline crossed the soft skin, her head slowly shaking because she had felt something... she had felt the *jump*.

"Aw, you like dolphins still!" Seema suddenly exclaimed, her pitch rising as she pulled a small glass figurine of two dolphins breaking through the molded water in a dramatic arrangement of motions.

"Yeah," Nyssa said quietly, her palm before her face while her mouth quietly sounded out the Low German word for 'jump'.

"You should be careful with that," Seema said without looking at her, her attention focused on the *Sea World* sticker on the bottom of the figurine. "You never know what could happen if you really mean it when you say it."

"Do you speak a lot of German?" Nyssa inquired, dropping her hand to her side.

"Quite a bit, and Latin, Farsi, Urdu, Spanish," Seema shrugged, taking a seat in her computer chair that rested before a gray-metallic desk. "And I can get by well enough to ask what time it is, find a restroom and where to eat in a spattering of other languages."

"Wow!" Nyssa's jaw dropped.

"*Et tu?*" Seema giggled.

"*François,*" Nyssa replied, shrugging. "For seven years now. I will start learning Spanish in the fall."

"Too cool!" Seema widened an authentic smile.

"Yeah, well, I only know one other person who speaks it fluently enough to enjoy it," Nyssa responded with a hint of disappointment. "Back when my dad was making really good money, he was going to take me to Paris for Christmas, and the main part of his gift was so that I could speak the language until I was blue in the face, but my mom put the kibosh on that."

"That seriously sucks," Seema sighed, eyes dropping to her toes. "How is your father doing? I remember him and Lady Agatha keeps pictures of the three of you in the parlor when, well, you know… when your parents were together."

"She does?" Nyssa brightened, liking the sound of that; it is good to be remembered. "He's good! He's bouncing around the west coast right now putting in networks for some international company."

"Does he still do his artwork?" Seema asked, still having the illustration of a teddy bear which was made to look as if wrought from colorful balloons twisted together.

"Yes, he does, it's his hobby, but not like before," Nyssa pointed to a large thirty-six by twenty-four-inch framed picture of an elaborately designed toy train hanging on the wall just above her bookshelf. "He made that for me while he was away and sent the image to a local place to have it printed for me."

"Oh my, wow!" Seema's face stretched in awe at the colorful print; the detail of the train was so elaborate that you could almost read the foundry stamp on the tiny rivets of the boiler.

She quickly moved towards it for a closer look, her eyes dancing over the intricately modeled wheels and the ornate steam whistles both fore and aft of the shiny bronze boiler. Below the image was a small, beveled oval cut from the matte and, in a perfect script, read: *'The Toy Train'* and beneath that, it stated: *'For my darling, Nyssa.'*

Seema giggled and pointed to the salutation.

"Now *this* is beyond awesome!"

"I know!" Nyssa smiled, feeling warm. "I don't remember what program he uses to do things like that, but he once showed me a picture of the wireframe, kinda like the innards of the picture, but in three-D and I couldn't make heads or tails from it."

"Way over my head," Seema laughed and moved back to the desk, taking up her seat again next to Nyssa.

"Mine too," Nyssa nodded. "He told me he made it for me because he's always thinking about me and wanted me to have something special to think about him when he was traveling. I don't see him as much as I would like, but we keep in touch all the time by phone and internet.

"Here let me show you."

Nyssa moved quickly towards where Seema was sitting and grabbed a foldable chair that leaned next to her closet and opened it next to Seema and sat down. With a quick shaking of the mouse the flat panel monitor came out of *Sleep* mode and glowed into life. With a quick double click on her browser icon the World Wide Web exploded into life.

"Do you use MyBook?" Nyssa asked, her eyes focused on what she was doing as she rapidly clicked in her extremely long password. Her father—being a network security person by trade—had long since convinced her the importance of long, complicated passwords for everything; always setting it to something only you knew and could remember, but long and complex using capitals, numbers, and special characters. For her, any letter 'a' was an '@', an 'e' was a '3' and an 'l' was either an exclamation point, or a numerical number one.

"No, Lady Agatha doesn't think the diversion would do me very well," Seema partially lied, leaving off the part that there are those who sought people like her and to advertise your life was *not* in her livelihood's best interest.

"That sucks," Nyssa replied, clicking, and after the password was clicked in, her homepage loaded, and Seema produced an *Aww* sound when her picture loaded showing her and her father smiling cheek to cheek in the image.

"That is such a great picture of you two!" Seema beamed, leaning in for a closer look. "You have his eyes and nose… mouth too."

"Yeah, everyone tells me that," Nyssa smiled. "I miss seeing him all the time."

Seema thoughtlessly reached over and gave her thigh a gentle, compassionate squeeze and a smile in which Nyssa returned and mouthed a 'thank you'. After a moment, Nyssa clicked on her main

115

photo which brought up a new page of a multitude of photos and sub albums. On one such album entitled *Family,*

She maneuvered the mouse and clicked.

The album opened to several small thumbnail pictures, mainly of which were of her with her mom and Randy, some with her and her cousins in Chicago, but the last four were of either just her father or her with her father.

"Who are they?" Seema asked, pointing to a small grouping of smiling faces in thumbnail images beneath her picture.

"Oh, those are my *'Buddies',*" Nyssa said absently with air-quotes motioning with her two first fingers on each hand.

She maneuvered the mouse and clicked a small hyperlink stating **Show All** causing a window to pop up on top of the previous one and display a long list of thumbnails and names.

Seema's eyes grew wide, and a soft sound of surprise escaped her throat.

"Maynard Drelling?" Seema whispered, her hand slowly pulling back from the monitor, her eyes full of recognition. "Angelica Wooten?"

"Hmm?" Nyssa sounded and then produced a low giggle. "Yeah, those are old friends of my mom. She told me to add them for some reason and that they would love to see how I have come along over the years. I don't remember them, but she said they all knew me when I was just a baby, so you know… what do I care, right?"

"Right," Seema nodded, whispering her response, her eyes slowly looking over faces and names of recognition: Joseph Pratt, Kendall Holmes, Marcy Longrove… names she knew not out of fancy or premonition; No, these people were pure Consortia through and through.

"I think it's a sly way my mom's keeping me honest on here," Nyssa shrugged, clicking the mouse pointer on the **CLOSE** icon, and shutting down the list box. "I mean, she knows she can check on my page from her own login anytime she wants too, but I tolerate her little game; it's kinda obvious they are all secret-censor spies for her."

Seema simply nodded and then swallowed.

She was not allowed personal pages like this because she was still a fledgling. Until a certain age, young people of Magic had to be hidden to prevent them from being proselytized by the Anathema (or any of its sub-sects). Still, here she sat with proof and concept that a fledgling was allowed to broadcast herself despite the rules. Perhaps it was because Nyssa herself was not learning or practicing Magic, or probably since the veil of naiveté existed over Nyssa's entire family, the Consortia had to be like Alice through the *Looking Glass*; outside, looking in and monitoring from afar. Either way, Seema did not know; this question was a Lady Agatha-level inquiry to which she may—and more than likely not—get an answer.

While Seema's mind poured over the questions which had no answers, Nyssa went on about the pictures of her and her dad.

"Those are really good pictures," Seema nodded, clearing her voice, and scrubbing her mind clean of her previous thoughts. "Did you let him know that we were coming?"

"No, not directly," she shook her head. "Between playing maid for the last two days getting the house ready for your visit, and sleeping, I haven't thought much of anything else. However,"

Nyssa maneuvered the pointer to the top of the screen to Inbox, where the menu cascaded down. A quick point to 'Compose,' followed by a click, and a message box appeared. She entered her father's name, hit Enter, then mouse-clicked on the Subject line, typing in: *'Guess who's here?!?!?!'*, followed by rapid tabs to the main body section, where she began feverishly keying away.

"Wow, you type fast!" Seema beamed, her eyes rapidly darting from the blurred moving fingers as the letters formed words on the screen.

"Yeah, I picked my speed up chatting with my dad online over the years," Nyssa smiled, eyes focused on the screen. "Sometimes, depending on where he is, we can video-chat; other times, well, it's the 'beat up on the old keyboard' routine."

"That's really awesome!" Seema glowed, reading off the message as Nyssa typed. When the message was nearly complete, Nyssa paused just as she entered, *I will send you a pic,* and looked curiously at Seema.

"Can you and I take a group-selfie to send him?" Nyssa's expression was full of life, eyes wanting.

Seema held her eyes for some time and then glanced at the screen.

"I don't know if I should," she whispered back. "Lady Agatha…"

"She doesn't like you having your picture taken?" Nyssa's brow furrowed, full of confusion.

"No, we take pictures all the time," Seema licked her lips, begging to find the words which would explain away but not entirely explain the situation. Her mind raced over the last thing Lady Agatha said to her before exiting the car, a statement Seema had promised to keep, and that was: *'You are not to tell her what she is or what she can do, and by all your prowess do not do anything to draw attention to yourself.'*

"Well then?" Nyssa's eyes were now pleading. "My dad would love to see a pic of you and me and trust me; no one will see it but him."

Seema was slowly shaking her head and then released a long, heavy sigh, "Fine, just one."

"Great!" Nyssa clapped her hands together and then moved in close towards, the tips of her fingers running through the edge of her hair, neatening it. "Okay, look straight ahead."

"Where's your camera," Seema looked around perplexed.

"Right there," Nyssa pointed quickly to a small clip-on camera fastened on top center of the panel. "It's a webcam, but it can also take stills."

"*Ohhh-kayyy*," Seema drew out and shrugged. "Just one, right?"

"Right!" Nyssa added and the two moved in close. "Now smile!"

The pair produced stunningly adorable smiles; their eyes partially squinted as their cheeks did the work. With one out-of-camera-view hand, Nyssa clicked the mouse, and a soft '*ka-chink*' sound broke from the speakers. A moment later, a small window opened, and the system drew the captured still on the screen from top to bottom.

"Now that's a keeper!" Nyssa smiled, giggling.

"Yeah, that's a really good picture!" Seema agreed and joined Nyssa's giggle with her own.

Nyssa leaned in slightly on the table and with a rapid order of clicks, drags and more clicks, the image disappeared, and she finished up the message; explaining that she was sending a picture of them two.

"So," Seema sounded, a nervous tone lacing it. "Only your dad can see that picture, right?"

"Yeah, only him," Nyssa looked at her, a peculiar *'Are you serious?'* expression on her face. "Of course… it's really secure."

And with that, Nyssa clicked Send, and away the message went in the form of hundreds of thousands of little bits to its destination. Seema watched it blink away as Nyssa hummed with a soft song playing through her stereo and nodded confidently that the email had been sent.

After a moment Seema nodded too, convinced that no one dark would discover their presence and smiled along with Nyssa, joining the hum-a-long.

Relaxed and enjoying each other's sisterly time together all felt safe in the home in the burbs, but regardless to anything put in place to provide security, Nyssa failed to mention to Seema that her father always told her that nothing—especially in the world of the internet—is *ever* truly secure.

*

Twenty-five miles to the east and a few more to the north, the door to Seth's study parted, and Mica's round face appeared. He was sitting in his chair with one hand on the armrest while the other held the silver case intently.

"Teacher?" she spoke softly, almost whispering and not knowing if he was *Trancing* or not.

There was a simple rule in the house, and that was under no circumstance save the end of the world was at hand, was anyone to disturb him when he was *Trancing*.

When a senior person of Magic *Tranced,* they didn't simply meditate, allowing their mind to travel off to some ethereal plane of existence. No, their mind_*REALLY* went off somewhere, and to disturb one in that state could be devastating to the individual [like, we are talking a stroke-level event, to say the very least].

Seth had told her once as a bedtime story—one which would likely keep any child awake after hearing it—about a man named Halifax Peregrines, whose name Peregrines just happened to mean '*wanderer.*'

Halifax was *Trancing* once, as he did most often, and his pig-tailed pupil (which Seth had altered the story enough to state that it was a little girl much like Mica at the time... with pigtails) had stirred him quite rudely and irresponsibly.

"*And do you know what happened then?*" he had asked her as she held the edge of her covers tight just below her nostrils, her head shaking in unwanted anticipation. "*His mind was severed from his body, and he walked the Earth aimlessly not knowing how to get back to his 'self.'*"

"*I'm sure you are curious what he did after that, aren't you?*" he had asked, this time her head shook *No* as her body did the actual shaking. "*I will tell you regardless. He haunted that little girl with pigtails until she went mad!*"

After that, Mica never interrupted him ever again (nor slept well for some time following), and only up until the previous year to date, did she dare peek into his study after a certain hour. Now, she rarely thought of it anymore, but that night after the story was over, she was so terrified that Seth's mad spirit was going to haunt her that she laid awake shaking the entire night.

The poor girl even wet herself for fear of leaving the confining safety of the bed covers.

"Yes, Mica?" his voice echoed back, monotonously.

"I've got her," she said quietly, inching into the room only to be stopped by Seth's rising hand in the distance.

She could barely make him out in the shadows, but the blue aura that danced the edges of his hand clearly said, *Hold*. She shuffled her feet and then stood still, only to rub her ankle with a socked foot where a bandage sat, the center an off-red where blood was scabbing from a little bite wound. It had been itching something fierce for the last hour or so.

"Explain," called his voice, emotionless.

"I, um, hacked her father's profile online… it was easier than I thought; his password was predictable."

"And what of it?" he asked, hand lowering.

"Well, I figured if the Consortia did contact her, this Nyssa would probably contact her father."

"Smart thinking, Mica," he said. "And did she send him news?"

"The girl sent a picture to him… a picture of herself with the mage-brat, Seema," she replied, her eyes sparkling violet. "They are there with her now."

Seth stood so quickly that his motion was a blur and his eyes on the case, "Are you sure?"

"Yes, Teacher," she nodded in the dim light. "There was a message with the picture… they are staying the weekend."

Odd, he thought, glancing at the low-lit fire. *I didn't feel you come to town, Agatha.*

"Should I inform the others?" she asked.

"No, not yet," he said, glancing back at the case and then to her silhouette in the doorway. "Tell Pia to get out there, better yet, no; I will go. You two seem to have a problem completing things, especially when it comes to little dogs."

Seema's head dropped to her feet and nervously she rubbed her bound wound with a toe.

"Very well, Teacher," she whispered and turned to the door, head hung low. In the corner of her eyes, she felt tears rising and threatening to fall. She was trying so hard to win his overwhelming acceptance and affection from him that it was tearing her apart on a daily level.

"Mica," he whispered after her, his tone soft.

"Yes, teacher?" she paused, glancing back.

"You did very well tonight," he replied and after a moment he added: "The other day was not your fault… Pia should have known better. You are to be commended before the Order."

"Thank you," she smiled feeling warmth grown in her chest.

"Now leave me as I prepare," he finished and she nodded, closing the door behind her.

She stood looking at the large, carved oaken door for a moment, a gentle smile on her lips and with softened eyes a single tear of happiness fell where ones of sorrow normally trailed.

Alarmed by their presence, she touched the surface lightly with her fingers and smiled.

"Thank you, Father," she whispered, and with a little more pep in her step than usual, she skipped down the hall, beaming.

CHAPTER EIGHT

Devil's Dance in the Moonlight

-1-

The house was nearly silent as Agatha moved through it, her steps never making the slightest sound, even on the two stairs that creaked near the top landing. She moved like a thief in the night but did not intend to steal anything except for a glimpse of the moon. There had been so many things coming to light recently that the archmage felt drained without it, and halfway down the stairs, Agatha convinced herself that she would do much more than steal a quick peek.

Instead, she would bathe in its splendor.

As she stood before the sliding doors to the backyard, she paused with her delicate fingers on the handle as a muffled sound came from upstairs. Randy and Christine were having back-and-forth slumber-mumbles which drew a thin smile to her lips.

"Deeply sleep," she whispered, motioning her hand towards the stairs and the second floor fell silent.

With a soft click from the latch—the locking mechanism now free—she slowly slid the door open and stepped out into the cool night, sending out a mental *'thank you'* to Nyssa for if the storm had never come, this night would have been horribly balmy.

The moon was alone and indeed full as it hung in the western sky; the distant scattering of clouds were hours from intruding on its glow, and the mere sight of it drew an uncontrollable smile, and she giggled softly despite herself. She closed her eyes to it, stretching her neck so that her face could get as close to the light as possible, much like on a bright sunny day. Her eyes moved over the darkened windows in the houses neighboring her friends,' and with soft waving motions, she passed from one home to the next, summoning them all to *'deeply sleep'* as well.

She wanted and needed privacy so to enjoy her time with her moon.

Agatha slowly strolled across the deck, descended the three steps, and out onto the dew-laced grass in her bare feet, her hands moving with grace as she stripped off her nightgown, dropping it to the side.

Once she reached the center of the small yard, she raised her palms to the moon, humming softly through smiling teeth, her nude body glistening in the light. Her soft pale skin began to dance and shimmer in the light, assuming a soft glow that matched the moon, and she giggled soundly as she wrapped her arms around herself.

"Oh, hello, my moon," she spoke with a lilt, but the moon did not answer her; only the night bugs whispered their music in the bushes, shrubs, and the garden. She gently rubbed her shoulders and arms in the moonlight as if she was applying a soft lotion. "And don't you look quite spectacular tonight?"

As she bathed in the moonglow, her mind played over the events leading to this night, a night that whispered odd things about confrontations, betrayals, and Magic. The Consortia knew for a long time about Nyssa, just as she herself knew about her arrival long before she was born.

From the moment Agatha first walked into the dorm room occupied by Nyssa's mother, Christine, at the University of Illinois in Urbana, she knew. She had felt it much akin to someone dropping something heavy on your shoulders. The *elan vital* was *not* Christine herself that she was sensing—this peppy little freshman standing before her as she continuously rambled while unpacking her luggage—no; Agatha felt it come from *within* her, channeling from someplace and sometime yet known; a feeling that she knew could only come from a child yet born.

Regardless of the Consortia's axiom regarding happening upon someone of naïve Magic—to mind them like a hawk and to protect them without the intimacy of a bonded relationship—, the two of them still did become best of friends, which carried on through their college years. The fond affection towards one another prospered even when Christine had gotten married, Agatha being the Maid of Honor, and then later to Nyssa's birth.

On that day, Agatha's long-standing sensation that there was something within her friend that bested even the very word *Special* had proven to be true.

She leaned into the light, her fingers rubbing in the moonbeams into her knees and calves as she thought about that special day in October when Nyssa was born. Her brothers and sisters in the Consortia were convinced that there had been nothing at all particular about the moon's alignment to the sun and that Mars wasn't in any special relationship with Venus even to expect anything extraordinary on that day.

On that late October evening when even the night bugs had chosen slumber rather than perform their chirping calls, Nyssa did come about, and oh, how the brethren were so wrong!

Nothing special? Well, let us just say that the world has never been quite the same.

"Do we instruct her?" a younger Agatha had asked her then mentor as she looked into a small makeup mirror in the hospital restroom.

"No," returned the voice, wise and patient, but there was some level of anxiousness in the tone. Luther was a prodigy in his own right, a staunch advocate for playing by the rules, but then now, with the birth of Nyssa, the rules and the book they came in were worth nothing more than toilet paper wrappers. *"For her to be here,* now, *is very wrong."*

"It being wrong does not *undo her being here,"* Agatha had spoken respectfully hoping to draw forth reason, but she could feel her pressure gauges climbing. *"This is a fact which we cannot ignore."*

"We will watch her carefully and guide her away from the World of Magic until she is too old to have any power over it." Luther nodded in confidence towards his insistent course of action. *"For anyone to even attempt to instruct her would be the primer to the undoing of everything. Something is terribly wrong in the World of Magic... she should not be."*

"And yet she is here," she had replied, dabbing the corner of her mouth to straighten her lipstick as a ruse just in case someone entered the washroom and noticed her.

"Unfortunately, you are correct," Luther's voice responded followed by a long silence.

"*Unfortunately?*" Agatha had squawked, almost eating the tube of lipstick; she had been a younger, more modern person of Magic at the time after all. *"Are you nuts? She is born to make even Houdini look like a child's coin trick!"*

"*Precisely,*" Luther had sighed, his patience thin. *"More so a reason that she should never breathe Magic, for everyone's sake; Us and Them."*

"*And what if Magic flows from her regardless,*" Agatha shook, daring to smash the small compact (which in turn could have had so many adverse effects, including her ability to see or talk ever again [destroying a *Reflector* during mid-conversation has never had a happy outcome]). *"Magic* cannot *be bound by our pure desire alone!"*

"*Then pray, Agatha, that the stars are aligned in our favor if such a day comes!*"

And that was that.

When the *Reflector* faded, Agatha spent several minutes staring into the toilet water, making it spin backward at an alarming rate to calm herself. She knew her task regardless of how ridiculous it sounded. At the same time, her Consortia brethren focused on their endeavors to return the Earth to its normal course instead of plummeting into the Sun. They had predicted '*nothing special,*', but at least they had prepared for the worst (after much persistence from Agatha to do so) and got *precisely* what they had not bargained for: the worst.

Luckily for everyone, however, on the day of Nyssa's birth, the whole of the Consortia was standing ready, for if they had not been, well, let us just say that Global Warming as we know it now would have been the last concern on everyone's minds.

Exhaling heavily as she stood, stretching tall with her hands extending to the moon again, she knew her premonitions about Nyssa were all true, which meant time was quickly running out. The girl would need to be taught.

"And that my glorious moon," she smiled at the moon, wiggling her fingers and thumbs at the orb playfully. "Is that."

With her 'bathing' complete, Agatha smiled and gave a graceful curtsy towards the bluish orb, and as she walked back across the small lawn, she froze mid-step. Something was wrong in the night's air; the noise of it suddenly became almost deafening. All the night bugs had fallen silent at once. Dew glittered on her tingling skin as hairs climbed upright, sensing.

"Your magnificent body has not aged a day, Lady Agatha," the voice came from the shadows, and as calmly and with calculated motions of being nonchalant in the effort, Agatha turned towards the sound, smiled, and continued to gather her nightgown.

"Spying on a bathing woman from the shadows, Seth?" she produced a soft chuckle, retrieving her nightgown from the grass and then calmly began to don it. "If you had wanted to see me naked, I am sure you could have sought it through Magic instead of creeping around the shadows like a thief."

Blue glints sparkled in the shadows as Seth came into the moonlight.

"I do so in order to be a thief, so to steal treasured glances of thee, Lady Agatha."

"You tease well with clever words, Seth," she smiled, but behind the teeth, she wanted to curse herself for as she fastened the top button to the nightgown, she was alerted to the fact that her brooch was sitting safely in its case in the bedroom inside.

It was not the source of her Magic—that was something tucked safely away in her *elan vital*—but it was her instrument, her conduit, her talisman, that one thing that allowed her to channel it in a pure, pristine form. If Magic was needed now—and she was sure it would be—she could do it at only a fraction of her usual strength, and many conjurations would be rather sloppy.

She had no doubt that Seth had *not* forgotten his trusty cigarette case.

"You have beauty in your presence almost every day," she continued seemingly without care of his presence. "Are you telling me that you still shun her love and do not steal peeks at her?

"Speaking of which, is Pia lurking around in the shadows back there as well?"

Seth's aura flared and then waned at the mention of Pia's name as he stepped close.

"No. She is away tending to things."

"A solitary personal visit, then?" Agatha smiled hands at her sides. "That is not like you, Seth."

"Where's the girl?" he said flatly, his eyes trailing up the side of the house to a darkened window above.

"She is safe; that's all you need to know," she answered just as flatly as received. "So why don't you go help Pia tend her wounds? I heard Marley had had a nice little snack of her rear end yesterday."

"Agatha," Seth blinked, staring at her; a wicked smile grew on his lips. "Step aside, and I promise I will leave you and your little *filius-populi*-chance-child, Seema, breathing."

"After all those nice compliments, you present me threats?" Agatha shook her head, adding several *'tisk'* sounds to accentuate her sarcastic sadness.

Her right palm flared open, fingers outstretched, and a deep amber glow danced on the skin.

"You know very well that the girl has been marked and blessed since birth, just as this house and every place the child goes! You have no power over her here!"

"I know of the Consortia's enchantments, crone," Seth growled, his hands becoming blue fists. "Truly a waste of effort."

"Insults?" Agatha was breathing heavily now, the glow at the tips of her fingers sharpening to a fine point. "Now I know you didn't come just to look at my bare bum."

Agatha's hand jerked up to her hip, and light exploded outward, the amber fire shooting in a perfect point from her fingers, much like a hurried shot from a quick draw dueler in the old west. The Magic raced home, filling the yard with light, only to reach Seth, who opened his hand, deflecting it and sending it aloft over the house. Moments later, a few miles away, a hapless semi-driver dozing in his sleeper cab on the side of I-290 was thrown from his little bed as the trailer he was hauling exploded.

For every action, there is always an equal and—usually unhappy—opposite reaction.

Seth looked down at his blue palm and smiled, "I suppose that I am lucky that you weren't really trying, huh? No mystical amulet tonight?"

"*Slappen!*" came a German-accented voice from the darkness and a sharp clap rang in the air as well as between Seth's ears, spinning him around sharply. He found himself one moment standing and the next on all fours, his right cheek blazing as if he had been slapped across the face with a barber's strop.

A small hand dangling a satin band and an ivory brooch appeared before Agatha's eyes as Seema stepped close, her large almond eyes resembling tiny thin strips as she beamed towards Seth.

"*Filius populi-chance child?'* Did he just call me a bastard?"

"I do think so, Seema," Agatha replied quietly, the anger she should be feeling towards the girl for interfering would have to wait (depending on the outcome of the night, of course).

"You forgot this, my Lady," Seema said flatly, and Agatha took it and then clasped it behind her neck quickly.

Seth stood, hand coming from his jaw, eyes finding Seema.

"I have been slapped before, child, but that was a good one."

"Be glad all I could see was your face," Seema spat back, her hands at the ready, the small brooch in her hair pulsating. "I wanted a place a lot further south than your jaw!"

Where is Nyssa?' Agatha's mind quickly yelped in Seema's mind.

'Sleeping,' Seema's voice echoed the answer.

"Not for long," Seth cut through heavy laughter, his teeth streaked with blood as the wound inside his cheek leaked. "Soon she will be wide, *wide* awake; trust me, bastardling."

"Forget this!" Seema barked, her right hand open and pointing back towards the rose garden, her left shooting forth towards Seth, and from the tips spiraled a glowing tangle of wicked red thorns, the air crackling like fire as they moved. Usually, Seema would have *sought* something other than a plant to do her bidding, but they were dead, having drowned in the storm after all.

Seth ducked and dodged as he danced to his left, his hand coming up as blue flares shot from his hand towards Seema, bearing home quickly towards her chest, and luckily for her, Agatha's hand interceded, barely. The Magic Seema was aiming broke away into shimmering pieces when the blow came, hot and heavy as all the air escaped her chest in one audible cough. Agatha spun on her heels as the impact knocked her hand away, the remainder of the Magic lifting Seema upwards and back, slamming her against the side of the house.

In a brilliance of a smidgen of a second, Agatha's mind recollected the sight of a significant split in the street just two blocks from them and channeled: slamming her hands against the ground and rapidly the earth jaggedly split, throwing up sod, dirt, and stones. At that exact moment, just two blocks away, the asphalt closed, saving the repair crews one thing on their mighty list to do. It met Seth's shoes, and with a loud *pop* like a bursting balloon, and by the grace of a jiffy of time, he leaped up and backward, his hand slashing the air towards Agatha, flinging her. Winded, Seth glanced at the tips of his thousand-dollar shoes and wiggled the toes, which showed through the singed and split leather, ensuring they were all there.

"That! Really! Hurt!" Seema was growling as she pulled herself up, her eyes ablaze with a sparkling mixture of reds and whites, the clasp in her hair a pulsing beacon. The ground began to tremble as her eyes narrowed; one hand slowly rose towards him as the other

sat flatly pressed against the house wall. Agatha had time to look up as she pulled herself from the ground, and she couldn't prevent what she saw brewing in the girl's mind.

Put simply: it was about to go down.

"Seema don't!" Agatha tried.

"Krossen!" Seema surely did—her voice deep and barbaric—having spoken the Low German word for *crush*, the side of the house tore away and whipped around her, flying forth in a mass of heavy chunks and splinters.

For a brilliant moment, Seth's eyes became saucers, and Agatha would later smile at the fact that she could have sworn she heard him utter the word *'Shit!'* as he blued just before the wreckage slammed home on top of him. The noise had been chaotic, the debris blinding like the soup of a tornado, and as the silence slowly fell, the pandemonium was quickly replaced by Seema's infuriated panting; one hand still extended, the other no longer touching anything at all.

Agatha was quite relieved that she had enchanted the neighborhood to deeply sleep.

"Seema," Agatha spoke softly as she approached, her hand gently taking the girl's extended and shaking arm, her heart melting at the sight of her young pupil, face full of rage as terrified angry tears streamed her cheeks. "All quiet now."

She was still panting, her eyes aflame as she looked towards Agatha, then towards the hole in the side of the house she had made, and then reality flooded in. Terrified, sobbing quickly broke from her throat as she lunged into the welcoming embrace of her teacher. Although she had been practicing Magic for as long as she could remember in preparation for days such as this, now that it had, the sensation was overwhelming.

"Now, I am mad," Seth's voice came from the yard as he pulled himself from the wreckage, the air filling with deep pulsating blue. He was brushing off splinters, insulation, and shards of glass from his clothing; his suit was a tattered mess. The back of his hand came away bloody as he wiped his brow. "Little witch, I will have to kill you now."

Seema's jaw dropped at the sight of him. Her quick brain assured her that: *Yes*, indeed, she had slammed at least two tons of house atop of him, and *No*, instead of making him gut-squirting squish, she had drawn out his most profound rage.

Agatha turned and instantly moved into a defensive prize-fighter stance, putting herself between the direct line of sight of Seth and Seema. Slowly Seth's hand drew from his tattered suit jacket his case, the highly polished and etched surface sending off his blue light across the yard in broken pieces like the reflections from a disco ball. His body began to bulge and swell grotesquely in places, his head slowly swelling and becoming inhuman, and his fingers stretched, tendons popping.

Seth was pissed indeed, no doubt about that.

Agatha took in a deep breath, her mind rapidly flipping through a catalogue of items in her mind that she had seen recently, accepting one then disregarding it: no, not that one; that will not do; too simple that one, and still finding nothing adequate. She could feel the case glow and vibrate; her internal organs began to tremor with it, and whatever incantation Seth was mumbling about, she was sure it would be the curtain call.

"Are you, my teacher?" Nyssa's voice came from behind them, far away and distant like a dreamy child entering her parent's room in the middle of the night with an inquiry born from a dream.

Agatha and Seema spun around to find her standing in the gaping hole in the house, one hand lazily rubbing at an eye and then slowly looking about herself, her expression wide and blank.

"Nyssa!" Seema spat out and moved towards her, and while Agatha was a Lady and did not use foul language, much like what she swore she had heard Seth utter early on, her mouth motioned out the single word in an inaudible whisper: *'Shit!'*

Seth stopped in mid-utterance, his hands slowly dropping and his body reducing, forming back into his human self.

"I see Pia and Mica didn't quite fail after all," Seth smiled, sliding the case back into his breast pocket and then slowly advanced towards Nyssa.

Agatha quickly flared a hand towards him, and light flashed, her mind stopping on a catalogue page of hammers. Seth motioned in front of his face as if he was shooing away a gnat, deflecting the Magic, which found its home against the side of a large elm tree, blasting away several inches of the trunk in a shower of Magic and splintered wood.

"Enough of that, Agatha, the night is mine."

The air hung in a quasi-stillness, and for what it seemed, even all the clamor of their engagement seemed to fade without so much of an echo.

"Nyssa, Nyssa, Nyssa," he smiled, hands coming up as he moved towards her, his face a gentle glow. "I am so glad to have finally met you."

"Is he, my teacher?" Nyssa whispered to Seema who was moving her away. Seema shook her head frantically as she attempted to keep Nyssa moving, while keeping a glowing hand pointed towards Seth. "I mean... he *looks* like my teacher."

"Lady Agatha is your teacher, Nyssa!" Seema whispered sharply towards her, giving her a light shove to move her past the edge of the hole in the wall. "He is evil!"

"The girl does not know what she says, child," Seth beamed, sidestepping Agatha, his welcoming arms before him. "Come to me, Nyssa and we will go home to your sister."

"Do I have a sister?" Nyssa blinked at Seema, eyes curious.

"*Yes!* I'm your sister!" Seema shot back.

Agatha's hand swung down, and the chain link fence that had once been on the side of the yard suddenly appeared before Seth, who paused in his advance, his eyes glancing about it, and then shook his head.

"I have grown tired of this, Agi," he said flatly and motioned his hand in a wiping motion, the fence crumpling into a jagged metal mass which flew towards her; an object which she was lucky to avoid the direct impact of. It did wing her, however, catching her by her shoulder and throwing her into the shadows.

"*Do not touch her!*" Seema screamed, her mind locking onto an image of quite a giant bomb strapped to the underwing of a fighter plane. It had been a dated image from sometime during the Middle East conflict, so where and when the ordinance was at that moment (or one like it), she did not know, nor did she care.

She was young and very, *very* angry.

Seth paused, sensing her mind.

"Move girl," he spoke flat albeit concerned at what he sensed in the girl's mind.

"Or what?" Seema spat back, a hand pressing against Nyssa's chest to keep her back as she attempted to move towards him, drawn.

"You know *what*, brat!" he roared back, his hands coming up in a blue blur, Seema's fingers expanding as the image of the bomb became real.

"*Seth!*" came a thunderous voice, snapping his attention to his left in time to see a purple fist blaze towards him, catching his jaw and knocking him back in a blaze of sparkles of brilliant light.

Seth's hand blindly flashed Magic, which crackled in the air, missing its target and detonating the corner of the garage. He corrected himself, eyes scanning for prey only to be shoved in the lower back, propelling him forward as a yellow orb collided with him and exploded.

"We will have none of that!" came another voice, and as Seth spun towards it, his hands ready, the whole of the world began to shake.

"*Enough!*" Agatha commanded as she strode from the shadows, her shoulder bleeding from under the torn pieces of her nightgown from where the fence had struck her. She was calm, but her eyes glowed with rage.

Marco and Amora stood on both sides of him while Seema pressed against Nyssa, attempting to move her back into the house. Seth's eyes darted angrily between Agatha, Marco, and Amora, his mind calculating his odds while his gut told him they didn't look good at all.

"Good to see you two, Marco," Agatha said as she advanced, stopping in between the couple, and closing the circle to having Seth surrounded.

"Likewise, Lady A," he smiled and giggled to himself knowing that she loathed him calling her that.

"We would have been here sooner," Amora said quietly, glancing at her husband with a thin devious smile. "But Marco was insistent about breakfast in Paris today... Umm, I mean tonight, or... what time is it now?"

"*Shut up!*" Seth barked, spit flying from his lips.

"You were not wise to come here tonight, Seth," Agatha said flatly; glowing. "Portal on home now while you can; the whole of the Consortia is undoubtedly on their way now."

"*Never!*" Seth spat. "She is coming with me!"

"They have bewitched her, My Lady," Seema said, struggling to keep Nyssa in place.

"Come to me child!" Seth screamed to Nyssa and then froze as the humming of several raised hands rose in the air.

Two flashes in the shadows blinked, and from the depths, the form of Maynard Drilling walked, a finger pushing his glasses up higher on his nose, a small lapel pin pulsating a soft yellow. To his right, Angelica Wooten appeared with a yardstick in her hand that rapidly vibrated orange. Seema knew the two well and was happy to see them both, even though Angelica—who was a grammar schoolteacher known amongst many a student about that tool's menacing existence—had used that very same yardstick on her knuckles years ago when Seema would daydream during her tutoring sessions.

Seth's eyes met those of the newcomers who quickly took up around him.

Agatha was not spitting tongues when she said the whole of the Consortia was on its way.

"Fine, Witch!" Seth spits, moving to the side, his hands ready and his eyes keen. "Keep the little wench but hear this! Mica's Magic still works inside her, so she will never be one of you!"

"You have lost, Seth," Amora snapped, her dangling earrings blinking opalescent colors. *"Now piss off!"*

Seth stood upright, his eyes blazing rage, his finger extending towards Nyssa, "Mark this day, all of you! The Anathema will not allow her to be taught by you!"

With that, Seth clapped his hands around the case, and in a blue blink, he was gone. Soon the yard was filling with Consortians as more and more arrived, turning the small space into a mob scene. Besides those who had already gated, they were joined by the likes of the brazen Li Qiang Ding of northern China pulling at his silver beard, Adimu Mwangi of Kenya with her fierce eyes of golden amber, and Amka Eetuk of the Innuits (whose name sardonically means "one with a friendly spirit" however any who had ever crossed her knew quite the opposite of such graces).

There were scores of them from all edges of the world, and more were surely still gating to the gathering. This was no convention, however; Seth was lucky, for it was about to be a butt-kicking event of epic proportions if he had remained.

"Marco, send them all back!" Amora whispered sharply as she moved towards Agatha, her attention drawn to the shoulder wound. Agatha was waving her down and expressing that she was fine as

Seema was struggling to support Nyssa, who, in her drowsy sleepwalking, was deciding it was time to go back to bed.

Marco moved deeper into the yard with raised hands and began to express words to disperse the crowd, many of which were grumbling about, missing all the excitement as they reluctantly blinked out of sight.

"Are you alright, Agatha?" Angelica spoke quickly, gently taking Agatha's arm and exploring the wound.

"I am fine... I'm fine," she responded, calming herself.

"I see that Seema has gotten angry again," Maynard mused, adjusting his glasses as he inspected the gaping hole in the wall which climbed up to the substructure of the second floor. "That is going to cost a pretty penny, plus two."

"I-I didn't mean to! I—" Seema stammered, helping Nyssa into a deck chair where Nyssa slouched to one side and began to softly snore.

"Well, it looks like it did the job for at least a little bit," Maynard added in attempts to console Seema's guilt.

"Lady Agatha!" Seema cried, shaking Nyssa's shoulders. "What is wrong with her and what did he mean *'Mica's Magic still works inside her'*?"

Agatha moved quickly and placed her palm on Nyssa's forehead, closing her eyes and concentrating. She was sensing deep within the turmoil rolling inside the girl's mind, filled with both glorious light and stygian depths of nothingness.

"There is some, not a lot, but enough," the archmage whispered, her head slowly shaking with a disconcerted expression.

"Marley interrupted the planting," Amora whispered, moving in close as well. "Can you purge it?"

"Agatha! Would you sit still so that I can heal your shoulder?" Angelica demanded, fidgeting with Agatha's wound.

"Leave it," Agatha shrugged her off, her mind focusing on Nyssa's. "It will prove to be beneficial soon enough."

"A gaping hole in your shoulder proving to be beneficial?" Angelica squawked, confoundedly bemused. "How in the he—"

"Umm, Angelica?" it was Marco who was kneeling next to a man named Rusty Menden who was one of the Consortia's oddest characters. He *was* a man of Magic, there was no doubt, but what exact *kind* of Magic no one was quite certain. Things happened around him, usually odd and unfortunate things. Still, as Agatha and others are quick to point out, it keeps the World of Magic perfectly balanced and makes for humorous stories after-the-fact (and after the healing).

"What?" Angelica snapped.

"It appears our good Rusty here has gated in, well…"he trailed off, moving to the side a bit to show Rusty bent in an odd fashion with a hammock passing through his midsection.

"Oh, the stars!" Angelica's hands went up and she quickly moved towards him. "I told you before that you need to know where you are going to portal!"

"I saw pictures of this yard two months ago on the internet," Rusty protested, daring not to move. "On that satellite imaging site, the one you always talk about."

"You gated using two-month-old pictures?" Angelica was near livid, her hands rummaging in her purse. "I should take my stick to you! I have told you countless times to use Google Earth!"

"Hush, everyone!" Agatha whispered sternly to everyone, focusing and the yard went quiet.

There was a lot of darkness and confusion in Nyssa's mind forming a torrid storm which was battling against her soul. Mica's charm was strong but incomplete, thanks to little Marley, and if he had not intervened, the hexing would have been permanent. Agatha probed her mind, searching every nook and cranny to locate all the anchors of the charm's web, softly sounding *'Hmm'*(s) and *'I see'*(s) as her hands moved about Nyssa's head and neck.

Agatha straightened, her eyes finding Seema's wide eyes hungrily begging for an answer.

"Well?" Seema begged, nearly dancing as if she had to pee.

"Amora... remind me to send over several large soup bones to Marley as a gift," Agatha smiled, her eyes trailing down towards Nyssa's sleeping face.

"So, does that mean she's okay?" Seema begged once again.

"Yes," Agatha said softly, petting Nyssa's hair. "I have removed much of what was planted; however, I fear she will have bad dreams for a while."

"Stop moving!" Angelica's voice rose and the sound of a yardstick striking a thigh rose sharply in the air with a brief cry of pain.

"Lady Agatha?" Amora urged, her hand motioning to the collective people of Magic loitering the yard as more flashes blinked as more People of Magic appeared.

"*Oh my!*" Agatha spat out and stood sharply with widening, nervous eyes. "Too many are coming! *Way too many!*"

Marco dashed into the yard with waving hands, his mouth repeatedly calling out towards the new arrivals: '*Too many! Too many!*' and with surprised cautious expressions of guilt, the portals blinked closed again.

"Thank you all! You were all spectacular tonight!" Agatha raised her hands to those present as she hurriedly attempted to do a head count and felt her throat tighten when the number was twelve, five over the allowable number. "Please, quickly return to your homes, and I will update you all come late morning."

One by one, they nodded and said their goodbyes. With a sharp wink of different colored light, they blinked off to unknown destinations, the last of which was Angelica and Rusty, who, having unhooked the hammock, guided him towards the shadows he waddled uncomfortably.

"Will he be alright, Angelica?" Agatha called after them.

"Yes, yes, he will be fine," Angelica waved back, and with a swish of her stick, a brightly lit doorway opened before them out of nothingness, showing a rustic kitchen beyond. Seema double-blinked at the sight of it, for she had never seen that Magic before. The two stepped in, and the doorway closed behind them with a faint *swooshing* sound.

"That was close," Agatha sighed as she rested her palm to her abdomen in attempts to control her rapid breathing. It *was* close, there were too many People of Magic in one place in Time, and with the number who were still answering the call, something dire was going to happen making a broken house seem like a discarded wrapper on the ground.

"Really close," Marco nodded feeling nervous and ashamed. "I didn't think when I sent out the distress."

"Maybe the girl's presence countered the Rule?" Amora added from the sidelines as she scanned the yard, her mind replaying a snapshot of a dozen mages filling the space and not once did her mind see the danger.

"I don't know," Agatha shook her head as her eyes held the sleepy form of Nyssa. "Just don't know."

"Well, then," Marco joined them, wiping his hands together. "That sums up the evening then?"

"Not quite," Amora addressed, pointing up towards the gaping hole in the house and Seema immediately dropped her head towards her feet.

"Settle, Seema," Agatha said with a faint smile. "As I have told you before: all things happen for a reason, and this time, it will prove to be more beneficial than ever planned. Marco, Amora, we— Seema, Nyssa, and I—will be leaving in the morning."

"So, you will be teaching her then?" he asked with a smidgen of anticipation lacing his tone.

"I have no other choice," Agatha sighed. "In another year, I wouldn't even worry; most of her mana would have dissipated by then, but now: having already conjured unconscious Magic and the Anathema hungry for her power, what else am I to do?"

"Right then," Amora nodded. "Shall we get her back inside then?"

"No, Seema and I will manage," Agatha shook her head. "You two should go now and stay on your guard; Seth rarely leaves with a bloody nose, let alone with his tail tucked. He will be hunting for revenge."

Amora nodded, producing a courteous curtsey and Marco flinging a quick open finger salute towards her, then took up his wife's hand and kissed it.

"Lunch in Cairo?" Amora asked.

Hand in hand, they looked at each other and shrugged, sharing a common thought.

"Why not," Marco responded and in an opalescent blink they were gone, leaving the three of them in the yard.

Agatha stood staring at the wounded tree, her fingers rolling amongst the palm, thinking.

"Should we get her inside, My Lady," Seema asked softly. "Dawn will be here soon, and the moon is almost gone."

"You take her in," Agatha replied. "Don't worry, she will walk, all you have to do is guide her."

Seema nodded and coaxed Nyssa into a standing position, pulling her up with both hands while walking backward to guide her, adding calming words as if speaking to a slumbering child like: *Just a little step here… THERE YA GO!… Almost there,'* and so on.

"Seema?" Agatha spoke after her as she coaxed Nyssa to step over the threshold of the now 'newly redesigned' open-air kitchen.

Seema paused wide-eyed.

"When you get her into her room, I want you to keep her and yourself clear of any windows… better yet; I want both of you under her bed."

The almond shape of Seema's eyes transformed into that of wide circles, and her mouth dropped open without a sound. She hadn't the foggiest idea what Agatha was about to do; Lady Agatha had always been one to say what she meant and meant what she said, but whatever she was about to do undoubtedly would be grand.

Seema began pulling Nyssa along faster, quickly moving her out of sight.

Agatha looked towards her moon, which was slowly being consumed by clouds in the far western edge of the sky, creating a soft, wide blue corona; its glow coming through in small pulses through the branches. With a heavy sigh, she moved towards the large elm, which now had a gaping wound in its trunk several inches deep, and its life sap was flowing from it much like blood. She rested a palm against the bark just above the wound and could feel its pain.

"I am so sorry for what has happened," she whispered to the injured elm, eyes closing and her stomach filling with guilt. "More so for what I am about to do, but painfully it is for the best for every living thing. I will take one of your seeds and nurture your memory."

She stood for a moment with silent tears running her cheeks and regarded the moon once more, her mind focusing on a faraway storm full of wind, rain, and most importantly, lightning.

"Forgive me."

A blinding flare exploded from her hand, producing a sharp thunderclap that raced through, splitting the trunk in a jagged maze of singed wood. With a ground-shaking tremor, the tree broke forth, crashing into the house above the gaping hole Seema had produced, crushing in the roof, and pushing into Nyssa's bedroom. The sides of the house crumpled and sagged, bulging in places under the stressful weight which sent many of the boards flying into the yard.

Windows flexed and burst outward in a shower of glass tinkled to the deck, followed by several of Nyssa's lava lamps, stuffed animals, a computer, half of the desk and chair, and dozens of books closest to that wall.

Agatha stood amongst floating wood fiber and smoke, weeping soundlessly as her shoulders rose and fell with heavy panting until all went quiet.

After a moment, Seema's muffled voice coughed down to her, "Umm—*We're okay!*"

Nodding, Agatha moved towards the house, pausing to stoop down to gather up a branch that bore a healthy clutch of samaras near the leaves. Her hand waved over the stem, and she selected one and held it tightly in her palm. She will keep her promise and plant it so the tree will live in another place and time.

As she entered the home, slowly ascending the stairs towards her guest room which bore part of the elm's girth, she contemplated the stars' order of things and how things seemed to happen for a reason. She had sensed the seed in Nyssa's mind and the looping words *'I do not want to go with them'* ordering her destiny, but now—as the order of the stars, Magic has proven once again—things have happened, and now with no house, she will have no other choice *but* to go.

It was predestined, maybe… or perhaps it was simply: Magic.

CHAPTER NINE

Pandemonium

-1-

Nyssa flung herself from under her platform bed in what can only be described as absolute, fish-flopping terror as her head and arms banged, smacked, and rebounded off the wooden slats. As her throat began to sear with an ongoing scream, her mind never questioned *Why* she was under her bed in the first place, let alone regarded the swelling lump above her brow line. No, it only considered the impossible possibilities as she gawked eye-to-eye with the jagged trunk of the elm tree that once sat in the backyard and now was less than a foot from her face inside her room. There was to be no more looking out her window with a fond distance, wondering where the squirrels were going or how the bright red cardinal longed for its mate; oh no! She could sit back comfortably against her headboard and ask them up close and personal in a quasi-surreal kind of way.

Seema had been waiting for the moment when Agatha would snap her fingers and release the neighborhood from their deep slumber, the occasional *'Almost there'* acknowledgment coming from her in the other room extending her anxiousness. She had positioned herself on the floor in a sleeping bag just at the edge of Nyssa's bed, precariously beneath a menacing one-ton branch that had found part of the house's superstructure to support itself. When Agatha assured her that the moment was close, she lay there nervously; her ears anticipating the sound of the crackling wood in the tree's final motions toward the earth.

As Nyssa began to scream, there had been no time to consider if Agatha had said anything; the high-pitched shrill of her voice could very well possibly raise the dead. Seema could feel the tone reverberate through her lungs and rebound off her chest cavity, and time would pass as the two girls stared into each other's faces to realize that she was screaming too.

The moment Agatha placed things in motion, she sought the world for a similar thunderous crashing chorus to mimic how it had sounded when the tree struck the house. Instead of finding just one barbaric noise, she summoned a complete montage of them which exploded together in a ballad entitled *Pandemonium*. The archmage made sure that the neighborhood shook violently so to assure that there was no mistake that something terrible had occurred.

"WHAT THE HELL?!" seemed to be the words of choice which not only broke from Nyssa's throat after a quick break from the screaming as well as from her mother and Randy who raced down the hallway, pushing the bedroom door open.

The room was a complete warzone with tattered books thrown about the floor; her desk and computer a pulverized collage of plastic, metal, and gadgetry; her collection of various colored and sized lava lamps was shattered on the other side of the room, sending their liquid contents splattering the split floorboards and walls; tree branches and leaves were strewn everywhere resembling an indoor garden which had run amuck and took over.

"I don't know!" Seema screamed back, her eyes wide in horror, which held more truth than made-up expressions; a terrified culmination of the showdown just moments before with Seth and the barbaric, neighborhood-awakening production Agatha had conjured attempted to be lies in her eyes, but they were quite wide and aware with panicked truth.

"Is everyone ok?" Randy demanded, moving in on Nyssa and Seema, who held each other tightly. Her mother began to cry despite herself, and she shook violently as she grabbed up the two girls, absorbing them into her bosom.

"I think so!" Nyssa cried, a peering eye darting around her destroyed room past her mother's shoulder. The carnage had also collapsed in her closet, tangling up many new school clothes which had hung there with the price tags still on them. "What happened?"

"I don't know!" Her mother was sobbing, rocking the girls back and forth. *"Randy?"*

Randy had already shot through the house and exited to the yard, rounding the trunk and easily maneuvering through the gaping hole in the side of it. His pace slowed to a careful tiptoe, his eyes wide and calculating the damage, his lips moving in a continual loop, mouthing *'Oh my God'* repeatedly, speaking to no one in particular as his eyes scanned the jagged split in the thick trunk.

"Randy!" a voice came from the rear of the yard to where at the small fence that separated their property from their rear neighbor. There stood the McCall's—Beth and Oliver—who in their robes looked utterly terrified and confused. "Are you alright over there?"

"Yeah," he said, moving towards them and turning back towards the house. "Damndest thing I have ever seen!"

"How did that happen?" Beth gasped, her eyes attempting to take in everything at once.

"I don't know," Randy shrugged slowly, his mind in a dreamy state attempting to comprehend the moment. "The tree had to have been damaged in the storm the other day and finally came down."

"You are insured, right, buddy?" Oliver added, giving him a slight nudge, his tone light as an attempt to brighten the moment.

"Yeah, you bet," Randy nodded while his brain rapidly scanned their insurance policy through his mind. *Fire...? CHECK! Flood...? CHECK! Storm...? CHECK, CHECK! Big elm tree plowing through the back of the house...? Umm... umm...*

He would have to recheck to see if that was checked or not.

"I thought a train was rolling through the backyard," Oliver insisted, his hand reaching up and waving to another neighbor, this one from the house to the right. "Everything's alright, Carl!"

Carl Ransburg was an extremely tall black man with the features of a teenager but with deep, premature wrinkles. He had taken early retirement from working the stock market because of the high stress and noise working the floors of the Mercantile Exchange downtown, his eyes bobbing over the edge of the fence and wanting a double dose of his anxiety medication badly right then. In one instant that morning, all the stress and noise of the decades spent at the Mercantile Exchange had been delivered to him in one sudden blow.

He simply nodded, his eyes bobbed along the carnage and then he moved back towards his home.

"No one got hurt over there, did they?" Beth inquired and as if a switch had been thrown, Christine was calling down to him from the hole on the second floor as Randy was shaking his head 'No'.

"*Randy!*" her voice terrified. "Agatha is hurt! Come quick!"

In a blink, Randy boosted away from the fence and crossed the yard, his feet seemingly never touching the grass before he found himself leaping over the last step inside to the second floor. He might have sucked as a stepfather, but no one could ever question his deep-set parental humanity.

Agatha was sitting on the edge of the bed in the guest bedroom with a hand near her bloodied shoulder, her head nodding in continuous reassurance to everyone that she was alright. In the light of the room, Seema noted that the wound looked painful but not as bad as it had looked earlier that morning in the darkness of the yard. The girl played her part, insisting that she needed to get Lady Agatha all that she could desire, including (and heaven forbid) a hospital resulting in Agatha's persistent 'No's' and eventually giving her a sharp, little wink and informing her that a glass of water would suffice.

"This is just horrible!" Christine cried sitting on the bed next to her friend, doting over her.

"Believe me, I am fine, everyone," Agatha was smiling and then regarded the solitary branch which had punched its way through the wall of the guest bedroom. "Let's go downstairs and away from this tree."

They all moved to the ground floor, and upon Christine's insistence, they continued out to the front yard to be met by the sirens of an oncoming fire engine. Randy stood idle as paramedics tended to Agatha, who firmly stated that a trip to the hospital was completely unwarranted. His concern was genuine, only glancing up as neighbors gathered far and wide to investigate the source of that thunderous, shuddering noise that had ripped them all from their slumber.

Nyssa and Seema were sitting in the grass near Agatha, who was resting in a chair that Randy had brought out to her from the front porch. Nyssa's eyes were wide and blank with shock while Seema rubbed her back, comforting her with soft coos of reassurance. Her mind did not quite comprehend the morning events, and Seema's words came to her in a faraway mumble that made no sense at all.

Something was hiding in all the chaos; the flashing lights of the ambulance, the firemen moving back and forth with picks and hoses, and the gas company employee waving a sensor assuring that there was no gas leak. It was there, however, shadowed. Just a continual blur of visions of a man and a voice whispering occasionally about him teaching her something, and when she would focus on any particular segment, it would fade like a dream under the blare of an alarm clock.

The sun was in its seven o'clock position and was already beginning to pour out its heat, but luckily Nyssa could care very little less this time.

-2-

"Then it is settled then," Christine said with gentle authority as Nyssa and Seema walked up the driveway, the two of them pulling on iced coffee drinks which they had been sent away to get so that the adults could talk.

They stopped just shy of the open garage door where Randy had set out several folding chairs and a card table lined with bottled water and a beer for himself. He was bouncing between the cell phone, which he had plastered to his ear, to questioning a worker who led a manned crew working on removing the tree from the side of the house. The one thing Nyssa did appreciate about the man was that he performed well under pressure, and since the cataclysm that morning, that was all there was.

"What is settled?" Nyssa inquired, her eyes moving from one set of eyes to the other.

"You are going to go stay with Auntie Agatha and Seema for a while," her mother replied, sitting.

"I am?" Nyssa jerked, eyes full of curiosity, her eyes shifting between Seema and Agatha.

"Yes," her mother said.

"For how long?" she inquired, taking a seat.

"Until before school starts," her mother said confidently.

"Why?" Nyssa continued, her mind doing all the talking.

"*Why?*"her mother's eyebrows rose, head cocking to one side. "Have you not seen the back of the house or your room? That's why. Why she asks… *hmph!*"

"No, no, no, that's not what I meant," Nyssa pressed, leaning forward. "It's just… well, I don't know… do I have to?"

A short but heavy quiet fell upon the moment as side-eyes and shifting weights of uneasiness hung over the drive.

"You don't want to visit Auntie Agatha's'?" Her mother asked, confused, her eyes looking about. Seema held Agatha with a pleading expression, her mind begging her teacher's brain to do something to help Nyssa see past the confusion in her mind. All the while, Agatha held her gaze on Nyssa. "She has everything there. You know this!"

"Yeah, I know," Nyssa sounded distantly, a fog heavy in her mind.

She wanted to go, desperate to rid herself of the boredom she has had so far this summer, but there was something; something in her that prevented the excitement which should be exuding from every pore.

"Um, yeah, and we have four new horses!" Seema glowed suddenly, her hand coming across the table and taking Nyssa's. "You still love horses, don't you?"

"Well, yeah," Nyssa blinked, a minute ping of excitement jumping only to have something dark in the shadows leap forward with claws ripping it back down. "But what about help around here?"

"And what do you think you could do?" her mother spat sharply, hands of frustration rising. "The house is unlivable and your father and I—"

"Stepfather," Nyssa interjected with a grumble.

"—is going to have to stay in a hotel until they get that tree out of the house! You're going and that's final!"

"You know, Nyssa," Agatha spoke quietly, her voice coming in low and gentle beneath the tone of the conversation. "The Fairy Garden is still there."

"It is?" Nyssa whispered back, her eyes finding Agatha's and a gentle coolness flowed over her skin.

There was something about the woman's aura she could not quite see but acknowledged, nonetheless. A glow perhaps, as if her Auntie sat before a brilliant light, but she was under the shade, so it was probably nothing, exhaustion more than likely, or could it have been...?

Agatha slowly nodded over the rim of her glass and with each slight rise and fall of her head, Nyssa's heart pumped stronger with delight.

Her mind flashed to a time when she would sit on the edge of the reflecting pond in the Fairy Garden, her tiny fingers carving the surface of the water as she sang *Shall We Dance* just like her grandmother on her father's side had taught her, serenading to the Fairy Princess and the little guardian gnome, Mr. Phipps. Her mind was filling with happy memories, which burned away at the fog in her mind, brightening the corners and sending a bolt of rage and pain through the owner of that whispering voice in her mind.

She would go, yes, to that place where she once dreamed of Magical things, while weaving holly flowered crowns for her and Seema to wear and rubbing the pollen of buttercups on their cheeks and noses.

Yes, despite the voice she would go!

In a burst she leapt from her chair and dove into Agatha's arms, happy tears streaming her cheeks and laughing. Seema wrapped her arms around her waist and squeezed, overjoyed.

"This will be great!" Nyssa pressed her head into Agatha's neck and kissed her smartly right above the satin choker.

"I am so glad you are happy, Nyssa!" Agatha laughed back, squeezing her. Her mother raised her palms again in a frustrated *'can you believe this girl'* fashion and then shrugged.

"Can't believe you had to twist the girl's arm for a month away from home," her mother huffed, head shaking as she moved to follow Randy and the tree removal people into the house.

"This is going to be so cool!" Seema beamed and the two girls clapped a high five.

"Oh my god, I don't know what I was thinking?" Nyssa laughed, shaking her head. "Horses? Auntie Agatha's? *Duh!*"

Agatha sat drinking her iced tea with a thin smile on her lips watching the two girls who, save their complexion and hair, could easily been sisters. She glowed at their youthful excitement and their composure and enjoyed it for what the moment could bring her.

Quietly, she placed her hand on her wounded shoulder, touched the brooch with her fingertips, and whispered. A gentle breeze cut through the open garage door, bringing an itching, tingling sensation that crawled over and into the wound and stood still. All healed and one less thing to worry about, she sighed as the thoughts of what lay ahead for them ran through her mind.

Smiling, she leaned back into her chair, listening to the girls' glee over all the cool things they were going to do and then thought of Seth.

"Nice try, Seth," she whispered, taking another sip of tea. "Take that."

CHAPTER TEN

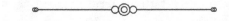

Conspiriation over Blood

-1-

Seth and Pia hissed in unison while Pia's steady drawing motion eased the two-inch nail from Seth's body, just behind the collarbone. His was out of sheer pain, searing hot and unforgiving, while her sounds came because she could guess how badly it must have felt. A small silver tray on the edge of the wading bathtub had a nice heap of splinters, glass, wood, and now the two-inch nail.

"That's all of them," she grimaced, dropping the surgical-style tongs on the tray. Seth grunted an answer and then slipped deeper into the warm water.

If it had not been for the healing oils and herbs which covered the surface, the water's color would have a nice rusty color from all the little bleeding wounds on his body (just as yours would be, too, if you had had the side of a house slammed atop of you).

"You know, I could have had Mica draw them out; her abilities have matured quite well, and she could have had this over with an hour ago."

"Pain builds character," he lied to her as he cupped two hands of the bath water and splashed it on his face.

Why his comments were a lie was simple: Seth didn't trust *anyone*, not even his long-passed teacher, to use healing Magic on him, let alone to have his student! That would show a submissive dependence like a dog on its back exposing his belly, and he would rather die than be dependent upon a pupil regardless of the agony of having Pia do the work (even though deep down he purposed that the woman was enjoying it).

"Bull," she snorted back, turning and using the rim of the sink vanity as a support to lean against, arms folded.

"Yes?" an eyebrow rose to accentuate his question after an annoyed moment of silence which he could no longer bear.

"Well?" she replied.

"Well, what?" he vaulted the question right back.

"Exactly!"

The game was afoot!

"You speak in riddles, woman!" Seth sneered, irritated and he attempted to sit upright only to halt his motion due to the pain running the length of his back. "And you test me while I ache and bleed… not a smart thing to do right now, Pia."

"Apologies," she conceded in almost a whisper, shifting the tray on the sink, her hand cupping something indiscreetly from its surface. With a sleight-of-hand that would best any street magician performing for quarters, the object was gone.

She moved back towards the wading tub and sat at its end, her eyes showing a brilliant green, more intense than usual. Seth watched her approach, following her complete form as she moved and then locked onto those eyes.

There was no doubt that Pia was thinking something wicked.

"It is a rare thing to ever see you injured... I thought a little light humor would spark your mood."

"Well then you have thought wrong," he said flatly, his tongue playing with the nasty split along his gum line.

He had known ahead of time that when he gated to the house in the burbs, Agatha would not be alone. Much like any teacher of Magic, their pupil was always present, but he had not expected in the least that the little brat could deliver such a wallop. As he pried away a piece of loose skin, flapping at his gums using his teeth and tongue for leverage, he assured himself that he would *never* make such an ill-perceived error again.

Pia looked at him momentarily, studying him, then released a noise that sounded quite like a *'huh'* from the back of her throat and shrugged.

"What is on your mind, Pia?" he inquired cautiously with a slight feeling of unease by her look for he was unable to sense exactly from where the wicked eyes wandered.

"Oh, nothing much, My Lord," she spoke calmly, never blinking. "It is more what is in my eyes than what is on my mind."

"And what do you see?" he urged the question.

"I see that little inerudite girl has taken up homestead with the savant girl and Agatha," she said softly, playing with a clump of herbs along the rim of the tub.

"It takes your gift effort to see the obvious?" Seth replied harshly and then he laughed. "Now I see where Mica is picking up her bad habits; I should keep you two apart more often now."

162

Pia produced a slight smile as thin as a razor, but her lips had no humor amongst them unless a blade's edge could be considered humorous. She continued:

"Well then, you must also have surmised that Agatha would have taken her to Luna House then?" Seth nodded with a smile. "And then you must also know that no one other than whom Agatha wishes can enter Luna House, which means Nyssa will go on to train, and there's not thing-one we can do about it?"

Seth had forgotten that, and his sarcastic smile disappeared; no, that point was something that had not crossed his mind. Everyone along the ranks of both the Anathema and the Pax Consortia knew that Agatha was perhaps one of the mightiest archmages in the world, a woman capable of performing the most potent of Magic without so much as an effort. It had even been rumored that part of her aura contained one of the last and most coveted Vestiges, a remnant wisp of ancient pure Magic.

No, he knew they had her, and without fail, they would train her in haste so that by her coming age, she would clearly be in the ranks of the Consortia and, therefore, immutable to the Anathema's enrollment. He did not, however, consider the possibility—and the only logical step Agatha would take in the matter—that she would harbor Nyssa at Luna House, which as Pia so calmly had put it, would make the girl untouchable by anyone: physically or magically.

"That presents a problem," Seth said through clenched teeth.

"That it does," Pia nodded, her eyes twinkling. "One which really doesn't have an answer."

"Then what ideas do you pose since your eyes are blazing?" Seth demanded.

"Simple," Pia smiled, shrugging. "We put someone inside the Luna House."

"Inside?" Seth's voice came with a mixture of sarcasm, intrigue and disbelief laced with rage (weighed more heavily on the latter). "I think I should start locking the wine cellar. No one can enter without Agatha's desire; you have said this yourself!"

"She would want what we give her," Pia whispered, her eyes growing wide. "Oh yes, indeed, she would want it badly because of her motherly instinct and the overwhelming sense of affinity towards the young and the broken."

"The young and the broken," Seth was staring at her, lost in the riddle.

"Exactly!" she smiled wide, her eyes aglow. "I guarantee that she has a huge place in her heart for the young and the *broken!*"

Seth's eyes locked onto Pia's, growing wide as well; the sparkling green he saw before him soon faded to a rapid montage of horrific images of Mica being knocked, thrown, battered, and thrashed by his hands and Magic. Seth witnessed the ultimate pain of terror in his pupil's eyes, not so much as what he had seen in past pupils whom he cast out their souls quickly into the *Yondsphere*. Oh no; this was long and slow. Seth was observing her heart shatter into countless pieces before him, her soul broken as the one thing in this world she loved—himself—was in the process of killing her.

The image faded with the sound of Seth's distant laughter and Mica sprawled on the ground... young and broken.

Seth suddenly shuddered and jerked his body away from Pia's gaze, panting.

"*Enough!*" he gasped heavily as if drawing first breaths from holding it too long. "What is this you show me?"

"A possibility, that is all," Pia replied, breathing laboriously as she wiped the sweat from her brow, dabbing some on the tip of her tongue to reward her for performing yet another perfect *seeing* feat. "A possible direction of the future."

"I cannot do that to Mica!" he shouted, water shifting in the tub in a splashing wave. Pia quickly brought an erect index finger to her lips, silencing the room.

'*You will have no other choice!*' Pia yelled in his mind, desperate for him to see reason. '*Agatha will take her in, but only if she believes that you have cast Mica out, but Mica would have to be convinced of it as well! We could not use Magic to mask it! Agatha would see through that like glass! The only true mask is the utter pain of betrayal and the self-loathing of failure!*'

'*I could not do that to the girl!*' Seth barked back into Pia's inner consciousness. She could sense his heart fluttering and faltering for she knew quite well that Seth loved the girl as his own. '*What you are suggesting is for me to destroy every glint of Life in Mica's soul! It would destroy her!*'

'*Only until the time is right, Seth,*' Pia soothed; convincing. '*When the time is right, we—that is you—will inform her of our ploy and in time she will forgive you. You are not the only one who can see that the child adores you like a puppy does its master. She will understand and forgive and then do what is requested of her in the end. She is pure Anathema after all.*'

With that, Seth looked at her blankly, his heart throbbing with the pain and guilt of harming Mica wracking his soul, and he hadn't done anything yet. What he was feeling was a parental-loving feeling, and it sickened him, and the only image he could find in his mind was of Mica as a small child who once sat cuddled in his arms, whimpering when she had hurt herself practicing Magic. It was a time when the typical Anathema Teacher-Student mentality was tossed out the window, and Seth would take her up, soothing her pain and fear. The thought of him doing what he saw in the pseudo-premonition in Pia's eyes was devastating.

Pia's eyes dimmed and she stood.

"Take pleasure in your pain that you will have to do the same to me, Seth," she smiled the words quietly, her eyes a flat green now, staring at him. "The whole act will have to be as convincing as the Apollo moon landing and then some."

Seth's pain flared away in a sensational wave of sudden rage and spite, his eyes narrowing on her, his mind picturing him doing what the vision had shown him to Pia instead of Mica, and his heart warmed to the pleasurable aspects of it.

"Yes, Seth," Pia's smile grew wider. "Think of it: Every time you hurt your sweet Mica; you get to then hurt me twice as much."

There was a long silence as the two held each other's eyes and then Pia turned towards the door.

"I will go prepare for it then," she nodded and slowly moved towards the door and Seth quietly watched her go. If eyes really could shoot daggers, Pia would surely be dead.

"Oh, and what of this?" Pia paused and lifted the tray full of bloody shards. "Shall I discard it?"

"No, leave it," Seth said quietly, sliding down into the water, eyes closing. "And rinse your hands before you leave. I do not wish my blood to end up in some sort of Haruspex root."

Pia smiled, dropping the tray and turning a knob on the sink, which she rubbed her hands together, removing any dried blood.

Once her hands were neatly dried on a face towel, she produced them both front and back towards Seth for his inspection.

"Good, now leave me," he said, and Pia left the bathroom without another word, a hand moving to her sleeve and tapping, feeling the shape of the bloody two-inch nail securely hidden there.

Slowly she pulled the door closed behind her and moved up the hall towards her room, smiling.

CHAPTER ELEVEN

─◦◎◦─

Road Trip and the Explanation of Modern Magic

-1-

Despite Seema's attempts to get Nyssa to understand things, Agatha finally broke in and told her as bluntly as it could be said: "We—you, Seema, and myself—are Magic."

Nyssa sat in the back seat next to Seema with wide eyes as she held Agatha's serious expression in the rearview mirror and then trailed to Seema, who was nodding convincingly. There was silence in the car; even the wheels on the road seemed to not make a sound as they rolled along I-39 heading north towards Wisconsin. Her mind wanted to burst from its container, to run away from this sudden out-of-this-world confession she had been slammed with.

Nyssa slowly closed her mouth, which had been hanging open for quite some time, and if they had been outdoors, it was more than likely a fly or two might have taken up residency there. Her body tingled as Agatha spoke about all the events leading up to their visit and the destruction of her house, with Seema occasionally adding to parts of the story which she had played a hand in.

"You smashed my house?" Nyssa broke in, unable to listen any longer, her shocked expression directed at Seema, who squirmed in her seat and dropped her eyes, guilty of the fact.

"No, I didn't smash it," Seema licked her lips and gave a slight shrug. "I kinda blew it up. Lady Agatha and the tree squished it."

"You squished my house?" Nyssa's shot towards the rearview mirror to find Agatha.

"No, well, I kinda dinged it is all," Agatha responded.

"Dinged it?" Nyssa's mouth hung open quivering in disbelief. "I no longer have a bedroom!"

"I saved your picture your dad made for you though," Seema added quickly, hoping that this fact would bring some comfort. "It's in the trunk."

"He could have printed me another one!" Nyssa exclaimed, forcing Seema's eyes to drop back to her lap once more with guilt.

With a sigh, Nyssa pressed back into her seat, her eyes finding nothing, in particular, to focus on as her head slowly motioned a continuous *'No.'* If she was to sit in this car for the next four hours, she would go mad and show it.

"The house!"

"Did you like living there?" Seema asked quietly, her fingers rolling over each other nervously.

"What?" Nyssa hissed as her temples pulsed.

"I mean, didn't you mention to me last night that you desired not to live there?"

"Well yeah, but—" Nyssa tried and then fell silent.

Agatha focused on the road ahead, her hands in the ten and two o'clock position on the wheel, humming softly. Nyssa's mind was a torrent of thoughts, confusion, and realizations that pounded against her senses as if tormented in a long surreal dream.

If all of what they were telling her was true, then that could only mean—

"I made that storm happen, then?" Nyssa said in a whisper, glancing at Seema, who was nodding, and then to the mirror again, where Agatha simply delivered her a wink.

"Yeah, and it was bad ass!" Seema gave her a wicked smile, giggling despite herself.

"*Seema!*" Agatha scolded; the corner of her mouth twisting but there was no anger resting behind it.

"Sorry," Seema mumbled towards the front seats and then placed her hand on Nyssa's knee and spoke quietly with a smile: "I was *really* impressed."

"Thank you, but how did? I mean, all I said was that I wished it would rain and—"

The car jerked suddenly as Agatha's foot unconsciously pumped the brakes, and Seema's hands shot forth, covering Nyssa's mouth.

"Don't wish!" Seema almost screamed it, her eyes wide with fear.

"What?" Nyssa jumped, suddenly terrified eyes bobbing in their sockets.

"Don't wish!" Seema said quickly, eyes showing anxious fear. "People of Magic *cannot* ever wish! It's against the rules!"

"I'm sorry!" Nyssa quickly returned as Seema calmed, moving back into her seat. "I didn't know that a *wi*—I mean, that doing that is bad. Wait... what rules?"

"The rules to Modern Magic," Seema said quietly. "You will learn them and follow them just like we do, like everyone of Magic *should* do."

"So, there are more of you, I mean us?" Nyssa begged as Seema nodded.

"You have already met Marco and Amora," Agatha spoke from the driver seat as she dug around inside her purse with both hands.

"Auntie Agatha!" Nyssa gasped, her eyes on the unattended steering wheel.

"Relax, I am still driving," Agatha dismissively waved with one hand, her eyes in the void of her purse. "Consider it cruise control with an attitude."

"Magic," Seema whispered and gave her a confident nod.

"Who are Marco and Amora?" Nyssa nodded back to Seema, not understanding a thing, while her eyes occasionally glanced toward what Agatha was doing and *should* be doing.

"You met them the other day," Seema said to her, getting a shrug and a confused look in return.

"Remember a little wiener dog not far from your house?" Agatha sighed, sitting upright with a smile widening her mouth, having found what she was looking for—a stick of gum.

"*Them?*" Nyssa's mouth became a cavern in the shape of a perfect 'O'. "That couple walking with their dog in the rain?"

171

"That's them," Agatha nodded, resuming her physical control of the helm.

"I knew there was something odd going on with them!" Nyssa laughed to herself. "The woman gave me some chewing gum."

"Buttery-Sweet-and-Sours," Seema nodded, sticking out her tongue while producing a gross out face as she dipped slightly so not to be seen by Agatha's reflective eyes.

"Yeah, that, I guess," Nyssa nodded. "It made my stomach feel better though, and my cramps went away."

"*Ugh!*" Seema's eyes rolled as she pressed back into the seat. "I know all about that stuff... I don't like the taste, but it is an instant cure to cramps; they make really good bubbles too!"

"So, they were umm—Magical people, then?" she asked and got a pair of nodding heads for her reply. "That's so weird."

"They thank you, you know," Agatha added, chewing away on her gum. "They said that you gave them a day's worth of catching up; they've been so busy lately."

"Okay, but why were they walking in a storm?" Nyssa asked with an almost sarcastic tone.

"Simple," Agatha shrugged. "They wanted some alone time."

"Alone time... in a violent storm, really?" Nyssa begged sarcastically.

"Why not?" Agatha shrugged. "Would you go out walking in that storm to disturb them?"

That got her, leaving her mind blank and numb.

"I guess not," Nyssa whispered and shrugged.

"Well then, there you have it." Agatha finished with a smile.

After a quiet calculating pause, Nyssa spoke: "So if I made it happen, by wish, I mean, wanting it, why now?"

"What do you mean?" Agatha proposed, curious.

"Well, I have you know, *wished* for things in the past and nothing ever happened," she shrugged.

"Oh really?" Agatha said, letting go of the wheel and turning around in the driver's seat so to address her directly. "Nothing?"

"Man, that really wigs me out when you do that," Nyssa said quickly under her breath and then continued. "But no, not to my recollection."

"Hmm, interesting," Agatha smiled, glancing between Nyssa and Seema. "Did you ever wish for something not to happen that you were absolutely stubborn against, like your father taking business trips?"

"Well yeah, but—"

"And what happened?" Agatha inquired, eyebrows rising.

"I don't know," Nyssa thought hard. "Times I really wanted him to be home, the trips were cancelled somehow."

"*See?*" Agatha pointed out.

"But I wished that my parents did not get a divorce," Nyssa spat out, near angry tears. "And *that* still happened!"

"I know," Agatha sighed and turned back to the wheel. "That still happened."

"Well then, where was this *'Magic'* then?"

"Seema?" Agatha directed as she flicked the turn signal to change lanes around a slow-moving pickup truck.

"That's also against the rules," Seema said quietly. "Magic cannot control the human heart without dire consequences."

Nyssa sat idle momentarily, her arms folded and her breathing hard. Usually, it was easy to push away thoughts of her parents' separation (and ultimately divorce), but only in the privacy of her room or personal space. However, When the subject arose around other people, the saddened feelings always brought on anger. Her mind trailed back to when she was just little and sitting in her bed with the pillow pulled up, tears streaming her face as she heard her parents argue. The words *'divorce'* and *'I'm leaving'* stabbed through her little soul ruthlessly and without mercy.

Nyssa pulled up her knees in her seat and buried her face in them.

"Nyssa?" Seema said soothingly, touching her arm. "Everything okay?"

Nyssa nodded and then wiped at her cheeks, eyes peering through the window and after a short while, she finally broke the silence, returning her attention back into the car, "Why do you call it Modern Magic?"

Seema licked her lips, "Should I tell her?"

"Go right ahead," Agatha smiled. "Let's see if you have not forgotten anything."

"You see, it's Modern Magic because Magic—you know, the Hocus and the Pocus—has changed over the millenniums, and more so, diminished," Seema explained, taking a deep breath.

"Is there really Hocus Pocus?" Nyssa quipped, shocked.

"Well, not so much the Hocus anymore, but there still is a many a mage who can stir up some pretty good Pocus!"

Seema burst into wild laughter at her own joke, joined by Agatha who produced a healthy chuckle despite her 'concentration' on the road. Nyssa smiled, half laughed, attempting to get the joke, and waited for Seema's laughing fit to pass.

Once subsided, she continued.

"There was a time when Magic flowed so freely that if you were a Person of Magic, you could utilize it just as easily as you could use a cup to scoop water. At one time, there was so much of it that you could actually *see* it flowing through things, requiring only innate talent to channel it and do with it as you wished."

Seema paused, her palms down, her expression full of curiosity as she gave Nyssa a moment to process before continuing.

"Now, that's an important piece of this history that you must really understand and know if you are to understand anything today. Once again, it *used to* flow freely, but now, almost none at all; hence the Rules to Modern Magic."

"Rules," Nyssa whispered in concurrence, her eyes wide as she took in the lesson.

"You see, there had always been rules to Magic which everyone who practiced it had to obey, but the problem was that some People of Magic cut corners—cheated basically—and abused powers they had been blessed with for personal gains. Once that started happening, the World of Magic was split between Us and Them, and soon natural Magic began to fade from the world."

"Who are these *Them*?" Nyssa whispered; her attention focused on what Seema had to tell her.

"Dark warlock sects and orders which for over five hundred years make up the Order of the Anathema," Seema continued, leaning close; whispering: "Cursed Magic."

"You mean they go around like the evil witches in storybooks?" Nyssa asked puzzled. "You know, making the world dark, kicking small animals and eating up happiness wherever they found it?"

"*Kicking small animals,*" Seema snorted in retrospect, shaking her head. "Too funny, but no not like that.

"The Anathema are not so much 'evil people' as they are simply greedy sorts who run and control just about everything in the world—or desire to do so—and they use Magic as a tool to get what they want, ya know?"

Nyssa shook her head slowly, not knowing.

"Okay, many of the big oil companies, trading houses, law firms, ranchers, railroad barons, shipping tycoons, arms dealers, those types." Seema sought her brain as if she had a stack of *Newsweek* magazines to point out examples of. "Just about every major conflict, natural disaster, or environmental catastrophe you hear about on the news can be directly or indirectly linked to them in one fashion or another. Even political figures high up are either Anathema or have direct ties with them, and of course, we cannot forget the 'specialized' social groups."

"Sort of like *Big Brother is Watching* slash *New World Order* kind of thing?" Nyssa hoped for clarity as Seema nodded.

"Big Brother indeed," Agatha interjected and then fell silent.

"So, then things like the Gulf War… that was just a ruse of this Ana—Ana—"

"Anathema," Seema assisted.

"The Anathema, yes, thank you," Nyssa nodded, continuing. "They are using Cursed Magic for what: *Oil?*"

"In that case, yes and no," Seema shrugged. "Human conflicts are always going to happen; that's the natural order of humanity, and there is really no way of stopping it, but where you can see the Anathema's role, you have to look at who exactly is benefiting from the war itself: Consulting firms, construction companies, oil conglomerates and arms manufacturers, certain politicians; all of them. That's where members of or those in cahoots with the Anathema do their bidding up to, if not including forging the tensions of the war itself so that said industries and individuals can prosper."

"So, if they all belong to this Anathema-club-thingy," Nyssa mused. "What does that make us?"

"The Pax Consortia," Seema announced proudly, extending a hand which Nyssa took and shook, her eyes narrowing with a slight confusion. "The association or society of peace... Pax means *Peace* in Latin."

"I see," Nyssa nodded with a smile; clarity is blissful when it is overwhelming. "So, then what are the rules and how many are there?"

"Ok, there are six basic rules," Seema said, turning more towards her and holding up a fist. "And what I mean by basic is that they are easy to understand, and they all reflect upon the first rule which is the golden rule of Modern Magic. Also, there are a lot more rules than the six main rules, but they still reflect upon the first six and all of them may not violate the first one.

"Understand?"

Nyssa shook her head *no*.

"Alright, I may lose you a bit," Seema smiled.

"You already have," Nyssa sighed.

"Okay, let me explain a little better," Seema swallowed and took a deep breath, popping up the index finger on her fist. "The first rule of Modern Magic is *the* rule as in the *'God Rule'* and one that can *never* be violated under any circumstances of proper responsible Magic. That rule states:

> *"Much akin to science: Something cannot come from Nothing; if you were to conjure something in one place, it must come from someplace.'*

"Get it?"

"Sort of," Nyssa thought, her face twisting in confusion, then shook her head. "No, not really."

"Put it like this," Seema's eyes trailed up and to the right, searching the creative side of her brain. "Let's say that you and I were walking along, and you suddenly got thirsty, and you decided to conjure up a spring of water so to quench your thirst. If you didn't know *exactly* where the water was coming from, and you did not focus on that source, as well as the amount you wanted, in essence, a lake on the other side of the world could suddenly dry up."

Nyssa's jaw dropped.

"Are you telling me that's what I did?" Nyssa's mind flashing back to the storm and the newscasts about Tropical Storm Claudette; how it was in the Atlantic one moment and then the next, *Poof!* She was pounding Chicagoland Suburbia USA.

"Uh huh," Seema was nodding as was Agatha. "You wanted rain and boy did you get it!"

Seema broke off into another fit of laughter as Nyssa sat feeling her stomach fall to her feet. After a moment, Seema regained herself.

"Okay, so now you know the first and most important rule," Seema was giggling, enjoying her tutoring position. "Which I may add, you broke that rule in like a kabillion pieces—"

"*Seema!*" Agatha hissed.

"—but let's move on." Seema was holding Nyssa's attention purely for anticipation effect towards the conversation and then popped up a second digit of her hand. "Okay, rule number two, which I pretty much already spoiled for you, but here goes:

"'You cannot successfully conjure something unless you know exactly where it is coming from. If you do not, chances are that the repercussions could be severe.'

"I-E the conjuring water at Point A could drain a lake on the other side of the world, for example. This reaffirms rule number one."

"Ok, got those," Nyssa nodded, shame still rubbing the edges of her conscience.

"Good!" Seema clapped and then finger number three popped up. "Rule number three:

'Magic is to be used wisely and not squandered since there is not enough left in the world to balance things out, and some Magic is to only be performed when there is Free Magic available, and even then, only when absolutely necessary. Even when there is Free Magic one should be careful to not consume more than there is, or the consequences could be severe.'

"Henceforth, rule number one still implies and governs all the other rules."

"That makes sense," Nyssa nodded.

"Yep!" Seema beamed, producing digit number four. "The fourth rule is pretty straightforward, and one I would think is common sense, but it goes:

> *"Magic cannot be used for personal gain because doing so is Magical theft even if used to influence personal gain, the primary rule has been violated because such gains were achieved from another existence and does not belong to you.'*

"And this is the one rule, I take it, as you have explained, the Anathema violates without a problem?" Nyssa said sourly.

"You have taken it in correctly," Seema nodded.

"Okay, what's the fifth rule," Nyssa asked, taking it all in like a greedy sponge.

"The fifth rule," Seema began, her mouth twisting a bit in confusion. "Is one I always thought should really be the first rule, but then again all these rules were written some time ago. Never mind, that's just me, but it states:

> *"People of Magic are not allowed to wish, covet, will or foist for anything that cannot be achieved through normal means and or time, for doing so can and will cause severe trepidation and will stand as a direct violation of rule number one.'*

"Umm, that was you… *BIG TIME!*" Seema added, holding back the laughter and although she could not see Agatha's eyes peering into the mirror towards her, she could feel her gaze burning into her skin.

"Yeah, thanks," Nyssa rolled her eyes. "I get that one now."

"And... and... *the sixth...*" Seema fought for her words, holding back the laughter, "Is...

> *"Magic is never to be used to coerce the human condition, whether for love or for vice, life or death, and any attempt to do so can shift the balance of all Magic and tumble everything down.'"*

"Wait! What do you mean, *'tumble everything down'?"* Nyssa blinked.

"Just as it states," Seema replied, all humor racing from her face. "Everything as we know it. Snap-crackle-pop, *'help me, I'm falling'* down."

Nyssa sat quietly for several minutes, rolling the rules around in her head and finding a connection from one to another, but most assuredly, all of them reflected upon the first rule. The pang of guilt was heavy in her gut because as she sat and thought about it, she had directly violated five out of the six and had probably come close in the past to that one as well.

"So, what are the consequences to directly violating the rules?" Nyssa asked and a part of her expected to find Seema starting the count back over with other rules to be spelled out.

"Well, umm, I think Lady Agatha will need to explain that one to you," Seema sat back, her eyes looking forward.

"Alright girls," Agatha said with a chipper tone, the sound of the turn signal coming to life as the vehicle began to veer to the right. "We're here!"

"What?" Nyssa shook her head, sitting upright and looking about through the windows. They were no longer on the highway; the four lanes with the multitude of cars having been replaced by a double lane road with no ground markers, the highway lights replaced by heavy trees lining the ditches on both sides and even the air was different; cleaner. "We have only been on the road for like, twenty minutes!"

Her eyes found Seema, who was beaming a broad smile at her, her cheeks curved so high that it narrowly pinched her eyes into slits, followed by a childlike giggle. Agatha looked back at her as she completed her turn and slowly steered the car up the long gravel drive towards the main house, which could barely be made out through the trees lining the driveway in the distance. Agatha gave her a subtle nod, and she slowly sat back in her seat, her head shaking slowly in the confusion.

Magic, she thought to herself.

"Yes indeed," Agatha spoke back to her with a nod.

-2-

Overall, the large Victorian-style house was just as Nyssa had remembered it by shape and form; however, everything about it was just wrong.

The once grand, linear memories had faded over the years, but now standing in the drive a hundred feet from the porch, everything returned to her like a rushing flood. She should be beholding a glamorous house; the copper on the roof and tiers should be sparkling in the sunlight, the flowers rounding the edges should be in full bloom, and everything about its exterior should be exuding happiness and glee and now run-down, saddened dilapidation. Even the ornate carvings along the trim, which once held so much detail that, as a girl, she would spend hours circling the house only to find something new in the designs, were now eaten away and covered by twisting runaway ivy.

The large front porch, which wrapped around to the back, was once a brilliant shining whitewash as the car rounded the drive, and the double-facing porch swings should be hanging sturdy on their iron chains. Now the paint on the porch was faded gray and cracked like hardpan, the chains on the swing rusty loops, and on one swing in particular, the chair had been eaten through, and the whole contraption hung in an odd, dangerous tilt.

The front doors were always her favorite because the arched faces were made of beautiful stained glass, save the heavy oak frames. Each held a scene in which a large moon was divided between the double entryway and beneath, on both the left and the right side, held a fairytale design of fairies dancing in the moonlight. Now, pressboard covered one side completely, and on the other, a hodgepodge of regular plate glass and tinted plastic sheeting mended old wounds.

What she was looking at was a large run-down shack.

Nyssa stood almost in tears.

"Nyssa, get your bags," Agatha instructed. Seema, who was already at the rear of the car attempting to pull Nyssa's luggage from the trunk, held a strained look; using two hands to struggle with one of them.

"What in the hell happened to the house?" Nyssa could barely speak, and the words came out in a sudden, gasping squeak.

"What do you mean?" Seema grunted, shifting Nyssa's bag into a better position.

"Lu-look at it!" Nyssa pointed, eyes wide with disbelief.

"*Huh?*" Seema looked towards the house from around the edge of the trunk and then giggled furiously.

"What's so funny?" Nyssa huddled down with her palms up and open as if she was about to tackle her.

"What you are seeing—" Seema calmed, erasing the giggle from her throat to not only be very convincing, but impressive to the newbie as well. "—is what is known as a *façade noire*, or dark mask. It's Lady Agatha's 'Roaming Salesperson and Burglar Distractor'."

"You mean, it's not really—" Nyssa began.

"Real? Nope. You will see as you get closer to the house." Seema's head disappeared back under the cover of the trunk followed by soft sounds of a struggle.

"When I get closer to the house," Nyssa whispered to herself, awestruck.

"Lady Agatha invoked it about two years ago when we were continuously badgered during breakfast and dinner by John Deere and Holland tractor salesmen. It was really annoying."

"Bu-but why make it look like, well—Umm…" Nyssa tried to find the right words, her hand pointing and twisting as if attempting to pull the words from the very air.

"Crap?" Seema giggled to Nyssa's nodding. "Think about it; if you were a traveling salesman or a thief, would you think anyone that lived there had any money?"

"I guess not," Nyssa half smiled, moving slowly towards the rear of the car.

"What did you pack in here?" Seema grunted; her small hands seemingly unable to catch a good grip on the luggage even by the handles.

"Well, just about all that was left over from you smashing my room," Nyssa smiled and kicked the front of Seema's shoe playfully.

Seema rolled her eyes in response, and the two hoisted it out on its wheeled end, pulling up the tow handle, and they sighed in unison. Nyssa narrowed her eyes at the house as they moved up the cracked and weed-strewn walk.

"Are you sure it's not like this all the time?"

"You'll see, trust me," and with that Nyssa did begin to *see*.

It started with the wrap-around porch, which seemed to jiggle and cascade in the distance, and she froze in mid-step when her eyes caught the motion of several broken railing posts beginning to mend in on themselves and the cracked panes pulled together, fusing into a solid state.

"*Whoa!*" she gasped, taking several steps backwards to watch everything reverse back to its state of dilapidation and then forward again to watch everything mold back into grandeur. "Did you see that?"

"Kinda cool, huh?"

"This is amazing!" Nyssa beamed.

"Yep," Seema nodded, motioning her to continue forward up the walk.

Soon the hanging swing rose on its own, the chair rising and reattaching itself to its brother's links, and the rust melted away and became a thick, dark iron color. The pressboard on the left door faded out as the pristine cut and beveled colored glass began to show through, and soon both doors held the astounding story images they had always portrayed. Nyssa stood on the edge of the walkway, which followed the wraparound porch, absorbing every detail of lattice edgings that had hollowed shapes of stars and moons in different phases.

By the time she had reached the bottom stair, the house—Auntie Agatha's house as she remembered it—was back, and it was brilliant.

"Come girls, quickly now," Agatha was speaking halfcocked over her shoulder as she crossed the wide porch, and before she could reach it the door swung inward on its own.

Nyssa, still relatively new to all these shows of Magic, stood slack-jawed for a moment until the tips of Seema's fingers pressed upwards on her chin.

"You know, you do that a lot," Seema giggled and nudged her into motion towards the house.

"I thought you said that Magic should only be used when absolutely necessary," she whispered as Agatha disappeared into the house.

"Right," Seema smiled. "And opening a door is quite necessary unless you want to smack your face into it, right?"

"Right," Nyssa responded almost under her breath.

There was going to be a lot to be learned and understood as she could see.

"Come on," Seema encouraged as they drew closer.

"By the way, you really have got to teach me that olive trick!" Nyssa whispered and Seema immediately began to nod rapidly.

"Not now," Agatha called from somewhere inside the house. "That's for later on, now come quickly girls!"

"Man, she has some good ears," Nyssa said quietly, and Seema answered with another nod.

As they ascended the wooden stairs, Nyssa closed her eyes to the sweet scent of fresh cedar and cinnamon flowing from within, carried aloft from a cool, internal breeze.

"Auntie Agatha has central air?" Nyssa asked with a peculiar frown, only to be met by Seema's blank stare which turned into a gentle roll of the eyes and a giggle.

"C'mon, you'll see everything much clearer in a moment," Seema urged her on and as they crossed the threshold of the doorway, Nyssa stopped frozen, her eyes scanning up and up to the double staircase which rounded the edge of the grand hallway.

A deep burgundy carpet ran the center of the foyer, which split off into two runners, each carefully situated in the center of the curving staircases. The staircases were lined along the wall with arching stained glass, every pane holding its own brightly colored story. Nyssa's eyes trailed even further up to the large, glass-capped ceiling rising more than thirty feet into the air, the day's light beaming through the colorful plates and facets, making the whole foyer glow.

"I—I don't remember *any* of this," Nyssa stammered unable to move.

"Lady Agatha has been busy preparing it for your arrival," Seema said quietly, setting the bags on the floor. "Wait until you see our room! Oh, and when you walk through the atrium, mind the turtles—" she added in retrospect. "—she learned that you like turtles, and boy are there a *lot* of turtles."

"Turtles?" Nyssa said distantly.

"Welcome back to *Casa de la Luna*, my child!" Agatha proclaimed and Nyssa's eyes fell from the ceiling to find Agatha standing at the juncture where the two staircases met on the second floor. "You are now home!"

Seema stepped past Nyssa, who stood motionless, her mouth opened yet again; however, this time, Seema allowed her to gawk.

Slowly and effortlessly, the door closed behind them with a gentle click.

-3-

The room Agatha had prepared for the girls was right out of a catalog, with a dash of mystical heaven sprinkled on the top. Seema had expressed that she had not been allowed to see it until the day they had left for their visit to Chicago, and then it was difficult for her to pull herself away from it even after Lady Agatha had begun to get stern. Her old room, a decent-sized rectangle for a teenage girl, was sufficient, having all the necessities anyone would need: a bed, a dresser, an armoire (for her dresses and long coats whenever she *had* to wear them), a dressing mirror, a rug, a window, and a closet; basic.

The new room was no less than that of a master suite.

The arched ceilings rose to a height that Nyssa had to almost squint to see the tops, each curved beam alternating between dark and light blues. Curved skylights had been cut in the sides of each ceiling wall, filling the room with an even gentle light. The walls were a soft periwinkle that seemed as if it had been coated with a clear, yet opalescent, glaze. Many friends and family pictures were decorating the walls, most of which were from the girl's youth and others from Lady Agatha and Seema's several trips abroad.

"Those are some of my favorites," Seema glowed proudly; being an amateur photographer with the eye of a professional. "I took those in Venice last year. It was amazing!"

Each girl had a large bureau dresser crafted from white pine and cedar; the soft clear-coat varnish perfectly set the room's light color off. Each dresser had its own large mirror, which angled slightly forward to give the viewer a perfectly reflected view of oneself. On the top of each sat a large cherrywood box to keep their precious and personals in, and next to those sat a crystal pitcher on a base stand with three glasses each.

In the center between the two halves of the room was an intricately sculpted fireplace that rose nearly five feet at its mouth; its sides ornately carved with shapes of stars and moons. Lined up on the mantle were a collection of seven crystal eggs, each anointed with colored stones of various cuts, and inside them swirled a colorful plasma: each one a different color of the rainbow. Not one of the eggs matched the other besides their size, except for the center one, which stood twice the height and double the girth of the others.

Nyssa's eyes danced in its presence as it pulsated with a kaleidoscope of swirling colors.

"What are those?" Nyssa gasped with wide eyes as she neared them.

"Those are *Night Casks*," Seema said absently, unzipping one of Nyssa's bags which had been laid flat on her bed. "You open one and out comes the *Night Vision*. They are an aftereffect of Old

Magic… more like specters really; shapeless, but the show they put on is amazing!

"You will see tonight."

Nyssa withdrew her hands without touching them and chalked up another *To Do* event on the growing list in her mind.

"Auntie Agatha made all this?" Nyssa said, her jaw dropping and then she closed it suddenly for fear of being mocked by Seema once again.

"Yep, and the adjoining changing rooms," Seema pointed to the left and the right where a door stood partially open each one individually crested; one with an ornate *'N'* and the other an *'S'*. "I think she made my bathroom bigger than yours, or maybe it's just the light… who knows."

Nyssa glided across the polished wood floors and the large, centered rug towards the door standing ajar with the crested *'N'* on it and pushed it completely open. Inside was what was stated: a personal changing room with full-size triple mirrors, a small makeup table, two very comfortable chairs, and a rolling clothes bar so to hang your best on as you dressed, all of which were illuminated by four tall rectangle windows which were frosted for privacy. To the right of the main door sat entry to the bathroom, where besides its size of a master bathroom instead of one for a teen, it was simply a well-put-together space.

Nyssa walked back into the bedroom proper, her mouth hanging open regardless of what Seema might say.

"This… this is, uh—" Nyssa tried, pointing behind her.

"Impressive? I know," Seema giggled, imagining she must have looked the same when she saw the layout. "Agatha went a little crazy,

I think. She came with a stack of interior design magazines and went to work on them with scissors and glue until she had made a collage of what she wanted it to look like. After a lot of banging, creaks, cracks, and a few explosions, she came up with this."

"Explosions?" Nyssa gasped.

"Yeah," Seema shrugged. "There was a lot of trial and error, kinda like at a hardware store mixing the color periwinkle; no one ever gets periwinkle right on the first batch. I thought she had blown out a wall or something… sorry again about your house."

"Who cares about that?" She was laughing as she grabbed Seema in a sisterly hug, then turning next to her, arm in arm. *"Just look at all this!"*

"Well, I think Lady Agatha will be pleased to know we both like it."

As the two girls laughed and awed over their room, their voices racing along the hallways and around corners, Agatha was sitting in the library enjoying her tea, her heart swarming with the sound of their joyous voices laughing in unison once again, and with a gentle tip of her cup, she signed a silent *'You're welcome'* with a smile.

CHAPTER TWELVE

Settling in

-1-

Nyssa was sitting on the swing suspended in the center of the gazebo on the rear side of the house, her mind and body completely numb from the grandeur and Magic shock. As Seema explained, there was so much of it in Agatha's home that it even overwhelmed her whenever she and Lady Agatha took trips away.

"For me, it's like rereading a book after a long time," Seema explained when Nyssa had complained of feeling lightheaded. "You know, you start reading it, and although you are familiar with the story, everything seems new and fresh? For you, well, you haven't been here in eight years; you must feel like you are on a nonstop rollercoaster."

Nyssa half-sighed, half-huffed out a single chuckle, her head slowly shaking in a dreamy, intoxicated fashion. That's precisely what it did feel like a rollercoaster, but one that zipped and whipped and spiraled along at phenomenal speed with flashing colored lights which stretched out all around her.

Her mind trailed off, and she began to think about her dad, and she wondered what he was doing right then, what city he was currently bouncing through, and, more importantly, if he was thinking about her also. He had often told her that he thought of her all the time and had explained that she was his *'Light'* and that the world would be much darker and uglier if she was not in it. The echoes of his words comforted her only to a degree because other than the phone, email, and one-on-one chat sessions on the internet, his physical presence had not been felt since the Fourth of July earlier that month.

Nyssa knew she loved both of her parents equally; there was no question about that, but she did know that she loved them both differently, a mental tug-O-war she tormented herself with often. In return, she knew that they loved her emphatically, and her best interest was at the forefront of their minds, but much like her affection towards them, she received their love individually.

Her mom played the heavier hand, sometimes seemingly in a dictatorship role, and minded everything she did that her mother considered risqué. On the other hand, her dad was calmer and more open-minded, wanting her to remain a child as long as possible. He had often soothed her teen frustrations with logic, first listening to all she had to say with the most minimal number of interruptions, only to come back with words that explained her mother's point of view, which would get Nyssa agreeing with her mother's stance without realizing that she was.

Teen angst abated yet another time, and Win-Win for the parents.

If there had been a choice, Nyssa often figured, she would have rather lived with her dad than her mom, but in the end, she would understand the basic facts that this wanton wish was based on the anorexic time she spent with him. Maybe if she lived with him full-time, the tables would turn on her, and she would think the other way around.

The grass is always greener, her father's voice whispered to her, and she slowly nodded; drudging up enough physical energy to give the swing a slight nudge with her foot.

"I like to dream... Yeah, yeah, right between the sound machine," Seema was singing *Magic Carpet Ride* by Steppenwolf—quite loudly and a bit off key—which was one of her songs on her digital music player.

The girl had been listening to it for over an hour; the plugs were firmly pressed into her ears, and the volume was to the max. Each time a new song would begin to play, her sudden burst of happiness resembled that of a child in a candy store who had five dollars in their pocket, and all the sweets were a penny a piece.

Nyssa gave her a stealthy smile, and she watched her bop and move on one of the gazebo's edge benches, her eyes closed to the music as if picturing every word and beat. She had thought about showing Seema the MENU option so that she could select whatever song she wanted to hear instead of letting the whole list play but then thought better of it. The poor girl might just go into digital music apoplexy and never recover despite all the Magic in the world.

It didn't really matter, though. Once the battery inside the player ran dry, that would simply be that. At Auntie Agatha's house, there would be no way to recharge it; the one crucial item, the charging stand, was crushed under several tons of crumbled house many miles away.

Slowly Nyssa returned to her solemn state, staring off into the nothingness. She sighed, and thunder boomed overhead, startling both of them despite the volume Seema had the player on.

"Oh crap!" Seema shouted, startled, ripping away the earplugs.

"*I didn't do it!*" Nyssa immediately protested hands up defensively.

"I know, silly," Seema smiled, looking over the railing of the gazebo towards the sky. "Wow, it's really going to pour."

"I thought everything here stayed sunny and warm," Nyssa addressed, joining her at the railing.

Seema turned to her with a pleasant smile and shrugged.

"It has to rain sometime, ya know?" Seema giggled and Nyssa nodded in agreement.

With that said, the rains did come.

-2-

Auntie Agatha was in the kitchen heating water when Nyssa entered, her face twisted in an unpleasant expression mixed with pain and irritation. She had forgotten to bring her menstrual medication, a taboo she had learned in school when sitting through a boring lecture when the cramps set on. For all she knew, she could have looked high and low for them and never found them if the thought had crossed her mind before their departure, for more than likely, they were a crushed mess beneath the wrecked side of her house.

"That bad?" Auntie Agatha inquired, eyebrows rising.

"*Yes!*" Nyssa hissed, taking a seat at a small round kitchen-nook table. She eyed her fingernails on her right hand looking for any sign of white but only found nubs; she often bit her nails around this time every month for some reason. "And I don't have anything for it!"

"Well, you do, and you don't," Agatha responded, moving the tea kettle to the side. "We all do."

"Magic again?" Nyssa sneered at her aunt's mood and idle chitchat as she would anything near her now (the timing notwithstanding the latter).

"Of sorts," Agatha nodded, moving towards the refrigerator, and opening the door. Inside the light came on and Nyssa made a contradictory sound which sounded more like an '*uh-huh*'. "Something wrong?"

"Seema told me that you don't allow electronics in the house," Nyssa licked her lips. "She said that you didn't—"

"Trust them?" the archmage finished her sentence as she turned, holding a container of orange juice. "I don't, but some things are a necessity, and others are not. Now, unless you like drinking warm orange juice and sour milk, how else would I keep them cold? Magic?"

Nyssa gave a slight shrug as she nodded.

"I see you have a lot to learn about that subject," she said, moving to the counter and pulling two glasses from an above shelf. "There are things about Magic that exists in electrical devices, and that thing is natural and has always been here. Electricity, whether you follow your science books or not, *is* a natural occurrence just like Magic; therefore, it is to be used as such, but used wisely."

"But just about everything in the world runs on electricity," Nyssa egged on, confused. "So, if that's the truth, why don't you have regular lights, or a television, or even a microwave oven?"

"*Microwaves?*" Agatha's voice rising to almost a high pitch, her face screwed up in an expression as if she had just smelled something foul. "Dear child, everything comes out soggy or half-cooked with one of those. Ever try to defrost meat in one of those things? *Ugg!*

Half is frozen while the other side has started to cook. Miserable devices microwaves are. Never on your life, child."

"I am not a child," Nyssa grumbled as another hammer fall cramp shot her lower belly, forcing her to lean forward a bit. "I hate it when people call me that."

"Calm yourself, Nyssa," Agatha said calmly, unhurt, and slowly she began to pour the glasses full of juice. "It is a word of endearment, not a persecutory comment about your age or demeanor."

"Whatever," Nyssa grumbled so quietly that it almost sounded like her stomach was growling.

"Why don't you go have a seat on the back porch and I will bring you your remedy."

"Fine," Nyssa sighed, slowly pulling herself up into a standing position and moved towards the rear door to the kitchen. "It's not going to be that 'buttery-sweet-sour' stuff, is it?"

"No, as I said it will be a kind of Magic," Agatha raised one glass to show her. "A natural one... nice and simple."

Nyssa simply regarded the glass of orange juice with a blank stare momentarily, and then walked through the screen door separating the kitchen from the back porch and stepped out drudgingly into the rain-filled air.

-3-

The gnome stood guard in the falling rain near the garden's miniature gate, garishly smiling with wide eyes just before the iris beds, to the left of the petunias and to the right of the narrow cobblestone path.

It had only moved twice for as long as Nyssa could remember, and each of those times, Auntie Agatha had insisted that the gnome, Mr. Phipps, did so to get a better overlook of the garden.

He was on guard, after all.

Nyssa sighed without any real conscious effort as she regarded Mr. Phipps with a frown. After the last week of bad happenings leading up to now, she so wanted to *see* the little gnome move, even just a little bit, a slight gesture that might drag her out of her deepening funk.

Sporadic, fragmented memories of her younger self blurred through her mind like heavy soup, showing her hazy images of herself playing in that very garden where she used to have long afternoon conversations with Mr. Phipps and then danced amongst the cobblestones with the two garden fairies, Renée, and Regina. There were even times when she brought lemonade to the yard on the really hot days, and they all would sit in the shade of the mulberry tree at the garden's edge and gossip about The Bee King, Eldirt Fuzzy-Bunny, and Think-a-Way Squirrel. In those times, she was—

"Such a stupid kid," Nyssa sighed again; breaking off a small piece of a twig she mindlessly played with and tossed it at the silent gnome.

"Who is the stupid kid?" Agatha's voice came through the screen door as she exited with two glasses of orange juice on a tray.

Nyssa straightened and then relaxed, producing a slight shrug, and then leaned back in the chair, her eyes finding nothing particular to look at.

"Just thinking out loud, I guess," she replied, her eyes drifting to the two garden fairies that hovered in place on their thin glass stems.

"You weren't referring to yourself, were you?" her aunt's eyebrows rose as she set the glasses on a small table between the two porch chairs and then occupied the empty one.

Nyssa pressed her lips tightly together, her tongue moving back and forth against their insides as her mind scanned through a list of conversational pieces until her eyes found the gnome once again.

"His paint is fading," came the new subject, almost in a whisper.

"Whose?" Agatha's eyes darted until finding what Nyssa was looking at, then raised her glass and took a quick sip. "Well, one of these days, he will cooperate and let me touch him up."

"He's just a stupid garden gnome, Auntie Agatha," Nyssa spat out without even thinking as she rolled her eyes away, and by the time the rolling stopped, Agatha added without losing a beat:

"A crafty gnome, yes," Agatha nodded. "But far from stupid."

"Well, maybe it should be kept in the shade so it wouldn't fade!" Nyssa retorted, irritation growing in defiance towards the idea that anyone was playing off her youth. "It hasn't been moved for as long as I can remember!"

"He'll move when he wants to, you know this." Agatha shrugged passively.

"I am not a little kid anymore, Auntie Agatha!" she growled, her head snapping away with closed eyes.

She hated this stage in her age timeline where she was old enough for a load of responsibilities, but not old enough to be considered anything more than *a 'child'* when it suited the adults.

Nyssa slouched down deeply into her chair as warm air escaped her throat in the form of a long, irritated *Grr!* She wasn't necessarily upset with Agatha; relatives other than your parents were allowed to pamper—even *baby*—the younger ones, a thing all children pick up at an early age. This was an earned right of adding 'Auntie' to the adult title of one's life, and even though Agatha was not a blood-aunt, the right still remained; a right that, in most cases, carried no veto power by the parents (especially when afternoon ice cream was in order, to have breakfast cooked just the way you liked it, or the extra hugs and kisses of affection on a dreary, wet afternoon).

"You're right, Nyssa, I was just trying to cheer you up," Agatha said softly as she rose from her chair, wiping her hands together then gathering up her glass. "Well, there's your juice... I will just leave you with your thoughts."

To call the jolt of guilt that exploded in her stomach a *pang* would be a tremendous understatement. Nyssa knew that she had been stressing over one too many things for several weeks now and that she had been taking it out on any and everyone she came in contact with, but Auntie Agatha?

Enough was enough.

"Auntie Agatha?" Nyssa spoke softly as she turned in her chair to face her. Agatha paused briefly, meeting the brown, wide and anxious eyes fixated upon her. "I guess I have been a little crabby lately and there's a lot to take in all at once... please stay out on the porch with me?"

"Of course, I will," Agatha smiled as she returned to her seat, allowing the slow rhythm of the rain to soothe the air for a moment.

"These last couple of weeks have really, well, sucked," Nyssa broke in, breaking that rhythm.

"How have they, umm... 'sucked'?" Agatha probed, forcing down the smile that dared to show.

"Everything," Nyssa replied quickly, adjusting herself in her seat so to better face her aunt. "First, Mom wants to sign me up for all these summer activities—as if I am not busy enough—as she stated: 'so you won't be bored'. Bored? So many of those things she wanted to sign me up for are lame and she's worried that I might get bored?

"Ever since I was little, she has been signing me up for things like that without really asking *me* if I wanted to do them or not, and if I complain about them, she lays down enough guilt that I agree to doing them."

"That's no good," Agatha added, taking a small sip of juice as her mind trailed back to a day when Seema sounded much the same.

"It's not!" she agreed earnestly, nearly squealing it. "Doesn't she realize that *sometimes* I don't want *something* to do *all* the time? That sometimes I just want to veg?"

"Veg-ing can be good at times," Agatha nodded as she half understood the reference.

"*Exactly!*" Nyssa rounded the understanding between them to complete the full circle, only missing the two-finger eye-to-eye hand motion to show that they were on the same page. "That's what I wanted to do, veg, and not have every moment sucked up with what she wanted me to do, plus that crappy job!

"I am going to be a junior in the fall and the last thing that I want to do is to spend my entire summer at some sports camp, or music program or volunteering at the local zoo, which that one wouldn't really be that bad, though."

"At a zoo with all those animals?" Agatha's eyes widened. "No, that one doesn't sound bad at all.

"Let me ask this, though, Nyssa... have you ever had this conversation with your mother?"

"Only like a thousand times," the girl huffed. "We get as far as me telling her what I would *like* to do and then the fighting starts."

"Hmm, that does sound a little bit like her," Agatha nodded, reminiscing about a time in college when the two were trying to figure out what they were going to do for spring break.

Looking back, the two had done all the things Christine had wanted to do, but considering at the time, she was observing the future mother of something grand, she simply went along with it.

"Well then you know where I am coming from," Nyssa sighed.

After a quiet moment between the two, Agatha introduced, "Have you ever tried to turn the tables on her?"

"What do you mean?" Nyssa's eyes narrowed, liking the sound of turning the tables on her mother but not quite understanding the angle.

"You know, killing her with kindness sort of thing?" Agatha spoke as Nyssa shook her head, which was accompanied by a sold shrug of confusion. "It's simple, really: Instead of telling her what *you* want to do, try asking her what *she* thinks would be something good for *you* to do."

"Well… no," Nyssa answered, her mind not finding a single instance in her memory banks. "I guess I have never done that."

"You have to understand, Nyssa, that every parent finds it difficult to let go of that little, always-dependent child they now see as this growing adult who lives in their house. They long to be called 'mommy' and 'daddy' once again instead of simply 'mom' or 'dad.'

"Even with Seema, I have had difficulties letting her grow up. Sometimes, when I look at her, I wonder what she had done to that skinny-legged, big-headed child who used to come running whenever she skinned her knee or cried out my name in the middle of the night when the bogeymen came. "No, it is quite difficult, and although I have only had her for most of her almost sixteen years on this planet, I cannot remember a time when she was not here. It is very difficult indeed."

Nyssa sat staring at the gnome for quite some time, her mind echoing Agatha's words and finding sense in everything she said. In the end, she also found herself feeling a bit guilty and suddenly missing her mom.

"Trust me, she misses you too, Nyssa." Agatha said, taking a sip from her glass.

Nyssa shot her eyes to her, mouth hung in surprise. With a smile of fond relief, she moved across the small table to give her Auntie Agatha a thankful hug.

CHAPTER THIRTEEN

Late Meetings, Betrayal, and of course, Night Trips

-1-

"There are those who feel your handling of this matter has been quite irresponsible, Lady Agatha," the monotone voice came as directly and bluntly as a hammer fall.

Agatha was sitting upright in her tall chair, her hands calmly laid on the armrests as her eyes stared back into those of Langdon Drellic who, just like the other five present at the evening council, were there, but not there at the same moment.

Back in the early nineties—when word throughout the technological world was all abuzz about the advances leading towards video conferencing—Agatha had sneered at it with a sarcastic laugh. She then expressed how, in the World of Magic, they have been doing that for more than two thousand years without the high-priced service charges. In what could have clearly been Agatha's ten thousandth projection meeting, if they had been paying by the hour all these years, the bill would pay off the country's national debt and the world's tab entirely.

She listened patiently as Langdon droned on about her *'handling of this matter'* with her teeth clenched the whole time.

"And I for one must concur with their displeasures," Langdon was finishing, addressing the others who were present, but not present. "Or am I alone in my sentiments this evening?"

The projection of Langdon scanned over those who were also 'present' in the large study. To his right in the curved arrangement in which Agatha had set the chairs was Maynard Drelling, who occasionally reseated his large glasses on his nose, and at the far end was Angelica Wooten, who sat cross-armed and irritated (a staunch advocate against projection meetings because she preferred things to happen face to face and up close and personal where you can smell their breath, as she always put it). To his left sat Marco and Amora, who always shared a small leather loveseat with little Marley snuggled in between them, and at the far end of that side sat Rusty Menden, healthy and well, a clear sign that Angelica was quite successful in removing the hammock from his midsection.

"The only ones who share those sentiments, Langdon," Marco spat out. "Are those who hide behind Magic as if it were a shield!"

"And you are implying?" Langdon said monotonously, drawing out the word 'implying' in a very snooty fashion.

"I imply nothing, Langdon" Marco licked his lips several hundred miles away while his doppelgänger's projection did so accordingly. "When evidence is on the hands and the wall, there is no implication!"

"Gentlemen," Agatha spoke quietly, her fingers pressing solidly between her eyes. It had been quite a long night as it were and what she didn't need now was bickering to add to her already thudding headache. "This will get us absolutely nowhere and quite quickly I may add."

It was still raining from earlier that day, and she had not seen her moon, even for a wink, and the lack of its aura was wearing on her soul. She had considered leaning in while the two men fought, whispering towards Angelica's projection whether it was three bay leaves or four you needed to add to the parsnip tea to kill a headache, but she thought better of it. She didn't necessarily care whether it was three, four, or ten; all she wanted was this night and her headache to be over with; quickly.

"Do you know," Agatha spoke quietly with an edge of irritation lining her tone. "That every time that I have ever witnessed a projection squabble, I have humored myself with the thought of what would people do if they felt they had to come to blows? Would you swing wildly at nothingness in your dens or study's, knocking over lamps and chairs mindlessly in your irritations?

"If so, would you then realize that you would look quite foolish to anyone who was a witness?"

The two men suddenly froze in mid-bicker and then looked at Agatha, smiling thinly, her eyes only on Marco. Marco calmed quickly and gave a slight nod as the reality of everything promptly hit the top floor without further coaxing. Calmly, he relaxed back against the cushions.

"Sorry, Lady A," he smiled and one of Agatha's eyebrows rose sharply. "I mean, Lady Agatha, yes, forgive me."

Agatha held Marco for a moment longer as Langdon returned to his monotone rant about her mismanagement style, her head ever so slightly shaking back and forth with a motion of disbelief, thinking to herself that Marco still had that explosive fire inside him like when he was a teenager. He was never one of her 'adopted' pupils as he was simply someone else's student, which she guided along his final stages.

Marco was a fosterling of Magic, the lost pupil of an archmage who died before completing the apprenticing task, along with the rules of Magic. That should have also been the end of Marco's education in the magical arts. It had never made much sense to Agatha (nor did it to many other people of Magic) that if the teacher dies, the student must return to their everyday life as a half-breed construct between normal and magical.

The rule had been set by ink and pen a long time ago, mainly as a safeguard for the teacher from an afterlife of guilt. In the most superficial wording of the rule: if the teacher is dead (especially if the student's ill-guided Magic happened to be the culprit behind the teacher's death), that's it! *You're out!* When death found poor Anton many years before, Marco's fate was sealed, but as with everything, there is always a stipulation blowing around to counter such terminations.

In Marco's situation, he was lucky that Anton didn't simply wake up dead one morning from old age, no. Anton unfortunately fell ill after being murdered by an outside aggressor, which made the previous rule null and void.

Simple, just like everything should be.

"And with that, Lady Agatha," Langdon was still droning on while Agatha's mind was busy in the past, and for an act of melodramatics supposedly to draw those present into some sense of anticipation, he slowly took a sip from something, swallowing and releasing a soft, *'Ahh'* for good measure. "My main question of concern is, what are you going to do about it?"

Agatha blinked several times having heard her name spoken, "What am I going to do about what?"

"Excuse me?" Langdon gasped, his eyes narrowing. "Did you not hear a word I have said about the girl? About this 'Nyssa' child!"

"I don't plan on doing anything but teaching her what she should have been taught years ago," she said flatly, ending it and receiving several nods of approval from others 'present.'

The nerve of him.

"I do not think that you heard—" Langdon started.

"No, I heard you clearly," Agatha finished. "What *exactly* do you propose we do with her, hmm? Send out a projection to the Anathema and tell them that the girl is broken-Magic so we are not going to teach her, and neither should they?"

"I uh—" Langdon stammered out of embarrassment.

"Should we stave off such possibilities and simply kill her now?" the archmage said as her mind twisted out darkened questions which made every projected eye on her shift uncomfortably. "That would be an Anathema way of handling the situation: *'We can't manage it so let's destroy it!'*"

"I am not suggestion that we ki—" Langdon's lips raced to finish his sentence only for the head to be bitten off once again.

"You listen now!" Agatha snapped, leaning forward in her chair, her finger pointed at his projection. "And all of you listen as well!

"I really don't care whether any of you see the possibilities in Nyssa or not, but the fact remains clear that not only does she have potential for wondrous things, but she also has the potential to tear it all down.

"We are not talking about a few forest fires or a maelstrom appearing where it should not; *No!* I am talking apocalyptic levels here, and recent events should show you *exactly* what I am talking about!"

Agatha took a deep breath and scanned the intensely alarmed expressions around her. She had never been a confrontational woman, taking the road of calm democracy above all others, but everyone present *had* to understand the possibilities and the dangers.

Calming, she softened her tone and continued:

"It was only a matter of time before the Magic flowed from her... no, let me clarify that: *burst* from her, and as we sit in our high mansions and conduct idle parlor tricks, Nyssa was bringing forth the Magic that all of us combined would have an effort in doing.

"Imagine the chaos if I didn't intervene?" Agatha paused so to allow the weight of the possibilities to settle on them all. "Visualize if she happened to be *in* downtown Chicago with millions of people milling about instead of several thousand in a sleepy suburb? Imagine something even direr; imagine if *'They'* end up instructing her and not us?

"Imagine the world then... *all of you!*"

For that moment, everyone, including Langdon Drellic, was picturing all that she had said in crystal, high-definition clarity.

Agatha sighed heavily and then continued:

"I had assumed that all of us with our given talents had moved beyond the ideologies of our common brethren." Agatha added quietly as she regained a calm heartbeat. "We all hear of it, all the time, and it is pathetic."

"What do you refer to, Lady Agatha?" Amora asked quietly with a guilty tone, and although Agatha's sharp words had not been directed towards her, the feeling was there, nonetheless.

"How often do we hear about things that are 'could of, should of and would have done situations?" Agatha replied, her eyes scanning. "How many times do we learn that those who have the power to make change only do so *after* something terrible happens?

"Just two weeks ago, a small child was run down in a street where all the residents in the neighborhood had complained about the traffic lights, and those of authority did nothing about it. Now, with a child's death on their hands, guess what? They put in new traffic lights, increasing the speeding fines in the area, and of course, more patrol cars are on the streets to catch violators."

"That is horrible," Amora whispered, her eyes lowered to her floor.

"Yes, tragic," Maynard added followed by accompanying nods all around.

"*That is us!*" Agatha said sharply, her palm striking the arm of the chair, startling them. "We are those people who have the authority and the power to challenge such things, yet we wait until it is knocking on our own front doors before we raise a finger to do anything about it.

"Our actions may never be Anathema, but they are surely lower and darker than theirs in our cowardice!"

Not even the clock on her wall dared to click out a sound. Marley had had enough of the sharp tones, and he jumped down from between Marco and Amora and disappeared out of projection.

Agatha breathed quickly, sitting upright again and attempting to slow her heavily beating pulse. She knew she didn't need to convince all of them of the obvious, but she damn well wanted to make sure that the message was sent home.

"And you have explained this to the girl—to Nyssa—all what she has done?" Angelica asked quietly; she was one of the ones who didn't need a lot of convincing that the sky was blue and the grass green, but she did require at times a little more explanation of the *Whys*.

"Of course," Agatha said calmly, her hands returning to the armrests. "She had every right to know what she has done."

"Right, right," Angelica nodded, her hand busy scribbling down notes (a persistent thing of the wise older teacher to do). "And has she been taught anything as of yet?"

"The six basic rules, yes," Agatha replied.

"*Oh!* Splendid then, splendid," Angelica smiled, producing a rapid nod to everyone 'present' as her hand scribbled so fast that it seemed blurred. "That is the most important step towards tutoring."

"Lady Agatha," Amora spoke softly, her tone showing respect in an awe-inspired fashion. "You know that Marco and I commend and fully support your efforts in this endeavor, but the one most important question needs to be answered, one I am sure even the Anathema is wondering now as well, but is—"

"Is she the Next Coming?" Agatha interjected with a question and all of them, save Langdon, replied with a slow nod.

"We all really need your guidance on this one, Lady A," Marco said quietly and attempting a soft smile to encourage her along. "I don't think anyone is prepared for the possibilities, maybe not even an answer."

Agatha slowed her thoughts, having come back upon the fork in the road of her mind. It had been more than twenty-five years since she had walked into that dorm room at college and felt the aura that could only be described as magical bliss, a mere tip of a teaspoon-taste of what *pure* Magic tasted like. For twenty-five years, her mind repeatedly tormented her soul with the same nagging question, and only now had she been put in a position to even dare to speak these thoughts publicly. Behind her eyes, she could only see Luther, her teacher, and mentor, shaking his head in rapid disapproval.

She sighed softly and laid it out for them all.

"For more than twenty-five years I have felt nothing less than surety that this girl's mother had a mana of pure Magic.

"Yes, this girl is the very one."

Agatha did not know what to expect as reaction whenever she dared to speak her thoughts, but what she got was a clear indication that she had at least accredited many of their fears.

Maynard tilted his head forward, his glasses sliding to the very tip of his nose, his eyes wide with disbelief; Angelica's hand froze in mid-stroke, and the pen between her fingers rolled away while her writing hand began to move instinctively, scribbling invisible jargon without the acknowledgment that there was no instrument to do so; Rusty's mouth worked so rapidly and uncontrolled as a combination of denial, nervous laughter, and faltering disapproval attempted to rush from his throat all at once, and sweat exploded on his forehead resembling large water droplets on a recently washed car; Amora gripped her husband's wrist so tightly that the edges of his knuckles began to pale, her head pressing firmly against his shoulder for comfort; Marco, on the other hand, simply smiled; excited to know that there was indeed a challenge in the life of Magic for them to handle.

As for Langdon, despite his mouth parting enough to see the shadowy shape of his motionless tongue, he simply lifted his cup and took another long, slow drink.

"So, the timeline is off, then?" Maynard asked Agatha directly while making several attempts to right his glasses without realizing that his head's downward angle was going to counter any such movements. "Magic really has been distorted over the millennia?"

"Yes, Maynard," Agatha said calmly, attempting to soothe his evidently rising nervousness. "The timeline is very off, more so in the last twenty or so years, and for that, I do not know why, nor does the lore. In the end, I am afraid that, in many ways, the lines of Magic have been broken. With that, so to calm your fears—if I am correct, and Nyssa is the Next Coming—she is also the one who can mend it."

"*If* she's the one," Langdon injected, his eyes narrow and burning at her from his projection.

"*If?*" Marco turned towards his projection and Agatha began to picture the two of them again going at it in some bizarre projected fisticuffs. "What more proof do you need, man?"

"Believe as you all wish and be fools with it!" Langdon stood quickly. "This girl is nothing more than a possessor of happenstance-Magic regardless to how lucky—or unlucky—she was to conjure the storm."

"Langdon you must see reason!" Amora protested.

"Reason to what?" he nearly laughed at the blear-witted possibility of the idea. "That this girl is one of the lost Vessels of Pure Magic?"

"*A Vessel?*" It was Rusty who spoke up, his eyes locked onto Agatha with pure hopeful wonder.

"Well, I see you even have the eccentric caster convinced," Langdon huffed, shaking his head in disbelief.

"Langdon, there is still much to be discussed," Agatha attempted, but she knew the response already before she even uttered a single word.

"Then I pray you all enjoy your little discussion," Langdon sneered and made a motion with his hand, blinking out his projection. If Agatha was sure of what she had seen, his hand held a single middle digit towards her as it moved.

"Well, I see Langdon still knows how to tantrum his way out of things," Marco added with a smile, breaking the sudden silence following Langdon's departure.

There was nervous laughter around the room; even Rusty took part in it, his vote cast with the majority that a Vessel indeed had surfaced.

Agatha smiled in response to the comical break in the mood, and slowly she lifted her own cup of robust black tea. As she sipped, her eyes trailed upwards toward the skylight, longing for a hint of her moon to grant her even the slightest sensation of peace.

All she got in return was darkness.

-2-

Besides the steady sound of falling rain, the house was quiet.

Nyssa and Seema were staring at each other from across the bedroom in anticipation; two sets of wide eyes and cheesy grins bore through the darkness. They were eagerly waiting for the right moment to open the casks and see what the visions had to show them.

Despite her on and off day, Nyssa had not forgotten about them.

"Now?" Nyssa whispered, excitement boiling in her belly.

"Not yet," Seema whispered back, hopping off her bed and moving silently to the door without so much as a creak. If you were a parent requiring a flaw such as a squeaking floorboard to alert you when your children were moving about when they should be in bed asleep, Luna House is not the place to raise them.

Floorboards never creak there.

Seema parted the door slightly and looked down the long hallways towards the opposite end of the house where Agatha's bedroom sat. The door was closed, and there was no other light save a very faint glow coming from underneath. Seema closed the door and moved towards the center of the room, where she stood at attention, taking a deep breath.

"A-hem, my dear sister, Nyssa, for your first night back at Luna House after many long years, I wish to announce that the Lady of the house has retired!"

Nyssa gave a rapid round of applause as Seema took the bottom edges of her long night shirt and produced a salutatory and thankful curtsy. In Nyssa's excitement, she stood next to her bed only to be stopped by Seema's outstretched palm, signing for her to *'Halt.'*

"Please sit for a moment, my dear audience of one," Seema announced loudly and proudly. "As I explain the magical wonders of the Night Casks and what resides inside!"

Nyssa sat back down with a playful pout and watched Seema move to the mantle, where she stopped to the side and held up two hands: oddly resembling a shorter, darker-haired version of Vanna White of *Wheel of Fortune* with her hands up towards the crystal eggs.

"Take a look audience! Yes, take a look at how beautifully crafted each cask is, and I would like to point out for you that there is no two exactly alike, nor are there any matching sets in all the world!"

"Yes, they are quite lovely," Nyssa added, performing the role of the captivated audience perfectly.

"Right you are, my lady, right you are!" Seema smiled widely, giving an extended pointing finger towards Nyssa to heighten the moment. "They are lovely, as they are rare, for this set—which goes by the name of... of... of Bob, is one of the last re—"

"Wait... what?" Nyssa interrupted; her head cocked to one side with a face full of curiosity. "Did you just say that the cask-set's name is *Bob?*"

"What?" Seema paused; eyes confused.

"Bob... you said the cask-set's name is Bob."

"Well, yes! Bob!" Seema proclaimed, attempting to get back into character.

216

"Well, isn't that an odd name for them?" Nyssa inquired, folding her arms with a doubtful expression on her face.

"Well… well…" Seema tried and then sighed, raising a single eyebrow towards Nyssa, and then continued flatly, the character gone. "Look, I couldn't come up with anything special for them, okay?"

"Okay," Nyssa replied sheepishly.

"You sure?" Seema reaffirmed and received rapid nodding from Nyssa as a reply. Seema raised her hands, palms up, her face expressing clearly *'Are you sure, you are sure?'* look, and Nyssa quietly did the silent invisible zipping of the lips, then turned the imaginary key and flicked it across the room. "So, we're good then?"

"Mm-hmm," Nyssa sounded through lips that were pinched so tightly that they disappeared.

Seema could not help but crack a smile and then she cleared her throat, bringing the character back.

"Alright then, providing there are no more comments from the Peanut Gallery—" Nyssa snorted out a laugh, covering her mouth with both hands, "—Bob here—" more snickering followed by a vise grip press of her hands over her mouth, "—Bob is one of the last remaining complete Night Cask sets in existence!

"Now, take a gander at this center cask egg," Seema flowed along the mantle with a fluid movement as she followed the directions of her own words. "This one here—"

"Is that one named Irving?" Nyssa cut in with the best foreign accent she could muster—the tone a mixture between that from West London and Northern Belfast—and then burst into a laughing fit.

Seema's hands shot to her hips as she glared at her, where Nyssa immediately performed the invisible zipper-lock-throw signs and placed her hands in her lap. Her face turned an odd shade of orange-red as she held her breath tightly to subdue the laughter. Seema rolled her eyes and then shot out a pointing index finger from her hip as if it were a gun in a quick draw showdown.

"I see we have ourselves a heckler in the audience," Seema sneered and then stood straight in her most proper stance and voice. "As a matter of fact, it is named *None of Your Business*, thank you very much."

That was it, laughter exploded between them and climbed until Seema squatted low to the floor, an index finger to her lips trying to hush them both up.

"Okay, okay, woo—" Seema gasped, attempting to calm herself. "—she'll hear us."

After a moment, laughter became giggles which soon became wide smiling with the occasional chuckle and eventually a simple exchange of digressive sighs.

"Alrighty then," Seema continued, wiping the laughter-borne tears from her eyes. "Now, the Casks are very special, and they are rumored to be of pure Magic, ancient remnants of that time when the world was flowing with it. A time when many of us were wizards and warlocks, simple mages and mongrels, and any female practitioner of Magic was known either as a witch, a bruja, an enchantress, a sorceress, or a hag.

"Personally, I don't think either one of us constitute being a hag, do you?"

"No, not at all," Nyssa firmly agreed, shaking her head to enunciate her claim.

"Me either," Seema said absently, her eyes moving up and to the right to ponder briefly. "However, an enchantress does sound rather intriguing.

"Anyway, first a little history," Seema licked her lips and began moving down the line of eggs explaining like a tour guide in a museum. "The Casks were crafted throughout the millennia, each in different regions of the world by people of Magic who—even though thousands of miles and hundreds of years separated them at times—suddenly had some sort of epiphany that they should craft one.

"If you think about it, it is almost like with the pyramids, you know? They all have the same basic shape but can be found all over the world, built by different cultures and sometimes centuries separating their conception but yet, there they are."

"I have often wondered about that myself," Nyssa was nodding, forehead bunched in thought. "Always thought that odd, pyramids that is."

"Me too," Seema sighed, then shook her hands to get back on track. "Anyway, when it comes down to the Casks, the creator would bestow a single, absolutely pure fundamental essence of Magic.

"And do you know what the odd thing is about the creator of each Cask once the Magic was bestowed?

Nyssa shook her head, captivated by the history lesson.

"Each and every one of them ceased to exist," Seema's eyes grew wide and moved hands and fingers in an exploding, scattering motion.

"What the...?" Nyssa squeaked. "They what: disintegrated?"

"No one knows," Seema shrugged. "All that is known is *Poof!* Gone! Never to be seen again, leaving only a glowing Cask where they once were."

Nyssa stared across the room at the Casks, her mind toiling with a morbid understanding and then her eyes grew wide.

"Are you telling me that those people, people of Magic, their ghosts are... are in those?"

"Maybe," Seema shrugged, regarding the one closest to her as it pulsated yellow. "As I said, no one really knows, but I will tell you this, later on as the world started to come together through travel and commerce—especially in the World of Magic—and mages spoke to other mages, and the old tales from one culture were told to another, people started putting two and two together and always coming up with one solution: Don't wanna go poof? Then don't build a Cask!"

"Thank you," Nyssa smiled and shivered as she pictured herself spending eternity in an egg. "Mental note taken, and it is locked in."

"Very good," Seema nodded. "Alright, now that we have a little historical information laid down, let's move on to introductions."

Seema moved to the far end of the mantle and struck another showroom pose; a hand extended loosely towards the first Cask which pulsated blue.

"This one is *Blef*, or Blue in Anglo-French, dating back to the thirteenth century making it one of the oldest surviving Casks in the world." She paused momentarily to allow it to sink into Nyssa's mind and then she continued down the line. "This next one is *Growan*, which is a derivative of the Old English word meaning to grow and hence the color, green."

Nyssa moved from her bed for a closer view, taking up a comfortable cross-legged position on the edge of the rug before the fireplace.

"Moving right along," Seema smiled, her hand gliding along the surface of the mantle and stopping before the bright pulsating yellow Cask. "This feisty guy here is *Yelwe*, Middle English for yellow."

"*Yelwe*, ha... that's cute!" Nyssa smiled.

"I think it thinks so too," Seema eyed it and moved on, skipping the larger center Cask, and then moving on to the next one. "Whenever you pay the slightest attention to it, it starts glowing like that."

"*Yelwe*, the spoiled one," Nyssa confirmed with a nod.

"You got it!" Seema laughed and continued. "Okay, this red baby here is *Erythros* which is Greek for as I am sure you have guessed it, *red*, and his neighboring buddy over here is *Kyanos*, another Greek native which means *cyan*.

"All I know is, if what happened to their creators is true, well, the Greeks didn't learn from their mistakes the first time."

"No kidding," Nyssa agreed wholeheartedly.

"And our last fellow is *Naranga* based off of the Sanskrit meaning for orange tree."

"What about the big one there?" Nyssa pointed towards the center Cask. "What's that one called?"

"Oh, that one," Seema sighed, taking a step back and knelt next to Nyssa on the floor. "Well, you wouldn't believe me if I told you."

"Sure, I will," Nyssa encouraged. "Promise."

"Well, you're going to laugh but, that's *Bobbe*."

"Bobby?" Nyssa looked at her as if she had gone insane. "As in Bob... really?"

"Yep, *Bobbe*, with an *E*," Seema smiled. "It derives from the Middle English word pronounced *bobbe*, which is akin to the word bob, which means a bunch or a cluster. The transitive meaning goes further to then mean—and don't you laugh—but transitive to *nosegay*, or, a bunch of flowers, hence the prism of colors."

Nyssa snorted a quick laugh and then studied the swirling, mingling multitude of colors coming from the Cask.

"Hmm, nosegay... bob... *Bobbe*... it fits."

"Yep, that it does," Seema agreed and the two admired the Casks in silence for a moment.

"Alright then," Nyssa looked at Seema with a smile. "Now that I know a little bit about them—and we have been properly introduced—what's next?"

"Simple," Seema shrugged. "We open one."

"That's it?"

"That's it," Seema smiled, standing, extending a hand down to Nyssa who took it and pulled herself up.

"No spells or anything?" Nyssa looked at her curiously.

"Nope, we just take one down and put it in the center of the floor and take the top off," Seema shrugged and moved towards the mantle with Nyssa in tow.

"That sounds too simple," Nyssa shook her head, unbelieving.

"I know, right?" Seema smiled, her eyes moving from one to the next.

"So how many have you ever opened?" Nyssa said in almost a whisper at Seema's shoulder.

"Well, all of them except for Bob here," Seema said, shrugging. "I guess I have been too chicken to open him up considering he has the colors of all of them in one place and I will put it like this, just one color is enough to deal with let alone a Vision that has everyone."

"I can see that," Nyssa nodded and then added: "When was the last time you opened one?"

"Oh, maybe about two years ago," Seema replied, thinking hard about the dateline. "They used to be in my old room, and Lady Agatha gave them to me not long after you and your family stopped visiting. You know when things got bad between your parents? She said they were a gift to cheer me up on nights when I was lonely."

"I am so sorry, Seema," Nyssa said softly, rubbing her shoulder.

"It's not your fault," Seema gave her a reassuring smile. "Nor anyone's fault really. Lady Agatha is and always will be as close as to being a mother I ever had, and she has always been a mother first, teacher second. You were the only thing I have ever had that closely resembled having a sister, so… well… anyway, which one?"

"I don't know," Nyssa said with heavy uncertainty, eyes moving from one to the next. "So, you just chose whichever?"

"Well, yeah, sort of," Seema paused, finding her words. "You see, each Vision shows you something differently, but not simply like looking at a television. You are actually *there!* As for me, I learned to open certain ones depending on my mood at the time because of what's going on in the Vision. Usually, the subject matter is the same, like *Blef* shows you incredible night scenes, while *Yelwe* tends to be bright day scenes, usually somewhere in Europe with castles and fluffy clouds.

"It has been said that they are remnants of what their creator's saw in their day-to-day lives, like going to the market, or the gentle breezes coming from a lake, or love's first kiss."

"Really?" Nyssa's tone was full of surprise. "You see it?"

"And feel it, almost as if you are inside the viewer," Seema nodded.

"So, odd question then," Nyssa pointed to two of them. "What if you were to open, let's say, *Blef* and *Naranga* simultaneously; what would happen?"

Seema laughed beside herself, "That's an interesting little story; when I was like eleven, I got pretty brave of myself, and I opened *Blef, Growan,* and *Erythros* one right after the other, and well, let me put it like this: after Lady Agatha herded them back into their proper Casks, I slept in the gazebo for a week while she rebuilt my room."

"You're kidding?" Nyssa's mouth dropped.

"Not at all," Seema smiled. "Lady Agatha then took them away from me until I was fourteen as punishment."

"Damn," Nyssa said in almost a whisper. "So, the Visions don't get along then?"

"Nope. Specters fight like little kids all wanting the same toy, but then again, they are a set. We know that they are a set even though they don't look anything alike, because they can only exist around the right kind of Cask, but once the tops are off, it is all about the right balance.

"Back then, if I had just opened let's say *Blef* and *Erythros*, everything would have been peaches and cream, but it was *Growan* who started it… didn't you *Growan?*"

The Cask, *Growan*, said nothing as a reply to the accusation.

"So, some can be opened together then?" Nyssa pushed on, curious.

"Oh, sure, but once again it is all about the right order and the right mood." Seema found herself staring into wide eyes of eager curiosity, the expression telling her she had better explain and quickly. "An example, take *Erythros*, he is red, the color of love as well as the color of rage and war, right?'

Nyssa nodded.

"Ok, let's say I come in and I am in a really bad funk. Usually, the best way to get out of a funk is to have wicked thoughts until you use up all the anger. In that case, *Erythros* is your candidate because it would show you just that. Same goes if you had a crush on someone and were feeling all giddy about it, well, there you have it; open *Erythros*."

"That seems pretty straight forward to me," Nyssa could not help but giggle.

"Precisely, but it makes me kind of wonder what kinds of lives did the creators live if the tales about these things are true, you know?"

Nyssa nodded in agreement.

"Anyway, the colors do match what humanity sets them out to be: green equals envy, red love, etcetera, so if your mood is off, it may show you things that you may not want to see, and if you combine them, you have to make sure that the mixture is right, or just like a selfish child, one will pit against the other for your attention.

"I could only imagine what would happen if you came in here with a broken heart, you know, red-with-rage but still in love with that person at the same time, a-k-a *Erythos*; the person you are in love with left you for another, so add *Growan* with envy; you feel all sweaty and nasty because the day was so bright and hot, now you have *Yelwe* and so on and so forth, but basically a cornucopia of moods and emotions, and *then* you open all of them. Man, imagine the mess!"

"You don't breathe much when you talk, do you?" Nyssa smiled and the two started to laugh.

"No, not really," Seema smiled, gulping two voluminous breaths. "You don't remember when we were little, I would talk so fast and so long that I would get dizzy and pass out?"

Nyssa almost screamed laughter, the memory bursting through her brain in 3D clarity.

"*Oh my god*, I almost forgot about that!" Nyssa was attempting to whisper but with little success. "I remember once you passed out on the tree swing and smacked your face on the ground!"

"Oh yeah!" Seema found a new memory too and attempted to choke back the laughter. "Too funny… well now it is. Then, it hurt something fierce."

"I know," Nyssa finished, and their laughter slowly idled away.

"So, what did you mean about them only existing around the right kind of Cask?" Nyssa inquired retrospectively.

"Well, it's kinda like you and me, really," Seema thought deeply. "If one of us happened to be a spoiled little brat who got whatever they wanted, let's say you and the other was a compassionate child who understood the word 'sharing,' etcetera, which is me, of course, well, we would have always been fighting and never wanted to see each other again.

"Just like friends, there must be the right fit, or there's no substance to the friendship."

"Hey!" Nyssa flicked the girl's knee, her face full of surprise and hurt. "That's not true!"

"I'm kidding, honest!" Seema attempted, producing a wide grin to show her sincerity.

"Fine! Brat! I get what you are saying," Nyssa huffed and returned a thin smile. "Besides your insults. In my case, my dad always tells me that there is a big difference between *'Friends'* and *'Associates'* and that he has very few *'Friends'* but lots of *'Associates'.*"

"Not sure if I follow you," Seema interpolated, a little lost.

"Well, what he says is right," Nyssa continued. "A *'Friend'* is someone you think about for no reason when they are not around, which is *not* you, and know you are thought of in return." — Nyssa stuck out her tongue at her sister quickly— "These are the ones you can count on being there when needed and they want nothing in return."

"You're being funny," Seemas attempted, but Nyssa continued.

"'*Associates*' are, I am referring to you now, are just another person on the street you have to deal with."

"*Touché, mon ami,*" Seema giggled, accepting the jibe. "I deserved that, but yes! Very good point! You really have a wise father."

"I know," Nyssa said with a comforting smile, her shoulders rising proudly.

"But I see your comparison and you are right," Seema nodded. "Most Casks are associates, but only so because they are an essence of Magic, and some are actually friends because there is a match. If they match, great, but just like friends, you can only have certain ones around other ones some of the times or in the right setting."

"Perfect, now it even makes more sense to me."

"And me as well," Nyssa concurred. "So, when these were being matched up, did someone have to do a trial-and-error process of elimination? You know, like put one Cask close to the other to see if they got along like pets?"

"Exactly," Seema nodded, happy to see Nyssa was seeing the World of Magic through clearer eyes. "And if it didn't match, they would push each other away like two magnets when the identical poles are facing one another. This process works until you have a set of seven, but never ever one more than that."

"Why not?"

"Have you ever heard of Chernobyl?" Seema's eyebrows rose.

"Of course," Nyssa nodded. "The nuclear plant that melted down in the Ukraine, everyone has."

"Well, you get the same kind of thing with Magic," Seema shrugged. "That's why you will never see a conference of magicians at some convention center. Also, as you have noticed, we are all taught the old way: Master and Apprentice and in rare cases like you, me, and Lady Agatha: Master and two Apprentices."

"Then that explains away my next question," Nyssa mumbled.

"Which was?"

"Well, I was wondering why, you know," Nyssa licked her lips, hunting for the right words. "Why didn't Auntie Agatha simply make some sort of school here? I mean, her house is big enough for like twelve, maybe even fifteen students. If Magic—goodly Magic—is out of balance, wouldn't that be the most logical thing to do? Teach them by the masses sort of thing."

"I know what you mean, but it doesn't work that way," Seema explained patiently. "Just like Chernobyl with the core melting down and everything, it happened because the control rods started to melt, and they could no longer contain the reaction as it reached critical mass.

"In our case, you cannot have all that Magic in one place at one time without it reacting against each other. In the old, *old* days, when Magic was everywhere, you could have a ton of magic folk loafing around, talking politics, and nothing would have happened. Then it was just commonplace because there was enough Magic to control the effect, much like how the control rods work in a reactor. Now, try to picture eight, nine or ten mages in one place, and all that

Magic flowing and intermingling and stewing and boiling, in the end—"

"*Boom!*" Nyssa finished her sentence and Seema nodded.

"Boom is right, and you wouldn't want to be there when that happens. The fear of it is even present when the two sides quarrel—which thankfully doesn't happen too often anymore save the other night at your house that is. What happened and what *should* have happened, didn't, which was odd to say the very least."

"I don't follow," Nyssa's forehead scrunched with confusion.

"There were dozens of mages coming to help," Seema licked her lips, her expression dire as her eyes widened unconsciously. "That 'boom' *should* have happened, perhaps so catastrophically, that your storm would have been an afterthought before we all were vaporized."

They sat silently for some time following the revelation.

"Anyway," Seema cleared her throat in an attempt to draw them both away from the murk of dread. "When there is a fight, and people on your side come to your aid, if the playing field is already balanced, which normally means someone is going to be the underdog in the fight, the arriving party must sit it out for fear of causing a reaction.

"There have been times in the past when quarreling mages had to do it kind of like tag-team wrestling." Seema smiled and then added. "Let me tell ya, it sure beats watching wrestling hands down."

"You've seen wrestling on TV?" Nyssa looked surprised.

"Many times," Seema produced a guilty smile. "Well, not directly. Don't tell Lady Agatha, but I sometimes pry through other people's eyes so I can see and experience things I am not allowed to.

"Man, I feel so sheltered sometimes."

"Yeah, I was kind of wondering that earlier, how you knew all the songs on my music player."

"Well, now you know," Seema smiled and stuck out a pinky. "Pinky-swear you won't tell?"

"Pinky-swear," Nyssa laughed, looping her pinky around Seema's and then they brought their knuckles together to seal the promise. "*Wow!* I haven't done that since I was a kid!"

"I know, me either!" Seema glowed.

"Okay, here's my quick rundown to see if I get it all:

"Seven Casks make a set, but only if they match up and never more than seven or boom?"

Seema nodded and Nyssa continued her roll.

"They all have weird names, which represent their color which in turn represents their moods, which in another turn means you have to have the same or similar mood to match their color which matches their mood or in a way you get a boom?"

Another Seema-nod and Nyssa kept on going.

"There can never be a school of Magic because if you were to pile up all that magic in one place, they will react badly towards one another and so then, once again, get a boom?"

"Big boom!" Seema nodded with a wide smile.

"Also, you have become a psycho disturbed eavesdropper who watches fake wrestling through other people's eyes and we both remember you face planting off the swing when we were kids.

"Did I miss anything?"

"Except for you to breathe yourself," Seema gave her a concerned look and then giggled. "Your face is all red."

"Yep," Nyssa said as she leaned forward; placing her head near her knees to catch her breath, her head filling with light, tingling air. "Forgot to breathe."

"I know that feeling," Seema giggled at her and with careful tiptoe steps, they inched closer to the mantle.

"Okay, all better now," Nyssa slowly stood erect, her eyes finding the Casks before her once again and whispered: "So when do I start learning all this *Magic*?"

"You are already learning," Seema whispered back with a smile and nudged her with her shoulder.

"So now we choose one?" Nyssa asked, excitedly.

"Now we choose one," Seema nodded.

"So, what kind of mood are you in right now?" Nyssa inquired, just to be sure.

"I am in a happy mood actually," Seema answered. "You?"

"A brilliant mood," Nyssa smiled.

"Alrighty then," Seema beamed.

"Alighty then," Nyssa echoed as she studied the Casks on the mantle, rubbing her hands together. "Now we choose."

-3-

"Mica!" A sharp whispering voice cut through the darkness, stirring her, and pulling her towards the edge of consciousness, but still far away and distant. *"Mica, wake up!"*

"Whu-what?" Mica mumbled as she peered through the haze that separated her dreams from consciousness and found Pia sitting on the edge of her bed, the woman's eyes holding fear.

"You have to wake up now, girl!" Pia was near panic in her tone and expression, and she shot a glance over her shoulder to the door.

"Pia, what's wrong?" Mica sat up quickly, her eyes darting about the shadows in her room.

"Shush, Mica! Keep quiet, but we have to go… *now!*" Pia took her by her wrists, pulled her out of bed and instantly the blood raced from Mica's head, splashing dizzy waves over her mind.

She faltered but regained, shaking her head to clear her mind.

"Did something happen?" Mica whispered back to those brilliant green eyes of Pia. "Where's Teacher?"

"Just get dressed," Pia pulled her towards her bureau and began snatching open drawers. "I will explain everything on the way."

Blinded by confusion and a rapidly rising flood of panic in her mind, Mica began pulling off her nightgown and pulling on clothes in a hectic frenzy.

*

"Where are we?" Mica begged as the aura from gating slowly dissipated and the shapes of large trees and the smell of open land filled the voids.

Pia didn't respond; she grabbed up Mica by her wrist and shuffled towards the outcropping of trees, nearly dragging her along.

Mica's eyes scanned everything around her to gain her bearings, but the one thing she knew clearly was they were no longer in the city. Pia pulled her along until they were but a few feet from the trees, where she paused, raising a hand towards the old oaks, her eyes deepening.

"*Fortificare!*" she commanded, and her fingertips sparked. Mica stood in awe at how the trees twisted and bent closer to one another, their branches intermingling and becoming quite the vegetative fortress. "Quickly, before they close off the gaps!"

She tugged on Mica's wrist, and they quickly moved towards the narrowing space between two large trunks, running the last steps just in time.

Pia was panting in the darkness,

"*Lucere!*" Pia commanded and bright light filled the outcropped fortress made of trees.

Mica looked about herself, her eyes finding the details of the space very confining, for every trunk had found another to wrap around and mold to; even the canopy above showed no gaps. Mica turned in a circle, her mouth hung open in amazement at what had been done, and she stopped to find Pia staring at her with wide eyes.

"We are safe, for now."

"From what, Pia?" Mica's voice came out nervous and small.

"From Lord Seth," Pia said flatly as she rummaged around in her shoulder bag. "Do you have your talisman?"

"N-no I left it back—" Mica stammered as blind confusion really set in.

"*Shit!*" Pia hissed, her hands coming up and covering her eyes for a moment. "We are so screwed! How do you expect to protect yourself, Mica?"

"*Pia what are you talking about?*" Mica was nearly screaming, her eyes rapidly shaking. "What do you mean safe from Teacher? What has happened?"

"We failed him, Mica," Pia said quietly, dropping her hands from her face.

"What do you mean we failed him?" Mica was almost crying.

"They got the girl," Pia explained, her voice cracking with fear. "And you failed to plant the seed in her mind. Seth is beyond pissed."

"Bu-but I can just explain that—"

"He is beyond hearing excuses, Mica," Pia said flatly. "He wants restitution."

"You mean Teacher is going to hurt us?" Mica's eyes were so wide with fear that they almost took up her entire face. She could feel her body shake uncontrollably and she suddenly wanted to throw up as her belly soured.

"No, Mica," Pia said solemnly. "He's going to kill us."

Hot tears began to roll the sides of Mica's cheeks in a steady flow, her body frozen with fear as she watched Pia move about the trees with her palms inspecting their protective barrier. Mica's mind rolled slowly like a spoon stirring thick beef stew, torturing her with the pains of guilt, terror, and remorse that Teacher, her teacher, was angry with her. She began scrolling through all the wrongs she had committed, finding many that got her a harsh scolding but never something dire enough to warrant real pain or the threat of death. She had witnessed retribution for failure in the eyes of the Anathema before, but those events were spawned by heavy financial losses or betrayal, never for simple things and never—

"Pia, I need to see Teacher," Mica cried, her face wet with tears and her nose running.

"Mica, do not think of him," Pia hissed, thundering down on her and shaking her by the shoulders. "It will make it easier for him to find us!"

"But Pia—" she began but was immediately silenced by a sharp open slap which rung in her ears.

"Enough!" Pia growled at her, their faces mere inches apart. Mica was holding her fiery cheek firmly, her eyes full of sudden shock and fear; she had just been assaulted, a thing no one had ever dared to do prior, making the situation all too real. "You need to stop thinking of apologies and start concerning yourself with living! He is not going to care about anything you have to say! You are lucky that I even came and got you before he showed up or you would be in pieces right now!"

Pieces? Mica's mind begged and began to picture it for her to see, forcing her stomach to double flop.

Slowly she stooped into a squatting position, her mind foggy and blurred as it begged for understanding and rationalization but finding none of it. Could the man who she thought of as a father have the intent of harming her?

No, her mind would not accept it; Pia must be confused; perhaps this was a training exercise; perhaps—

The fortress of trees began to tremble and creak, bringing down a shower of healthy leaves on their heads. A heavy moan came from one side, and the trunks started to bulge inward, flexing grotesquely until finally succumbing to the force on them with a sudden, explosive cracking. Heavy chunks of bark and ripe wood showered them like shrapnel from a bomb, and in the large hole from which the trees once grew stood Seth, his eyes blazing, his aura a pulsating blue.

"*Oh shit!*" Pia screamed, her green glowing hands coming up before her in a defensive posture.

"Never so right, Pia," Seth growled, his right hand coming up while the other held his silver case which was crackling blue fire.

The beginning of the end had come.

-4-

A kaleidoscope of colors burst from the top of the Cask as *Bobbe* erupted forth with such fury that the whole room seemed to shake with its energy. High-pitched whistles and swooshing sounds clipped the air as the colorful plasma masses dipped, spun, and shot through the air.

"*It's beautiful!*" Nyssa was screaming over the noise *Bobbe* made as it filled the room.

"*I know!*" Seema screamed back, her face a wide-open smile, her hands clapping to the display of Magic.

Bobbe clashed and splattered along the walls like the Indian celebration of *Holi* where large volumes of different colored *gulal* powder at them. They huddled together in excitement; their hair being tossed by an invisible wind as the colors whipped and burst around them.

"What happens now?" Nyssa screamed; the sounds *Bobbe* made resembled that of a passing freight train.

"You have to command it!" Mica screamed back. "Tell it to show you something!"

"Like what?" Nyssa shrieked with laughter.

"Anything!" Seema replied with her own laughter. Nyssa thought for a moment, her arms wrapped around Seema's waist, searching for something, *anything* that she could command the Vision to show her, but instead chose vagueness.

"Show us something grand!" she commanded and in a rapid fusing of colors, the whole bedroom faded away and became a splendid night scene of Paris.

Nyssa and Mica both gasped as they found themselves hovering over the skyline with at least a hundred feet of open French air beneath their feet and slowly they followed a prismatic ball of light which was *Bobbe* in tour guide form.

"Oh my God this is so amazing!" Nyssa gasped and slowly released the excited grip she had on Seema's waist.

"I know, right?" Seema responded through rapid giggles, playfully pedaling her feet in the emptiness.

"You can smell the restaurants!" Nyssa laughed.

"Smells wonderful!" Seema agreed, smiling as they soared, the winds rustling their clothing and hair as they approached the Eiffel Tower which was aglow in the distance.

"But it shouldn't be nighttime in Paris right now!" Nyssa called out to Seema who was almost touching distance away.

"I know," Seema nodded. "You told it to show you something grand so what could be grander than nighttime in Paris?"

"You're right!" Nyssa screamed back and then both of them screeched with joy when suddenly *Bobbe* dived downward with the two of them in tow.

-5-

Am I flying? Mica's mind asked her as the ground blurred under her and then filled with exploding fireworks as she slammed into a tree on the other side of the clearing.

Unconsciousness toyed with her, taunting her from the shadowy darkness that was creeping in on her with clingy hands and sharpened claws. Somewhere behind her in the clearing an awesome fight of Magic was underway, showering her with bits of plasma of various colors. There was a moment when she no longer knew who she was or where in time her life resided, but the sudden piercing scream from Pia brought reality back to her quickly.

She was in a clearing of some unknown field, and she was in the process of being murdered.

Slowly she crawled around on her hands and knees so to see what was going on behind her, her eyes blurry with tears and pain. She was panting heavily; the last blow of Magic had knocked the wind right out of her lungs and the fresh air returning to them burned like acid.

"No," she muttered with a bloody mouth, and she spat in attempts to free her voice that needed to beg.

Pia was pulling herself up from the ground, her hand pointing behind her where a thick rope of greenish plasma was projecting

239

towards Seth, who in turn was shielded by a giant blue orb encompassing him. He was smiling at Pia's attempt, holding him at bay but causing no damage; Pia, on the other hand, looked utterly disheveled, her hair a sweaty mess, and blood ran from an egg-shaped wound beneath her left eye. The orb surrounding Seth pulsed and flexed, and in one sudden wave, Pia's Magic backfired and struck her in the back, skipping her over the ground like a rock sent across a pond.

Mica took in a deep breath and screamed: *"Teacher no!"*

Seth's glow diminished in a blink, and he turned towards his fallen student and for a moment his heart wanted to split in two. He was there, as planned, hurting the one thing in life that he cared for and loved; a sadistic ruse so that he and the Anathema could remain on top.

'Stop listening to your heart!' Pia's mind screamed in his head; her projection so strong that he could feel the pain that she was experiencing now on the other side of the outcropping. *'It must be believable! You have to really hurt her!'*

Nodding, he slowly advanced on Mica, who had sat back on her haunches with both her hands up and fingers spread, a physical protest for him to stop. She was sobbing as her head shook in disbelief, and for each tear that fell and for every whimper that escaped her, Seth wanted to break his own back into a thousand pieces for what he had done and would do to the child.

"Tuh-tuh-teacher plu-plu-please stop," Mica begged, and all Seth's eyes could focus on was her badly bashed and bloody lips as they pleaded. "I am so suh-sorry… plu-please don't hu-hurt me anymore."

Seth paused, his body shaking, his soul damning him in every language that he knew and even in ones he did not. He wanted to cry himself, to snatch up his dear pupil and cuddle her in his arms, to beg for her forgiveness and explain everything to her. Seth knew that he could not do any of these things if the plan was to work. He knew that he had to break her.

Slowly he bent and gripped Mica by her hair and pulled her up; the whole time she attempted to touch and hold him, her eyes and mouth begging for his affection.

"You have failed, Mica," he spoke through clenched teeth, the whole time he wanted to scream as he pulled his own teeth out.

"For-forgive me, please?" Mica was near hysterical, sending daggers through Seth's soul. "I am so sorry!"

"I am the one who's sorry, Mica," Seth whispered and closed his eyes.

Suddenly Mica began to shake violently and scream as pure Magic flowed from Seth's hands into the girl. Her whole body blazed with the feeling of ground glass searing through every fiber of her body as she slowly rose in the air several feet; the Magic of Seth now born by pure disdain for his own actions.

"Father!" she screamed as consciousness dissipated, her mind racing to that dead place where everyone eventually goes.

Seth released an animalistic roar and pushed the Magic away, sending Mica soaring across the clearing.

He could bear this no more and all went quiet in the clearing.

Seth was panting as he stood with clenched fists, his eyes pinched shut and daring not to look at what he had done. Slowly the lids parted, and he sought the distance where his little pupil lay in a smoldering heap.

"My dear Mica," he whispered and crossed the clearing quickly and stopped short as she came into clear view. She was breathing ever so slightly, the air entering and escaping her lungs in a raspy congested wheezing, her body broken and singed by his Magic and her soul obliterated by his betrayal. "What have I done?"

"What was needed to be done, dear Seth," Pia's voice came from behind him, and his head snapped towards her, his skin warping and bulging with rage.

"Say nothing to me, woman!" he growled, attempting to control the metamorphosis his body begged to undergo; to bear that creature from his dark mana which had been twisted and warped after decades of practicing Dark Magic. He wanted to show her what it looked like when it was looking at her; oh, he wanted it to come so badly and to teach the woman once and for all what pure rage looked and felt like.

"Calm yourself, Seth," Pia snapped back, adjusting her grip on her battered arm. "Mica lives, and we will move on and soon we will have the girl in our ranks and put this all behind us."

"I should have never listened to you and found another way!" he barked, slowly squatting next to Mica, his fingertips on her cheek.

"There was no other way," Pia said softly behind him. "We must go."

"Mica, I am so sorry," he whispered, moving matted hair from in front of her partially closed eyes.

"Are you sure that they saw this?" he demanded.

"Yes, Seth, they saw it," Pia nodded.

"They had better!" he snapped, turning his head, and peering right through Pia's eyes. "For if I have done all this for naught you will truly know what it means to piss me off!"

"They have seen it," she insisted. "And we had better be gone before they get here."

Seth turned back to his fallen pupil, his heart aching with every wheeze that escaped her lips. Pia centered herself in the clearing and closed her eyes, waving a hand before her and opened a portal gate.

"Do not take too long," she whispered and stepped through the gate.

Seth leaned forward and kissed Mica on her sweat-soaked forehead, trembling with rage and remorse.

"I pray you will understand all this someday, my dear Mica."

Slowly he stood and walked towards the portal gate, never looking back.

-6-

They swooped in low over the tops of café umbrellas, and although they were technically not there, their passing rustled napkins from the tables and sent them into flight. Over cars and lovers holding hands, they flew, dipping under streetlamps and climbing over buildings. *Bobbe* pulsated rapidly, and the vision before them changed, and from one moment, they were speeding along the streets of Paris to the next, they were buzzing the tops of raised plateaus of the Grand Canyon.

It was daylight now, and the multicolored layers of aged carved stone of the canyon swept under them, their forms never casting a reflection on the Colorado River beneath them.

They felt like eagles soaring with the ground and heavens at their disposal for pure amusement.

"This is so amazing!" Nyssa burst out in awe as she looked at Seema who was nodding rapidly with a wide cheesy grin.

They rose high and slowed over the mass of the canyon itself, and everything calmed to a gentle hover as they took in the pure splendor of it all.

"I could just stay here forever."

"I am with you there," Seema agreed. "Look there's people rafting down there."

"Think they can see us?" Nyssa asked quietly.

"Nah, we are really not here," Seema explained and slowly hovered closer to Nyssa. "Technically, we are probably staring at the rug on the floor right now."

"This is so weird," Nyssa mumbled and kicked her feet several times for clarity. She never felt the floor and was happy to know that some visions could seem more than real.

Colored lights flashed and flickered to their right like lightning in the distance, drawing their eyes.

"Huh?" Nyssa sounded and they maneuvered themselves to look. In the distance was an anomaly; an outcropping of trees sitting in a wide-open grassy field and the air around it was a blanket of night filled with twinkling stars.

From beneath the canopy of trees bright bursts of multicolored plasma streaked forth as if fireworks were being set off.

"What's that?"

"I don't know," Seema squinted towards the distance. "*Bobbe*: what is that you show us?"

Bobbe didn't reply; it simply pulsed twice and then slowly moved towards the outcropping, pulling the girls along. As they neared, the explosive display took on sounds, and somewhere through it came screaming, and even worse, something was roaring. *Bobbe* brought them directly above the outcropping, and the canopy parted, and what they saw below them was pure horrifying chaos.

The woman Nyssa had seen on the bus the day she had brought the storm was deflecting a barrage of blue bolts streaking towards her, sending them off in all directions that exploded when they encountered the surrounding trees or ground. There was a man Nyssa could have sworn she had seen before, firing blue daggers from his hands as he advanced on the woman.

"I know that girl!" Nyssa gasped past her pressing hands. "Her name is Mica!"

"I know her too!" Seema squeaked, terrified. "That's Seth's pupil!"

"What is he doing to them?" Nyssa begged, confused. "Is this how they train?"

"*No!*" Seema blurted out, her head shaking rapidly. "This is not training at all! He's fighting them!"

"Holy crap!" Nyssa screamed as she saw Seth make a gripping motion in the air towards the older woman and squeezed, her face shooting towards the sky in pain as her body rose into the air.

He motioned to the left, followed by the woman's body as if attached by marionette strings and then quickly thrust his clenched hand towards Mica and the woman flew that direction, slamming directly into the girl who turned in time to catch the weight full force. Upon impact the two tumbled through the air like bowling pins, landing with heavy thuds.

"Is this really happening?"

"Yes!" Seema called to her.

"Can't we do anything?" Nyssa begged.

"No!" Seema cried back, her hands at her own throat, unbelieving what she was witnessing. "As I said we are not really here!"

"But he's killing them!" Nyssa cried, tears filling her eyes as she looked down on the torment below.

Seth made a wide circle motion with his arm and as it came around, a blue pulse leaped from his hand, striking Mica in the chest, throwing her backwards.

"I don't want to see this anymore!"

"Bobbe!" Seema screamed at the orb which was pulsating softly nearby. *"Take us home!"*

Bobbe pulsed and flashed, speeding up and becoming almost blinding and everything before their eyes blurred, accompanied by a heavy static sound and the voice of Mica screaming after them *'No!'*

*

They were standing in their bedroom, their bodies trembling with fear and their eyes locked onto each other's, their faces damp from tears. Seema bent and retrieved the top to the Cask and set it in place, locking *Bobbe* away in his home.

Neither one spoke a word, their minds unable to find the steps to fulfill such a task, but they nodded to each other and then shot towards the bedroom door, screaming for Agatha.

CHAPTER FOURTEEN

Exigency

-1-

"Agatha!" They both screamed as they burst into her room, their faces sweaty and eyes terrified. She was standing near the windows talking to Marco and Amora who were there in physical presence, and in Marco's hand he held his pocket watch which was glowing brightly in between his clenching fingers.

"We already know, girls," Agatha said solemnly to them as they stood stark in the doorway. She turned back to Marco, placing her hand on his shoulder. "You must get to the girl quickly, Marco."

"I will," he nodded, his voice serious.

"Take heed," Agatha said, gripping his shoulder for strength. "He may still be there."

"I will be ready if he is," he nodded, stepping away from Agatha.

"I have already summoned Angelica," she whispered. "She will be here when you return with the girl."

"Let us hope that her services will be needed," Marco replied solemnly and then nodded as the watch pulsed once and the two of them were gone.

"Auntie Agatha," Nyssa was shaking as her tears ran. "It was horrible!"

"I know sweetheart," Agatha said, raising her arms to the girls who ran and flung themselves into her bosom.

"He was killing them!" Seema sobbed, her mind a mess.

"Let us pray that he was not successful," she whispered to the girls' heads, rocking them back and forth. She turned her head towards the windows as dread crept along her limbs making her numb.

How I want to see my moon, she thought to herself, closing her eyes, and resting her cheek on their heads.

-2-

"She's alive," Marco said quietly over his shoulder towards Amora who was standing guard with her hand held high above her head with an orange glow providing much needed light. "Barely."

"Where is the other?" Amora mused, scanning the trees around them. "That minx-woman, Pia?"

"Don't know," Marco shrugged, gently turning Mica's head by her chin. There was a nasty purple bruise covering the left side of the girl's face which was mostly masqueraded by a tacky layer of drying blood. "Knowing her she turned tail and ran, leaving the girl to die."

"Is she going to live?" Amora asked with a flat tone, her focus on her eyes and ears for any warning that would provoke her mana.

"Don't know that either," he replied and then slowly gathered Mica up as delicately as he could. "What did you do to provoke Seth's rage, little one?"

He straightened, seeking direction, the mere effort drawing out an unconscious whimper of pain from the girl's throat as shattered bones ground together. Marco made several '*Hush*'-ing sounds and then bettered his grip.

"We must get her back quickly," he said turning to his wife who nodded and flashed the ground with her hand, and they were gone.

-3-

"Quickly, take the child to Seema's old room," Agatha directed rapidly as they appeared in her study.

Without a word, they moved hastily down the hallway led by Seema.

Marco gently placed Mica on the bed and was shoved out of the way by Angelica who set a large handbag on the mattress.

"Oh, my child, what did he do to you?" Angelica whispered and placed her palm on the girl's chest and then forehead. "That bastard was really trying to kill this child!"

"We know," Nyssa whimpered, gripping Seema's hand for support. "It was so horrible! She was begging him to stop!"

"You two: out!" Angelica nipped at them. "This is no place for young people to be right now!"

"Yes, Seema, take Nyssa to your room," Agatha insisted, taking them by their backs and ushering them towards the door.

"Muh-mercy please?" Mica whimpered unconsciously and then began to convulse.

"Agatha please get them out of here!" Angelica demanded and began to rummage in her bag. "Marco, I will need a lot of hot water!"

"Right!" Marco nodded and moved out of the room quickly, followed by Amora who eased herself in between Agatha and the girls and placed her hands on the small of their backs.

"I will tend to the girls, Lady Agatha," Amora insisted and continued the ushering movement. "Stay and assist Angelica."

There was little protest from the two, and despite the morbid fascination which spurred their curiosity to want to stay and watch, both were happy that they were being forced to leave.

Seema was sobbing as they moved along the hallway, joined by Nyssa whose tears ran silently. Amora was gently rubbing both of their backs to comfort them, and once inside the bedroom, she moved them both to Nyssa's bed where they sat holding each other's hand.

"Is Angelica going to be able to help her, Amora?" Seema begged with her mouth and her eyes. Amora's eyes moved from one set to the other of pleading eyes, not wanting to lie to them but not wanting to tell the truth either.

After a moment Amora took a stool from the end of the bed and sat on it, releasing a long sigh.

"I really don't know, girls," she said quietly, her eyes finding her knees and not wanting to look into those pleading eyes any longer. "She's in really bad shape. If she had been attacked by another I would say yes in a heartbeat, but this is Seth's Magic; it doesn't come much viler than that."

"What of the woman," Nyssa asked eagerly. "There was another one there fighting him."

"Pia," Amora nodded and then shrugged. "There was no sign of her. She either fled the area or—"

"He blew her up?" Nyssa finished Amora's sentence and got a slow nod as a reply.

"It was so horrible," Seema sobbed, slamming her face into Nyssa's shoulder.

"I know girls," Amora soothed as she nudged her way between them, holding both of them in her arms with slow, gentle rocking. "I am so sorry that either of you had to witness such a thing."

As Angelica worked her healing Magic on Mica, using Marco as her gopher for every little thing she needed, and as Agatha projected out to the dozens of other members of the Consortia, Amora sat on the bed, rocking them until both had fallen asleep.

Quietly, Amora maneuvered them both under Nyssa's blanket and tucked them in, then gently petted their hair with her hand as she sat on the bed's edge. She considered letting them sleep alone, safely tucked in the bed, as she went to assist Angelica in any way needed but then thought against it.

She was looking at the Cask and at *Bobbe's* aura inside it. She was familiar with *Night Casks* because she had three of them herself when she was a child, but never had they ever shown the viewer terrors such as the one he showed the girls that late night.

In the end, she had a sensation of mistrust crawling her skin that night in the bedroom, and quietly without disturbing their slumber, Amora cast them to the *Yondsphere* and then took a seat on the stool, standing guard over the girls.

It was going to be a long, long night.

-4-

Pia limped into the guest bedroom of Seth's home and flicked on the light next to the bed. She jumped, startled, to find Seth standing next to the doorway, his eyes locked onto her with a wicked smile.

"Seth, you scared me!" she panted and attempted a smile. "So-so they have, umm, collected Mica and—"

"I know," he said calmly and slowly shut the door. "Your plan is working to the letter, I am impressed."

"Oh, well, thank you," she stammered out, her pulse racing as she watched Seth slowly cross the room towards her, his eyes bright blue. "In a week she will be up just like new."

"Yes, she has always been a fast healer," Seth said quietly, his grin widening. "But you know, there is something missing from your scheme."

"There is?" Pia's voice came out high pitched, almost whiney. "What did we miss?"

"The part I am going to rectify now, Pia," he said, his voice climbing to a growl. "The part about me hurting you twice as much as I hurt my Mica!"

Pia's screams raced down the hallways of Seth Manor, shaking glasses in the kitchen and trembling plants in their pots in the living room and oh how was Seth taking pleasure in what he was doing, just as Pia had foretold that he would.

By the time he would be finished with her, it might be two weeks before she would feel anywhere like new again; perhaps even a month.

CHAPTER FIFTEEN

Waiting Days

-1-

It had been two days since the arrival of Mica and two long days of waiting.

Nyssa and Seema were sitting on the grass near the Fairy Garden, practicing simple Magic by moving small stones. Seema had expressed that Nyssa's gift was similar to hers; being a myriad caster meant she could do almost anything.

"Don't focus too hard on making the stone move," Seema explained. "The stone has its own energy and doesn't need yours. All you need to do is to coax the stone's energy a little, just a nudge, and it will take over from there."

"It's mana?" Nyssa conjectured, her brow a lined ridgeline full of curiosity.

"Mana, exactly!" Seema smiled brightly.

"Ok, I am not sure that I understand this 'mana' thing," Nyssa shook her head while her eyes moved from between the rocks and Seema's eyes. "Doesn't it just mean Magic?"

"No, it's not the same thing but they are related," Seema sat forward, and she had no problem translating Nyssa's confused face to mean that more information had to be given. "Put it like this, it is kind of like the Soul, but not so much in a Biblical sense."

"Like, *The Force?*" Nyssa chirped.

"In many ways, I suppose," Seema shrugged. "But I'm more of a Trekkie, but yeah kinda like that."

"I'm with you," Nyssa smiled dryly. The heavy mood of the day weighed heavily.

"You see, mana is an energy that resides in everything: people, animals, and even inanimate objects like the stones here. It is what makes up everything in the universe, right down to the atoms and quarks for they too have mana. It's the life energy which has many mythological names depending on where you are from.

"The Welsh called it *'awen'*, the Aborigines called it *'maban'* and the Greeks referred to it as *'ichor.'* Regardless of what it is called, it is still mana, and we all have it."

"It's just some of us," Nyssa hypothesized, eyes narrowing. "Like you and me, we just have a stronger version of it?"

"Yep," Seema smiled as the creases along Nyssa's brow smoothed. "I think you are getting it."

"So, in theory, that is the basic point to all of it?" Nyssa looked up; her face twisted with curiosity. "I mean Magic in general; just use the mana inside of something to do what you want?"

"In most cases, yes," Seema nodded. "If they are directly linked to the four elements of life then absolutely, but many things in life contain several if not all of the elements, you just need to learn which one to manipulate."

"So then with fire for instance," Nyssa's mind began to shape the information into common sense. "Fire is an element of life, but it also uses other things to be fire: air to breathe and earth to eat, well, things of the earth to feed upon like wood."

"Exactly!" Seema smiled.

"Odd really," Nyssa said absently.

"How's that?" Seema inquired, curiously.

"Well, this past year we had to do a paper on whether Fire was alive or not," Nyssa sat up, stretching her back. "If you think about it, Fire has all the characteristics defining life: it eats, breathes, and even reproduces. Most of the class did their papers on the fact that Fire is not alive, and it is simply a form of energy, whereas I, and only three other people, debated that it was alive, even though it doesn't show any signs of intelligence."

"What grade did you get on your paper?" Seema inquired.

"I got a B-minus," Nyssa shrugged, her eyes scanning the small stones between them. "It should have been an A, but my teacher said my paper should have been longer to express my point. Oh well."

"Yeah," Seema agreed, not knowing, but she understood. "Well, basically, then you have the elements of life down pat if you can see beyond the world of science and identify the life force in something. I just find it odd that most people are ignorant of the fact."

"I know, right?" Nyssa agreed. "It's kind of like with water. I once told my mom something my dad had told me when I was ten. How the same water you are drinking from the tap is what dinosaurs used to drink millions of years ago. She thought both of us were bonkers."

"It's the same water?" Seema's eyes grew wide.

"Yep," Nyssa smiled.

"That is too cool!" Seema giggled, liking the idea that she and a brontosaurus once shared the same gulp of fine H_2O.

"I know! My dad explained that: save being struck by an icy comet, all the water we will ever have is here right now, and we should take steps to preserve it if we want to preserve ourselves. He's really nature-conscious like that. I mean, he's not a tree hugger or anything, and he jokes that if you want to save a tree, then eat a beaver."

The two of them roared laughter until their sides hurt.

"Too funny," Seema snorted. *"Eat a beaver.'* I wouldn't tell that joke to Lady Agatha if I were you; she's beyond a nature lover."

"I won't," Nyssa shook her head, smiling. "You know, I have been curious about one thing."

"What's that?" Seema sounded, placing the rocks in the shape of a circle.

"Why doesn't Auntie Agatha have any kids? I mean, she's a very beautiful woman and I am sure there are men who would flock to her."

"Well," Seema licked her lips and sat upright, leaning back on her hands. "There are people of Magic and then there are *People of Magic*, and many of them in the world don't even know that they have the gift."

That familiar bunching along Nyssa's brow formed again to show her confusion.

"Let me backtrack a little first so you will better understand," Seema took a deep breath, palms down as she focused. "The World of Magic is divided into two basic types: *Simplus,* or those having simple Magic like being a Seer or a Healer, and then there are those like Lady Agatha, you, me, and that Mica girl upstairs who are known as *Myriads,* or those who possess many gifts of Magic."

"So that girl, Mica, is kinda like you and me?" Nyssa attempted.

"Pretty much the same other than what method she has been taught," Seema winked at her. "But you see, it does go a little bit deeper than that."

"How so?" Nyssa said quickly as she made another attempt at the stones.

"Well, look at me and you," Seema explained. "We were both born with what is called Good Mana in our beings, so we will attract those instructors who are also good. When Mica was young and taken in by Seth and the Anathema, she would have had to have possessed Bad Mana. We call a female *noviciatus* of bad-mana, *Mala,* or Spanish for 'bad.'"

"*Wait!*" Nyssa said excitedly. "That's what Amora called me when I first met her and Marco and their dog. She said I was a novu-novi—"

"A *noviciatus,*" Seema giggled. "She called you a 'newbie.'"

Seema broke into a wild fit of laughter and fell backwards into the grass.

"That is too rich!" Seema guffawed, covering her mouth with her hands.

"Ha-ha, very funny," Nyssa said, sticking her tongue out at her. "So, I am a newbie, so what?"

"Oh, relax," Seema smiled, nudging Nyssa's knee. "We all have to start off somewhere. I might have had more instruction than you have, but I am far from being considered a serious mage, let alone an arch-mage."

"Fine," Nyssa sighed, pretending to be mad. "Anyways, so then how does this explain Auntie Agatha and no kids?"

"Well, a Myriad—one who is also very powerful—can never have children," Seema shrugged.

"Why not?" Nyssa sounded shocked.

"It has something to do with the Magic," Seema shrugged again. "It makes the body sterile because it consumes us entirely."

"So, then that means you and I, well..." Nyssa managed to mutter.

"More than likely, no," Seema sighed. "We will probably not be able to have them either."

"Well then, that will make my mom happy to know," Nyssa said solemnly. "As soon as I started liking boys. That was one of the main fears that one day I'd come home and am like, 'Hello Mom, guess what? You are going to be a grandma.'"

"*Really?*" Seema asked with a twisted look of disbelief on her face.

"Yes really," Nyssa said leaning forward. "The idea of sex is so far from my mind that the only way I could get pregnant now is by Divine will, and well, after what you just told me, I guess that might not happen either."

"Sorry," Seema said quietly. "But you did want to know."

"No, I am fine with it I suppose," she shrugged. "There are always plenty of kids in the world who need adopting; lots of them in our own country."

"Absolutely," Seema smiled. "Just look at me, if it wasn't for Lady Agatha, well, who knows what would have happened to me."

"How did you happen to come under Auntie Agatha's care?" Nyssa questioned along the new line of the conversation. "If it's not too personal that is."

"No, it's fine," Seema sat forward and took a deep breath. "In my case, I was just about three years old when an earthquake ripped my small town in Pakistan, killing my family. I don't have any memories of it, but Lady Agatha told me that I used to have some wicked nightmares about it when I was little. Lady Agatha arrived in the area later that day after she sensed a great rift in the air of Magic, and she gated there to investigate."

"And that rift, was you?" Nyssa assumed.

"Exactly: Me," Seema smiled gently. "She found me under my crumbled house, screaming at the top of my lungs with the whole building collapsed into a shell around me. She said my mana was pouring out of me so thickly that she could *see* it flowing in streams and stop looking at me weirdly... I didn't cause the earthquake. It was a natural thing."

"I wasn't thinking anything," Nyssa whined, her palms coming up flat showing that she posed no threat. "Never crossed my mind, honest!"

"Uh-huh," Seema said through her twisting mouth.

"However, you did blow up my house," Nyssa added, and the two shared a brief burst of laughter with that, and Seema tossed a stone toward her. Out of pure reflexive actions, Nyssa shot up a hand to deflect it, and the rock zipped away with a soft hissing sound like a bullet having never touched a thing.

"Did you see that?" Nyssa squealed; her eyes wide and mouth hanging open.

"Yes, I did!" Seema laughed, astounded. "Man, you did that without even trying!"

"That was so cool!" Nyssa giggled; her eyes locked in the general direction that it went. "And it was so easy! I didn't feel a thing but a wisp of a nudge."

"Want me to throw a bigger one at you to see if you can do it again?" Seema proposed, producing a sinister smile.

"Umm, no," Nyssa shook her head. "I don't think I will take my chances on that one."

"Good idea," Seema giggled, and was soon joined by Nyssa's sounds of amusement.

-2-

Nyssa had been closely following Seema's instructions, but her mind toiled over the mounting questions which begged for answers.

"So then how did this Seth guy get Mica?" she asked flatly, breaking the concentration of the tutoring session. "Did he find her under a pile of bad cabbage or something?"

Seema fell quiet, her eyes locked onto Nyssa's with a desperate look of determination.

"What?" Nyssa laughed.

"Really want to know?" Seema asked her and Nyssa nodded. "Alright, here it goes, but it's not pretty.

"When the Anathema detects a child of Magic, regardless of the will of the child's mana, they take the child by force, and if that means killing the parents in the process, so be it; all the better to them."

Nyssa's mouth was a cavernous space of silence as her head shook slowly in disbelief, "So you are telling me Mica was kidnapped?"

"Yep," Seema nodded, leaning back on her hands.

"What happened to her parents?" Nyssa said, her voice cracking with disbelief.

"I don't know," Seema shrugged. "I don't think anyone does, other than Seth. For all I know he could have simply stolen her away in the night, who knows. Maybe he did it forcibly, which is more of a senior dark mage's way of doing things."

"Do you think she knows this?"

"More than likely: no," Seema answered. "If you ask her, she will probably tell you that she was an orphan or was abandoned by a mother who left her to fend for herself. Regardless of what she tells you, you can be certain that something darker is in the center of the truth. I don't think it would be in the best interest of Anathemians to tell their pupils that they murdered their parents, and *voilà!* Here you are!

"It's sad really." Seema finished with a soft sigh.

"So why do you think he did that to her?" Nyssa pressed on in an attempt to match morbidity with common sense, her voice quiet as a whisper. "I mean, you know, trying to kill her?"

"Well, she was one of the ones trying to convert you," Seema said. "I suppose after the butt-kicking Lady Agatha and I gave him, he had had enough. The Anathema's method of punishment for failure usually results in someone's death."

"I am glad I am not with them then," Nyssa shook her head in disbelief.

"Isn't that the truth," Seema agreed.

"So, what happens now with her?" Nyssa asked. "I mean once she is all healed up and such."

"I don't know," Seema sighed. "I suppose Lady Agatha will take her in and probably attempt to persuade the 'mala' out of her."

"Can that really be done? I mean, if her mana is bad, can she be converted?"

"Sure, it can" Seema nodded. "We haven't reached our maturity yet and until then we can be coaxed in either direction."

"I don't follow," Nyssa shook her head.

"Let's put it like this," Seema sat forward again and spoke while using her hands to help enunciate her point. "One of the reasons a teacher keeps their pupils so close to them is so that they cannot be swayed by another, especially someone from their own order who may want the pupil for their own. People of Magic can be selfish sometimes, and I heard Lady Agatha once refer to it as being about as tempting as a shiny object to a kleptomaniac.

"You don't see that happening too often with the Consortia—I mean, it *does* happen occasionally—but the Anathema has been known to magically fight over a brightly gifted child. Lady Agatha once told me that the Archimage who possesses a gifted child has been known to simply kill him or her to avoid any drastic confrontations."

"*Shit!*" Nyssa gasped.

"Shit is right," Seema nodded, her eyes darting about herself to ensure no one could hear her '*French.*'. "For us Myriads, we are even more sought after because no one really knows what our limitations are, and much like the hungry klepto, the arch-mages are salivating over our potential worth. We are targets, especially by the Anathema, hence why I have been homeschooled, and I am rarely out of direct sight of Lady Agatha.

"In your case, you were hidden even before you were born, and Lady Agatha always kept a close eye on your mother."

"What do you mean '*a close eye*'?" Nyssa's voice questioned with a defensive, interrogating tone, her brow rising. "You mean when they were in college together?"

"Well then and afterward as well," Seema continued with a slight error of caution brought on by Nyssa's tone. "You know… when your mom was carrying you and after you were born. Kind of part of the reason you and your family vacationed here so much."

"So, Auntie Agatha isn't really my mom's friend?" Nyssa sneered as she pushed defensively for her mother's good name.

"Oh no! They are great friends!" Seema shook her head, realizing that her words did not come out as intended, bringing a cold sweat to her skin. "I mean, it was pure luck that they ended up roommates, and yes, at first, she got to know your mom really well to keep watch of her, but regardless, it didn't stop them from becoming close. I don't think Lady Agatha intended any harm by staying close over the years, I mean, she loves you and your family, but she also was trying to protect them. I mean, if the Anathema knew of you, then all of you were in grave danger, don't you see?"

"Yeah, I guess so," Nyssa said sourly, then shrugged, and a sudden pang of guilt hit her in the midsection when her mind realized that people standing guard like Auntie Agatha, Marco, and Amora were putting their lives in danger by simply protecting her. "So, I was hidden then?"

"That was the plan," Seema said softly. "The idea was that you would reach maturity at eighteen, which would make you un-teachable, hence protecting you from this world. After that, you would be *special*, not Jerry Lewis special, but special in your own right. You know, you might be one of those people who always got what they wanted, always had the best streaks of luck, or maybe the type who could always find what was lost but no *real* Magic.

"That was the hope at least but then, well, you kind of blew your top and invoked a tropical storm where it did not belong."

"Yeah, I suppose that would get a lot of people looking my way, huh?" Nyssa said, producing a wicked smile.

"Yep," Seema giggled at the thought of the storm. "And personally, it wouldn't matter what discipline of Magic I was teaching, I wouldn't make someone like *you* my student who could do that."

"Oh hush!" Nyssa snapped, poking Seema on the knee with her finger and the two began to laugh.

-3-

"So, here's the thing I am quite curious about," Nyssa leaned forward, her eyes narrowing and focusing on the dilemma on her mind, and Seema carefully allowed the small flame she had invoked in her palm to die away.

"Sure, what's up?" Seema smiled; she did enjoy being a junior teacher after all.

"I am a person of Magic, just as you are, and that girl Mica is and of course, so are people like Auntie Agatha, Marco, Amora and Angelica, right?"

"Duh!" Seema sounded and giggled.

"Well, if we are magical," Nyssa continued while ignoring her sarcasm. "Does this mean our parents or someone in our bloodline are magical as well?"

"Ahh, excellent question!" Seema nodded, feeling slightly bad for her sarcasm. "You know, when Lady Agatha explained what had happened to my parents in Pakistan, I wondered the same thing myself. I was like: 'If Magic saved me, and I am my parent's child, why didn't they have powers to save them as well?'

"She broke it down like this—sort of like I kind of explained to you—that all of us have mana, just some of us shine more. I had assumed that at least one of your parents, or maybe even your grandparents, had to have been mage or archmage in order, you know... their kids to also, *have it?*

"But no, we are flukes; we just sort of happened, and there is nothing in the lore that can explain rhyme or reason to it."

"So, we are accidents then?" Nyssa produced a scowl with that one. "Kind of like unwanted children?"

"Don't treat it so black and white, Nyssa," Seema shook her head with a smile and gently tapped her arm. "Lore expresses that we are very special, more special than the average bear, even more so than the above average person who walks amongst mankind. I mean, we are not like some sort of 'chosen people,' although that's exactly what the Anathema think all people of Magic should be: rulers instead of followers, shepherds instead of sheep."

"Is that what started the big rift between the two sects?" Nyssa asked, her mind beginning to put the pieces together. "The Anathema wanting to control everything and breaking all the rules along the way and the Consortia trying to counter everything the Anathema did?"

"You've hit the nail right on the head," Seema smiled. "At one time, there was no Anathema or Consortia, just lots and lots of various sects worldwide. They had all sorts of names, usually that of the region they were from, and there was even one called the Order of the Righteous Clowns, if you can believe that one."

"Righteous Clowns?" Nyssa's questioning tone was accompanied by a solitary eyebrow which climbed up to her hairline.

"Yep!" Seema chirped with a giggle. "They were circus folk and for some reason one drew the others together and from what the lore states, they were magnificent performers. I am talking Cirquè du Solei looking like babies rolling over on their sides.

"Anyways, right around eleven hundred or so, there were some who grew tired of working for what they wanted and began to covet things like wealth, land, women and men, and power, and slowly but surely, mages quickly understood that if they had all this magical power, why not simply use it to get what they wanted. That was the beginning of the end of the era known as The Harmony of Magic, and those with wicked passions in their heart began flowing to one side while those who still believed that Magic is simply a part of life went to another."

"Man, this is so interesting," Nyssa sat in awe; she, like her father, was a sucker for history. "So, when did the two sides really start, you know, fighting?"

"Well, the fighting was always there," Seema continued as her mind rolled along dusty pages of historical texts and scrolls. "We are human, after all, but the real fighting began when a grand archmage named Theodore Granyx created the Pax Consortia in a vision of reuniting the World of Magic. He hoped a union might pull the spreading sects back together.

"It started to work, and those who had stolen and coerced worldly goods using Magic began to cease their coveting ways, and many even began returning what they had taken. It seemed like the World of Magic was balancing out until a wicked man named Victus Anathema came on the scene with both heels."

"Wait," Nyssa was shaking her head with some confusion. "Anathema was a person?"

"Oh yeah, he was once," Seema nodded. "And thankfully he was so full of vile Magic he never had any offspring."

"When was this?" Nyssa leaned forward and hung on every word Seema said.

"This was in the early fifteen-hundreds, and he would be damned if he was going to lay back and let the sheep of everyday mankind control what he had done, let alone give back what he had taken. When Victus showed up, that's when all hell broke loose.

"There were grand fights between the two sides, and many mages were killed in the process, including Theodore Granyx, who was murdered by four of his own Consortia members who had recently begun to follow the other side's beliefs."

"Dear God!" Nyssa gasped, her hands flying to her mouth. "That's a downthrow of Caesar-type move!"

"Exactly," Seema nodded slowly. "But Granyx and the Consortia suffered much worse than Caesar because once they had Granyx beat, lore states, they removed his heart and liver while he was still alive, and then they nailed it to the door which led to the Halls of the Consortia Elders: the place where the Consortia met in counsel."

"Holy shit!" Nyssa squirmed, wrapping her arms around herself as her mind pictured it. "That's horrible! So that's when the Anathema we know and love now started calling themselves that, from this Victus character?"

"In the long run, yes," Seema nodded as she played with a reed of grass. "But the name came in martyrdom after the death of Victus in the fifteen-hundreds."

"So, we got him... the Consortia that is?" Nyssa asked excitedly; good triumphing over evil, *(hells yeah!)*.

"Not directly," Seema shrugged. "The Roman Catholic Church actually is the ones who finally got hold of him and burned him nicely at the stake, but yes, the Consortia played a part in his demise."

"What, for being a witch or something?" Nyssa asked, blinking.

"For being the spawn of the devil," Seema looked at her with a solid face. "Anathema means in loose definition: 'Cursed', and to be Anathema meant you had to be cursed by the authority of the Church. It's a real word in the dictionary, did you know? Anathema, that is, but the word did not enter the English language or any language until the coming of Victus."

"Wow, I didn't know that," Nyssa shook her head, her mind filling to its capacity with the onslaught of information. "That is too weird. So, the Church got pissed at him and that was that?"

"Not at first," Seema sighed, her brain tiring as well. "Have you ever heard of The Peasants' War?" Nyssa slowly shook her head. "Well, the Peasants' War happened between fifteen-twenty-four to twenty-five where hundreds of thousands of peasants, farmers, townspeople, and even lesser nobility rose in revolt towards the higher nobility. At the time, it was the largest war Europe had ever seen and would ever see until the French Revolution hundreds of years later.

"Modern history books tell us that the true leader of the revolt was a man named Thomas Muntzer, and yes, he had a big hand in it and was executed for his crimes, but there was someone higher up than Muntzer pulling the strings and guess who that was?"

"Victus?" Nyssa squeaked and Seema nodded with a smile. "But wouldn't Victus be on the sides of the upper nobility, which if history taught me anything, included the Church?"

"Not in this case, no," Seema licked her lips and continued. "Ever hear the phrase: *The enemy of my enemy are my friends*?"

Nyssa nodded.

"Well, there you have it. Like today, the Anathema is wrapped up in all sorts of world power and domination; heck, even the stock market is teeming with them in their pursuit of control, and much like ill-tempered children, they will also throw tantrums, even at the expense of ruining a whole economy or starting a war to get what they want.

"Regarding the Peasants' War, Victus wanted more influence and control of the nobility, but instead of taking the slow road of political process and planning, he began stirring up the furor in the peasants who rebelled against all those he wanted power over. He figured that when it was all said and done, he would waltz in, pick up all the pieces, and run it all."

"But that didn't happen apparently," Nyssa injected.

"Nope," Seema responded. "The Consortia did one thing they never expected, and they took sides. With the Consortia's help, the higher nobility pushed back against the rebellion, nobles began making separate peace treaties throughout Europe, and the revolution slowed."

"So, our side did someone else's bidding then?" Nyssa's face was twisted sourly as if she had just smelled something distastefully rank.

"Oh, no, not so much as that! Surprisingly, some Consortia were of higher nobility as well. I mean, just because we don't use our Magic for self-gain doesn't mean we are poor. You have to remember People of Magic don't choose their parents, and even today, many are born to wealthy, influential parents."

"I see," Nyssa followed, but her eyes remained cautiously narrowed.

"Anyway, to make this long story short, after the rebellion was quashed and the words of the Doctrine of Divine Rights of Kings were rewritten so people moved on, but the Roman Church and the Consortia were not content that the Peasant's War was over. Even though the apparent culprit behind it was now dead, they knew there was something darker in the shadows, and in a year, they had finally tracked down and captured Victus and had themselves a little barbeque."

"That is so wrong, Seema!" Nyssa burst into a wild fit of laughter, her head shaking in morbid disbelief, her eyes squirting tears. "Barbeque; man, that is too funny."

Seema giggled, "Sorry, but all true."

Giggling, the two returned to the practicing of minor Magic in silence as Nyssa's mind relaxed having many of the nagging questions answered for her.

-4-

The girls had been practicing all morning next to the garden, and not only had Nyssa perfected moving stones, she was able to get them to 'jump' just as Seema had done with the olives during their visit to Nyssa's home more than a week before.

They had taken cover under the gazebo when Seema had announced that she had to bring the warm rains for the Fairy Garden, and after a few hand gestures and something uttered in Low German, a gentle shower softly pelted the property. Seema had promised her that she would teach her how to do it as well— especially since more than likely it would end up being her chore in the future to do anyways—but Nyssa had vehemently declined the tutoring having stated that she had brought enough rain already to last her a lifetime.

"So, you do this three times a week, huh?" Nyssa asked distantly as she sat on one of the cushioned side benches under the gazebo top, her hand extended out into the falling water.

"Usually," Seema nodded. "Always depending on where rain is falling in the world and how much."

"So, this goes back to *Something* from *Nothing* thing, then?" Nyssa looked at her, her mind slowly beginning to unwrap all of the enigmas of Modern Magic quickly. "The first rule?"

"Precisely," Seema smiled. "There is a trick you will eventually learn and that's how to seek what you are looking for. At first it can take you a while just to do something simple, but once you get the hang of it, it's almost instantaneous and poof: you have it."

"So where is this rain coming from?" Nyssa asked, looking upwards where the heavens hung blue, yet the rain seemingly coming out of thin air.

"The sky," Seema smiled at her and then burst into laughter.

"Seema has a lot of jokes today," Nyssa shot back and stuck out her tongue.

"I'm sorry," Seema giggled, calming herself with rapid breaths. "It's just you make it so easy sometimes, but to answer your question, this rain is from the Amazon… smell how fresh it is."

Nyssa closed her eyes as she extended her neck forward towards the rain and breathed in heavily several times.

"Wow you are right, it does smell fresh," Nyssa smiled and waved her hand in front of her nose with a twisted expression. "They need this over Chicago sometimes, let me tell you."

"Too funny," Seema smiled. "I prefer the rains from the Amazon, and they do fall in abundance there; much better than other wet spots of the world."

"So, you bring them, uh, invoke them from other places too?"

"I used to from everywhere, but learned my lesson quickly," Seema smiled, her mind traveling back. "About four years ago, I invoked rains falling over Hong Kong..." Seema paused, shaking her head slowly, "...not recommended."

"Why not?" Nyssa laughed.

"Way too much pollution and smog," Seema replied. "Lady Agatha scolded me for a solid week after that one every time the breeze would shift towards the house. She said we would live in a Chinatown district if she wanted to smell a million car mufflers and soy."

"Ha! Served you right!" Nyssa laughed, enjoying the joke being on Seema for once.

"Yeah, I suppose," Seema smiled, her eyes narrowing. "I fixed her though."

"How?" Nyssa was beaming.

"I brought rains that were falling over a pig farm in Nebraska," Seema giggled. "And all the windows of the house were open that day... Lady Agatha almost had a bird."

The two of them burst into wild laughter.

"Oh man I bet she was so pissed!" Nyssa laughed, wiping her damp cheeks.

"I think 'irate' would be a better word," Seema smiled. "She told me that she would be better off if she sold me to wandering gypsies or cast me into the *Yondsphere* after that. For a while I think I believed her, so my pranking days ended."

"*Yondsphere?*" Nyssa urged, having heard the word mentioned numerous times by several people now. "Is that a nice Magically way of saying hell?"

Seema giggled, her head cocking slightly.

"Umm, no. The *Yondsphere* is the 'in between,' neither here nor there. Picture if you can a chaotic realm full of happenstance mayhem where down is up, up is down; backing up is moving forward. It's an insane place of twisted magic which was purged from this world centuries ago in hopes to keep Magic balanced."

"Sounds like a funhouse at an amusement park," Nyssa tried her best to correlate what she knew to what she was now told.

"Something just like that," Seema stretched. "All you need to do is add a Cheshire Cat with the body of a pink hippopotamus, have an intoxicated Dali be the interior designer, and the Mad Hatter with an axe as mayor, and you're pretty darn close.

"The *Yondsphere* is forever, plus two days and yet, no time at all."

Nyssa was not as much staring at the girl as she was gawking. Seema nearly recoiled at her expression as she slowly and quite carefully leaned in, placing two fingers under Nyssa's drooped chin and lifting it closed.

"I think we will go into the *Yondsphere* in depth at a much later date," Seema spoke softly then their attention was drawn away.

The large French doors on the back of the house opened, and Marco stepped out onto the patio with his face up towards the falling rain, where he stood for several minutes, absorbing the warm splashes. Since they brought Mica into the home, he had barely left, having only gated away once that either Nyssa or Seema could recall.

He looked extremely worn and very tired.

"He is really worried about that girl," Seema said quietly as they watched him from over the railing of the gazebo.

"I know… I can tell," Nyssa nodded, watching him run his fingers through his hair so to allow the water to run where it wished. "He reminds me of how my dad gets whenever I got really sick; just a state of constant worry."

Marco noticed the girls in the gazebo and waved, slowly moving through the falling rain to them.

"Hello, ladies," Marco said quietly, attempting to produce a cheery smile. Marco found another cushion to sit on, his hands wiping away the water from his face. "By the smell of it, I sense that Seema sought the rainforest today."

"Sure did," Seema smiled; happy that her work was noticed and appreciated.

"The Fairies will be happy for it," he sighed and then coughed lightly, and Nyssa could see that the man had apparently not slept in days.

"How is Mica doing?" Nyssa asked quietly, concerned.

"To be honest, young ones," Marco sighed, removing a handkerchief from his hip pocket, and dabbed away at his brow. "She is not doing very well at all."

"But she will get better, won't she?" Nyssa pressed, her shoulders weighing down from the heavy news and expression borne on Marco's face.

"Angelica has done all she can for her," Marco said flatly with his eyes finding something in the distance.

If the girls were younger by just a few years, he would have made every attempt to lie, to falsify his smile, and to brighten his tone, but even then, he would probably fail in any level of deceit. Children are intelligent creatures who can see through anything because they watch the eyes of adults, and their eyes never lie. No, these teenage girls have had a lifetime—however short so far but a lifetime nonetheless—to know when an adult was not telling 'The All.'

"I am afraid it is now up to her body and spirit to do the rest. Seth has done more than break her body; *he* has also broken her soul.

"I think she is giving up." Marco finished, dropping his head.

"Is there anything we can do?" Seema asked, her voice soft and little, like a mouse.

Marco gave them both a comforting smile, "The compassion I see in both of you is overwhelming, little ones. For now, I think that is enough either one of you can do for the moment."

"Well, we could gather her some nice flowers from the Fairy Garden?" Nyssa pressed, her eyes shifting between Seema and Marco for encouragement.

"Yes, and we can let in the rainforest breezes," Seema nodded. "That always cheers me up."

"Well then that sounds like a good plan, girls," he smiled and stood, stretching out his back slowly which popped and strained like a knotted and worn leather belt. "When you visit her, mind not making too much noise; she needs all the rest she can get."

"Promise," they agreed in unison.

"I must be off," Marco said quietly and slowly moved towards the gazebo steps. "Amora has not seen me in days."

"Make sure you rest, Marco," Nyssa spoke after him and he smiled at her, adding a reassuring nod. Marco made his way back into the house while Nyssa and Seema headed for the Fairy Garden for flowers.

CHAPTER SIXTEEN

———◦◦◦◦◦———

Fairy Fête of Gnomish Behavior

-1-

"Remember," Seema said quickly, licking her lips, her eyes afire with their plan. "You are going to have to convince the Fairies to let you pick their flowers, like when we were kids."

"I-I don't remember doing that," Nyssa shook her head, confused in her own memories which showed her nothing.

"Don't you remember getting bitten by Regina when you were seven?" Seema asked her.

"She bit me?" Nyssa said surprised, her eyes locked in the center of the garden on the violet fairy Regina who was suspended on her glass rod, forever locked in a ballerina's leap.

"Yes, right on your finger," Seema giggled. "You cried for like an hour and you wouldn't step foot back into the garden for a week!"

"What a rude little bit—" Nyssa said rhetorically and distant but failed to finish her sentence. "So how do I convince them then?"

"Man, you really don't remember anything," Seema shook her head as her hand came to her forehead. "And you really think a life of television and digitized music has given you a fruitful life. Tisk, tisk."

"Seema!" Nyssa was pleading. *"Tell me!"*

"Fine… pushy, aren't we?" Seema stuck her tongue out at her. "You have to sing to them like you did when you were little. Remember you used to sing that Kookaburra song your grandmother used to sing to you?"

Did you? Nyssa thought to herself distantly.

Yes, her grandmother had sung that song to her many times, just as her father had learned it when he was just a boy, but she had not thought of the tune or the words for many years, ever since her grandmother passed away several years before. It used to soothe her energetic mind when she fought the sleep pixies that dared to make her slumber, and it eased the grumblings in her belly whenever her stomach hurt, that she remembered, but singing it to the Fairies?

She could picture herself doing it but had no memory of it.

"I really don't remember a thing, Seema," she said quietly, her mind saddened by her own memories of childhood exempt of these few defining details. "Sorry."

"Look, it's simple," Seema pointed towards the reflecting pool. "Once you go into the garden—requesting permission from Mr. Phipps, of course—you go and sit on the stones near the pool and sing to them. Don't forget the last part; it's the *really* important one. Once they are relaxed simply ask them for some of their beautiful flowers and there you go.

"If you forget that step, well, I will make sure I get out the mercurochrome for the bite marks."

"What are you going to do while I am doing all this?" Nyssa reached out and took her arm as Seema attempted to move off.

"I am going to go open the windows to Mica's room," she smiled. "And get a vase for the flowers. Relax, you'll be fine, and I will know if something went wrong by your screams."

Seema moved off, giggling at the thought of suddenly hearing Nyssa's cries of pain in the distance, and headed for the French doors to the back of the house. Nyssa watched her go, her mind rolling over the thoughts of being attacked by little fairies stuck on glass tubes and how that would look on the evening news.

News flash ladies and gentlemen, she pictured an anchorman declaring. *Today a young woman was mauled by angry fairies and…* and so her imagination faded as she concentrated on the words to the song.

"Kookaburra sits in the old gum tree-E," she sang softly to herself, her mind searching for the right words. *"Merry, merry king of…* damn it!"

Slowly she moved towards the gate to the garden, her mind seeking through locked and rusty filing cabinets of her past.

*

Mr. Phipps was standing just to the left of the gate with his beaming smile and bright eyes staring at her; motionless.

He wasn't standing at the gate earlier; she distantly thought to herself and then dismissed it. She hadn't *seen* him move, but that doesn't deny the fact that he had moved. Fragments of childhood were present far and few in between in her mind and being reminded by Seema that she had to have permission to enter the garden was one thing that she knew quite well.

She had forgotten once, on an early bright sunny morning when she was almost nine. She had entered the garden quickly and stealthily to pull a prank on Mr. Phipps, who was facing out towards the gazebo and away from her approach. She had gotten in by stepping over the two-foot-high fence and tiptoed ever so quietly amongst the petunias and the ferns. The plan was to take Mr. Phipps' little wooden box, which had contained only a dove's feather, and when close to accomplishing her task, an acorn bounced off of her forehead. She yelped, surprised, her hand to her forehead as her eyes scanned the garden for the gnome.

Mr. Phipps was nowhere to be found.

Instinctively she looked upwards, assuming that an acorn had broken loose from a squirrels grasp, and found her forehead as a landing point, but no, to her confusion, there were no squirrels, let alone an oak tree; that was on the other side of the garden's edge. Shrugging, she reached for the box again, only to be pelted by numerous acorns, seemingly from every direction at once.

"Stop that!" she had screamed, her eyes searching about her, and there, between a small metal archway decoration, Mr. Phipps stood, his bright eyes twinkling and his garish smile beaming. She paused, eyes locked on his, and with a steady slow motion, she inched her hand closer to the box and glanced to ensure that she was on target, only to be pelted on the side of the face.

"Ouch!" she had cried and looked for the gnome who was no longer standing in the archway, but to her right with a small pile of acorns near its terracotta feet.

Slowly, and without further to do, Nyssa went back to the way she had come and exited the garden and did not return until the next day in which she did so properly.

"Good day, Mr. Phipps!" She said as brightly as she could as she squatted down in front of the little gnome. "And what a fine rainy day we are having, aren't we?"

The gnome said nothing; it only smiled at her.

"I would like to go into the garden to see the Fairies, if that's okay with you?" Nyssa continued and waited, only to get nothing but a smile and twinkle in return.

"Nyssa!" Seema called down from the bedroom window; the double windows swung outwards. "What's taking you so long?"

"I am not sure what I am supposed to do!" She called back to her. "I asked him for his permission, now what?"

"Did he hit you with anything yet?" Seema inquired.

"No!" Nyssa called back.

"Well then you're safe," Seema giggled. "Go on in!"

Seema disappeared from the windows and Nyssa slowly turned back to the gnome who was now standing sideways next to the gate which had been swung inwards.

"Thank you, Mr. Phipps," she smiled, standing, and carefully stepped into the garden while giving the gnome sharp glances in anticipation of flying acorns. No missiles flew, and as Nyssa followed the stone path toward the reflecting pond, she heard the gate close behind her with a metallic *Clink!* Quickly she spun on her heels and looked, but the gnome was nowhere to be found. "Now *that* is awesome."

Nyssa followed the path and moved close to the reflecting pond, where she sat on carefully stacked stones fashioned to resemble a small bench. She carefully adjusted herself on the small seat, vaguely remembering that Auntie Agatha had made these for Seema and her when their bodies were still small. The colorful Koi was lazily swimming, occasionally breaking the water's surface to collect some tasty insects they could only see. Nyssa smiled warmly as the soft Amazon rains fell on her and the garden, and she closed her eyes to the sounds and the smells of it mingling together.

"Hello, my dear Fairy Princesses," she said softly, her eyes parting lazily, her smile broadening. Renée and Regina were just as beautiful as she remembered them, each made from multicolored glass; Renée's body was mainly blue while Regina's was violet, and their wings were the most detailed stained-glass pattern she had ever seen. Their delicate faces held bright smiles, and their hands poised in elegant gestures as Renée's pirouette and Regina's graceful leap hung permanently in motion. "I have come for some of your beautiful flowers, my ladies, so that they may brighten a hurt girl's soul. I have a song for you, of course, so hopefully, an exchange can be made?"

And neither one of you had better bite me, either! she thought after the fact and stared at the fairies. There was no reply, so she closed her eyes, gently clearing her throat and concentrated on the words and began to sing:

"Kookaburra sits in the old gum tree-E,

Merry, merry king of the bushes he-E,

Laugh, Kookaburra, laugh, Kookaburra,

Gay your life must be."

Rustling sounds broke her concentration, and she opened her eyes and gasped deeply to find Regina hovering just inches from her nose, her delicate wings fluttering in the rainy air. At the same time, Renée was squatting, her tiny feet propped on the end of her stem and her face in her hands, looking at her.

"You *do* move!" Nyssa gasped in a whisper, her eyes moving from one to the next in disbelief. "It wasn't a childish daydream."

Regina smiled and swooped in and patted her gently on the tip of her nose and then backflipped and dove, taking up a lounging position in the bow of a large Hosta leaf with her chin resting firmly on the back of her interlaced hands.

"You want me to continue?" Nyssa continued and was answered by soft, squeaking sounds and little rapid nods. "Okay then—"

Nyssa licked her lips and began to repeat the words to the Kookaburra song, slowly and softly, her voice carrying across the garden and tickling the flowers, which motioned and moved towards her as if to hear her words better. The Kookaburra song ended, and she started in on another song her grandmother used to sing to her: *The Cannibal King*. When the verses of the Cannibal King having more family with the *"Boom, boom, Grandma!"*(s) and the *"Boom, boom, grandpa!"*(s), the two fairies began to giggle, which nearly got her giggling as well. As she sang, she nodded a little towards Mr. Phipps, who was now standing at the edge of the pool, smiling at her.

Soon *The Cannibal King* became *Madame Librarian* from *The Music Man*, which then became *Shall We Dance* from *The King and I*; all the songs from musicals that she remembered her grandmother singing to her and all the while, her heart filling with warmth and love. She paused briefly, cleared her throat, and then focused on her throat to produce the proper notes to her finale, *Climb Every Mountain*, from *The Sound of Music*. Slowly Nyssa closed her eyes and began. This piece had been one of her favorites as a child, and whenever her grandmother had sung it to her, she would close her eyes and picture herself rising high in the air, effortlessly climbing like a soaring bird on the winds.

Nyssa carefully opened her eyes only to find Renée and Regina sleeping comfortably, Renée having taken up a small spot on the Hosta leaf and had curled into a little ball on her side. Cautiously, she scanned as she softened her tone to almost a whisper, and it seemed the whole garden had fallen into slumber, and even Mr. Phipps leaned oddly against the stem of a tall fern as if he were napping.

The song ended and Nyssa waited for a moment.

"May I pick some of your beautiful flowers, fairies?" she whispered, and Regina lazily waved her hand to her in approval and then returned to her sweet slumber.

Nyssa gently moved amongst the patches of flowers picking tulips and daffodils, geraniums and petunias, and a handful of baby's breath. Then she quickly tiptoed towards the gate so to avoid disturbing their sleeping. Once the gate was closed silently behind her, she whispered a *'thank you'* and hurried towards the house.

-2-

Seema was holding the vase out the window in a streaming flow of water from one of the gables above as Nyssa entered the room as quietly as she could with the flowers held delicately in her hand.

"So, you didn't get bit this time then?" Seema smiled, bringing in the crystal vase which was half-full of rainwater.

"Put them right to sleep," Nyssa smiled brightly for having accomplished the unimaginable in an imaginable world. "Is the vase ready?"

"All set," Seema nodded, and she placed the vase with water on the nightstand next to the bed where Mica slept.

Although they had been back and forth through the room several times, both had been too busy to actually *look* at the unconscious girl. As they focused on her, their mouths dropped simultaneously in shock at the sight of the bruises along her cheekbones and eyes. Nyssa swallowed hard enough for Seema to hear it, and they moved in silence as they arranged the flowers as pretty as they could.

"My God," Nyssa whispered, shooting a sideways glance at Mica's face. "Look at her."

"I know," Seema whispered back, shaking her head in disgust. "But she doesn't look as bad as she first did."

"Yeah," Nyssa sounded back as she matched up colors as best that she could, accenting the blues with the reds and so on. "You know, she doesn't look... *mala*."

"I know," Seema nodded and paused long enough to look Mica over. "She looks just like a normal girl, like us."

"Do you think she will attempt to blast us if she wakes up?" Nyssa followed up as her mind went to extremes.

"Well, she doesn't have her talisman," Seema shook her head and then stepped away from the nightstand, followed in action by

Nyssa as they critiqued their work. "And even if she did, she would be more worried about where Seth was than us two."

"Good point," Nyssa said quietly, her eyes studying the round face lying in the bed.

When she met her on the sidewalk that day after the storm, she seemed like such a cool, genuine person that she might have gotten to know on a friendly basis and maybe even hung out with. Those were the *'Would be-Maybe'* circumstantial possibilities, but now—after all that had happened and what this injured girl had tried to do to her—all that could go through her mind was that she was now looking at the enemy.

Nyssa sighed quietly and shuddered, trying not to think of it.

"Get a bad vibe?" Seema asked softly, nudging Nyssa gently.

"No, not really," Nyssa said and moved to a narrow sitting bench near the far wall where she sat with her elbows on her knees, thinking. Seema joined her with a look of concern on her face.

"Then what is it?" Seema pushed lightly.

"It's just when I think back on all the wondrous, magical stories from when I was a kid," Nyssa began, sitting upright with her back against the wall. "You know, wizards, castles, dragons, and things of the like, you knew that there were the good and bad people, and the bad people always got it in the end.

"I know a lot of that is the Disney way of doing things, but over time as I would hear about how screwed up things were in the world, I often drifted back to those stories as some escape from all that was real, ya know?"

Seema simply nodded, understanding.

"In freshman year, we started reading the fairytales as the Brothers Grimm wrote them," Nyssa continued, slightly turning to face Seema better. "The stories were just like the ones I remember watching as a kid or my mom or dad reading to me from a picture book. Those stories were the *real* ones, dark and full of despair. Although good vanquished bad, the endings tended to be harsh. Even look at *Alice in Wonderland*; the movie is full of wonder and shenanigans, but the *real* story, the way Lewis Carroll told it, was rather dark.

"I had always wanted to live in the world like many of those stories thinking they were one way, but now I am living it, and the mirror image is not the same as I had expected. There are no *'happily ever after'* kinds of endings, but *wham-blam* in-your-face kind of endings. I mean, I can see why Disney changed them so as not to scare the crap out of kids."

"So, you don't see all this as the same kind of thing, then?" Seema edged on, drawing the conversation out of Nyssa.

"No, this is a lot worse, I think," Nyssa said flatly, her eyes meeting Seema's. "In this story, people really do die or get really close to it like Mica, and I am starting to feel that 'Good' is not always the winner in the end. Darker yet, I think 'Good' has the real struggle in this story; struggling to keep its head above water in shark-infested water."

There was a long silence between them until Seema's body rapidly shivered, "I think I see your point."

"Sorry," Nyssa added. "I have been known to be the killjoy to moods at times."

"You're honest," Seema shrugged. "And you say how you see it. There's nothing at all wrong about that. I guess I have never

289

looked at the frailty of it until now with me sitting here thinking about it while looking at her lying there like that."

Gentle Amazon breezes flowed in through the windows sending the curtains to billow upwards from the window seals. Seema cracked a smile and nodded in the curtain's direction.

"Let's see what we can do about this ending then."

Nyssa and Seema moved to the end of the bed, and they could feel the warm breeze caress their skin as it carried the freshness of nature with it. Seema quickly took Nyssa's hand, her face stretching a smile as her eyes sparkled.

"We're going to try something," Seema whispered to her. "Something I think may work."

"What's that?" Nyssa was ready for anything, but oblivious to it all.

"Remember the olive trick?" she smiled, and Nyssa nodded. "Well, what if you and I focus on good things, like the warm breezes and the smell of the rain, and then bring it into ourselves? Once we can feel it, what if we project it into Mica?"

"Kind of like giving her a jump start?" Nyssa squeaked, her mind filling with possibilities.

"Yeah, just like that," Seema grinned. "I mean, it couldn't hurt now, could it?"

"I don't suppose that it would," Nyssa smiled back and slowly they looked at Mica who had not stirred. "Alright, how do we do this?"

"Okay, close your eyes and follow what I tell you," Seema whispered, and the two of them closed their eyes. "I want you to picture the warm breeze flowing over the canopy of the great Amazon rainforest. I want you to picture the leaves rustling and the birds coasting along the jet streams effortlessly."

"Alright," Nyssa nodded, eyes closed and mind picturing exactly what Seema was referring to.

"Can you smell the fresh flowers?" Seema asked and Nyssa noised that she could. "And smell that Amazon rains; pure, unpolluted, and untouched. Breathe deeply, take it all in, and when you have it in, concentrate on picturing it is glowing beneath your sternum."

The two girls took in a long, heavy deep breath and held it, and in the pit right behind her sternum, Nyssa pictured all of that green foliage and colorful birds and the vase full of various flowers all drenched in that perfectly pure water falling from the sky. There it pulsed and grew warm, the edges tickling the sides of her lungs like a feather tip, and without any instruction, Seema gently squeezed her hand, and both of them opened their eyes which focused on Mica's chest.

"Gumpen!" Their voices came monotonously, propelling them backward as the Magic flowed from them, casting pure light that slammed home into Mica's chest, forcing her body into an odd arch as the Magic seared into her soul. For a moment, neither of them quite knew how they ended up sprawling on the floor. As they sat up, they found Mica's figure sitting in bed as their eyesight crested the bed's edge. Mica looked about herself with wide, confused eyes, her body shaking in ever so slight jerks as the Magic finished its journey through her being, and when her eyes happened upon the two sets looking back at her, slow tears rolled her cheeks.

291

"Am I su-safe?" Mica squeaked softly, her eyes darting about her.

Nyssa and Seema looked at each other with open mouths of surprise which formed wide smiles and nodding they returned their eyes to Mica.

"Absolutely safe," Nyssa beamed. Mica let the floodgates go and dropped her face in her hands as she wept, and quickly, like two old dear friends, Nyssa and Seema went to her for comfort.

*

"Lady Agatha?" Seema said quietly as she approached where Agatha sat reading *The Color Purple* on a comfortable bench in the atrium. A small box turtle gave her a mild glance in its slow-moving life, and if turtles could shrug it would have.

"Yes Seema?" Agatha said without looking from the pages.

"The girl, Mica," Seema smiled brightly as the excitement danced in her eyes. "She's awake!"

-3-

Agatha was nearly running when she entered Seema's old bedroom with her teen pupil in tow, her eyes a wide expression of surprise about Mica's fast recovery. Nyssa had been sitting on the foot of the bed talking to her when they entered, and she quickly raced to calm the girl who moved up towards the headboard with a sudden terrified expression on her face.

"Relax, Mica, relax" Nyssa soothed with a calm steady voice, her hands gently pulling at Mica's which had crisscrossed her chest defensively as her body shook like tree branches in winter's wind and rapid whimpers crept from her throat. "Everything is alright; no one is going to hurt you."

Mica's eyes darted between Nyssa's and those of Agatha who stood several feet away from the edge of the bed with her palms up and fingers spread showing no intent of harm.

"This is my Auntie Agatha, Mica," Nyssa whispered and smiled. "She is the one who sent for you and brought you here."

Mica slowly relaxed, allowing Nyssa to ease her arms down to her lap where she fumbled with her fingers. Agatha dug in deep and found the mother inside of her soul and produced a smile full of bright tulips and sunny days as she calmly moved to the edge of the bed and slowly took a seat there.

"Hello, young Mica," Agatha said softly. "I am so glad to see you awake. I am Lady Agatha, and this is my home. Here, you are safe."

Mica's eyes danced in her sockets as the waters rose against the dams of pain and relief, and in no time at all the tears began to flow. Instinctively the two moved towards each other as Agatha opened her arms and allowed Mica to dive into her waiting embrace.

With slow, gentle motions Agatha rocked back and forth as she stroked Mica's hair and soothed her quiet sobbing with a soft humming tune.

"But you are Consortia," Mica managed through her trembling mouth. "You're not going to hurt me?"

"Never in a day, young Mica," Agatha soothed; closing her eyes as she rocked and hummed.

Seema took a sitting position on the edge of the bed behind Mica and gently rubbed her back as Nyssa leaned forward with the side of her head pressing gently on Mica's arms which wrapped tightly around Agatha's body. The three women of the Consortia sat there for quite some time, comforting Mica until her tears dried and for once fell into slumber borne from the confines of safety and love instead of torment.

CHAPTER SEVENTEEN

Decisions, Dreams and Damnation

-1-

Seth was standing on his balcony, his eyes staring in the distance over the tops of the maple trees of the property and seeing nothing but Mica in his mind. Outwardly, he was strong and bitter in stature if anyone cared to meet with him regarding business. Still, on the inside, he was a tormented soul in which his mind continually reminded him with visions of what he had done.

In the days since his betrayal of Mica, his mind attempted to rationalize his actions by reassuring him he had done 'the right thing' and that 'there was no other way,' but he knew he was lying to himself. Those were Pia's words, not his. Although the ploy had worked—the Trojan Horse had been planted firmly inside the nest of the Consortia's haven—his heart was condemning him regardless of whether the grand solution led to a positive outcome.

Softly, he sighed and opened his hand where a small picture of Mica sat contained in an oval frame and he shuddered at the sight of it, snapping shut his hand and pinching his eyes together so tightly that it hurt.

"I am beyond damned," he whispered, his mind repeating the dying words of his teacher in his mind about being a harsh teacher himself. Slowly he opened his eyes and looked out across the treetops again, his head shaking slowly. Perhaps Pia was right, and Mica would truly understand when all of it came to light. Maybe she would even laugh at it, calling the plan brilliant and give him that wicked little smile with twinkling violet eyes like she always had when something devious was in the air. Perhaps— "What if she never forgives me?"

His mind thought of Pia then, and his heart raced and pumped with rage. That woman was cunning and persuasive, and it was she who formulated this idea and tricked him into carrying it out. She was even more vicious than that of all the Anathema combined, and because of her his Mica lay with the enemy bloodied and broken.

Seth growled and spun away from the balcony's edge and stormed into the house, his eyes blazing blue.

Seth would do it; he would kill Pia once and for all despite the years of devotion and her apparent affection for him, finishing what he had come close to doing days before. It had felt right; his body had coursed with the pure intent of ripping the woman who had devised all of this to shreds, his spine had tingled with excitement with each cry of pain that escaped her, and his heart pounded feverishly with each drawn drop of blood. He cursed with a roar and kicked the large desk in his parlor, flipping it over with such speed and force that it shook the house's very foundation.

He will kill the woman without a second thought!

Yet no, he couldn't, and so he paused. The plan was not yet complete! The Consortia had possession of the Next Coming, and without a doubt, they were teaching the girl that very moment as he stood panting with rage. If the tables were turned, he would be doing the same, and if he had had Nyssa under his thumb, would he have had much need for Mica in the end? Would his affection wane from

Mica and wax towards Nyssa in tenfold time as he taught and nurtured the living, breathing form of pure Magic? Wouldn't Mica note this and despise the girl and her teacher—him—in the process? Wouldn't what had recently occurred happen regardless of when and why, but as a point of inevitability written in the annals of a time long ago?

Seth blinked and pondered, his pulse softening, and his breathing slowly returned to normalcy.

Yes, he thought to himself. *Fate is in control here.*

Calmly he opened the connecting doors to his study to another room. Inside, Pia was pressed up against the headboards of a bed, her green eyes wide with terror from the clamor of the slamming desk and the roaring which bore from his lips. She was expecting Seth to pounce her, for the Magic inside of him to metamorphose him into that creature only the dead have ever truly seen, but she found a pleasantly smiling face looking at her with eyes soft and comforting.

"Stand fast!" Pia shrieked, her eyes scanning for her talisman, but it was nowhere to be found.

"You can relax, sweet Pia," he said softly as he stepped in the room and shut the doors behind him. "I have come to pay aide to you and to enjoy your company as I have so many times in the past."

Pia's eyes watched his every move suspiciously, her heart thudding in her chest. She had been lying in bed for days, her body a complete tangle of the human form, expecting that at any moment Seth's guilt would have the best of him and he would come seeking proper retribution from her. Slowly he moved to the edge of the bed and took a seat, his hands moving slowly and taking one of hers, which shook like a terrified small animal at the feet of a rabid beast.

"All is right as rain, Pia," he said softly, slowly bowing and kissing the back of her hand which was spotted with bruises. "And I think your plan was brilliant."

-2-

Nyssa walked along the emerald-colored marble path that centered the atrium, the sides of which were a shallow aquarium of plants and Koi, the occasional frog which disappeared under the surface when you passed, and just as Seema had told her: there were lots and *lots* of turtles.

Nyssa had fallen in love with the ancient creatures when she was a little girl, having the honor of taking home her classroom's pet water turtle to tend to over the summer because of the fantastic job she had done caring for it during the school year. She knew when autumn came that the turtle would have to return to the school, and she dealt with that fact from day one, but for an entire summer, she knew that Bubbles, as she so named him, was hers and hers alone.

As she walked along the straight pathway, which branched out every twelve feet towards the atrium's edge, she marveled at all the detail in its design. Potted lemon and orange trees sat in sizeable square planter boxes at the edges, with deep green moss bedding beneath them. On these beds of soft foliage, several of the turtles rested. She smiled as she identified one genus after the other and then giggled as she passed a box turtle resting lazily near the walkway with stubby little legs hanging over the edge.

Her eyes traveled over every detail of her surroundings: the green glass ceiling curved at the top, the emerald pillars that rose from the waters and climbed up high, and the brass water spigots that protruded from the pillar's sides, pouring water into the aquarium below.

Agatha was reading a book as she sat in a high-backed wicker chair at the atrium's center, where the path connected to a large round patio made of the same emerald marble. She had to climb two steps to get to the main patio floor, and from there, she slowly moved to a matching wicker chair opposite Agatha with only a small, round wicker table separating them. All Nyssa had known was that Auntie Agatha had to speak to her about something of great importance, a phrase that rolled from Seema's lips almost as seriously as someone delivering devastating news. She had inquired as to why Auntie Agatha needed to see her, and her only reply had been two words: *The Atrium.*

As Nyssa sat down, Agatha closed her book, removed a small pair of reading glasses, and produced a thin smile.

"Seema told me that you wanted to see me, Auntie Agatha," Nyssa said in almost a whisper as nervous acid crawled along her stomach lining in expectation of bad news.

"That I do, Nyssa," Agatha smiled, setting the book onto the small table and then leaned all the way back in her chair, studying her. Nyssa's eyes shifted back and forth, waiting for Agatha to speak, to tell her why the request was so serious, which would in turn explain why her feet were sweating inside her *Skechers.*

Agatha's smile broadened and she took a deep breath.

"Your parents," Agatha began, intertwining her fingers on her lap. "Your real parents are coming for a day's visit."

"They are?" Nyssa blurted out, shooting forward suddenly as if she was pushing out her words. "Oh man, is that all? I thought I was in trouble for something, or someone died."

"No, not at all," Agatha chuckled. "You have done nothing but right since you have gotten here and I assure you that everyone, even Mica—partially thanks to you—is quite healthy."

"Okay, but why was Seema so serious then?" Nyssa relaxed, sitting back, adding a carefree shrug to enunciate her words.

"Because when your parents leave in a day," Agatha said flatly. "They will be leaving you in my care: permanently."

Nyssa's throat closed off her breathing so quickly that the gasping sound she made was clearly audible like a sucking *Pop* sound.

"I am?" Nyssa said in a whisper.

"Yes, Nyssa," Agatha said quietly. "You are."

Confusion rolling downhill without brakes raced through her mind, flashing past the pros and the cons as they sat on the sidelines rooting her on. If she went home, she would have her friends, school, and all the amenities to which any regular teen had grown accustomed, if not dependent upon. If she stayed, she would have the World of Magic at her fingertips, her reacquired sister to care for and be cared by in return, and of course this house, with the fantastic atrium and the fairy garden and the horses in their stable and—

"Really?" Nyssa squeaked and Agatha nodded slowly. "Forever?"

"Only until you have made your passage into magedom," Agatha replied, her tone pleasant but direct. "And then you can do as you please for the Anathema would have no power over you in any attempts to convert you."

"But that means like two years!" Nyssa exclaimed, her mind tumbling like clothes in a dryer.

"You do like it here?" Agatha broke in.

"Well, yes, of course!" Nyssa was nearly rambling. "But I mean no more school, no going to senior prom, no more sports, no learning to drive... and... and *boys!*"

"Sacrifices, yes," Agatha said quietly and then her face became as blank as printer paper. "But then I can assure that you will still be alive by your eighteenth birthday, as well as your parents, to see you come of age."

"What?" Nyssa lashed out, her cheeks blazing with rouge.

Agatha slowly stood, walked to the edge of the patio, and peered down to the walkway's edge where Koi had gathered in a spot where something tasty had fallen in, and she closed her eyes towards the truth. Truth, she had learned a long time ago, might be the best policy, but it rarely looked grotesque and hideous. She knew she had to show; no, she had to *make* Nyssa see it for exactly how and what it was; white was black, and black was white.

Sighing, she turned to Nyssa, her hands at her sides.

"Seema has told me that she explained some of the tyrannies of the Anathema, no?" Nyssa slowly nodded in reply, her nostrils flaring as her innate defense mechanism had kicked in upon the mere mentioning of her parents' mortality. "Then you should then already see the reasons better than I. If you return to the world of Common Man, the Anathema will hunt for you, and if they feel they cannot have you, they will kill you."

"But—" Nyssa attempted only to be stopped by Agatha's quick moving tongue and raised 'pause' signing hand.

"*And*, Nyssa," Agatha commanded. "If they have to go through your mother or father to do so, they will do it without even batting an eye. I am trying to get you to understand that you have become a major threat to the machinery which they have relied upon and controlled for so long. They all understand, of which none more so than Seth, that their establishment of order can not only be shaken but can be brought down as well."

"They would kill my parents?" Nyssa muttered out, her eyes shifting but seeing nothing but the faces of her mom and dad.

"Painfully, yes," Agatha nodded and then returned to her seat.

"But what will stop them from hurting them anyway?" Nyssa was near frantic tears. "I mean, they could surely use them as a tool! You know, kidnap them or something?"

"We have that already taken care of, Nyssa," Agatha smiled, relaxing.

"Huh?" Nyssa froze as light shone at the end of this tunnel of confusion before her. "You do?"

"Yes," Agatha's smile broadened.

"Ok, I am lost," Nyssa said exhausted as she leaned back into her chair.

"Your parents will arrive both bearing great news," Agatha said with chronological foretelling preciseness. "Your father has finally landed that full-time job he has been seeking for years enabling him to get off the contractor bandwagon, but with one catch: it will be out of state. He will hope that you understand, which you will, but he will assure you that you two will spend more time together because of this new stable job.

"Your mother will have just as equally fantastic news that after all the years of producing prize-winning roses the Conservatory in San Francisco had extended her a tenure there with a complete relocation package to boot, that it is an opportunity that she cannot pass up.

"There will be conversations concerning you; about your school, your friends, and the sudden move, and they both agreed that homeschooling by me will be the best bet for everyone. And before you ask the obvious, how your parents moving to other states will protect them, there's an added benefit. The places they will be working just so happen to have devout Consortia employees watching over them. As a matter of fact, both will be living in areas that contain perhaps the highest concentration of Consortia in the whole world, and that is also where your mother and your stepfather will be raising your little brother in sanctuary."

"Little brother!" Nyssa popped up like a blade exiting the sheath of a switchblade. She stood trembling in shock, her eyes wide as saucers. "What little brother?"

"I am sorry to be the one to tell you this," Agatha said quickly, an edge of uneasiness passing over her. "But yes, your mother is expecting… they just got the news themselves."

"Hu-how do you know all this?" Nyssa begged, confusion tears rising to eyes.

"My girl, we are Magic after all," Agatha replied as calmly as she could. "We see things."

"You did this?" Nyssa asked in an accusative tone as she pulled her knees up towards her chest as her eyes narrowed at the woman. "You made this happen?"

"Well, not your mother and stepfather making you a little brother," Agatha replied, wanting to giggle at the thought but choked it down and continued. "That is something they did on their own, but the other things, yes; I had a hand in it all."

"But *why?*" Nyssa bellowed, the tears flowing now.

"As I told you, Nyssa," Agatha said without any regrets. "To protect you as I have been protecting you since long before you were born."

Nyssa's mouth was quivering rapidly, her eyes shifting sharply to the left and right, trying to find sense in all of it as if she was trying to decipher hieroglyphics on the walls of a pyramid. Part of her mind understood everything the woman was telling her, and in some distant way, it all had made sense, but the remainder of her brain was still stuck in first gear and fighting to find the clutch so as to shift up.

Needless to say, there was a sharp headache forming between her ears at the moment.

Nyssa slowly slouched back in the chair and brought up her hands before her which she held palms up for a moment and then let them fall to her thighs; she had nothing left to give or understand.

"Follow me, Nyssa, and try to understand," Agatha gracefully sat forward, her face kind and understanding. "Do you not find it odd that two people of Magic, Marco and Amora, just so happened to be strolling along just a mere few blocks from where you lived?"

No answer, just darting eyes.

"Never found it strange that your house compared to thousands of others still had power during the storm so that every amenity you enjoy still functioned?"

Silence from Nyssa still, but there was some clarity in her eyes.

"Even better, look back on your entire life; has anything terrible, save your parents' divorce and your grandmother's passing—which you know could not have been interfered with—ever happened in your life?" Nyssa's eyes fell to her lap, and she slowly shook her head. "We have always looked after you and your family for all the reasons you already know, and I will apologize only for the fact that this has all hit you abruptly and at once, but I will never apologize for what has been done."

"No, I understand," Nyssa said quietly as she wiped her eyes with a lazy hand. "Thank you, Auntie Agatha; I'm sorry for being selfish right now."

"*Selfish?*" Agatha chortled, her hands coming together is a loud clap. "You are perhaps the least selfish person I have ever met, Nyssa; even your name personifies good-natured and helpful."

"I know," Nyssa said, sniffing back the remnants of her tears. "It means little elf or brownie; my dad named me for that reason."

"Precisely!" Agatha smiled. "When he told me what your name would be, it filled my heart with joy. Just know that all your concerns right now are completely understandable and as well, completely human."

There was a long silence between them, only the sounds of the falling water and the occasional croak from a frog entered the air. Nyssa slowly advanced through the cards of information she had just been dealt, her eyes focusing on an embroidered flower on the right front pocket of her shorts.

"So, I will be homeschooled like Seema, then?" Nyssa said in a murmur.

"Of course," Agatha responded with a gentle smile. "And you will learn here more than your school can hope to teach you."

"Can you teach me Urdu?" Nyssa looked up to her, puzzled. "And Low German just like you did Seema?"

"And Russian, Cantonese, or any other language you wish to learn." Agatha's smile grew, and she motioned with open arms for Nyssa to come to her. Nyssa slowly stood and moved to her, taking a seat on Agatha's lap, her head resting on her shoulder. "Here, there is so much to learn, my child."

Nyssa played with the ideas through her head and liked all the possibilities that she saw there.

"*Soooo,*" Nyssa said, drawing out the word. "I am going to have a little brother then?"

"That you will," Agatha giggled. "And think of it, you will not be there to change diapers, or mind him while your mom seeks rest and surely wouldn't have any little hands touching your belongings."

"I like the idea of that," Nyssa nodded, picturing it and she gave Agatha a loving squeeze. "So, when will they be here again?"

"In two days, my little brownie," Agatha smiled and squeezed her back, her eyes closing to the moment and enjoying the love. "In two short days."

-3-

In his rarest form, Langdon Drellic paid a visit to Luna House to see Agatha in person later that day, by permission of course. Since Lady Agatha's bold and somewhat explosive statements regarding Nyssa being the Next Coming, there had been quite a bit of buzzing amongst the bees of the Consortia despite his staunch rebuttal of such ludicrous ideas. He knew he had to find an angle, or he'll find himself entirely on the far edge of being out of the mix. With a false smile hiding his incredulous state of mind, he produced a slight bow to Lady Agatha and dared even to grace her hand with a small honoring peck of his lips.

"I see that there must be something grand in the mind of Mr. Drellic this day," Agatha mused as they walked along the paths past stables where the horses played amongst themselves.

Even though Langdon was perhaps the most influential member of the Consortia—as well as its chief historian this side of Yesterday (having rewritten many parts of it to suit his own needs)—Agatha didn't trust the man as far as she could cast him (and under the right circumstances that would be pretty far indeed).

He walked on her right with his elbow slightly extended outward, and she, with delicate fingers, grasped it ladylike, and the two strolled as if there wasn't a care in the world. Deep down, she knew his real intent for a visit was out of hope that he could see Nyssa up close and personal, perhaps even to charm her away without Agatha's notice. Still, Agatha had already devised a counter for whatever the man could have surmised.

"So, she is tending to this Anathema cacodemon?" Langdon drew back to a previous notation in their conversation as they moved away from the cross-thatched fence which rounded the horse's trotting ground.

"Oh, she is by far not a devil, Langdon," Agatha laughed. "She is just a girl who has been shown the wrong hand by the wrong dealer. She has a bright light inside of her, you will see."

307

"So, you intend on nurturing this Mica, then?" Langdon continued, and Agatha could picture him surmising her expulsion doctrine from the Consortia as they spoke; him sitting in a darkened corner, scribbling madly by candlelight, his brow and palms sweaty with carnal delight.

"That I do, Langdon," Agatha smiled through her reply. "Providing that she wishes to be taught, but she has sanctuary here regardless of her wishes."

"The great savior of the strays and the unwanted," Langdon smiled to her, his voice pleasant but the point of his stinging tongue was well felt. "Speaking of which, I see Marco has your fire."

"Marco has always had his own, Langdon," Agatha shook her head to him, her graceful smile never leaving her lips.

"I see," he said quietly, his tongue working back and forth between clenched teeth as he thought. "Well don't you think that things have gotten a little, well: crowded for you?"

"Oh, not at all," she glowed a smile. "I have plenty of room and it is not like they are small children."

"That they are not," Langdon agreed, his mind twisting and screaming for him to get out what he wanted to say. Finally, with a sigh, he spoke: "Don't you think that it might be wise for the Nyssa girl to be trained by someone who has more historical understanding of who she is?"

"Like whom?" Agatha paused in mid-step, head slightly cocked in anticipation. "Angelica perhaps?"

Langdon almost spat when he attempted to calm his laughter, "Excuse me, Lady Agatha, but Angelica is a fool by her own right, and I would fear that our Nyssa would succumb to some ill-prescribed ointment resulting in her turning into something wet and wiggling."

"Who then?" Agatha asked sharply, but she already knew the answer to that. "You, Langdon Drellic?"

"It would be a heavy burden on top of my other duties to the Consortia," he said and then smiled. "But yes. Me."

To Langdon's surprise, Agatha actually held her midsection with both hands and bent forward into her laughter which came wild, fresh, and without remorse. Langdon stood with thin slit eyes, the pupils narrowing towards her contemptuous disrespect.

"Why do you find this so amusing, Lady Agatha?" he spoke through clenched teeth.

"Oh, I am so sorry, Langdon," she laughed and had to take a moment to calm herself. "But you? A student? After all your years of teaching no one? A female pupil on top of that?"

Agatha returned to her laughing fit until tears squirted from her eyes.

"I personally do not appreciate your sense of humor, Lady Agatha," he said dryly. "And pray tell me what does her being a female have one thing to do with anything? I have taught many students in my day."

"I know Langdon, and those are partially my points," she attempted and eventually got the laughing to quell until its afterglow was merely a smile. "For one, your day as a teacher of Magic has long since passed, and secondly, you have never once instructed a female.

"As a matter of fact, I recall a paper you had released amongst the ranks about how you felt about women and how they should never be taught any Magic stronger than being a basic Seer and the battle of the sexes was a fight that should remain only in the world of normal people and *not* the World of Magic."

"Well, people do change over the years, you know?" he attempted to defend against the blatant truth against him, poorly.

"They do, I agree, but even when the web is gone, the spider still waits in the shadows," Agatha said flatly and sighed. "Alright, let us humor this idea for just a moment then. Let us say that I agreed with you and handed over Nyssa to your care and education; what is the first thing you can tell me about a girl's needs? Better yet, a *teenage* girl's needs?"

A long pause hung between them like fog.

"Any clue?" she added, waiting.

"I would do all that is needed of me," he said dryly, attempting to pass the idea off as if this was all trivial firsthand knowledge that any respectful person of Magic had already bred into their fibers.

"Oh?" Agatha quipped, surprised, and she sat on one of the white wrought iron benches scattered amongst her property. Langdon followed suit and sat as well. "So, you are ready to handle the mood swings of an emotional, developing, hormonal sixteen-year-old student then, are you?"

"All of those things can be contained and controlled," he rebutted flatly.

"Contained and controlled?" she resounded, her smile nearly vanishing. "You are suggesting that the human condition can be contained and controlled? Interesting. So, what will you do in about a month when her visitor comes?"

"Turn the visitor away for she will need her time to study," he replied quickly, knocking that blow down in a wink only to receive Agatha's slow sympathetic shaking of her head. "What?"

"I am talking about her menstrual cycle, Langdon," she said quietly as his eyebrows rose. "You know, her period? It can be quite messy, and I am not speaking just metaphorically either."

There was such a long pause coming from Langdon now that Agatha thought that she had stopped his heart.

"Messy?" he returned her point and she nodded.

"Quite," she said flatly and began to play with a fingernail. "But I am sure you will manage with providing her with plenty of dark-colored undergarments and bedding, that, or you will purchase a considerable amount of bleach and fabric softener."

"Undergarments?" his mouth moved without his permission. "Bleach?"

"Oh yes, bleach, and of course you will need to go and buy her those essential items too," Agatha tossed in another hand grenade to the melee.

"Essentials?" he muttered, his brain now the consistency of warm lumpy oatmeal.

"You know," she leaned towards him, cupping the side of her mouth with a hand, and then whispering. "Feminine napkins?"

"What?" he jolted back, eyes wide.

"Well, you can't have her bleeding all over the place now, can you?" Agatha laughed passively. "I mean think of *that* mess you will have to clean up!"

"She can manage that herself!" he declared defiantly.

"No, she cannot," Agatha shook her head quickly. "Especially not the Next Coming, she surely cannot. *You* must go to the store and buy them *for* her. Well, until you know what they look like, then perhaps you can invoke them, but that would be stealing, and we have rules against that."

Langdon was a quaking mess after that.

"You do know that our students can never leave our sides," she added in another nudge in her attempts to push him over his edge. "And under no certain terms are you to expect the Next Coming to go to the store by herself to buy them. No, you will have to manage all this as well as make sure that her linen is clean and—"

"*Enough!*" Langdon barked, his head swirling in thin air as his stomach flipped. "I see your point!"

"Oh, I thought you would," she smiled. "And to think if I had to explain tampons if that was her method of choice."

"Lady Agatha, please!" he said, standing. "Keep the girl and train her… keep them all for all I care, but you must keep the whole of the Consortia privy to her progress—"

"I shall," she injected quickly.

"And you be weary of that Anathema brat and keep her under a close eye!" he barked, his mind begging him to leave and damning himself for not having this conversation projected. "And we do *not* need to know of *any* of her monthly 'visitors' in *any* of your reports."

"That is not a conversation a lady will have in open company, Langdon," she gasped and followed it with a repetitive *'tisk'*-ing sound.

"So be it!" he growled and produced a rough bow. "I will take my leave of you and inform the others of my decision to have you instruct the girl."

"And such a wise decision it was, Langdon," Agatha smiled and stood as she watched him move swiftly back up the pathway and eventually out of sight.

Sighing through a smile, she sat back on the bench, her eyes watching the horses prance in the distance. Soon the smile became a giggle, then a chuckle, until eventually becoming a hearty, victorious laughter. She was confident this would be the last conversation on the subject and a vision no less every time Langdon lunched on tomato soup.

-4-

Nyssa and Seema walked Mica to the atrium, taking firsthand care to step on each side of her in case she got dizzy. Despite Angelica's healing spells, ointments, and unique Magic drawn from Fairy flowers and Amazon breezes, Mica still had a way to go.

They had expressed there was a surprise for her in which Mica drew immediately inward, instinctively suspicious of her hosts, borne out of years of brainwashing under the guise of Anathema logic that the Consortia tortured and killed any member of the dark sect upon sight. They had assured her of innocent intent and that she would love what they had to show her, and they even agreed that she would not be blindfolded or requested to close her eyes to see the splendor they had to show her.

"This is amazing!" Mica croaked harshly; her throat still strained from screaming during the attack. Her eyes were wide with amazement and darted about in their almost futile attempt to gather in every colorful detail simultaneously. "Look at all the turtles!"

"I know," Nyssa smiled and pointed to a pair which was lazily lounging on a large stone. "Look, I think those two are in love."

Mica attempted to smile and even dared a slight chuckle, but her expression remained weary and dark between the physical pain and waning distrust. Slowly Mica moved to the edge of the suspended walkway and slowly squatted down, her sore muscles moving like pistons without oil. She cautiously extended a small hand towards the two turtles who favored her with a long stare from the sides of their heads, but neither withdrew into their shells. Mica smiled at this because, for once, something did not recoil from her.

"They like you I think," Seema smiled, squatting down next to her, causing her to flinch ever so slightly.

"They are not normally this trusting," said Nyssa as she crouched down on Mica's other side. "You have a good mana; they can sense that, you know?"

"I-I-I," Mica sounded softly, her head turning between Nyssa, the turtles and Seema as she tried to find her words hidden so deeply beneath the fear and shame.

She wanted to scream, to damn Nyssa as well as Seema for their kindness and their words; how dare these two mentally torture her with affection only to later strap her to a flogging post with sinister grins on their faces.

How dare they?

"Yes?" Nyssa sounded, eyebrows up.

"Nothing; never mind." Mica finally whispered as she shook her head, dropping her eyes to the water below.

"She's right, you know?" Seema said to her softly. "All animals know when a good soul is near them; why do you think people-loving dogs growl or cats hiss at certain people when they might normally love everyone?"

"But—but I am Anathema," Mica whispered, briefly seeing the tear fall from the tip of her nose, which disrupted her reflection in the water. She wiped it away with a fast, harsh motion, angry at the idea that she had cried and, even worse, done so in front of *lesser* people of Magic. She was Anathema, after all, and these two Consortia brats with their pleasant upbringings, happy bedtime stories, and teachers who never yelled, never chastised, and never hurt you!

How dare these brats? How dare they?

Mica gasped for air, having not known that she was holding her breath for nearly a minute, and then sat back on the walkway and pulled her knees to her chest.

"You say all these things to break me."

"Break you?" Nyssa said sharply, a flare of anger rising but it was not directed towards Mica, however the suddenness of it jolted through Mica, causing her to flinch. "I think your bastard of a teacher has done that enough, don't you think?"

"Nyssa!" Seema whispered sharply which ended Nyssa's verbal onslaught, but the flare was still burning bright inside her.

"Suh-sorry," Mica whimpered as she buried her face in her knees as her body rocked back and forth, her fingers pulling at her own hair. "I just hate this! I am so confused! They haven't tortured me like you said they were going to do! This *is* torture! Damn it!"

"Torture you?" Nyssa blinked, her mind stunned by these words, and she didn't know if she should laugh at the idea of it or say nothing at all. Nyssa and Seema leaned back so that they could look at each other clearly out of Mica's sight if she happened to look up; Nyssa mouthed: *What the hell is she talking about?'* while Seema immediately replied with a rapidly shaking head, palms up shrug and mouthing back: *'I have no idea!'*

Mica nodded as her forehead rested on her knees, her hands pulling thick locks of jet-black hair down past her eyes.

"It is historic," Mica continued, her tone wavering with apparent fear and forced in attempt to sound brave.

"What is?" Seema asked, her face twisted with absolute confusion.

"The torture the Consortia is renowned for," Mica said in a rapid fire of grunts.

"We are?" Nyssa's voice rose sharply, her own face matching Seema's as Mica nodded her head once again. "Well, this is all new to us, isn't it Seema?"

"Hells yeah, this is new!" Seema spat out, and briefly Nyssa acknowledged that in some ways maybe, just maybe, she was a bad influence on Seema. "We don't torture people, Mica! What 'historic' lies have been said?"

Hells yeah? Nyssa repeated the words her sister just spat out in her mind and figured she would have a talk with her at a later date on the subject.

Mica looked up, her hands still holding her hair and then pivoted on her butt using her heels so that the three of them could face each other. The two sets of eyes bearing down on her showed no lies.

"You flog members of the Anathema," Mica whispered as she relaxed her grip on her hair and brought her head up slightly. "With leather dipped in rock salt and shards of glass. I was told that you continue to torture us even after we've talked!"

"Really?" Nyssa gasped as her spiritual cheeks stung with the open-handed slap of the rumor. Mica nodded and crossed her chest with her armss, her mind preparing her for the attack which must truly come now; she knew their secret. "I mean you did try to brainwash me, didn't you?"

"Yuh-yes but, I was told to!" Mica squeaked, her eyes widening with fear.

"And although you failed, that was still assault," Nyssa narrowed her eyes at Mica as she slowly leaned in towards the terrified girl. "Well, then I guess we had better get this torture started then."

It would have taken a high-speed camera to have captured who exactly recoiled first by Nyssa's profoundly serious and overtly dry comical comment: Mica or Seema. It might have also caught which of their simultaneous gasps escaped the two girls' throats, which came so sudden and sharp that even Nyssa flinched, but on that day, they were nonpresent.

"*I'm kidding!*" Nyssa's hands flew up, palms open and fingers spread, her grin nearly reaching both ears and her dimples sucking in so deeply it was as if she had pits in her face. Seema's eyes darted over her with a terrified shock of disbelief, whereas Mica's dashed just as well but laced with terror. "I am seriously kidding, Mica!"

"Oh, that was so wrong, Nyssa!" Seema scolded, a hand unconsciously sliding over and rubbing Mica's back soothingly while the other one shot out and popped Nyssa in the shoulder. "That was mean!"

"Oh my god, Mica, I am so sorry," Nyssa insisted in her attempts to sound sincere through the wickedness of the mood. "I am really, *really* sorry."

"That was mean," Mica whimpered, her lips barely moving and after a moment to both Nyssa and Seema's surprise, Mica began to smile which eventually became a chuckle, then laughter, which ended with an unexpected snort, which not only got Mica laughing again, but all of them.

"Now that snort was torture," Nyssa added, which got the three rolling again and again, and each time it seemed their laughter would abate, one or the other would add in something, getting the whole grandstand rolling once again.

-5-

That night, Mica slept soundly for the first time in days, her mind slipping into the solitude of her mind without fear or regret, and if one had been present to note, they would have seen her slide away with a smile on her face. She had had a fantastic day without torture or interrogation as Anathema lore had misled her to believe, and for the first time in her life, she had known what it was to be loved for who she was.

They had done just about everything imaginable including sharing fun bits of Magic which the other had not learned. Nyssa had sat on the sidelines watching with awe and wondering how many of the Magic was performed, but she was a fast learner, and had even modified some of the Magic on the fly.

Twice Mica had scorned herself when her displays had grown dark and devious, promoting the essence of Dark Magic in which she had so long learned, but upon realization, she was quick to change them up, and instead of producing things of darkness, they became things of light.

"Sorry about that," she had whispered when she had produced a small swarm of locusts that immediately sought the Fairy Garden only to be stopped by Seema's fast hands and mind, which brought a freezing gust of wind from the Arctic, ending their advance.

"No worries," Seema smiled, nudging one of the frozen insects with her toe with a disgusted look on her face. "Well at least you might have saved someone's crop somewhere in the process."

"Really?" Mica asked surprised and when she was met by two nodding heads, she felt better about her actions.

They had spent the day talking mainly about the contrasted views of the Consortia and the Anathema, and although at times Mica vehemently defended her upbringing, words of poverty, war, and starvation quickly closed off those avenues as guilt had set in. They were not trying to make her feel guilty; all they wanted was for her to *see* why a certain Magic was wrong, but a few times, Mica sat quietly and cried, having learned that some of her actions had made others suffer.

"So, by me selfishly wanting something in the past," she had whispered, her eyes daring not to look at them. "I have probably caused some of that starvation I see on TV?"

Nyssa and Seema looked at each other in an attempt to find words of less conviction, but in the end, they gave slow, steady nods. Her mind replayed a multitude of events like a library of videotapes, each showing her what she had done with so little effort, which had more than likely caused some suffering in the world. At one point, the guilt had grown so strong that her tears came near hysterics, only to be comforted away by Nyssa's and Seema's reassuring affection.

"Just because you did those things," Nyssa said softly as she and Seema wiped away her thick tears. "Doesn't mean you still have to, you know?"

Mica nodded and laughed and then focused on the thawing locusts on the ground with a slight smile and whispered: *"Animatus."*

Right then, the locusts began to move, climbing up on their rear legs, and with a single hand as if strings were attached, Mica wiggled her fingers, and three of the locusts began to dance, all the while Mica hummed a chipper tune. Nyssa and Seema began to laugh hysterically as they sat cross-legged in the grass watching the show, and Mica was so happy that she was doing something that brought positive joy to her Magic that she could do nothing but giggle herself.

Yes, they had a good day, ending with a fantastic dinner of pot roast and potatoes, creamed spinach, and dumplings followed by orange sherbet for dessert. Agatha had spent most of the meal listening to the girls talk and sharing stories, occasionally telling a few of her own to keep the conversation alive.

For Agatha, there was no need to talk but only to listen and enjoy the three sisters of Magic carrying on as if they hadn't a care in the world. At that moment, as they sat at a table in the House of Luna, they did not, and although she would share a smile when they laughed, her mind was far away and focused on her concern about

Anathema's next move. She refused to allow the thoughts any longer, for this was a moment of celebration at the very least, and soon they moved on to the living room, where they continued their conversations and enjoyed their after-dinner drinks of warm cocoa milk with crushed walnuts sprinkled on top.

Yes, Mica had a fine day, and she slept accordingly until the dreams crept in, dark and brooding as they slithered from the edges of her subconscious like a rancor vermin from the murk. It crept over happiness and replaced it with dread, obliterated hope and filled the void with despair, and slowly it took form in her mind's eye and became that of her teacher, that of Seth. He approached her as she stood in the grand hallway of Luna House, coming slowly to the edge of the porch stairs and looking at her intently over the distance to where she stood with open arms. She was terrified in her dream, and in the physical world, the sheets became moist with her perspiration.

"Come to me, my Mica," the Seth-figure said lovingly to her, his eyes blue and calm.

"No," the mind-Mica told him defiantly and dared to run but did nothing but suffer in fear. *"You are Hurt, you are Pain, and you did both to me, badly! I hate you!"*

"Those are harsh words that I do not deserve," the Seth thing whispered back, its head slowly shaking as it stopped at the base of the stair unable to advance. *"Remember all things happen for a reason and your reason is to allow me in so that I can bring you home."*

"Home?" her mirrored-Mica questioned and images of her room with all her computers, and posters of her favorite bands, and her twin voodoo dolls with the stabbed-out eyes flooded in. *"That's not my home anymore, you saw to that."*

"All but a ruse, my Mica," the Seth-shape hissed and slowly began to change; the jaw stretching downward and hanging open grotesquely, his eyes slanting backwards and growing dark and save not having a luminescent orb above his head, his face looked shockingly familiar to a hatchet fish. *"All you have to do is let me in, Mica and you will see."*

"You will hurt them!" duo-Mica screamed, her conscious mind begging her to slam shut the door and to run. *"I cannot allow you to do that!"*

"You will still have one of your sisters," Seth-it hissed, swaying back and forth. *"One is better than none… NOW LET ME IN!"*

Mica woke with a sharp scream in which she quickly strangled back with her hands plastering her mouth, her body shaking, and her breathing loud and audible as she attempted to calm herself through deep breaths through her nose. Her sheets were soaking with sweat, and her pillow was damp with tears that had come long before she had awoken, and as she sat there rocking back and forth on the bed in the darkness, she could feel the presence of him in the room with her.

"Why?" she cried softly, pulling the sides of her hair until her scalp hurt, twice hitting the top of her head with her fists. "Just leave me alone!"

The night carried on slowly and without whispers in the dark other than her mind begging for answers until she eventually cried herself to sleep.

As she dozed a second time and the Seth-thing came again in her visions, she was able to shut the door in her mind with only a slight hesitation and effort. It had asked her once for admittance, in which she paused momentarily, pondering the possibility for an unknown reason, and whispered back: *"I will think about it."*

For the remainder of the night, she did not dream again.

CHAPTER EIGHTEEN

A Family Visit

-1-

Just as Agatha had promised, in two short days, Nyssa's parents came to visit.

As it had been of years of late, whenever there was any form of family function in which she was already present at whatever particular location the event was held, her parents arrived separately; her father always arrived early to spend a little unabated free 'Dad and Daughter' time with her. He arrived at nine in the morning, rolling up the drive in a shiny new rental car, having flown into Madison, Wisconsin, just an hour before, and drove directly. He had barely exited the vehicle when her body slammed into his with open arms, nearly knocking them both to the ground.

"Hey, Dad!" her face a joyous painting of smiles, her voice small and full like a chorus of flutes. They stood embraced for what seemed like minutes as they slowly rocked back and forth. "Aw, you look like you are going to cry."

Her father smiled warmly and softly bopped the tip of her nose with a knuckle and kissed her on the forehead, "Just happy tears, little one."

The reuniting was grand as he entered the house, his arms absorbing Seema's hug with no less sincerity than his daughter's, which then moved on to Agatha, who then gently scolded him for his visit being way too long in the making.

"I know, Agatha," he smiled, but the guilt was in his eyes. He had no real excuse, and his feet shuffled nervously just as they had when Nyssa would sometimes inquire about the long gaps between his visits. He didn't have to dig down to know the reasons. Since the divorce, it had been simply out of shame of the separation that had kept him away; something he would admit if the issue was pressed.

Instead, Agatha simply smiled and gave him another hug and whispered softly in his ear, "Well, you are here now."

As they moved further into the large entranceway, Nyssa broke from his arms and darted towards Mica who was standing far off to the side and attempting not to be seen.

"Dad!" Nyssa said excitedly as she scooped an arm around Mica's and began pulling her towards the group. "I want you to meet a really special friend!"

"*Friend?*'" Mica whispered, confused, her eyes darting like scurrying mice.

With a smile, Nyssa quickly turned towards her and nodded so rapidly she resembled one of those little bobbleheads on the dashboard of so many taxi cabs.

"Dad, this is Mica," Nyssa proudly said as they stopped before him. Mica attempted a smile, but inside, she was a squirming mass of sickly eels in muddy waters. She wanted to run away. Nyssa's father gave her a warm smile, overlooking a few fading bruises which edged her jaw bones despite the delicate makeup Nyssa had applied. "She's our new sister!"

"'*Sister...*'" she muttered quickly, echoing the words but confused about their origin Mica's eyes moved between the girls and Agatha, full of questions. Still, they focused mainly on the light-skinned man before her who had kind—albeit tired—eyes, his reddish mustache curving with a pleasant, loving smile, all accentuated with a spattering of freckles.

"Hello, Mica," he said quietly and opened his arms. "Well, if you are one of their sisters, then you deserve a big hug as well."

There was a brilliant moment, one which could be categorized using only massive numerical fractions close to one sextillionth of a second [a sextillion being an actual and extremely large number having lots and *lots* of zeros], Mica hesitated, and as that un-recordable fraction of time passed, she too got a hug from Nyssa's father. She murmured a '*thank you*' and then moved away; this time, her face held a smile as gleaming as everyone else's.

-2-

In short order, Nyssa and her father found their alone time as they took a long walk amongst the grounds, the whole time Nyssa was an excited teenaged chatterbox, times two.

For Nyssa, it was not an uncommon action to hold her dad's hand, even at this age. To do so came as natural as breathing, a habit which started long before she could remember when she would grasp his two forefingers as they walked. As they moved, she talked of everything that had been going on in her life since the last time she had physically seen him almost three months before, and although most of it he had either already heard or read via phone, email, or text, to listen to it in person he could not be happier. Once she had dispatched all her mundane day-to-day's, she dove into the events which brought her to Auntie Agatha's (leaving out specific details, of course).

"And then you know that big tree in the backyard?" she added, never losing a beat as her mind locked away certain details of the storm weeks before. "Well, that thing came crashing into the house! My whole room was smashed!"

"Wow," her father added as his mind trailed back to when he first visited his child's new home. Then he had made a mental note that he did not like seeing an old tree outside his daughter's window, but now, just like then, he said nothing about the fact. "I am so glad you didn't get hurt."

"Auntie Agatha got a little scrape, but she is fine," Nyssa added and then fell silent as they walked. She had already heard the news of both her parents and fought desperately to keep her knowledge a secret. Her mind pondered when they would tell her, perhaps when her mother arrived or one at a time. Ideally, she would have preferred the group method so that she wouldn't have to put on the act of being surprised twice. "So, Dad, what's *new* with you?"

Her father gave her a quick sideways glance and licked his lips nervously. He had a feeling, small yet significant, in the back of his mind that she already knew and grew cautious of what he would say. Nyssa was quick and could pick up on something even before you thought it.

He called it her gift; she now called it something else.

"Well, I am not sure how much your Aunt Agatha has told you," *Smart thinking,* he thought to himself quickly and then continued. "But I have been given a job offer for a fulltime position."

"That is so cool!" She beamed and hugged him sideways, her arms wrapping around his waist and squeezing tightly. She *was* more excited for him now that it was his words telling her.

For years her father had gotten wrapped up being a network consultant, which at one time, he immensely enjoyed because it gave him diversity in his job. Still, after being on that bandwagon for a few years, he had found it impossible to get off it and to find something with more security than being nothing more than a temp.

"Yeah, Auntie Agatha kinda let me in on a few things only because I nagged her, but I think you should take it! It's such a good move for you."

"So, then you know about it being out of state as well?" he added as Nyssa nodded, and although he was relieved to see his daughter's acceptance, he was a little put off that she had all this information without it coming from him first. That also had been a customary habit since he and her mother separated: he was always giving the news too late, regardless of what it was. "And you are okay with this?"

"Dad, yes, of course," she smiled and double-hugged him sideways as they walked as if she was trying to squeeze the understanding into him. "I mean, I am used to you being gone, for work that is, but I know you will always call me, and you try to visit me whenever you can, and I know you love me.

"*And* I know you will buy me things!"

Nyssa stressed the last part with a beaming grin, her eyes twinkling up at him narrowly in thin, cheek-pinched slits. That got the two of them laughing despite the pangs of guilt reverberating through his chest like hammer falls which showed on his face as clear as day. He hated his career path more than anyone else, which led him to live the single bachelor's life resulting in having no one close to comfort his pains or to allow him to talk it out in moments of need. She leaned in tight and squeezed him lovingly, producing a smile only a child who utterly understood something could make.

"It's okay, Daddy," she said softly, and meant *Daddy* with the utmost sincerity spanning her entire young life. "I completely understand, so don't feel bad. You know you that are the best, right?"

He stood momentarily holding his daughter's eyes and saw nothing but the truth inside the sparkling orbs before him, and he slowly produced a smile that came from deep down inside. Slowly he took her into his arms and held her tightly, hugging his young adult daughter with a glowing radiance.

"When did you get so grown?" he said to the top of her head.

"You're not crying, are you?" she said, her face into his chest.

"Shut up, now," he smiled and squeezed her tighter.

-3-

An hour and a half after her father arrived at Luna House, Nyssa's mother pulled up into the drive. They all had been sitting on the porch swings drinking iced tea, some with mint, and others with lemon and two large trays of finger sandwiches of all types.

"The house is just as beautiful as I remember it!" her mother proclaimed as she walked from the drive. Agatha had sent away the *façade noire* an hour before her father had arrived using broad swooshing arm movements towards the two stone pillars standing at the mouth of the drive, and the whole of Luna House and its grounds showed off its splendor to the world.

"That was pretty amazing," Nyssa glowed as the ugliness of the façade seemed to melt away like so much sidewalk chalk in the rain.

"Are we still safe?" Mica whispered to Seema as her eyes darted the distant tree line for danger.

"Of course," Seema chirped and spoke dismissively towards the idea of being in danger. "No one can enter these grounds unless invited."

"By anyone?" Mica continued.

"Oh no," Seema adjusted herself on the swing so to get a better look at the new arrivals. "Only Lady Agatha has that power."

"Oh, okay," Mica nodded and fell silent.

"*Christine!*" Agatha released a playful squeal as she moved from the steps meeting Nyssa's mother halfway up the walk with open arms, and the girls shifted peculiar glances to one another.

Agatha held a confident, elegant composure at all times, and this sudden burst of excitement was entirely out of character, especially since they had recently seen each other during their visit to Chicago. The girls could do nothing but shrug and watch.

"I am so glad that you made it!"

"I just don't know how you do it, Aggie," her mother said shaking her head, not all too surprised that her mother had nicknamed her as well.

"Are you Seemie?" Nyssa leaned over and whispered to Seema who gave her a playful shrug and the two giggled. Nyssa looked at Mica with a playful smile and continued, "You will be Micky by the night's end, I promise!"

The three giggled as they attempted to regain their *proper* air.

"Took longer than expected then?" Agatha responded to Christine's comment as she walked with her up the walk.

"All that construction!" Christine exclaimed, her head shaking once again. "It must have taken you all hours to get up here."

"It took quite a while indeed," Agatha responded as they climbed the steps, and she gave Nyssa an innocent 'inside wink' which got Nyssa smiling.

"Hey, Mom," Nyssa smiled and got up and gave her a hug that lacked the heavy squeezing effort she had towards her father earlier.

They always saw each other as the main reason for the lackluster greeting; the other was that her mother was not an advocate of public displays of affection.

"I am glad you made it here safely. Where's Randy?"

"Oh, he's back in Naperville getting things ready," she stated as she took a seat in a beautiful white wicker high-back on the porch. "Mainly with the insurance adjuster and things of the like, but we will discuss that and other details later."

I already know, Nyssa smiled and returned to the swing.

Once all the welcoming greetings finished, Nyssa's mother settled her eyes on Mica, who held a nervous stranger's smile on her face the whole while.

"So, Mica," her mother addressed, her eyes scanning the girl from top to bottom. "Are you are related to Aggie?"

"Well—" was all that the girl could manage before Agatha interrupted.

"She is my God-niece," Agatha passively said as Nyssa was walking between them with a small tray of finger sandwiches, and she smiled when Nyssa made a motion with her eyes towards her mother, which screamed: *Do something about her!* "She will be summering with us this year as her parents vacationed abroad."

"Oh, well, that's nice," her mother said quietly, shaking her head to the spread of cucumber and cream cheese sandwiches; she hesitated and then took one anyways. Nyssa never liked her mother's cynical method of introductions when she met new people, significantly younger new people. "So, have you been enjoying yourself then, Mica?"

"Very much so," Mica responded nervously, understanding the lie, and knowing she must follow along.

"What do you like the most?" Nyssa's mother continued.

"Umm, the turtles I think," Mica responded honestly and smiled. "Uh, Aunt Agatha has a lot of them, and Nyssa she, well, she's been teaching me all about them. I named one Dipper because he, well… he likes to dip his head in the water."

"Has she?" Christine asked surprisingly and regarded Nyssa with a wide look. "Well, you do have a good teacher then; she has had maybe four or five of them since she was little, haven't you Nyss?"

Nyssa nodded as she returned to her seat on the swing next to Mica with Seema on the other end.

"My God, you three could almost be sisters," her father noted with a comfortable smile, having truly spent the moment to look at the three of them.

Nyssa, as stated early on, was a cornucopia of multiracial blood. Although Seema was Middle Eastern by descent and Mica had Northern European features through and through (with a shadow of something else mixed in for good measure), their ages, characteristics, and personalities could easily be mistaken for relatives.

The three smiled shyly in response as Agatha nodded in agreement while her mother cocked her head to one side in judgment.

"Hmm, I guess I can see that," Christine finally added, but always with a counter when it involved her ex-husband. "But I see more cousins than sisters, but close."

Her father simply bit down and nodded, taking a sip from his lemongrass tea. Nyssa swallowed hard on a piece of cucumber sandwich as her mind sought hard for something to change the subject. She had a gift of noticing the small tendons in her father's face flex when he had a lot to say but chose better on doing so, but that fuse was short and the detonator tricky.

"So, Mom," she blurted out quickly having found the key to not only move the conversation on, but to open the doorway to the reason for her visit in the first place. "Did your rose garden survive all that flooding from the storm?"

"Oh no, they all drowned," she said passively, but lit up, nonetheless. "Which brings us to some terrific news!"

"Oh?" Nyssa sounded, eyebrows rising with an added false expression of curiosity. "Drowned roses?"

"Yes indeed," her mother beamed setting her glass down. "Well, no, not the drowned ones, but I have been extended a tenure at the San Francisco Conservatory!"

"Really?" Nyssa added and swallowed softly, preparing herself for her award-winning act.

Now, should I be excited or play the brat? The words raced through her mind, and although she had already decided days before on her reaction, now that the time had come, she couldn't quite make up her mind. She chose both: the excited brat.

"Does this mean I will attend California school now?"

"Well, no," her mother attempted to hold her smile, her expression growing uneasy. "What I mean is, as I have talked it over with your father as well as your stepfather, and of course your Auntie Agatha, we have decided that it would be best—at first of course—that you remain here and be homeschooled.

Go for the confused look, she thought and cleared her throat. *That always wins.*

"Home schooled?" she attempted, her voice squeaking twice to hold back her laughter. "At Auntie Agatha's... homeschooled?"

"Only until Randy and I get settled," her mother said so rapidly that there shouldn't be spaces in between the previous words of this sentence.

"I see," she said softly and fell quiet with all eyes on her. Her face twisted from one contemplative expression to the other, until her eyes happened upon her mother. "Any other news than that?"

Christine's jaw dropped suddenly which almost got Seema giggling for she now knew where Nyssa got the slack-jawed expression from and quickly she returned a smile to Nyssa clearing her throat.

"Well, we can discuss the other things later just you and me, but what do you think about everything so far?"

"Umm..." Nyssa attempted another look of confusion which soon failed as a smile crept the corners of her mouth, transforming her dimples. "...it sounds good to me."

Both her parents sighed with her acceptance: her father for purposely failing to inform her outright earlier of their decision and her mother for not having to fight it out as they had done on so many other subjects in the past. Mica squeezed Nyssa as Seema squeezed Mica, and Agatha softly clapped her hands together a few times, applauding the overall approval.

"That went surprisingly smooth," her mother added quietly to Agatha who provided her with a little shrug, and they all laughed together.

"So, when is your baby due?" Mica asked suddenly with a happy sincerity, and everyone froze with their jaws hanging, even Seema's mouth was cavernous; neither Agatha nor Nyssa had told either of them. Mica sat quietly with a partial smile on her face, her eyes moving from one set of wide eyes to the other with a cautious curious glance. "What?"

Well, as you can imagine that the relief all of them shared that the conversation was going to remain a smooth-running machine flashed away like gasoline to the match, or the other way around depending on your view of things.

*

"How did you know she was pregnant?" Seema was whispering harshly to Mica as they climbed the curving staircase quickly having been dismissed by Agatha to allow Nyssa and her parents to talk in private.

"I could hear two heartbeats," Mica said almost in a squeal, confused and embarrassed for what she had said. *"Couldn't you?"*

"No!" Seema said quickly as they moved down the hall towards her and Nyssa's room, moving Mica through the door and shutting it behind them. "I mean that's a brilliant gift, but oh my! That was *not* the right thing to say!"

"How was I supposed to know?" Mica begged and truly, how was she to know? The Anathema had been her life up until now and the Anathema was not known for being tactful in the very least.

"Well, I umm," Seema sounded and then exhaled, losing all her wind and then shrugging as she sat on her bed with Mica sitting down next to her. "I guess you wouldn't... neither would have I if I could hear them both."

"Think they are mad at me?" Mica asked quietly as she stared at the bedroom door, expecting that at any moment someone was going to barge through it to scream at her or worse.

"No, no one is mad," Seema said quietly and then giggled. "But I think her mom pooped a little when you dropped the anvil like that."

Mica exploded with laughter, followed by Seema, who made her best attempt to cover her mouth, which was in vain; the chortling carried and rose. The two held each other's eyes for a moment, and Seema gasped as she saw the sharp color of violet in her eyes.

"Do your eyes always glow when your mana sparks?" Seema asked quietly, having learned in her studies that that is a telltale sign of the Anathema's intent of doing harm.

"Sometimes," Mica smiled and patted Seema's hand. "Especially when I am thinking something... naughty."

"And what are you thinking?" Seema said in a dry whisper.

"Nothing anymore," Mica shrugged slightly and returned her eyes towards the door.

-4-

Nyssa's parents had come and gone leaving her feeling empty and alone. Although her parents did their best to put on a cordial appearance, no one—especially Nyssa—was fooled that they were minding their tongues and attitudes at times, but every now and then, they glowed together like husband and wife. It might have been the occasional joke in which they both laughed at simultaneously. Perhaps when one finished the other one's sentences just as she had remembered them doing in the past?

Nyssa couldn't quite place it, but when those rare moments did shine, she could do nothing but sit there and smile at them silently.

The remainder of the day had gone by relatively smoothly despite Mica's outburst of knowledge that only her parents, Agatha, and herself knew. Nyssa explained it away by stating that her mother had a certain glow to her skin which was radiantly beautiful.

"Just a good guess, I suppose, Mom," Nyssa had lied but then returned the truth to her mother. "You do look radiant."

"Why thank you," her mother smiled with a blush and temporarily dismissed any notion that Mica was a rude young woman.

For two more hours, the three of them sat on the front porch acting as if they were a family again, and with all of the ice fields now broken apart and shattered, their little boat of quality time chugged along unhindered. In the end, her parents left at the same time despite Agatha's insistence that they might stay at least for the evening and find their roads in the morning but to no avail. Both had their reasons for leaving when they did—her mother's excuse was the construction she was going to face and her father's that he had a flight out later that evening was all it took—but at least they left with warm smiles on their faces.

After giving hugs all around, her mother rolled down the drive first, stating that she had better find an open smoke shop before reaching the border, having promised Randy that she would bring him back venison jerky.

Her father shuffled about a little longer to say his own personal goodbyes to her.

"I am going to miss you, my little one," he said half-smiling in attempts to hide his sorrow. They hugged for a long time next to his rental car without even breathing.

"I am going to miss you too, Dad," she said with a croak in her voice as tears gently swelled near her lids. "You know that Auntie Agatha's house sits in a dead zone, but I will make sure that I get a hold of you in two days to make sure you got there safely."

"Sounds like a plan," he smiled and nodded. "I will call your mother and let her know as well, you know, just in case you reach her before you get a hold of me, that is?"

"Yeah, I know," she smiled back and hugged him once again.

These were the moments she hated and dreaded the most; the goodbyes.

"You be safe," she added, wanting to scream it.

"Oh, you know me, baby," he smiled. "I always am."

With that he opened the car door and then paused, snapping his fingers quickly and then reached into his pocket for his wallet.

"No, Dad, I don't need any money," Nyssa smiled as she attempted to stop his actions.

"No worries," he smiled and winked at her. "I wasn't going to give you any."

The two laughed together, ending with Nyssa tapping the side of her head and sounding out, *"Duh!"*

"No, what I want you to have been something that has always been special to me." Nyssa's father said as he unzipped a coin sleeve inside his wallet and removed a small lock of hair entombed in an amber resin. Smiling, he held it out to her. "I hope you do not think this is morbid, but this is a lock of your grandma's hair."

"Really?" Nyssa blurted, confused, surprised, and in the end, morbidly curious. Her father quickly saw the expression and could

only manage what the child was thinking; that he had somehow removed it after her death a few years before.

"No, no, no," her father shook his head and laughed nervously. "I got this from your grandma's jewelry box back when I was in kindergarten. Remember me telling you she once had hair down to the back of her knees?"

Nyssa nodded slowly, her eyes never leaving the encased lock and her mind still wrestling with morbid thoughts.

"Well, she had kept a small piece of it," her father explained as he held it by the clasp, the top of which had a gold eyelet that would support a nice neck chain. "And when I was about five or so, she cut it and kept a lock as a keepsake. I snagged it when I started school because I missed her so terribly, and I carried it in one wallet or another since then."

"You've kept this since grade school?" Nyssa asked surprised, her eyes widening as her hands cupped beneath it but without touching it.

"Umm-hmm," he sounded with a guilty smile. "A few years ago, I had it set in resin and polished so that nothing would ever happen to it, but yeah, I have had it ever since. I never told your grandma or aunts I had it, but it has always given me luck. I think now she would like you to have it."

With that he placed the resin coated lock of hair with its clasp into her palms and the world shifted. The rush that raced along the edges of her forearms and biceps into her chest was almost electric, carrying forth a jolt that sent a flare off behind Nyssa's eyes which blinded her from the inside. In the brilliance of an infinite fraction of time, just shy of a Planck Second, Nyssa saw the whole world happen all at once, twice.

"*Whoa,* did you feel that?" Her father laughed nervously as his eyes looked about him and he rapidly fluttered his fingers to ease the sensation.

"Yes, I did," she said with as much as a whisper, her head turning towards Agatha who was smiling and nodding at her from the porch. When she looked back at the pendant, she could see it glowing golden.

"Must have been static build up," her father shrugged as he slipped into the science geek mode that she knew him well for. "Oh well. So, do you like it?"

"I love it," she nodded, her eyes staring at the lock and slowly they moved upwards towards his which were looking back at her warmly. "Are you sure you want me to, have it?"

"As sure as my love for you," he smiled and slowly embraced her, kissing the top of her head.

*

He soon left thereafter, giving the horn a double tap, and waved from the driver's side window. Slowly, he rolled down Agatha's gravel drive, with Nyssa watching him go until only a hazy dust cloud hung. Her eyes returned to the lock of hair which pulsated golden in her hand, and she could *actually* feel it like a soft beating of a heart.

"You now have one," Seema moved up close to her and giggled.

"What's that?" Nyssa asked with a whisper.

"You now have your mana-vessel," Seema nudged her with her shoulder. "I saw it spark."

"Huh?" Nyssa looked at her, confused.

"That is your talisman," Seema smiled and gently tapped her hairpiece made of red flowers and baby's breath. "It is the essence of who we are and our focus, and like mine that found me, yours has found you."

"My dad had it all the time?" Nyssa shook her head as it begged for answers.

"Seems like it," Seema beamed scooping Nyssa's elbow with her own and moved her towards the porch. "I personally assumed it was your music player since you cherish it like life itself; funny how a piece of our deep-set love is the answer to it all."

"Yeah," she whispered back as she walked with Seema to the porch; the pendant-lock of hair nudging her palm with steady, even pulses.

CHAPTER NINETEEN

Weighing of the Souls

-1-

"It is quite unfair that you won't let me in, Mica," the Seth-personal-look-alike said softly as he flicked small pebbles from the pile in his hand. He was sitting on the top stair of the porch, much closer than he had reached in previous dreams. Mica looked through the eyes of her dreaming essence at him as she stood shielded behind the screen door, and both of her minds were a tangled mess of confusion; the Mica in the dream and the one whose head it all was in.

Slowly the sheets of her bed began to moisten as her temperature rose.

"I cannot trust you," she said quietly in response, her eyes finding her fingertips to play with uneasily. *"What you did to me, to Pia, I-I—"*

"Pia is alive and well, Mica, don't you see?" The Seth-shape spoke and flicked its hand to the right and Pia appeared as a secondary image in her mind. The image he projected was of her working with vials and bowls and spoons concocting something that steamed and bubbled. *"Believe it or not, my Mica, it was her idea that this barbaric ruse took place."*

"Her idea?" The mental Mica scrutinized, her eyes narrowing on the vision of Pia who showed physical evidence of the damage

done by Seth just as she had had from the attack in the outcropping. *"I don't see the angle."*

"Mica!" He turned towards her quickly where he sat, his voice full of authority but not cruel. *"You are not a little child anymore. If all of this must be spelled out to you as if you were five, do you think that I would have you sit at the table of the Order?"*

"No," Mica whispered feeling the shame, her eyes dropping to her fingertips once again. The Seth-thing breathed heavily and then calmed, attempting a thin smile.

"I know what I did was barbaric and that you are very cross with me," he said softly as he tossed his handful of pebbles to the ground and calmly stood. *"But you do know the importance of us, the Anathema, to have that girl's power on our side, don't you?"*

"I am just as strong," Mica whispered as her eyes narrowed angrily and then made the tips of her fingers disappear into a fist. *"She knows only kiddie Magic! Who cares what she did that day, she is a fluke, you said so yourself!"*

"Yes, Mica, I did say that," he said calmly, palms facing her to show he meant no harm as he took one step towards the screen door. *"And yes, you are quite powerful without a doubt, and yet...*

"Imagine, though, how strong our little family would be if I, the father, with his two daughters, were all together? You on my right and Nyssa on my left? Do you not see this?"

"We would be a family?" she asked sincerely as tears welled up along the edges of her eyes as they slowly rolled up towards his.

"Yes, my sweet Mica," Seth-vision smiled widely, his raised palms extending outward to his sides in a large, anticipated embrace. *"A*

family of the father with his daughters who are sisters, you would like that wouldn't you?"

"*Yes,*" she smiled both in dream and in self as her respiration slowed and her body relaxed against the sheets.

"*Then all you have to do, my Mica,*" the Seth-form gleamed as he reached for the handle of the screen door. "*Is to let me—*"

"*Mica!*" Seema's voice shattered the vision in a thousand pieces with her voice and one heavy shake. Mica was sitting up immediately, her eyes wide and terrified as she sought the night shadows rapidly.

"What?" Mica squawked as she scooted back towards the headboard rapidly.

"You were glowing," Seema said sternly through clenched teeth. "I could see it from our room!"

"So what?" Mica quickly spat out defensively.

"And you were talking to someone," Seema whispered slowly, enunciating every word perfectly. "There was a channel open; I could sense it!"

"I wasn't talking to anyone!" Mica hissed at her and heaved forward, delivering a double open shove to Seema's shoulders pushing her back. "I had a dream!"

"That was no dream, Mica!" Seema leaned in towards her, her fists clenched. "What-did-he-want?"

"It was just a dream, Seema!" Mica huffed, her eyes narrowing towards Seema and violet rose.

"You just sparked again," Seema uttered softly and leaned back, her body slow and steady as she stood from the edge of the bed as if she had just happened upon a rattlesnake in the grass. "Mica, what's going on with you?"

"Nothing, Seema!" Mica glared, her voice becoming deep and monotone. "Aren't you worried about what is going to happen to you?"

"What?" Seema charged quickly, her eyes shifting over the girl in the bed as if she were a complete and utter stranger. "You-you don't have your talisman; you cannot hurt any—"

"Leave me alone, Seema," Mica said flatly as she kicked her legs from the bed and advanced on Seema until their noses touched. "I was just having a bad dream!"

"Fine," Seema whispered and backed away, never taking her eyes off those violet ones until the bedroom door closed in front of her.

Seema stood looking at the wooden door for quite some time without daring even to breathe. Her mind split into two defined halves identical to the other, but each screamed their cries of desperation: one half demanding that she kick the door in and cast the girl to the *Yondsphere*, and the other begged for her to find someplace small and dark to crawl into, afraid.

As she struggled with her two emotions, the sharp click of the bedroom door lock latching cracked the silence of the hallway, making her jump. She knew that Mica was standing directly on the other side of the door, her eyes peering through it and into her soul. Slowly Seema backed away from it, her eyes focusing on the handle as she sidestepped toward her and Nyssa's room and eventually broke into a run.

-2-

"I think there is something wrong with Mica," Seema whispered to Nyssa in the dark, shaking her awake rudely by her shoulders. Nyssa looked at her with one wide eye while the other stood at half-mast as it begged the body for a little more energy to make it climb to the top.

"What do you mean?" Nyssa grumbled back as she moved her hair from her face and with hands in her lap, she looked at Seema's excited expression with little less than care.

"She was dreaming, Nyssa!" Seema said rapidly, running the words together.

"That's what I was doing too," Nyssa replied sarcastically. "We do that when we sleep."

"No, not that," Seema replied standing, her hands in front of her which moved with each and every word. "Channel-dreaming as in someone was channeled to her."

"Who would channel to Mica?" Nyssa yawned and stretched, her half-slumbering mind humoring the conversation for a moment.

"Her teacher," Mica said quickly as she paced back and forth, hands moving. "Seth!"

"You mean the same guy we saw trying to kill her?" Nyssa asked, her right eyebrow raising inquisitively her voice caustically dry. "*That* Seth?"

"Don't be so sarcastic, Nyssa!" Seema stomped one of her feet as her voice rose sharply. "I saw her glow coming from down the hallway! She was talking in her sleep! I think she is plotting something!"

"What? Against us?" Nyssa scowled at her and rolled her eyes. "I am not trying to be sarcastic, Seema, but aren't we the ones who saved her life?"

"Yes, but there is the things that—" Seema stammered out the words, but Nyssa cut in quickly.

"Look, when I was younger," Nyssa said quietly, her voice softening. "I used to dream a lot after my folks split up, and I always talked, even cried, in my sleep. Look at what she has gone through; don't you think she will have a few, if not *a lot* of bad dreams?"

"Yes but—"

"And..." Nyssa continued gently but firmly. "All this is new to her. I feel like giving her the benefit of the doubt personally, don't you?"

Seema's mouth worked, but without words, she could only stand there next to Nyssa's bed with her palms up, eyes wide, and her mind drawing a complete blank. Deep down, she knew something was amiss, but it had no natural face other than that of Mica's, which she could only assume that she was a pawn in something dark and dire. After a moment, she sighed, threw her arms up, and sat on the edge of Nyssa's bed, sulking.

"This might not come out right, but..." Nyssa spoke softly as she leaned forward and placed a gentle hand on Seema's shoulder. "You are not a little jealous of her, are you?"

"What?!" Seema gasped as she flung herself away from Nyssa's touch.

"Seema," Nyssa attempted but to no avail.

"Me being jealous of what, Nyssa?" Seema said harshly as spittle flew from her lips. "That I now have the Anathema sharing the house with me?"

"That's not what I meant!" Nyssa squealed defensively, her palms up and shaking as if signaling *No.*

"Then what did you mean?" Seema growled as her head began to swim in the darker waters of feeling alone and without support. "You seem to know so much so tell me that!"

"Seema, stop!" Nyssa insisted forcefully, attempting to grab Seema's hands but missed as Seema drew them away. "You are not listening to me. I am saying that since she came here, I have been giving her a lot of attention and not you. I want you to know that that's because, you know, she came here in that horrible condition. You are my sister, and I want to spend every moment with you. It's she's kind of like that hurt bird you take in, and you pamper it back to health, is all."

"Fine!" Seema hissed, not looking at Nyssa as her eyes shot to the floor past her socked toes. "Don't believe me."

"It's not that I don't believe you, Seema," Nyssa attempted a smile as she rose on her knees and sat on her haunches in the bed and attempted to turn Seema's face in her direction with a gently pull on her chin. "It's just with all the things that have happened in the last month and a half, well, it seems all of us are not ourselves and well, I can guarantee Mica is not."

Seema—although having put up one hell of a fight against it— eventually turned and looked at her and found a worried smile on Nyssa's face with eager conviction. She knew what she had seen since the other day when Mica's mana sparked; she had seen it in the girl's eyes just as clearly as seeing the morning sun or the turtles in the atrium. She just knew, but did she? Had she had a spark of jealousy hidden deep down that she didn't even know was present? Hadn't everything in the last month and a half truly turned the whole world upside down twice and then back upside right again? Hadn't—

"Maybe you are right," Seema said quietly as she dropped her eyes shamefully.

"I think I am about this one," Nyssa soothed with a warm smile. "But if you'd like, we can both talk to her in the morning and see what she's like? You know, we will be like the other person's second opinion, you know?"

"I guess," Seema sighed, tired. Her head ached somewhere deep inside and now all she wanted to do was go to sleep. Slowly, she scooted to the edge of the bed and stood only to be stopped by Nyssa's hand.

"Can I get a goodnight hug?" Nyssa smiled, arms slowly coming up. Seema returned her smile with one not as genuine and leaned in and embraced Nyssa warmly, but her eyes remained open finding a shadow in the corner to focus on.

"But what if I am right?" Seema whispered to her as they held each other.

Nyssa didn't respond for she too had her eyes open finding a shadow in the distance, the shadowy edge of their bedroom door closing.

-3-

"And sign here," a thin young man spoke to Seth as he stood next to his desk, flipping over several pages of a binder that had been sectioned off with colored sticky tabs. His suit and demeanor said everything about him: the flat gray pinstripe fabric, the crisp cuff edges of his tailored white shirt, and the oval gold and black cufflinks with a deeply pressed monogrammed letter *M* in their center. Like the two men sitting across from him with their blank yet stern expressions, he was a member of the Merionethians, people from Charles' sect who had come to finish the business deal which was a ruse for the retribution of Seth killing him.

Seth released a slightly agitated sigh as he repeatedly scripted out his name, each time knowing that the presence of his ink and his name was signing over another twenty million dollars to them, and his mind's sadistic nature kept a running tally just to be sure.

That makes it one-hundred and eighty million dollars, his mind taunted him from the shadows of his mind making him want to curse and spit. He had known that, yes, there was going to be some sort of recourse, but he had never imagined this much for a Seer of so little consequence.

"And… here, here, here and here," the thin little man summed up the last, pointing to the various parts of the last page where he had to sign.

Seth glared at him momentarily, holding the late-thirtyish man's face and form in his eyes, imagining strangling him with his intestines. Seth smiled at this and, without looking towards the page, signed his name the remaining four times and closed the binder.

"Very good," the little man snipped and collected the binder with the letters LHC stamped on the front with the words '**Large Hydron Collider**' written beneath it, and twitched as he walked away and took up a position behind the two men.

"So, now that you have a *lot* of my money," Seth smiled as he toyed with the pen in one hand. "Are we all satisfied now?"

"We are," the men replied in unison and nodded and together they stood, their eyes beaming at Seth full of disdain and left, leaving Seth alone in his office to his thoughts.

Such a waste of money, Seth thought to himself as he leaned back in his leather chair and placed his heels on the desktop.

The Large Hydron Collider was the most significant manmade device in history and spanned the borders of two countries, costing billions of Euros (only to fail in previous years when they tried to start it up). He laughed at them then as he did now, picturing a group of cavemen tinkering around with something they had no idea what they had made in the first place. There were many things in which his kind, the Anathema, had assisted in their creation: the Transatlantic Railroad, the a-bomb, the Panama Canal, and NAFTA; all great things in their own right but summed up in the suffering of many, many lives.

"If it works," the voice of Mica echoed through his mind from a time when she was reading about the endeavor many years ago when she would sit behind stacks of *Discover,* *Newsweek,* *Time,* and *Popular Mechanics* magazines of which he ordered subscriptions for her in droves. *"It will not only be the largest nucleonic collider in the world, but they might be able to find the Higgs Boson: the 'God Particle.'"*

Seth had inquired as he often did when his little evil prodigy read in-depth on a subject he usually would never be interested in. As usual, he would sit next to her to see if any pictures satisfy the mental artist within the composition of an image to understand. There was an artist's rendition of the typical round accelerator with yellow signifying particle flow in one direction and blue in the other direction in which they were to spin protons near the speed of light only to smash the streams together.

"And what happens when they find this 'God Particle'?" he had asked her quite curiously because if it meant power, it meant control, and if it meant control, it meant money, and since he knew you had to spend money to get it, his investor mentality was quite peaked. *"What do they do with it?"*

"Not sure," the young Mica shrugged as she focused on the small glow in the collision chamber where all things met their end as well as beginning on a theoretical and quantum level. *"I guess so they know how it all started, you know, the Universe. Everything."*

"I see," he nodded, his mind still interested in her interest on the subject, but in the corner of his mind, he heard a large toilet flush and the sounds of coins and bills circling the bowl being lost forever in the sewers of waste.

He had patted her head and went on to other things as his investor mind shut down shop and went home for the night.

"I told you that Charles was going to cost you," Pia's voice came from across the room where she stood leaning against the doorjamb for support. She was still somewhat bruised from her ordeal with Seth, and her right leg stood bent with the tips of her toes barely touching the floor.

"Why are you out of bed?" he asked with a parental scolding tone, moving quickly from his desk to hers, in which he ducked under one of her arms and assisted her to the closest chair. As she sat with the occasional groan and grunt of pain, he carefully raised her feet and placed them on an ottoman.

"I deplore lounging about," she replied, her face twisted with pain as she better adjusted her position.

"You should let me summon some healers," he said quietly as he looked at her from his position on the edge of the ottoman, his eyes scanning her bruising which had been formed out of Magic and fists.

"I do not trust them," she said flatly as she crossed her palms on her belly and sighed. "Too much: 'eye-of-newt' and things of the like. I will heal naturally."

Seth nodded, patted her hands, and moved back to the desk in silence. Over the last week, he had seen her bruising turn from ugly to worse as they healed; an odd concept of the human body to fancy such a method instead of going from bad to good or at least visibly better. Deep down, he had some guilt for what he had done, but then again, it was part of a plan, and Seth so greatly loved an excellent strategy that he always nurtured to fruition to the letter.

"And what of Mica?" she called out. "Have you been able to reach her as she sleeps or is Agatha's Magic blocking you?"

"No, I have been reaching her," he said to her quietly as he poured two small glasses of a dark-colored liqueur; the air about him filled with the thick rich aroma of sweetness and anise.

"And?" She pushed him as he approached with a glass extended before him.

"And she listens for the most part," he finished, taking a seat across from her and tapped the edge of her glass. Slowly she brought it up to her nose and sniffed it, then gave him a perturbed look.

"What is this?" she asked with both brows standing up.

"Something sweet and warm for you, my sweet," he smiled and took a small sip. "Do you not trust me anymore?"

"I do," she whispered back and allowed some of the thick liquid to pass between her lips. Surprisingly, the taste was divine, and a warm wave of calm splashed over her. She nodded towards him in approval and then took a more sizeable drink. "Back to Mica, do you need me to channel her as well?"

"To what advantage will that bring?" he asked as he leaned back comfortably in his chair, crossing one leg with the other.

"None if you have everything under control," she replied and remained quiet for some time. "I will need to take my leave of your house for a bit."

"Now?" Seth inquired, his face widening in a sudden confused expression. "When we are this close?"

"I must go to the place of my teachers and heal," she said flatly with a shrug without looking at him as her eyes focused on the surface of the liqueur in her glass. "There is still Magic there even though none of them are."

"But I need you here!" Seth growled as he sat forward, his mind twisted with confusion, anger, and sadness. "Even if Mica turns off the Magic and aides me, the odds against us would be high!"

"Get one of the others," she replied with the same flat tone. "But you will not need any assistance if Mica does what she needs to do. I will be of no use to you in my condition and none of the healers here can do much for me."

"A few bumps and bruises are what this relies upon?" his voice came across full of sarcasm and irritation, his eyes narrowing.

"You did go a bit too far, even for you, Seth." Slowly Pia pulled up the edge of her slit black dress until her hip was exposed, and there glowed a raging bruise of deep red, purple, and black, which was edged with a sickly green. The mass of it rounded from the front of her hip and disappeared past the curvature of her right buttock. Seth stared at the wound he had delivered, his mind remembering the motions and movements that had drawn out the damage and echoed by the distant screaming Pia had released when it happened. During Guilt 101, Pia was the teacher, and Seth was clearly the untrained pupil.

"I see," he said as he dropped his eyes, his voice barely audible. "Are you hurt other places like that?"

"Why do you think I wear such concealing and restricting clothing, my Seth?" she replied with a question, her voice attempting to sound serious and caring simultaneously; to Seth, it was scornful blame, and he winced away from it. "Do not blame yourself, Seth, you were caught up in the moment, and I know you did not intend to cause so much damage to me. At first, I liked it… it was at least a form of physical attention from you, but even you can go too far."

The intentional spike that flew with Pia's words landed directly on the target as it, pierced his chest and split his heart. Anyone who had ever seen the two together knew there was a high degree of attraction. Still, it would have taken the viewer another moment to realize that Pia was the pursuer and Seth was the idle schoolboy who ran from the affection. It was not that he had not considered wooing the woman in the past, and by his realization, it would not have taken much, but it was *who* she was that had always concerned him. Just under that usually, beautiful, tanned skin and behind those brilliant green eyes sat a killer: a pure, unadulterated, maniacal, heartless killer that bothered him the most.

As stated early on, Pia was unique: a *Myriad-Haruspex* of an ancient order of haruspices from bygone Roman eras, who drew their predictions from the entrails of sacrificed animals which had gone by the name of the Denari, much akin to the ancient Roman coins. When Pia was young, not much older than his Mica, she had gotten in her head that she was unique, and the only way to be genuinely unique was to be the only Denari left alive on the planet. Within a year, Pia had hunted down and slaughtered her entire sect and achieved precisely what she had desired.

Seth could want and desire her all he wanted, but that fundamental murderous flaw she had turned him away from her (as would anyone).

"For how long you will be gone?" he asked solemnly as he watched the liquid roll around in his glass.

"For a while," she said passively and slammed the glass home in one swift gulp. "When I am right, I will return."

"I have soured you towards me then?" He added, his brows standing.

"Not at all, dear Seth," she said as she pulled herself up, her face showing the painful strain of every muscle and tendon in her body. "It would take more than an anticipated thrashing for you to foul my attention to you."

She moved the short distance to him with an apparent limp and then brushed her hand through his dark hair.

"But perhaps some time away may clear up some views you have towards me, and I pray that it does."

With that, she kissed the top of his head and limped towards the door, setting the small glass down on a table. He said nothing as she moved away despite his mind screaming to stop her.

She was his greatest ally next to Mica, and he was working diligently on reviving that bond, and that ally was leaving him for an untold time. For once, it crossed his mind that perhaps he really *did* want her, and he swallowed hard against the possibility that he was too late to see that potential grow.

Pia paused by the doorway and attempted a smile. She then left, leaving him in his study to dwell on everything alone.

CHAPTER TWENTY

***

Downfall

-1-

Despite her odd reoccurring mana sparks (always accompanied by a thin wicked smile), Mica seemed to be changing for the better. Agatha summed it up best when she told the girls that to change a person who has always known life to be one way overnight is impossible, and they cannot actually change her; all they can do is show her a different path and see if she follows it.

This satisfied Nyssa completely, who, as usual, attempted to see the good in everyone and everything before taking an opposing stance, but Seema went with her gut.

"I am just worried," Seema said softly as they folded towels in the linen room. "I mean, I don't know as many people as you do personally, but I do know the human condition. As I told you, I used to see through others all the time."

"You are still a little creepy spy with that," Nyssa giggled and then returned her attention to the lock of hair in its clasp which Nyssa had strung a thin gold chain through and held it before her. It was simple, but elegant and she was amazed at how much the color looked like her own.

"Stop that," Seema whispered back seriously, her eyes looking hurt. "It's not like I wanted to mind their business or anything. How else am I to see the world? Run away?"

"I didn't mean it like that," Nyssa said softly, hoping to calm the tension in the air. "Actually, I think it was a brilliant thing to do as long as no one got hurt in the process, and since no one did, there's nothing to worry about."

"Well, about that I don't worry," Seema shrugged as she placed a freshly folded towel on a pile. "Unless Lady Agatha ever found out, it's just Mica *seems* like she could be a really good person, I just think there is something behind all of it; something darker."

"Seema, Auntie Agatha summed it up the best," Nyssa insisted as she too placed a towel on the pile and retrieved a fresh one. "It's going to take her some time."

"I know," Seema agreed, but in truth she wasn't convinced, and her tone stated it clearly.

"Right now, she's with Auntie Agatha," Nyssa added, hoping the addition would persuade the conversation. "And don't you think that she would have sensed if Mica was, you know, rotten?"

"I would hope so," Seema sighed and then turned and leaned against the folding table. "Lady Agatha has such a big heart, too big at times I think, and if she had the chance to take in all the hurt and downtrodden souls of the world, she would have to build an island the size of Australia to put them all."

"Well, she took you in," Nyssa gleamed at her and peered out the corner of her eye for a response which she got in the form of a frustrated sigh and a glare which could have fried eggs. "Sorry, couldn't help it."

"What I mean is," Seema moved towards another basket of clothes near the back door and brought it to their work area. "We once had to go into town to get some things and Lady Agatha had seen this commercial that was playing in the local diner."

"Auntie Agatha ate out?" Nyssa asked surprised, her eyes wide and serious.

"I know, right?" Seema gave her a nod and then dumped out a basket of sheets that smelled of freshly line-dried air. "Despite her constant pursuit of 'the old ways,' she knows that there is a modern world out there, and she has to play her part in it.

"Anyway, we were having sandwiches and there was some sort of telethon on about starving children in Central America somewhere and I thought she was going to die. I mean she lost her appetite and everything and we had to leave immediately!"

"Wow, I didn't know she was so empathetic," Nyssa said quietly and dipped her head through the chain and allowed the lock to hang outside of her shirt. "Was she alright?"

"Took her three days to get the visions out of her head," Seema replied. "And she told me that we were never going back to that diner ever again; like that was the only place in the world showing the same depressing stuff, but yeah, she got past it. "

"Well, that sort of thing *is* sad," Nyssa looked at her, confused. "But Mica is not a starving child from Central America."

"*My point is*—" Seema stressed turning towards her. "—that Lady Agatha is sympathetic to all misery: good and bad."

"Huh?" Nyssa doubled blinked for now she was really confused.

"Man, I have never lived in a big city, and I am explaining this to you... sheesh!" Seema shook her head slightly annoyed. "Okay, there are homeless people in Chicago, right?" Nyssa nodded. "And it is sad to see them living on the streets, asking for money?"

"Panhandling," Nyssa interjected.

"Yes, that!" Seema continued, on a roll and ramping up. "Do you think *all* of them are homeless because they want to be?"

"Why would any of them, *'want to be homeless?'*" Nyssa shook her head.

"Exactly," Seema smiled and paused, hoping that she would get the point but found only a fog of confusion in Nyssa's eyes. "There are some who are homeless because they either lost their jobs, their homes; everything, right?"

Nyssa nodded following along so far.

"Okay, but there are some who lost everything because *they* put themselves in the situations to lose it: drugs, alcohol, crime, you name it, but either way the same result: they *are* homeless."

"True, true," Nyssa said and nodded.

"Lady Agatha wouldn't see the difference between the two," Seema finished, shrugging. "All she sees is homelessness and that she must help somehow. Mica is just like a homeless person, however leaning strongly on the latter example though. She didn't do drugs or alcohol to lose everything, but she was on the side of bad and there is nothing that the Anathema doesn't do which could not be considered a crime even after the fact."

"So, what you are saying is that Mica *asked* for the beating she got?" Nyssa spat out, almost defensively, her eyes wide with surprise.

"No, Nyssa," Seema said flatly, her eyes unmoving and serious. "What I am saying is that Mica became a poor, battered, homeless girl and regardless of whose side she may be on—Us or Them—Lady Agatha would take her in, provide her shelter, feed her, teach her our Magic and look past the reasons of how she ever got into the situation she is in the first place. She would do this *blindly*."

Nyssa stood looking at Seema for quite some time as she turned away and began folding pillowcases. No, she did not like the comparison between the two, much like she had never heard of someone hurting *'because they deserved it,'* but the truth was standing there in her face leaving her to accept it or not.

Truth, little one, her father's voice echoed in her mind. *It can hurt much more than any lie; remember that.*

She sighed and grabbed a pillowcase as well.

"I see your point," Nyssa said eventually and shrugged. "So, what you are basically saying is if Mica *was* up to something, Auntie Agatha probably wouldn't detect a thing, right?"

"I don't know," Seema mumbled; her mind feeling guilt for putting her teacher in such a light. "Lady Agatha is no way shape or form a dense person, I am just worried that if I say anything to her about it she will dismiss it as me being too protective and Mica just needing time to adjust."

"If you would like, we can both go to her," Nyssa smiled. "I mean, I see your point and all, so she might at least look into it if we are both on the same page?"

"Maybe, we'll see." Seema shrugged and focused on the sheets in front of her.

They fell silent as they continued with their chores, only occasionally asking the other one to take what they folded to add it to a certain pile of this or that. Seema was troubled, her mind spiraling through her convictions and her doubts; a young mind bent at the crossroads of being damned if she did and damned if she didn't, and as her mind spun, the occasional echo of Mica's voice would whisper in her thoughts from the night before.

"Aren't you worried about what is going to happen to you?" Mica's words crawled up her spine and she shivered the thoughts away.

-2-

Agatha said nothing as the two girls spoke, each adding their own points to the conversation; however, Seema had most of the floor. Between the two, Agatha could see that Seema was more sincere in her convictions, but she did not dismiss what was said like Seema had assumed she would. Patiently, she waited until Seema's argument had concluded before saying a word.

"I am not saying that she has done anything yet," Seema said finally. "I am just worried that she might."

"And you, Nyssa?" Agatha addressed her, who held a look of confident confusion on every pore of her face. "Do you also think there is something amiss with our Mica?"

"Well," she began, licking her lips and glancing between Agatha and Seema. "I didn't think so at first, but Seema has very valid points and I have to back my sister."

Agatha smiled thinly at this and pressed her lips together firmly to hide it. It had been many a long year since the two had spent this much time together and then the two were inseparable and whenever asked where one or the other one was, the response had always started with, *'My sister is—'* This had always warmed her and she knew deep down that it was this sisterly bond that would protect them somehow despite the fact that they were never to be in the situation that they were in now.

Fate is such an odd bird, she thought to herself and then stood, moving to the windows, and peered out across the rear yard towards the stables.

Mica was apparently having a wonderful talk with Sugar; a cream-colored mare whose mane and forelock were as black as pitch. Agatha had told Mica that that particular horse was a bit high-strung and nearly unapproachable, having come as an orphan from a farm where animals were neglected and abused. Mica never thought twice about what was said. She simply walked to Sugar with one palm up, her voice soft and gentle, and with a smile she commanded, *'Come to me, Sugar'* and so the horse did. All of them were surprised that she did and even allowed Mica to mount her, but then again, why should it be so surprising that two lost creatures from the same path of abuse would find each other in the end?

"I will speak with her," Agatha said quietly with a slight smile of admiration on her lips as she watched Mica brush Sugar along her neck and shoulder with even gentle strokes. Behind her was a dreadful silence and she could picture the two girls looking at her with hung mouths. She fought back a giggle at the image of them as she allowed them to stew at the idea of it for a moment. "Relax, girls, there will be no mention of either of you or what was said here today. Your Agatha does have some tact, you know?"

Nyssa and Seema physically expressed their satisfaction with this; both of them releasing long sighs of relief and producing smiles.

"Thank you, Auntie," Nyssa smiled and rose, nudging Seema to follow suit.

With that they left, leaving Agatha to her thoughts and contemplations as she watched Mica brush Sugar with the care and ease as a loving mother would her young. Although neither of the girls had made any personal statements towards her unyielding weakness for the downtrodden and displaced, Agatha began questioning her personal ethics in the matter dealing with Mica.

Had you gone about this blindly? She thought to herself and sighed softly. *Should you have simply turned away from her entirely?*

To these thoughts of personal damnable questions and others she did not know. Yes, the girl is young, and yes, she was brought to the very edge of death by one most vile, but could all of it had been simply a ploy, a ruse to convince the Consortia—to convince her—that Mica was no longer wanted?

Agatha shivered and moved away from the window shaking her head, damning herself for the thoughts, as she would no longer entertain such improbable possibilities.

-3-

The day was warmer than Agatha had expected it to be but the gentle breezes counter-balanced the temperature, as well as aided by the rich heavy canopy of trees spanning the grounds. Agatha moved steadily along the path leading to the stables where Mica was applying the finishing touches of strapping a saddle onto Sugar's back.

"You managed to get that on her yourself?" Agatha asked aloud as she approached, startling Mica who whipped around on her quickly, her eyes wide. "Oh, I am sorry, Mica; I didn't mean to startle you."

"Oh, that's okay," she responded and produced a nervous smile. "Just wasn't expecting... but yeah, I got the saddle on without any real problem... not as heavy as it looks."

"And you did it without Magic?" Agatha continued as she came up on Sugar and gently scratched between the mare's ears. "Very good job."

"No, no Magic," Mica smiled for she was pleased with herself and that someone noticed her handy work. "I am sure she is used to it being here, but I didn't want to, you know, frighten her."

"Very good thinking," Agatha nodded and took a seat on some stacked bales of hay. "But in regard to your presumption, believe it or not, there is very little Magic used on these grounds."

Mica paused in her motions and held Agatha for quite some time, her face twisted in a confused, suspicious expression wondering if the woman was putting her on.

"'Very little Magic'?" Mica echoed Agatha's words, unbelieving them and she looked about the area. "But I can see it everywhere."

"What you are seeing is called the Cascade:" Agatha smiled as she explained. "It is the glowing residue from a time when Magic flowed freely. Yes, there is a higher concentration of it here because there are so many of us in one place in time, but no, we of the Consortia know that Magic—much like many things on this planet—is a scarce necessary resource and it must be used wisely."

Mica was unconsciously rubbing Sugar slowly in long strokes, her eyes attempting to read deeply into what Agatha was saying to her and finding more confusion than answers.

"Are you telling me this or teaching?" Mica finally spoke with a suspicious expression on her face.

"Both in a sense," Agatha said as she placed her hands in her lap. "And neither in the end; idle talk is all it is, but what you take from it is up to you."

"In the Anathema," Mica began slowly, licking her lips as she carefully formulated her words. "We believe Magic is purely a tool put here for us to use and not the other way around."

"I know this, Mica," Agatha said calmly and carefully, knowing how there was a time such words would throw her into a rant of mass proportions. "And I know what has been said to you since your arrival here has contradicted all what you have been taught, but the truth is, because of that way of thinking is why there is so little Magic left in the world. This is why Seema and Nyssa have told you the rules so that you may better understand how Magic should be handled and treated."

"*The Rules,*" Mica huffed, shaking her head slightly as her eyes focused on the mare's coat. "They told me what they were, and I get what they say, but they don't make very much sense. We are powerful and others are weak, and even with the rules in place, I don't see why this is not taken to its full advantage."

Agatha took several deep breaths as she stood and slowly walked to the stable walls where Mica's riding hat was hanging on a hook. Slowly she retrieved it and admired the brim with a smile.

"I am so glad my old riding outfit fits you," Agatha said passively as she turned to Mica, looking the girl from head to toe. "Even the boots I see."

"Yes, they are a perfect fit," Mica smiled and looked herself over. "So, you were short too then?"

The two shared a giggle as Agatha placed the cap on Mica's head and fastened the strap securely under her chin.

"Oh, I was until I was about your age, and then *'Poof!'* I shot up," Agatha finished with a soft chuckle.

"So then there's hope that I won't be little forever then," Mica smiled back as she adjusted the small brim to sit better on her brow.

"That's the best Magic in the world, Mica," Agatha nodded. "Hope is powerful Magic."

Mica held her eyes for a moment as she absorbed the knowledge and the possibilities of what she said. She was so torn inside from being taught heavy-handedly under the Anathema where everything is 'Do-do-do', to now, where the lessons seem to come from everywhere and nowhere all at the same time with gradual nuances. Mica nodded and moved to the front of Sugar and adjusted the bridle. There was nothing wrong with how she had applied it, but it made a good distraction so to inch the conversation along a little further.

"So, then they know all this too," Mica began as she fidgeted with the strapping. "Nyssa and Seema that is?"

"Yes, they know all this," Agatha continued and found her own thing to fidget with by way of the edge of the saddle blanket. "Seema knows more so than Nyssa, of course, because just like you, Seema has only known this world. Nyssa is learning more and more every day, but just like you, she is torn between what she has been taught all her life and what sits on the other side of that knowledge rainbow.

"Trust me, Mica, I feel for all of you; all three of you are being forced to unlearn all that you have learned in such a short little timeframe. Nyssa is facing the understanding that the world in the storybooks is true, in a sense; Seema is forced to open her mind and heart to you who in her mind personifies as 'the enemy', and you, for having to deal with all of it."

"All of it?" Mica replied, her face full of questions.

"Of course," Agatha gave her a comforting smile. "Even if you don't unlearn what you have been taught, you *are* learning another way to do what you do, with forethought and reasoning instead of the rash spontaneity of simple desire or want. And if you look at your way of thinking calmly, you will see it is not only people like Seema and me who have been considered your enemies, but you said it yourself in regard to simple Man: Nyssa, up until recently, was nothing more than some creature that you had to lead and control much like sheep in a field."

Mica's hands had stopped moving along the bridle as she held Agatha's eyes suspiciously, drawn purely from her innate distrust towards mana of good. Slowly she began to nod as clarity set in.

"I think I understand what you are saying," Mica sounded and moved towards the saddle. Agatha took a step back to give her room.

"Hand up?" Agatha asked and positioned herself with her two hands intertwined in a cupping position hanging mid-thigh. Slowly Mica raised a boot and placed it in her helping hands and in one motion she was effortlessly sent in the air where she kicked one leg over the brim.

"Thank you," Mica whispered down to Agatha who moved towards the front of Sugar taking hold of the reins and began walking the horse away from the stables.

"You are more than welcome, my child," Agatha smiled up to her as she maneuvered the horse along the path which led alongside the gated trotting yard and out to open fields. "I am so glad you have decided to take her on a real ride instead of staying in the courtyard; you have ten acres of land to explore out there, so enjoy it."

"Yeah, I guess I am not all that afraid anymore," she said quietly down to Agatha who stopped the horse just past the wooden crisscrossed fence as her eyes locked onto nothing in particular in the distance. "I am safe out there, aren't I?"

"Of course, you are, Mica," Agatha said with a slight surprised tone, and her heart cried for the girl as she found Mica's eyes darting over the distance with genuine fear in her eyes. "Mica, listen to me: you are safe on these grounds from everyone."

"Everyone?" Mica pleaded with both her tone and eyes, hoping that that was true. "But the Consortia and well, I am, was, umm—"

"Your presence here is by my desire and all know that." Agatha said, her voice full of solid reassurances as she moved to the side of the horse and placed her hand on top of Mica's with a loving grasp. "No one would dare to question that, nor would have the power to do so on my land. You may be Anathema by birth into this world, but you have a good-mana inside there, and I can see it glow! All you have to do is let it shine, my child, and you will find your own place not only in the World of Magic, but in the world in whole."

Mica looked down at the thin fingers on her hand and then trailed them to the loving, begging eyes of the woman who trusted all too much. She was Anathema by birth and nature, that she knew, and although she grew affection to the woman's kindness, the dark shadows in her mind fought tirelessly against all of it.

"Maybe," Mica whispered and wiggled her fingers under Agatha's who quickly understood that affection time had ended. Agatha took a calm two steps back and nodded. Mica gathered up the reins and adjusted her cap once more and gave Sugar a little nudge in her side who responded by taking slow steps forward.

"Mind the northern edge of the creek!" Agatha called after her, taking slow steps in pursuit. "There is a nasty bee's nest in the tree there and many patches of burning nettles!"

"I will," Mica replied without looking and nudged Sugar's sides with firmer heels which got the horse moving in a gentle trot.

"How have you been sleeping?" Agatha forced out the question loudly after Mica, who suddenly pulled back on the reins and to the right, turning and stopping the horse in step.

"What?" Mica asked, her eyes narrowing.

"Are you sleeping well?" Agatha asked again, altering her words slightly and advanced several steps and stopped.

"Why?" Mica asked with an accusatory tone and for a brilliance of a second, Agatha saw what Seema had claimed: there was a spark of violet in her eyes.

"Oh, no reason," Agatha shrugged nervously, her mind formulating the lie which begged her voice to sound convincing. "It's just such a small room and all; stuffy at times. Just making sure that it is adequate for you."

"It is fine, Agatha," Mica said flatly, her lips barely moving. "I will ride now."

"Good... good," Agatha produced a wide-open smile and waved as she walked backwards. Mica gave Sugar a double-heeled sharp stab and barked out a *'Go!'* which got the horse moving into a fast run.

Agatha stood quietly on the grass at the edge of the field and watched her go, her hands on the sides of her face as her heart and mind begged for reassurance. Seema was right, things were going on inside Mica that was dark and shadowed, but she didn't know what. Only time could tell the outcomes of things, and she was stuck without a direction to follow. She could not send the child away for fear for her safety, and in the same fashion yet the opposite, she did not know how she could keep her there and ensure anyone's safety.

With a heavy heart and a clouded mind, Agatha slowly walked back towards the house with her watery eyes on the ground before her.

-4-

Mica rode until she was sweaty and her breathing labored, having put every effort into driving the horse to her maximum speed and using every muscle to stay on her. Sugar was fast and powerful, her hooves digging firmly into the rich soil and boosting off with every stride. As she rode, Mica screamed and cursed and cried and damned all that flowed through her mind like a raging river as it battled with everything simultaneously. Slowly, she relaxed her pull on the reins and allowed the horse to slow, eventually moving into a trot and then a slow walk. Crying as she leaned forward over the saddle horn, she repeatedly asked for death.

"I hate this! Why didn't I just die?" she cried aloud as her eyes narrowed on the edge of the creek through the blurry tears. She could feel Sugar's heavy breathing and she sniffed away the tears and sat up. "Want some water, Sugar?"

The horse's ears perked up hearing its name but gave no other response than that. She kicked her leg off one side and hopped down, feeling a brief jolt of soreness flare in her legs and buttocks. She had gotten used to riding a horse briefly in the trotting yard and still had soreness afterwards, but after that run, she knew she was sure to really feel it later once the muscles stiffened.

With reins in hand, she walked Sugar past the high shrubbery which grew along the creek's edge and down to the rocky shore where the horse had no trouble drinking after being led to water. There the animal stood gulping water at an alarming rate, paying no mind to the chubs and rainbow trout which swam before its nose just beneath its surface.

Mica stepped away and found her own spot where she removed her cap and knelt, cupping water up to her face in gentle splashes so to remove the running sweat and tears. She drank as well, having been told more than a week ago that the water ran clean, and after a satisfying drink she found a large stone to sit on.

Her thoughts were mangled and foggy as she stared into the smooth-running water of the creek, but she no longer had the strength to fight against them. Here she was a sixteen-year-old young woman with the weight of an old person resting on her shoulders as her mind produced a catalogue of guilt, spite, and rage before her as it flipped along the chronological mental pages only to stop at the end so to reverse the order accordingly.

How many people had she hurt? How many places had she had helped to destroy? How dare someone question who and what she was? How dare someone show her affection? They were a multitude of thoughts that came in slow, sagging Dali images which dripped into a mismatched puddle of thoughts only to form yet another damning question which had no answer.

Good-mana, she thought to herself and sighed and watched a meaty trout slide lazily in the shadows. *Good for whom?*

Without really thinking about it, she raised her index finger from her fisted hands and pointed it towards the trout which was lazily moving in the shadows. Her eyes barely sparked as she quickly moved the finger to the right as she concentrated on its tiny mind. In a blink the trout jetted to the right in the water and then returned to its lazy slow swimming. She jerked her finger back to the left and once again the trout followed suit.

Slowly, she sat up and extended her arm, her finger still locked on the motions of the creature and made quick right and left gestures in which the trout did the same. She smiled thinly at this, made a wide circle in the air, and watched as the trout swam out from the shadows in an arch, nearing the other bank, and then returned to where her finger pointed. Giggling, she quickly moved her finger to the left and then back to the right and twirled the digit once. The trout zipped to the left and back to the right, breaking the water's surface and performing a flip in the air as the finger twirled. Mica giggled guiltily at this and looked about herself with only Sugar present, who was busy munching on rogue alfalfa buds near the water's bank.

She was doing simple Magic, childish toying, which she used to do to the neighbor's cats when she was little. This was her game, her wicked little pastime, which caused no actual harm except when she ran Ms. Dobson's cat into an oncoming postal vehicle. It was purely an accident; poor timing was all; she should have had the cat zig when it zagged, or was it? Had she not thought to herself as she stood in the gated yard just out of sight with that wicked little grin on her face wondering to herself what must have been the last thing to go through the cat's mind before the grill of the vehicle did? Did it not tickle her on the inside when the cat released an uncontrolled shriek of terror as it made its final pawed steps toward this suicidal oblivion?

Did she not *feel* the cat's terror and take pleasure in it?

Mica's hand waved smartly towards herself, and the trout burst from the water and landed on the shore before her, its body immediately flopping in suffocating spasms on the damp ground. She stared blankly at the convulsing fish, watching how the gills begged for filtered oxygen, how the mouth sucked on nothing, and how its big wide eyes hung in terror. There were no feelings inside her as her heartbeat calmly to the event, but unlike with Ms. Dobson's cat, there was no pleasure in it, not for herself (and definitely not for the fish).

"Good?" she whispered, her ears focusing on the meaty slapping sounds of the trout's muscled body flopping in the mud. "Someone needs to define what 'good' means."

With that she flicked her hand back across the water and the trout flew, landing in mid-stream and quickly swam away. She sat staring at the water for a long time until her eyes held negative spots from the sun's reflections and turned towards the horse and found its mind.

"Go back home, Sugar," she said quietly, her face blank. "I will walk back."

With that, Sugar grunted with a nod, and slowly she trotted off towards the house in the distance. Mica returned her eyes to the running water and thought about everything calmly and slowly, utterly unaware that silent tears rolled her cheeks and then dropped from her chin.

-5-

Mica slowly crested the field edge, carrying the riding cap in her hand. She looked tired and worn, her face long and placid with the evident salty lines on her face that she had been crying. Nyssa and Seema stood together at the side of the stables with intent looks of concern while Sugar chomped on oats in her large stall.

Slowly she walked towards and then passed them as she hung the cap on its hook.

"Are you ok, Mica?" Nyssa asked with a voice full of concern.

"We thought Sugar threw you and you were hurt!" Seema added; her eyes and voice sharing the concern.

"No, we had a nice ride," Mica said monotonously as she slowly moved towards the house. "Where's Agatha?"

"She went out looking for you," Nyssa replied moving after her. "She was so worried! Are you sure that you are okay?"

"She's out looking for me?" Mica paused mid-step and looked around her. "That's nice. Yes, I am fine... I am very tired... I need to go lay down."

"Have you been crying?" Seema asked quietly, taking a step close to her, wanting to hug her but hesitant by the blankness of Mica's expression.

"Don't you ever cry, Seema?" Mica asked quietly. "I need to go lie down."

Slowly Mica moved off towards the house, her stride slow but steady and seemingly without thought or care. Nyssa and Seema drew close to one another unconsciously and took the other one's hand as they watched her go, both saying nothing but sharing the same thoughts and concerns for the girl. Despite their conclusions about her, she was a girl like themselves, one who was hurting badly inside and not knowing how to release it.

They would remain by the stables as instructed by Agatha to wait for her return. When she did, they would tell her that Mica was safe, but worried about her state of being.

Patiently, they were to wait in silence with only the hope that Agatha would return shortly so to ease the pains in their hearts.

*

Mica didn't crawl into her bed so much as she collapsed onto it, pulling the pillow up close to her chin, and tumbled into slumber. Her mind was exhausted and shattered having raced so hard and collided with so many contradicting thoughts that splintered them into an unrecognizable pile of refuse.

As the darkness enveloped her, she consciously wished that she would find her teacher in the shadows because despite the carnage he had created, he made simple sense of things.

One should always be careful of what they wish for.

–6–

"Even if I wanted to let you in," Mica's dream ego said quietly as she stood on the porch with her back to the screen door to the Seth-thing sitting on one of the porch swings. *"I cannot. Only Agatha can undo the Magic that surrounds this house; you know that don't you?"*

378

The Seth-clone nodded with a slight smile and gave the swing a nudge by boosting off one of his feet.

"And on top of that, I do not have Binky," Mica continued as her eyes dropped in shame having learned that any person of Magic without their talisman was as worthless as a bag of air. *"I wouldn't be of any real use."*

Seth-form shook his head, the smile remaining on his face, and he stopped the swing from moving with two solid heels.

"You do not need that bear to do what you need to do, my daughter." He smiled wider and slowly rose from the swing and approached her.

For a moment, the 'Fight or Flight' response kicked in, and her mind chose to flee, but with only a slight flinch towards the door, she stood still. Her eyes shifted between the floor and his approaching eyes until his form stopped its advance a few feet from her.

"No?" she whispered as both hearts began to beat faster; the one in her dream and the one plastered in the bed with sweat soaked sheets. *"Whu-what can I do? Wait! Daughter?"*

"Yes, my Mica," Seth-shape smiled with a slow nod and a dreamy hand slowly came up and touched her cheek.

She closed her eyes to it, her body shaking with both fear and excitement as her soul exploded with a mixed joy of acceptance and affection and the terror of what he had done to her. Slowly she pressed her cheek against the touch, preferring the sensation of fatherly attention over the fearful past.

"We are a strange breed are we not? We treat our pupils as if they are tools and as our knowledge vessels, only to cast you from our nests once you learn

to fly. I, on the other hand, know how to love. Forgive me for never ever truly showing you that I am proud of you."

Mica's eyes grew wide with surprise as a broad smile blossomed on her lips. These were words she had wanted to hear for more than fourteen years of silence-borne assumptions; she now knew the truth of his heart.

With hesitation, she moved forward, then stopped, eyes shifting amongst his eyes which held a soft blue she had never seen before, and then jetted ahead into his arms. In the embrace, she shivered wildly, unable to contain years of bottled-up emotions.

"Thank you, Father," she wept quietly, holding him tightly. *"And I love you too!"*

"I know you do, Mica," he whispered above her head.

"I am so confused," she cried. *"And I hurt so bad inside! I just want to go away and hide!"*

"There now, Mica," he whispered. *"The confusion is borne from your lack of knowledge of my plan, as well as the poisons these Consortia women put in your mind. Do not allow their wonton jabbering to betray the proper teachings in which you were raised; their methods are of the weak and the flawed."*

"They are?" she said muffled against his chest as her mind sought reassurance.

"Of course, they are, my Mica," he said back with the reassuring tone she was hoping for and he moved her away briefly to look into her eyes and wipe the tears away. *"I know what I did was wrong, but you know the reasons for it; you do trust me, don't you?"*

"Yes, I do," she replied, attempting not to produce more tears to be wiped away, but in her soul, she enjoyed the loving attention. *"I do trust you and you are wise."*

"*And I trust you too, Mica,*" he smiled to her, and he wiped away the hanging tears from her chin. "*And that is why you have the most important task, and you are the only one who can bring it all down.*"

"*How?*" she whimpered, returning to his arms. "*She is so powerful!*"

"*You have always had the power,*" Seth-thing replied and pushed her away gently so they could look eye to eye and tapped the side of her head gently with a finger. "*All of what you need is right up here, the same thing you used to do to me before I built up a tolerance against it. The thing you do to get what you want.*"

"*Nudge her?*" she replied with almost a whisper and Seth-form shook his head with a smile.

"*No, shove her, Mica,*" his smile grew wider and wider until the edges of his mouth seemed to disappear behind his ears. "*Shove her right off the edge of sanity if you have to.*"

"*Shove her,*" she echoed as he pulled her to his chest again and through his body, she could hear him sound an '*Umm-Hmm*' in acknowledgement.

Mica stepped away from him with glaring violet eyes, her lips twisting into a thin wicked little smile as her head cocked to one side and somewhere in the back of her throat a little giggle rose.

Turning, she opened the screen door and looked back at the eyes of her father and nodded.

"*I will see you tomorrow in person,*" Seth-form smiled and backed away. "*Not in this place of your mind, my daughter.*"

As the images faded, Mica found herself sitting in bed, the darkness of the room illuminated by her violet eyes and her heart filled with the love that showed in her glowing smile.

Unaided by need or want, she slowly laid back down and closed her eyes, where she slept soundly without visitors in her dreams.

CHAPTER TWENTY-ONE

Ragnarök

-1-

Marco stood next to the fireplace looking over the pictures Agatha had on its mantle and then chuckled quietly at a photograph of his younger self. The capture happened just as puberty started to take hold, giving him a thin mustache, which could have easily been mistaken for a smudge of dirt over his lip.

"I was so angry then," he said quietly and tapped the edge of the silver frame. "So full of confusion that I didn't even recognize my own shadow and wouldn't have cared less if it had tried to run away."

"You were never a *real* Pan," Agatha agreed as she looked up towards her half-moon from her window and sighed, saddened that its glow did not provide her with any comfort that night. Mica had been on her mind now for two days and her heart saddened by the thought of her with each passing moment.

"No, that I wasn't," he smiled towards her and crossed the study floor. "I couldn't wait to grow up thinking how much easier life would be when I got there."

"So, is it?" she asked without looking.

"No, it is not," he smiled again, shaking his head and took to her side and found the moon as well. "Actually, having to work, feed yourself, bathe, tidy up your messes and pay bills, well, I sometimes wish I was in Neverland."

"Then that would make me Wendy," she turned to him with a thin smile enjoying the comparative banter. "This line of thought would make you either a Lost Boy, or a Pirate."

"Aye, my lady that it would!" He glared with his best pirate voice he could muster and the two enjoyed a short laugh together. Agatha slowly returned her eyes to the moon as her expressions shadowed back to worry. "You shouldn't worry yourself so much about young Mica. She is going through a lot of change right now, not so much different than I did when I came to you."

"I know, Marco," she shook her head and moved from the window with Marco following and took a seat in one of the high-back chairs. "But you were different, and I was younger then; more bullheaded to think that anyone could tell me whom I was to instruct and more daring to bend the rules to my liking."

"Hmm, doesn't sound so different than now," he shrugged and took a seat and crossed one leg with the other. "Only difference now is the age thing."

Agatha opened her mouth, surprised, and scanned for something she could throw at him. Nothing would do, so only sharing in on the laughter that was exiting his lungs.

"You are still a brat despite being grown and wed!" She scorned him and did her best to look offended, but her smile continued to debunk that.

"I know," he smiled and leaned forward clapping his hands together and gave them a humble shake. "Amora tells me the same all the time, but she usually stays within reaching distance of something to throw.

"Now, Lady A, umm, Agatha, I know you are torturing yourself with this now, but in a short span of days or months Mica will start coming out of this poisoned shell. By your own words of her since she has arrived, she has made quite a few progresses towards this, am I right?"

"Yes, she has," Agatha nodded and leaned back, her mind exhausted thinking about the situation. "But there are those little things which concern me."

"What? The flaring of her mana?" he said quickly with a gentle smile of understanding. "The attitude she gave Seema? The dreams?

"Lady Agatha, the girl cannot simply walk into your halls and become a true Consortian overnight. She needs gentle molding and a lot of time to become that, if she ever truly does; you must remember she has been living on the other side of the street all these years and they play differently over there; we throw balls, and they throw rocks.

"Regarding Seema getting snipped at, well, you know she can get a little pushy from time to time."

"Yes, yes, yes, Marco," she sighed, her hands covering her eyes and pressing, praying that she could see the simplicity in it all which she knew had to be there. "Everything you say is true, even about Seema—bless her little big heart—it's just for a moment I felt something in her eyes, and it wasn't pleasant. Ugh! I just wish—"

"Watch that," Marco said quickly cutting her off, his eyes serious despite the smile on his lips.

"See what I mean?" she laughed dropping her hands heavily against her thighs. "I am a complete mess with all this. Yes, you are correct: No-wish thank you, I take that back, all I want is to stop worrying about all this.

"For you, Agatha, to stop worrying about what is right would mean that there was something truly wrong in the world," Marco smiled to her warmly. "And relax, that was a compliment down to the very core."

"I know," she smiled back, her eyes narrowing at him. "But don't think that I have forgotten for one moment that age remark."

"That would be another big surprise," he smiled thinly. "You to forget something, that is. Speaking of forgetting, I have been expecting some sort of retaliation from the Anathema for the whooping you put on Seth, but nothing. Is that something that has been troubling you as well?"

"No, not any longer; if there was to be something it would have happened days following that situation, but I figured he was too ashamed to let the others know that a woman and a girl hurt him. Moreover, they had gotten away with the prize. No, he is sour because of it, but there is nothing he can do to us, but he did take it all out on Mica and that vile Pia woman."

"I have done what you asked," Marco added, his head shaking almost immediately. "And no one, not even the Neutrals, have heard nor seen that woman since that night. The Seer in the Oquirrh Mountains told me that she had caught a glimpse of her essence on the winds somewhere to the south, but other than that, nothing. For all we know she is now vapor and that's what the Seer saw over Utah. Who knows?"

"You still have that morbid way of putting things," Agatha peered at him and struggled to contain her laughter. "But you are right, she is probably dead or hiding very well. Seth is not the type of person a lone cub wants to have mad at them and fail in the process of inflicting death."

"Do you think there will be a power struggle amongst the Anathema if word gets out about his multiple failures?"

"Oh, I don't know," Agatha shrugged, stood, and went back to her window in hopes a glimpse would do her some good. Her skin did feel better in its glow, but not perfect; the stress inside her soul was not allowing it to flow inside like it normally would. "That's what it is all about anyways, both 'Us' and 'Them': Who has the power? Whose power is greater and who will be next in line to claim or steal that power?

"Don't look at me with that hanging mouth," she added without looking at him and Marco closed his mouth quickly. "You do not need to tell me about the rumors floating around the Consortia's campfire about me and this house. If those like Langdon or any other wishes to seek my leadership role here in the Americas, they can have it forthwith; I am growing tired of the title and the responsibility."

"Well, rumors are rumors, Lady Agatha," he shrugged. "But loyalty is a hard thing to lose, and if that ever happens, you know, someone replacing you, we might find ourselves in the middle of our own power struggle, especially if someone like Langdon 'I eat out of dog's asses' Drellic assumes the role."

"*Marco!*" Agatha spun on him hissing, her eyes wide with surprise. "A responsible married man with language like that!"

"Sorry, but you cannot tell me you haven't thought something similar yourself." He smiled guiltily and loved it. "Maybe your vision included a yak's ass instead of a dog?"

"Nevertheless, you-you-you, oh shit, never mind!" she attempted to be angry and added in her own fun. The two laughed heartily and as Agatha dove back into her chair, her hands covered her mouth tightly trying to contain the laughter and her face was as red as a carnival balloon. "Did I just say that?"

"Yes, you did!" Marco laughed soundly and he gasped for breath as his lungs expelled it more out of shock for this had been the only time he had *ever* heard the woman curse. "Amora will not believe me!"

"You mustn't tell her!" she begged in gasps for she too choked for air. "Or anyone for that matter! Please, Marco?"

"Okay, okay, fine," he smiled as he leaned back in his chair satisfied. "I promise, but only if you promise to bake your famous butter cookies for me when I get back from Ireland."

"So, you are going then to Dundalk?" Agatha asked quietly and all humor raced from the conversation in a blink. Marco slowly nodded *'Yes'* as he still held a glint of a smile. "When are you leaving?"

"Tonight, not long after I leave you," he said quietly and retrieved two tickets from his inside jacket pocket. "Amora and I are booked on the nine-twenty flight out of Newark; we will gate to the airport and fly the rest of the way. Tonight, is a bad night for Magic; you can feel it in the air and neither of us trust it."

"And do you think the lore is true?" she continued, her tone a whisper. "Do you think the Hall of Covens really does exist?"

"Exists? Yes," he said quietly, and he put the tickets away and stood, moving before her and taking up her two hands in his. "But if it contains now, or ever, a vault of pure Magic is another story."

"You must be careful regardless," she said and stood holding his hands and hugged him. "If the Anathema even gets a hint of this there would be worse troubles than Nyssa to concern ourselves with."

"I know," he said with a nod and then glanced towards the door. "But to be honest I think Nyssa and the Hall are connected; no one, Us or Them, saw even the remote essence of pure Magic until it became unlocked in her. I keep thinking that she is the key to all of it and that excites and scares the crap out of me at the same time."

"I know," Agatha smiled and walked him to the center of the room and kissed him on his cheek. "You handle that for now while I handle things here at home, but I want you and Amora to stay ever so careful."

"We will," he smiled back and returned a kiss to her cheek and then paused. "You know, I can postpone this trip for a week or two, you know, hang around to make sure that everything here is alright?"

"Not at all," Agatha shook her head quickly. "We will be fine, I have dealt with teen angst before, and you should know that. And besides, if morons like Langdon Drellic caught wind of what you were doing, they would be all over it like flies on that very bad word I said earlier."

They shared a brief chuckle and Marco took several steps back from her.

"Are you sure?" he insisted as his pocket watch came into view and hung on its chain. "Once we are on that plane, you know that we cannot portal while traveling at those speeds?"

"We will be fine!" Agatha assured her and then gave him a quick wink. "I promise."

"Ok," he smiled and motioned his hand and the portal opened. Agatha could see into an airport lounge where on the other side, apparently in the corner of the establishment stood Amora with several bags of luggage around her feet, including a dog carrier where Marley was more than likely tucked inside. She waved in through the portal to Agatha who returned it, then tapped her wrist alerting Marco that time was short. "I love you, Lady A."

With that he stepped through, and the portal closed behind him in a blink. Agatha slowly moved back to the window and sought her moon which was hiding now behind thick clouds. She sighed heavily and looked at her hands and whispered to them: "And I love you."

-2-

Quietly, Agatha moved throughout the house prior to her bedtime, routinely checking on the sleeping ones to ensure they were resting, and then moved from fireplace to fireplace to send the flames away. Some of the fires came from furnaces within Kilauea in Hawai'i, others from great cauldrons of molten steel of one of the many foundries in the world, and others were shimmers from the Sun which she coaxed to stay around for a bit longer. She would dim all the lights, which were not quite lights at all, but essences of fireflies that she *borrowed* from the multitude that flickered in the world, and she would calm the waterfalls in the atrium so that the turtles may rest.

She followed this routine in this order every night, even before she had a houseful of girls, but this time she did it out of order by peeking in on the sleeping ones last.

Having had a long day, Nyssa and Seema were knocked out in their beds. She moved in like a thief in the night to ease Seema's leg back onto the mattress, a nighttime slumbering habit she had had since she was a little girl. She kissed her fingertips, pressed the mark on each girl's forehead, then quietly left and moved to Mica's room.

Tomorrow, she promised, she would expand Mica's room so that she could have all the space she wanted and go shopping for whatever the girl wanted to make the space her own. Agatha considered that the confined space might seem almost like a cell to someone her age, a kid's room, or a place where you put the undesired and wanted. With the understanding words of Marco echoing through her mind, Agatha knew very well that she desired Mica to be in their lives.

Quietly, she opened the bedroom door and peeked in, and Mica was nowhere to be found.

"Mica?" she whispered into the dim lit room but got no echoing reply.

She slowly moved in close to the bed and saw that it had been slept on but not in from earlier that day after the girl's ride, and a blade of terror crept along her spine after realizing that she had not seen her since. Quickly, she moved from the room to the hallway, ready to approach Nyssa's and Seema's room, when she froze, her eyes over the banister and across the large open hallway to find the front door standing open.

I didn't see that earlier! She thought to herself and quickly moved down the curved stairway and out onto the front porch. The night was dark and cloudy as she peered out into the darkness, and with a wave of her hand, the light posts lining the drive blinked to life. At the mouth of the main driveway down where it narrowed to the long drive that would take you to the country road, Mica stood still, her back to the house.

"Mica!" she called out as loud as she could without screaming it so not to wake the girls upstairs. Mica, in the distance, slowly turned her head towards her and then looked back down the drive.

Agatha moved quickly down the steps and out onto the lawn in a steady run as she held the edge of her long nightgown with one hand so that she would not trip on the fabric. The night's air was much cooler away from the house, and she could feel its damp crispness licking her skin as she moved.

As she happened upon Mica, slowing her run to a steady walk several feet from her, she could tell that something was genuinely wrong with the girl. She wasn't standing on the gravel drive as it appeared that she was from a distance, but instead, she floated over it by a mere two inches, and her body was surrounded by a violet glow so deep that it almost looked black.

"Mica?" Agatha whispered and took a step back as Mica rotated around towards her with a blank look, the irises of her eyes pulsing violet like a heartbeat.

"You know, Agatha," Mica said flatly; the sound of her voice coming a fraction after her lips moved like a bad dubbing job of a foreign movie as her feet settled to the ground. "I think you want to do something for me; I think in a moment you are going to want to do it really, *really* badly!"

Agatha could feel the girl's thoughts in her own, stretching and expanding from the soft center of her brain, and as she fought against it, that thing inside grew piercing claws that stabbed at the fabric of her mind. A faraway squeal escaped her throat as her hands came up to both sides of her head, and her knees buckled as her body jerked with spasms.

"Whu-what a-are yu-you do-doing, Mica?" Agatha begged as her body began to convulse.

"Nothing, Agatha." Mica smiled and extended a hand towards her and pointed towards Agatha's forehead. "All what is happening is your doing, don't you feel it? Now stand!"

With a flick of Mica's wrist, Agatha was snatched upwards into a standing position with only the balls of her feet gracing the ground. Ferocious pain raced through her, sharp and piercing as if shattered glass sat between bones and muscle, slicing.

"*Stu-awp!*" Agatha blurted out the disturbing slurred word as a large vein swelled the middle of her forehead and pulsed.

"The thing is, Agatha," Mica spoke as she moved behind Agatha with a thin wicked smile, her eyes blazing violet. "The more you fight me the more I will hurt you. If you want to fight it, I could care less; the only part of your sanity I need you for is to bring the façade down… All of it, down!"

"*Stu-awp!*" Agatha bellowed as her eyes leaked both tears and blood under the horrible convulsing stress of Mica's mind.

Regardless of her will, Agatha moved forward as if she were a marionette following her master's strings, and with each breath, she huffed back and then blew out the streaming blood which flowed from her nostrils.

"DO IT NOW!" Mica screamed both with her mind and voice, and in response Agatha's body writhed with it.

Despite all that she could muster to fight against the girl's mind, she could no longer hold against the flood of boiling blood in her veins, and her senses could no longer subjugate the searing, mounting pain. With one brilliant moment which flared and blurred the shadows which watched from their darkened edges of the drive, Agatha's hands jetted forward in a golden arc, and her mouth hung without movement as the command flew, bringing it all down.

The cacophony which followed—much like a vacuum cleaner being switched off and dying alone in a forgotten room whilst someone banged a heavy drum—moaned, filling the air with not the sounds of happiness but the slow droning rhythm much like the end of that Christmas favorite, *Carol of the Bells* when the sopranos drone off, and the tenors take over; leaving the listener wondering if it was St. Nick on his way (or something darker slithering down in the shadows of the chimney). To consider the sounds which accompanied the casting away of the façade as 'terrifying' would be ludicrous, but on that night—borne from the ripping tension of Agatha's muscles forcing the words out—terrifying was a simple bumping noise in the night and what raced across the whole of the world was the trumpeting call for the end of everything. The house shook as if a giant rose beneath its foundation and shuddered in its wake, angry at the existence of everything for being disturbed without the need of a little man or beanstalk.

No, what happened was pure rage transmitted through pureness and the ending result was chaotic bedlam.

The house's front doors blew inward and twisted against their hinges in a blink, snapping the thick brass metal that had hung there for over a hundred years without faltering. They dipped and bounced twice off their corners, passing each other as if dancing in unison to some hectic rhythm, and on the third tap, they rebounded from the floor and crashed together, exploding into a million shards of wood and stained glass.

Nyssa and Seema leaped from their beds with their eyes full of confusion and terror, neither knowing which exact direction was up, but both knowing that nothing was right.

"What the hell was that?" Nyssa screamed her begging demand as she moved without hesitation towards the bedroom door.

"I have no idea!" Seema cried as the house shook and shuddered once again as the air filled with the sounds of the stairs to the porch blowing away as if split with a gigantic axe. In a blink, she was at Nyssa's side at the doorway now hanging wide open. *"Agatha!"*

The two raced from the room and sped down the hallway towards the stairway, and as they rounded the corner, all the explanations were before them. Agatha was barely touching the large runner on the floor by the tips of her toes, her body flaring gold mana mixed with the colors of Mica's violet, which intermingled from her position behind the woman. Agatha's wide, strained eyes happened upon them immediately, and she began to convulse in every attempt to free her from Mica's mental grasp, forcing her veins to stand up clearly under the surface of her skin.

"Girls!" Agatha managed to scream past Mica's mental grip, only to be silenced instantly by pain.

"Stop them!" Mica roared behind Agatha and suddenly her mind filled with the image of a speeding train and the air that it moved.

Agatha's hand flashed upwards, and her mana arced towards them, erupting the stairs into jagged shards of splintered carnage.

"No!" Seema screeched, her hand flaring forward hastily as a corkscrew wave of red light shot from her hand, uncontrollably finding the carved walls, vases on tables, and stained glass to obliterate. As the golden wave from Agatha neared them, the two mana paths met and exploded, sending a wave of force that threw the two girls back against the hallway wall with a meaty thud.

Quickly, Seema's hand went up to the side of her head only to find her thick hair; her talisman sat on the nightstand.

Her heart sank.

"You'll hit Auntie Agatha!" Nyssa protested as she pulled herself and Seema up, shifting around the corner of the staircase out of harm's view.

"I am not trying to!" Seema yelled back over the noise of clattering wood on the floor below.

In a blink, Seema turned her heel and ran back towards the bedroom as Nyssa glanced around the hallway corner. Mica's eyes were narrow and locked, waiting for the slightest sign of life, and as Nyssa's face appeared, Agatha's hand popped up, and the corner of the wall exploded into fine chunks of plaster.

"Not that girl!" Seth's voice bellowed over the pandemonium; heavy and demanding. Mica relaxed and turned briefly as Seth stepped over chunks of doorframe that littered the entrance, his

heavily oiled snakeskin boots glittering in the dim light. "Kill the other one for all I care but keep her unharmed."

"Yes, Father," Mica smiled her wicked little smile as her eyes gleamed and glared at the color of her mana. "Are you happy?"

"I am ecstatic, Mica," he smiled as he came within kissing distance of Agatha and looked over her face.

Sweat, thick and running, gripped the woman's skin as if she had just come in from the rain, and wrinkles which were decades off from ever showing caved the beautiful edges of her skin. A light moan escaped her throat over the pained wheezing from her chest when he stepped into view, and her hand briefly jerked towards him, but Mica's mind was swift and halted any actions.

"Ah, Lady Agatha," Seth smiled and produced a slight bow. "Thank you for welcoming me to your home."

"*Fuckers!*" Nyssa shrieked as she bounded down the remaining stairs of the opposite staircase, her fist making a perfect ball, the thumb crossing the curved fingers and locking, the first two knuckles clearly standing forward as the arm corkscrewed back into the ideal text-book punch, just like her father had taught her to do so many years before. Mica watched all of this in a slow step-by-step demonstration of what it meant to throw a knock-out punch, and it would never be known if it was her thoughts or Agatha's, but the words *This is going to hurt* raced the edges of her consciousness and then stars exploded behind Mica's eyes.

The blow landed precisely where her father had always told Nyssa to deliver the first punch of any confrontation, right on the bottom eye socket, closest to the nose, resulting in your opponent's day becoming really fucked up in a hurry. Mica pin-wheeled backward with a heavy moan, and Agatha dropped like a bag of bricks once the lock of their minds was severed. Nyssa quickly turned her next fist towards Seth, who stood a foot taller than her, boosting off her toes and climbing, her fist arcing wide and fast. She briefly saw a smile on Seth's face before pain exploded through her body, and a fraction later, she found herself sliding across the floor; her body becoming a human broom to push along shattered wood as she slid.

"Very impressive, young Nyssa," he smiled, his eyes on Mica who was pulling herself up on her hands and knees, her head shaking in attempts to clear the pulsing wave of near unconsciousness away. "Imagine if you really meant it? Think about what you could have done."

"I meant it!" Nyssa pulled herself into a standing position and immediately assumed a defensive stance, fists in tight little balls.

"Do you really think you can hurt me that way, girl?" He laughed and took a step towards her.

"No, but I can!" Seema screamed as she leaped from the balcony, her mind finding the warm updrafts along the sides of the Swiss Alps, and she descended fast; the side of her head glowing red as her talisman hung snugly there.

With arms extended, a brilliant red pulse burst forth with uncalculated haste and rage flowing through her. An out-of-focused image appeared from somewhere in the world, and somewhere a hammer fell, hitting a bullet's primer with the intent of killing someone, but on that side of the world, there was a dud, but where she stood, the recoil launched her arms upwards. Seth took the mana bolt dead center, which slid him back towards the door, his snakeskin boots digging in at the toes and splitting the polished floorboards beneath them.

For a moment, Seema thought the fight was over as she looked at him, his hands to his chest with his body bent, but then he blued, bright and ominous.

"You know," Seth said with a tone full of sarcasm and wit, not knowing that if Seema hadn't had rushed the vision he would surely be dead right then. "I thought about killing you at her house, but now that's *exactly* what I am going to do!"

"Bring it!" She screamed forward and sent the gusts of the Alps towards Seth who clapped his hands together soundly and sent her Magic to his sides, blasting away wood paneling and old pictures from the walls.

"Enough! *Friosan!*" Seth commanded in Old High German, and with a wave of his hand, everything became still.

Seema was in mid-pitch of another bolt; her mind stuck somewhere between lightning and colliding tectonic plates; Agatha managed a weakened hand towards him, a sputtering golden arc drawn from the belly of the world which hung motionless and glimmering; Nyssa—full of rage much like the day when she brought the storm—only thought of death; her mind in the darkness where only evil things lived. She was bringing it forward with an open palm, even her color glowed with a brazen glare of pure white light, but then all things froze.

Seth stepped forward and looked about him, glancing at Mica who in mid-motion was bringing her own carnage in a jagged, white-violet wave, knelt frozen.

"Wow," Seth said and shook his head to all that he was witnessing and moved towards Agatha and slapped her hand down. In a sparkling shimmer the Magic dissipated into dim ambers on the floor which disappeared in hissing blinks. "You guys were really going to do a number on me, weren't you?"

With a snap of his fingers towards Mica, her motions continued forward. As the white-violet wave shot forward, Seth simply waved, knocking it to the floor, where it dissipated harmlessly into childish sparkles. She blinked repeatedly as her mind attempted to understand what had happened and then looked upon Seth, who was examining Nyssa up close and personal.

"Teacher?" she sounded as she stood; her hand moving up to her pulsating eye. "Why did you stop me?"

"All in good time, Mica," he said quietly and pulled the small gold chain and lock from its hiding place under Nyssa's shirt. "Interesting, she has her talisman, but nothing flowed through it."

"What?" Mica asked moving up close.

"She wasn't channeling her Magic," he said in admiration. "Either she doesn't know how or was not yet taught, but that really does not matter; look at her glow. That's pure Magic cascading through her... do you know what this means?"

Mica shrugged, caring more what her face was going to look like in an hour or two without an ice pack or a nice meaty steak.

"Mica, my child," Seth said with a shaking head. "I didn't think I needed to explain it out to you, but to make it simple, the rumors are true: she is the Next Coming, which means I was too quick to denounce everything. Silly me, but thankfully for us, she is not ready as of yet, for if she was, well, I am afraid that they would be cleaning the both of us off the walls for quite some time."

Mica moved close to Nyssa, and her good eye narrowed as she peered into the narrow-frozen ones of Nyssa's, which was a shimmering hazel and pupil-less. Mica's mind was filled with rage as her fists balled, and as her arm began to come up, Seth's hand reached out and snatched her by the elbow, yanking her back.

"If you happen to wake her with that blow," Seth said flatly. "I don't think I could stop what she was about to unleash, and your eye would be the last thing you would be worrying about."

Seth released his grasp and moved towards Seema where he stood before her with a wicked smile.

"So, what now?" Mica introduced, her mind pumping lava of anger and revenge. "Do we simply take her like this?"

"No," Seth said with his tone still caught in awe inspired bliss at Nyssa's glow. "Take their talismans and *nudge* those two quickly into chairs in the atrium and bind them; that freeze charm only lasts a few minutes.

"I have business with this one here."

Mica moved as commanded and first went to Agatha and unclasped the hooks that held the brooch in place and stuck it in her pocket. She turned to move towards Seema when Agatha's mind reached out to her with two damning words: *"Never child!"*

"Huh?" Mica paused, shaking her head, and looked back into Agatha's eyes and was alarmed to see the pupils narrow and the edges of the whites darting. Seth's freeze charm *had* worked for the most part, but it was evident that the older woman had casted something now he had spoken to counter it and it was working.

The foyer flashed golden with a loud popping sound.

The bolt that struck Mica in her side bent and threw her across the hallway, where she slid with a meaty thud into the oaken walls. Seth glanced up in time to see Nyssa's palm move towards him, delivering what had been originally intended. As it came forth, he recognized a glint of a shape that oddly resembled a bull's head before his body coughed out every ounce of air from his lungs. In a brilliant burst upon impact, Seth cartwheeled backward with tatters of clothing breaking away in smoldering strips and flung out through the doorway.

"Girls, run!" Agatha screamed towards Nyssa and Seema, who had recoiled to near tottering from the rapid blows that Agatha was throwing at Seth to keep him at bay, their minds clearing from the charm.

The two shot a glance at Mica, who kneeled shaken with her palms on the floor and head rapidly wagging off the blow and then towards the glowing blue light which came in through the doorway and grew in brilliance. Their attention shifting ended with the sound of the heavy growl coming into the house from outside, and terrified expressions happened upon Agatha, who was pulling herself up.

"Get out of here, *now!*"

They took heel and ran headstrong up the hallway past the foyer as a thunderous roar echoed behind them. Nyssa chanced a glance over her shoulder to see Agatha standing in a low defensive stance with golden glowing hands as the foyer behind them filled with a blinding blue.

"Where are we going?" Nyssa screamed to Seema at her side.

"The atrium!" Seema screamed back, her arms and legs pumping rapidly.

As they cornered the long hallway to their right, they paused to look back, only to see Agatha moving like a kung-fu master fighting an invisible foe; her blows flying in golden waves while warding off oncoming bolts of blue. There was an explosion down that way, and Agatha's cry of pain could be heard over it.

Nyssa felt as if she was floating as Seema pulled her along the west-wing hallway at top speed.

-3-

Seth—or the ever-changing shape that once was him—approached Agatha in heavy, lumbering steps, who was laid back across the floor, propping herself up on a large section of the stairway, trying to stand. His jaw grotesquely stretched downward as his forehead narrowed, pulling his eyes back in long narrow slits; his teeth extending and becoming translucent like frosted icicles hanging from a roof's edge. The constant growl that crawled out his throat reverberated through Agatha's body, shaking the organs to an almost nauseating tremor.

"*Youuu-arrre-a-foool, Agathaaa,*" Seth-thing growled and hissed, drawing out the words like a greased snake sliding on coarse sandpaper. "*Yoouu-arrre-gooinng-too-die-foorr-youurr-meddling!*"

"Stu-still a tuh-talker, Suh-Seth," Agatha stammered, attempting to smile as she stood, her face covered in sweat and blood. As she rose, she gathered a handful of splintered wood and glass, the sharp edges slicing clean into her palm.

She began to concentrate on what she had in her palm, focusing on the fires that melted the glass and the pain the trees suffered as they were sacrificed to become floorboards and stairs. With every intention of her being, she was concentrating on murder.

"I tuh-told you; you cannot have her!"

"DIE!" Seth-thing roared and lunged as Agatha's hand came forth and in a sparkling golden ball of glass and splinters that murderous bolt leaped.

It flew home, catching Seth-thing dead center only to burst away in a brilliant cascade of fireworks. Seth-thing began to laugh as Agatha's mouth trembled, and from the remnants of his clothing, an elongated dark and warped hand retrieved the cigarette case.

Laughing, he held it out towards Agatha for recognition.

"Dear God," Agatha gasped, collapsing back against the rubble.

"Wrong!" Seth-thing hissed, advancing on her. "He is not here tonight!"

-4-

"Agatha!" Nyssa screamed as the two skidded to a halt in the middle of the atrium and spun around towards where they came.

There was a loud roar and Agatha screamed and then everything fell silent.

"We have to hide!" Seema whispered so loud she might as well be screaming it and shook Nyssa by her shoulders. "Nyssa! Agatha can take care of herself!"

"What?" Nyssa looked at her with insulted confusion. "We have to go help her!"

"Right now, we have to help everything!" Seema said quickly, pulling Nyssa along. "If he gets you, *everything* falls down!"

Quickly, Seema pulled Nyssa along, her eyes darting about the atrium for places to hide, and then found a large ostrich fern with a massive outgrowth of maidenhair ferns at its base and pulled her towards it.

"Stay here!" Seema demanded as she maneuvered Nyssa behind the trunk and shoved her down by her shoulders. In Nyssa's confusion and terror, she complied without any hesitation.

"Where are you going?" Nyssa pleaded with tears in her eyes.

"I am going to go help Lady Agatha," Seema said quickly and reached towards the back of the outcropping and snatched up the soft growth by the handfuls which she dropped on top of Nyssa in attempts to camouflage her.

"I am coming with you!" Nyssa attempted to rise only to be pressed back down.

"*No!*" Seema scolded. "Remember: it will *all* come down. Stay here, I will be but a moment."

Seema snatched up another large grouping of foliage, dropped it on top of Nyssa's head, and then dashed off, heading back up the atrium's walkway towards which they came. She could see Seema speed off through a small gap, her tiny feet moving so quickly they were almost a blur, and her red aura trailed behind her.

Biting down on her lip and silently crying, Nyssa began to do the one thing she was never, *ever* supposed to do, and that was to wish for a solution to it all.

-5-

The Seth-thing was standing over Agatha's form, panting heavily with long streams of drool running from the edge of his hatchet fish-like jaw. Mica slid her back along the wall quietly, her eyes wide in fear, for she had never seen this side of him.

"Where are you going?" He growled towards her, and she froze with a start.

"I-I-I am, uh, going after them," Mica stammered through her words that crept from her throat in a whispering croak.

"They're mine!" He growled and pointed at Agatha. "I will take care of them! You stay here and finish this bitch off!"

"Yuh-you want me to kill her?" Mica blinked, her eyes finding Agatha's, which hung glazed and barely open as her body wheezed for life. Mica could see how the woman's Magic popped from her body in a helter-skelter randomness like sparks from a dying machine. Agatha's eyes slowly found hers, and she could see the woman's mind full of pain, despair, and still hope. "Like she is now?"

Without so much as a blink, Seth crossed the distance between them and Mica found herself airborne and dangling by one of his deformed hands, her body being throttled violently.

"Don't ever question what I command, worthless brat!" he screeched into her face, the edges of those icicle teeth grazing at her chin. "You kill her *now* before I kill you both! Nyssa is the only thing that matters here!"

Mica managed a gurgling *'uh-huh'* sound through her crushing larynx and a few rapid nods of confirmation. Seth flung her across the hallway, where she bounced twice before skidding to a stop, her hands to her throat, gasping for air through the pain. With a growl, he fixed his eyes on hers and narrowed, and without a doubt, Mica knew that he was quite sincere.

Grunting once, Seth leaped over rubble and began feverishly bounding up the hallway, occasionally dropping down on all fours to boost him along his way. Mica spat blood and stood through the haze in her head, her eyes locked on those of Agatha's.

*

Nyssa wished a lot of things in her frightened mind: She wished that none of this was happening. She wished that her father was there. She wished that they had never started to care about Mica. She also wished she could be more like Agatha and Seema.

Yes, Nyssa began to wish a flurry of things as noises began race up the hall to her small ears as she bit down on her fear which meant—just like her father—being afraid was the sure-fire way to making her very, *very* angry.

As sounds of carnage continued to roll and the ground shook, Nyssa's eyes began to narrow through the foliage towards the distance, building momentum as the rage trembled in her limbs.

Slowly, Nyssa began to rise up, the added foliage falling from her body as she moved, and her eyes narrowed becoming bright hazel.

Yes, she wished a lot, but now only her mind focused on *THE* wish until it had become a purely bright singularity in her mind.

Smiling wickedly, Nyssa wished that she could do all that Agatha and Seema could do, plus two.

-6-

"Suh-so," Agatha said in a raspy tone towards Mica who slowly approached her with a violet hand and wiped blood from the corner of her mouth. "In the end, you are truly an Anathema through and through."

Mica stopped in mid-step and coughed, her body was aching and her mind swimming in dark waters of confusion.

"You do not know me, Agatha," Mica managed a raspy whisper through her battered throat and the glow around her hand brightened.

"Oh, I do know you," Agatha nodded and managed to pull herself up into a higher sitting position, her eyes never leaving Mica's. "More so than you know, and I really wanted to one day share with you all that I do know."

"What do you mean?" Mica paused as her hand was coming up and the glow becoming a defined ball of violet light.

"You have the power, child," Agatha smiled thinly. "You don't have to do this… he doesn't control you anymore."

"Hu-he is my teacher, my father," Mica's words were soft peeps in the smoky, dusty air. "I don't want any more lies from anyone."

"We have never lied to you about a thing, Mica," Agatha said quickly. "Use your gift and seek my mind for the truth."

"I-I have to kuh-kill you," Mica attempted to find strength and her words sounded to have no more strength than a dead feather in the wind.

"Seek my mind first," Agatha said flatly, her eyes widening towards her. "Then tell me who you will want to kill."

Mica slowly shook her head but found her mind reaching out despite her orders. Like a wave of icy water, their minds splashed over one another's like two rivers colliding and mixing; each attempting to overcome the onslaught of the other until they calmed into a single flowing body. Her visions raced quickly and stopped at the image of a little brick house surrounded by tall bushes bordered by a knee-high stone wall. There were some small patches of flowers running the house's edge and a little fountain that sputtered water down a shimmering cascade of sparkling quartz chips.

The sound drew her closer at high speed to where she was now on the stoop just before the doorway, which was battered and split, the door which should have hung there lay broken and splintered on the floor inside.

There was moaning coming from inside, a male's moaning heavy and labored and full of pain.

Agatha? Mica's mind spoke directly to the joined one as she peered straight into the house and was met by a large entrance mirror. There she could see herself, short, stubby, and very young; her hair jet black with two tufts of hair on the sides of her head held by small white barrettes. She was in pajamas with little Elmos smiling back at her in the reflection, and there was a small bear, her eventful talisman, gripped tightly in her hand. Agatha's side of her mind said nothing in reply, but a soft nudge made her step into the doorway and the small house.

There was a crashing ensemble raging from a rear room of the house, and as the smaller Mica stood in the entranceway, she glanced towards the square-shaped living room where a stout man in shorts and a T-shirt lay crumpled in a mass that had one time been a coffee table.

"*Daddy?*" The mental-Mica whimpered and squatted down and touched the man's face which trembled by her very touch.

"*Guh-get out, Mi-Mi-Mica,*" the man attempted his body convulsing as blood flowed readily from his nose, mouth, and ears. Mica leaned back to see that she was squatting down in an ever-growing pool of blood which flowed from beneath him. "*Ru-run to the Cuh-Carter's duh-down the ruh-road!*"

Behind her raced a heavy roar and several heavy thuds against wood.

"*WHERE IS THE GIRL?!*" bellowed the inhuman voice which young Mica suddenly recognized.

"*Leave us alone!*" screamed a woman's voice in terrified desperation, her voice muffled as it bore through a closed door.

"*Mommy?*" Mica whimpered and suddenly she was no longer in the living room but pressed against the wall of a tiny child's bedroom, her bedroom of youth.

The woman was pressed against the door; her face stretched in terror and covered with sweat and tears, and in her hand was what appeared to be a butcher's knife. To her right, she could hear the whimpering cries of a child, and she got down on all fours and peered under. There, in the shadows under the bed, was herself; a mirrored image of what she had become in the vision, the child's eyes wide and bulging and streaming tears.

"*LET ME IN!*" the voice boomed, and the door flexed, forming an elongated split down its center.

"Are you me?" Mica whispered to the child-clone under the bed but got no response.

A heavy growl was followed by a severe impact as the door blew inward, sending the woman flying across the room towards her, followed by the door in three heavy chunks. Mica stood quickly and backed away, the small bear coming up to the center of her chest as her arms wrapped around it tightly.

There, in the battered doorway, stood the thing she had seen that very night in Agatha's foyer: the Seth that would be her teacher but transformed into that thing that bore the resemblance of the true hatred in his mana-soul. It was panting heavily, its narrow-slit eyes gleaming blue, its darkened muscles flexing on their own. It pointed an elongated finger towards Mica who stood trembling with the bear.

"COME TO ME CHILD!" it growled and quickly the woman dashed at the thing with the knife held high, screaming how she was going to kill it.

The young Mica watched in slow motion as the woman lunged and the thing lunged each other, and they collided; there was no competition between the masses. The thing's hands shot forward with clawed fingers slicing the air, slashing with rib-crushing, flesh-tearing brutality. It lifted the woman towards the ceiling, savagely thrashed her about, and, with a heavy grunt, slammed her down to the floor, lifeless. It stood panting over its kill, seeking any sign of life, only to be disturbed by a trembling whimpering from young Mica's throat. Quickly those narrow eyes shot towards her and then widened, and rapidly the thing shifted and morphed into the Seth she had known all her life.

"Mica," Seth said softly, his clothes hanging on him in tattered ruins and he extended a hand towards her as he approached. *"These people are nothing to you; I am and will be your teacher now."*

As the approaching hand neared, Mica began to tremble; both in the vision and the natural world, as she stood over Agatha in the foyer. The fingertips neared her face, and as they touched, Mica snatched herself away from Agatha in a painful shriek.

Mica lay on the floor, panting heavily as her body shook uncontrollably out of fear and rage. She propped herself up and wiped her face roughly with her forearm to remove the tears and found Agatha looking at her with a steady slow nod.

"Now," Agatha said quietly. "Who has been telling lies?"

-7-

Seema rounded the west wing's corner, began to race up the long hallway toward the foyer, and was immediately met by Seth, who was in mid-gait towards her. Seema screamed as she leaped as her glowing red hands came from behind in wide arches and clapped in the middle, flashing explosively and shooting forth. The combined bolt seared the air as it raced home, catching the Seth-thing in the hip and rocketing him backward in a corkscrewing, howling mass. As she landed, her right hand grasped the hairclip on the side of her head as the other shot forward, flashing red.

"Vindicare!" Seema screamed the Latin word for 'laying vengeance,' her mind not seeking the world for the images but instead deep down in her own soul and feeling the rage flowing through her.

The bolt raced forward, taking up floorboards in its wake but missing its target as the Seth-thing dove to the left, narrowly escaping the blast. They stood far from each other in fighting stances, their shoulders rising and falling in heavy pants.

"So," he growled, his body slowly shifting into the form of a man once again, clothes hanging in tattered ruins. "I think it is time to keep my promise to you girl. I think it is time that I kill you."

"Bring it!" Seema screamed at him, her body and mind exhausted.

"Here it comes," Seth smiled and pulled from his tattered hanging pocket his cigarette case.

-8-

Mica was racing up the hallway with angry tears streaming behind her. She had helped Agatha up, moved her out on the porch, and instructed her to call to the moon. The girl had never been told outright that Agatha recharged herself this way, but then again, she was not a stupid girl who didn't have eyes and could quickly put two and two together to get the sum.

"You need to stay here," she had desperately instructed Agatha, returning the woman's talisman to her. "I will go help them."

As Mica bounded up the hallway, her eyes narrowed to the brilliant explosion of red Magic, a muffled roar of the pain of Seth, and the sounds of his body banging against the floor. She might not have had her own talisman, but she could do Magic, providing that the fight would be up close and personal, which she had no doubt in her mind that it would be.

CHAPTER TWENTY-TWO

Mortality

-1-

The death of Seema was witnessed from a multitude of directions simultaneously, and there was no doubt that her passing was anything peaceful.

The cigarette case in Seth's hand pulsed once, and a blue spike extended from his right fist. Seema was advancing on him with her body vibrating red, her hands coming around in flared clawing arches, and she jumped up to cover the height difference. Mica was pulling up all the Magic she could muster as she pumped her arms and legs as fast as she could, hoping to cover the distance between them.

Nyssa was rounding the corner of the west wing, her hair flowing from the mana that coursed through her, and she froze once she saw what was happening.

The blue spike lunged forward, catching Seema directly below the solar plexus and slicing through and then exiting from her back, and her body curved around the blow as blood jetted from her open mouth. The two were motionless as they stared into each other's eyes, Seth's twisting to show his satisfactory smile and Seema's darting rapidly in a mixture of intense pain and shock. After a moment, Seth pulled back his Magic and allowed Seema's body to collapse to the floor below.

"NO!" Nyssa and Mica shrieked, and Seth attempted to look in both directions at once.

Nyssa's hands came up as she ran forward, white-hazel light jetting forth and twisting through the air towards him. Mica's violet aura haphazardly streamed across the distance, and her mind locked onto Seth's and shrieked through his brain with a tone as sharp as nails. His hands attempted to ward off the attacks, but in return, he found misery in a crushing onslaught that seared his flesh to the bone. He shot across the hallway, rebounding off the walls several times, and then came still in a wheezing lump on the floor.

Nyssa raced to Seema's body, coming to rest as she slid on her knees, her hands shaking, wanting to touch her sister and not to touch her at the same time. Seema lay motionless with wisps of smoke climbing from her singed nightshirt; her eyes were wide and glazed, and the sides of her mouth and nose were painted with blood. There was no open wound where the blue spike ran home, only a red mark where the Magic had entered to obliterate her heart.

Nyssa was crying soundly as Mica quietly advanced and then stopped several feet away.

"Seema, no!" Nyssa pleaded, her face planted on Seema's chest, and she shook the lifeless body in vain. Mica prepared words of comfort but decided against it and turned towards Seth who was attempting to pull himself up.

"You!" Mica growled softly and moved towards him, and the hallway became brilliant with Nyssa's glow. Mica spun towards it and shielded her eyes only to see an outline of what Nyssa through the brilliance was.

"YOU BOTH KILLED HER!" Nyssa roared from within the light and Mica was sent flying up the hallway with her arms and legs kicked out in front of her and she slid to a stop more than twenty feet away. Seth's eyes scanned for his talisman which was lying next to Mica's feet and clearly well out of reach. Nyssa's glow grew larger and brighter until the hallway blazed with it and filled every space, every nook, every cranny, *and* the nook's crannies, with light.

Her wish had come true despite her betrayal of the rules; all that Agatha and Seema had ever known about Magic, plus that of things they had never learned, swelled inside her mind and culminated into pure plasma borne from rage. Every single dark and dismal imagery that a sixteen-year-old could foster in their short life rushed in, flooding her mind with a melee of violence and revenge.

Nyssa's mind found the sounds of Seth's heart beating rapidly but healthy and then found the vision of Seema's lying still and obliterated in her chest. A Low German word was starting to rise from her lungs, a term that meant to jump, and her lungs filled with a massive volume of air to blast the word out so that even the angels in heaven would hear it.

"Nyssa!" Agatha's voice pleadingly commanded before her, using the wall as support. "Do not do what you are about to do!"

Nyssa held the breath and slowly moved her eyes towards Agatha as if through viscous syrup and her head cocked slowly to one side.

"He killed Seema!" Nyssa's voice came low, barbarically, and the house shook with it, bringing down plaster in chunks that had hung in place for over a hundred years.

"I know child," Agatha said quickly back. "But you cannot do what you are about to do! It's against the rules! What you are about to do is the Anathema way don't you see?"

"Then I am Anathema, then!" Nyssa screamed back and her eyes found Seth's once again. Two hearts in two different bodies were in her mind side-by-side and they were about to change places in a hurry. *"GUMP—"*

'No!' Mica's mind raced through Nyssa's, and she froze mid-command seemingly suspended in time. *'Not him, Nyssa, take this thought.'*

Nyssa stood rigid as her mind trailed from that of Seth's beating heart to Mica's, and everything seemed to slow to a crawl. Mica stepped slowly towards her, took one of Nyssa's extended hands, and held it momentarily, her eyes seeking Nyssa's brilliant hazel ones for understanding.

"Mica don't do this!" Agatha was screaming with every ounce of strength she could muster as tears burst from her eyes; her mind clear to what the girl was about to do.

'You all were good to me,' Mica whispered in Nyssa's.

Mica gently pulled her hand as she squatted down next to Seema's body and took up one of her lifeless hands.

'I do love you, Sister, and Seema as well. Be sure to tell her that I said that.'

"GUMPEN!" Mica and Nyssa screamed simultaneously, the word being forced from Nyssa's entrapped mind, and in a brilliant burst of energy, everything became white and faded to black.

417

-2-

As consciousness returned from the haze in Nyssa's mind, she slowly pulled herself up to see Seema sitting upright and crying silently with her hand on Mica's shoulder, who lay motionless.

"Nyssa?" Seema croaked and began to sob, and Nyssa scrambled on her hands and knees quickly to her and took her in her arms.

"My Mee-ka," Seth wheezed with his back against the wall, his body bloody and singed from head to toe. He wished that he had never chased so many desires of powers and wished even more that he had been a better father to the girl he had stolen, but on that day, at that moment, no wish that that man could fathom held any power.

Agatha appeared before him in a golden aura, holding his case talisman, which shook violently in her hand. As she pointed it at him, her mind chased the world for every clever, every dicer and mincer that there might be, and she could feel them culminate into a horrid vision that filled her soul with darkness.

"Never," she whispered sharply, attempting to push the dark thoughts as far from her as possible, but Seth's cherished case showed her only such.

As she raised his talisman above her head, the other forming a damning, pointing digit at his chest, the air around her crackled and popped minute bolts of energy haphazardly. Agatha's mind was in turmoil, yet oddly placid in so many ways. Dictionary pages flipped, memories of long travels were rediscovered, joys, sorrows, and pains; then, in one very peculiar memory-instant, it all stopped, and a wry smile edged her lips.

"Forever for you," her voice came flat, and Seth's battered eyes widened, sensing her mind and the horrid thoughts which comingled within.

"*No!*" he croaked, his weakened limbs attempting to rise for protection.

"*NGUSIR!*" the Sudanese word for 'banish' roared from Agatha's throat as both arms extended towards him in a brilliant flash; a horrid term in the World of Magic to be the receiver and the caster of.

Her energy struck his body like a hammer fall, forcing him into and up the wall, ripping him from it and suspended there, hovering and drawing out in every direction at once. His scream shook the walls to their foundations as his body disseminated into blue, pulsing globs.

In a blinding flash of gold and blue, Seth's *èlan vital* shot forward into his cigarette case forever trapped in his newly formed Cask prison.

Agatha marveled at the object, her mind filling with the bittersweet happenstance that she just happened to know how many a wicked mage actually ended up in one and a more profound pleasing realization that eternity is quite a long time indeed.

With a bright flare of golden light sparking from her fingertips, the Seth-Cask was sent to the *Yondsphere* forever, plus two days.

Calming, Agatha slowly moved to the three girls as tears began to stream from her eyes.

She knelt between them and took them in her arms, and they wept soundly together over Mica's body.

CHAPTER TWENTY-THREE

Closure and New Beginnings

-1-

They held a small, quiet funeral for Mica in Agatha's family plot, surrounded by fir trees on the edge of her property. Even the beautiful patch of land shared the somber mood which hung in the air like a thick fog, and although Agatha considered sending the natural falling rain away, she felt that it was necessary.

Marco and Amora were present, as well as Angelica, who cried soundly into her hand while being comforted by Rusty Menden, who held her close and patted her on her shoulder. They had not known Mica like Agatha, and the girls had gotten to know her, but their hearts were pained by the loss of such a young one who struggled so hard and long with herself between two worlds of Magic and choosing the light of the two to give her life for. Sugar stood without needing a bridle towards the edge of her grave, and the mare nudged the fresh dirt mound several times with its nose.

"Oh, Auntie Agatha," Nyssa cried, her head falling to the woman's chest and Agatha wrapped an arm around her with the other already snuggly-holding Seema who cried continuously there already.

"I know, my child," Agatha sniffed. "I know."

A partial-Magic man by the name of Roman Stewart, who Agatha had gotten to know over the years, stood near the head of the grave in full Scotsman attire with a vibrant red satin bag and three drones extending from them. No one knew precisely how old Roman was nor exactly where he was from, but he proclaimed he was Scottish and hailed from the early Moors of North Africa. He had missed his *coming* simply by age and overlooked like so many people who walked the earth to understand the gifts that they had been given. Still, his unyielding ability to make the impossible possible proved a worthy asset to the Consortia.

Marco nodded towards him, and he took up the reed of the mouthpiece into his mouth and began to play.

As the bagpipe music climbed into the trees, they all wept.

-2-

Back at the house, they had a small wake under the gazebo, which included other members of the Consortia with one condition: their talismans had to be left behind, and only simple gate spells could be used. For more than three centuries, this was the largest congregation of Magic in one place, and after some crafty meddling, Agatha found a solution to bend and break the seven-limit rule, and twelve were present. Although she knew that the number could have been tripled without threat because of Nyssa's abilities, she had felt that a larger assembly would lessen the moment.

The ceremony was initially quiet, with only a few mumbling conversations about how nice the rain had smelled and that one had not seen the other for quite some time. Seema decided to tell the first story about Mica, which got everyone smiling, followed by an even more humorous one that eventually lightened the mood to laughter.

In a short time, the stories moved back and forth about Mica and other lighthearted stories, which eased the tone of the day into one which was more easily dealt with.

There were inquiries about the three women's travels, and Agatha felt they could all use some time away to heal. The girls didn't know nor care one way or the other; to them, it was an adventure away from the house, which now held too many pains and sufferings. Marco and Amora were to be traveling again soon as they returned to Dundalk to continue their explorations.

Slowly they all departed with Marco and Amora standing before Agatha, each one taking one of her hands.

"We should have waited," Marco said quietly, his head hanging low and shaking. "I knew in it my mana that things were off."

"If we could predict everything," Agatha attempted, a comforting smile. "Then the world will be a heaven, and nothing would ever happen."

"We cannot say this has happened for any good reason," Amora said quietly, her eyes off towards the distance where beyond the trees lay the body of Mica. "She was just a child."

"I know," Agatha said quietly following her eyes. "But we can say that it happened and then learn from it."

Marco and Amora departed soon after with hugs all around and them reassuring the girls that they would love Ireland and see them there soon.

Once gone, the three women stood holding each other for a long, long time.

*

That night, when the air was cool, and the breeze carried the smell of lilacs and fir cones with it, Agatha moved through the trees in the moonlight and stopped before Mica's grave. Her eyes read over the epitaph, which was carved on the flat, white marble stone, which was topped with a carving of a half-moon.

The inscription read:

Mica

Our Daughter, Our Sister, Our Love

She sighed heavily, fighting back the tears, and then reached into the pocket of her long skirt and produced a single seed. She stood admiring the tiny elm seed in her hand at how all of life sat entombed in its shell.

Agatha glanced at the moon breaking through the surrounding canopy and then nodded to the seed she had been holding on to since that night in Nyssa's backyard.

"I will keep my promise I made to you," she sniffed back tears as she knelt several feet behind the headstone, and from her other pocket, she drew a small garden shovel and began to turn up soil.

When she dug out several inches of earth, she placed the seed in the hole and carefully covered it. She pressed a palm on top of the disturbed ground, closed her eyes, and filled her mind with all the love she could find there.

"Grow strong and tall and look after my fallen little one."

Agatha stood comforted as she surveyed the plot with soft tears streaming her cheeks. She nodded appreciatively to the path that rested silently beneath their stones and slowly walked back towards the house.

Trailing her, the night bugs began their simple songs as she moved away, weary of the day so to close out this chapter of life, yet hopeful towards the next to start another with two teenage girls who had grown up fast in such a short time.

End(?)

Until we meet again...

A VERY IMPORTANT AFTERWARD

*

Pia waited for quite some time in the shadows of the sultry night before approaching the little dilapidated house that sat down Double K Road on the edge of the tiny township of Cleo, Alabama. Cleo was not one of those townships where if you blinked, you missed it. No; it was even smaller where its presence in the world wasn't represented on any map, and neither word of mouth ever mentioned it, or you simply know how to get there.

The light coming through the curtained windows was dim and flickering meant that the person inside worked by candlelight, and for her, that was just fine (just in case her makeup didn't entirely cover up the bruises).

She adjusted her clothes smartly, wishing she had a full-sized mirror, and then pressed the palm of her hand smugly into her right hip joint until it popped. She shuddered against the flare of pain there but shook it off. Many nights before, it came close to dislocating, perhaps needing only another millimeter of motion to do the trick. Still, luckily for her, Seth had either grown tired or found compassion for what he was doing to her. She had thought about this many times since then and concluded that his mercy came due to the former.

She rapped smartly on the rusty screen door, which hung at an odd angle due to a missing hinge at its top, the noise of which stirred something in the shrubbery to her left, which surrounded the house. Her bright green eyes shot and fixated on the direction of the noise, and her body instinctively poised as if to pounce despite the pain screaming at her from every sore joint and muscle. Another rustle, a glimpse of motion, her breath caught short in her lungs, and slowly, a small cream-colored possum crawled to the shrub's edge and regarded her with an upturned nose. Slowly she exhaled and straightened, dismissing the little creature as it headed off to find something in the darkness.

A young boy appeared from the shadows inside and looked up at her; his face was as emotionless and distant as a child she had seen in so many pictures of children caught in war zones. He wore cut-off denim jeans above his bare feet and an oily T-shirt, which at one time had been white. He blinked once at her from under a large lock of brown hair that hung over his brow just above his eyes. Without a word, he reached up, flicked the hook latch on the screen door, and then turned back inside. Pia slowly took hold of a knotted rope fed through the hole where the handle had once been and slowly pulled the door open with a sharp creaking noise.

As she stepped inside the dim house, the little boy merely pointed to a tattered red chair nestled into one corner and then dropped to his knees in front of a small television set. Pia stood for a moment and scanned the innards of the house. Not much had changed in the many years since she had visited other than the arrangement and some furniture. It was all one level and very basic: living room, kitchen/dining area, and a back room separated by a row of hanging multi-colored beads. Candles of all sizes burned atop small end tables fashioned from stacked antique phonebooks and milkcrates.

She moved into the living room and sat where the boy had pointed.

He was watching a program about giraffes in the wild which came through relatively clearly on the old set. Perhaps the only thing she could see in the new house was the digital converter box on top of the set so that they could get any channels at all. A soft humming came through the beaded curtain of the doorway to her left, melodious and beautiful, accompanied by the occasional sounds of silverware rustling and water pouring. For several minutes she sat quietly, staring at the back of the boy's head and listening to the soft volume of the program. It had crossed her mind briefly if she should seek his mind to know what he was thinking, but when the boy's head slowly turned towards her with those blank eyes and shook 'No' slowly, she decided quickly against it.

Pia glanced at her watch, which read 1:21 in the morning, and then placed her hands in her lap. Soft mumbling in Creole-French whispered in the air, comingling with the sounds of the television, and after a moment, a breeze rushed through the space of the house, making the beads rattle, and the candles flicker. The little boy extended his arm and pointed towards the beaded doorway without looking away from the television.

Slowly she stood, her hip popping soundly, and she readjusted her clothes and stepped in front of the beads. Through the spaces, she could see a woman standing in front of a narrow worktable covered with bottles, bowls, and utensils in the middle of the rear room.

"Madame Josephine?" Pia said softly through the beads and the woman beyond slowly waved her in. As Pia slid through the hanging beads, a rush of heavy humidity and warmth laced with the acrid smell of cigar tobacco greeted her and she stopped, poised as rigid as she could muster.

"Pia of the Denari," the woman spoke with a broadening smile as she looked up from a large bowl on the tabletop, her thick Creole accent sounding dark and alluring.

She was young in form and stature, and by any glimpse, she was a woman in her late twenties with perfect bronze skin and long, thick curly hair. She was Creole through and through, and only around her eyes could anyone make the connection that she was a lot older than the youthful body that carried her. Her dark-colored halter top was wet about the cleavage as her neck funneled down sweat in the hot room, and her skin glistened with perspiration.

"It has been quite a long time, has it not?"

"It has," Pia smiled and nodded.

"And what is it that you seek from me this time?" Madame Josephine asked quietly, her head leaning to one side as she lifted a cigar from a small tray and pulled on it.

"Just a simple miracle, Madame Josephine," Pia smiled widely, pulling from her handbag a folded handkerchief in which she produced a long nail which was caked with dried blood nearly the color of pitch. She held it between her thumb and forefinger and then extended it out before her. "One which encircles this, providing you have any miracles left for me."

ABOUT THE AUTHOR

P.L. Hight is an American author who enjoys spending time with his wife, family, and friends. At one time, Mr. Hight envisioned himself as an astronaut, but upon learning the limitations of space travel, he left it to the professionals. In return, he imagined strange new worlds rather than discovering them by putting that imagination to paper.

A Chicago native having grown up on the city's far southwest side [as he likes to point out: as far southwest you can go and still be in the city proper], having come up in the magnet public school system and spent many hours embraced by his local library.

A part-time country mouse, he spent many of his youthful summers working on his relative's dairy farms in Wisconsin; learning and experiencing a side of life many never get to see.

COMING SOON

By

P.L. HIGHT

(Book two of Modern Magic)

Magic Most Foul

(and Book three)

Some Kind of Magic

Printed in the USA
CPSIA information can be obtained
at www.ICGtesting.com
LVHW090306011123
762649LV00059B/1407